Spanish
Serenade

Spanish Serenade

JENNIFER BLAKE

FAWCETT COLUMBINE · NEW YORK

A Fawcett Columbine Book
Published by Ballantine Books

Library of Congress Catalog Card Number: 89-91515
ISBN: 0-449-90421-7

Cover painting by James Griffin
Cover design by James R. Harris
Text design by Holly Johnson

Manufactured in the United States of America

First Edition: August 1990
10 9 8 7 6 5 4 3 2 1

For my husband, Jerry Ronald,
My sons, Ron and Rick,
And my sons-in-law, Roddy and Rob—
Southern gentlemen and heroes, all—
with love.

Spanish
Serenade

CHAPTER 1

Pilar Marie Sandoval y Serna knew that what she was doing was nothing less than madness. To meet the brigand El Leon, the lion of the Andalusian hills, by chance and in daylight was dangerous enough, but to invite him to come to her at midnight in a dark patio garden was to place her honor and her life in his hands. The danger did not matter; some things were worth the risk.

Pilar drew her shawl around her as she paced back and forth over the patio tiles. The night was chilly, as it often was in late December in Seville. That coolness was, naturally, the only reason for the tremors that ran over her in waves. Why should she fear El Leon? Her stepfather Don Esteban was far more despicable, a devil in human form, yet she didn't shake when she faced him. He thought he had conquered her, her stepfather, but she would show him. She would.

It was a quiet night. From the town streets beyond the garden wall came only the occasional rattling of a passing carriage as late revelers made their way homeward. Somewhere far away a dog barked. Nearer at hand, perhaps three or four houses down, a lovesick swain strummed a guitar, softly serenading his lady with an old Andalusian melody. The music was intricate and flowing, the voice low and deep, rich with suppressed longing.

The moonlight shone down into the enclosed patio,

filtering through the branches of the jacaranda and making deep pools of shadow under the glossy-leaved orange trees. It caught the water spouting from the tiered stone fountain, turning the splattering droplets to liquid moonstones. It traced the intricate pattern of the Moorish floor tiles and bleached the flowers of the trailing geraniums in their pots attached to the walls from rose to palest pink. Under its light the honey brown of Pilar's hair turned to gold, while her cheekbones were washed with a pearl sheen, and the warm chocolate brown of her eyes acquired more mysterious depths.

Pilar's pacing slowed. She stood still, listening to the distant serenade. There was something in it, in the man's voice, that drew an answering resonance from deep inside her. The empathy was unwanted, yet inescapable, moving her to tenderness and despair that was near tears. She felt she knew the serenader's pain, but also that he understood and shared hers. It helped, somehow, to still her apprehension.

The song came to an end. The last notes of the guitar died away, and all was quiet again.

Pilar gave her head a quick shake, as if to rid herself of the peculiar moonlight fantasy. Frowning up at that bright light, she moved deeper into the shadows under the loggia of the house. She must not be seen from inside. Her stepfather was at some official dinner, but her duenna was still up, working at her tatting. The duenna, a sister to Don Esteban who was terrified of her brother's shadow, thought Pilar was safely asleep. That was the way it must stay.

Where was El Leon? Surely he had received her message?

It was possible he had not; there had been so little time to give it, and no hope of repeating it. That she had found the chance at all was a miracle. Now she was in need of another one—that El Leon would answer her summons. He might well have decided against it. It would be nearly as insane of him to show himself at the house of Don Esteban Iturbide as it was for her to send for him. Her stepfather would kill him on sight, as he might a stray dog.

There came a quiet rustling from the palm tree at the corner of the patio garden. Pilar stopped, going still. She strained her eyes in the darkness until they burned, her every sense alert for further sound. There was none. It must have been the cool night wind coming over the garden wall, or else a bird disturbed in its rest.

Her chest rose and fell in a long sigh. She drew her shawl closer once more and resumed her measured pacing along the loggia.

The amazing thing was that her stepfather had not yet killed her. The deed would not have troubled him; he had murdered her mother, after all. Pilar had no proof that was what had happened, nothing except her suspicions and her knowledge of Don Esteban; still, she was sure that it was so.

Pilar had despised the strutting little man with his cruel eyes and pointed, perfumed beard from the moment her widowed mother had introduced him to her as a prospective stepfather six years before. She had not troubled to hide her feelings in his presence and, moreover, had done everything a girl of sixteen could to prevent the alliance between him and her mother. It had not helped; her mother had been infatuated. Don Esteban was a lonely widower and also a man of charm and address, her mother had said, smiling fondly down on Pilar, smoothing the silk of the girl's hair as she sat on a stool at her knee. There would be honor and privilege in being his wife, for he was destined for a great position at court in Madrid. With the weight of her wealth behind them, combined with his, the two of them would shine there. It was natural for Pilar to resent the man who would take the place of her own father whom she had adored, but she would grow used to Don Esteban in time. And in a year or two, when she was a bit older, it was possible there might be a marriage arranged between her and Don Esteban's son by a previous marriage.

Never, Pilar had declared. No, not ever. She had met Don Esteban's beloved son during a visit. The young man had cornered her in a darkened salon, sneering at her protests, squeezing and pinching her body, and had cursed her when she kicked his shins and ran away. She would never accept such a vicious, egotistical suitor—nor could she think the father any better than the son.

The choice had not been presented to her. Don Esteban had revenged himself upon her for what he called her meddling the moment the marriage celebrations were over. He had escorted her to convent school where he spoke personally to the mother superior, claiming that Pilar was wayward and spoiled and in need of severe discipline. He left instructions that she must be taught to respect her elders, to curb her tongue and stifle the unladylike fierceness of her spirit. Then within a few months had come the news of the death of Don Esteban's son in a duel. Pilar had been forced to stay on her knees in prayer for his soul for hours because she had dared to say aloud that she was glad he was dead.

In the end, Pilar had learned her lessons of obedience. She had learned to appear meek and compliant while rage burned inside her. She had learned to bow to a thousand petty rules while searching for ways to circumvent them. She had learned to accept punishment without flinching, assuming a smile of forgiveness even as she plotted vengeance. She hated the duplicity, but she learned.

For the six years of her incarceration she was not allowed to go home, never permitted to communicate with her mother. Still, Pilar heard rumors from the other girls who came and went. Don Esteban, it seemed, was of the old school which believed that women should be kept shut up in their houses as in the days of the Moors, a belief he had taken trouble to hide before his marriage. There had been

6

no shining at court for Pilar's mother, for her new husband decreed that his wife must not flaunt herself abroad, but stay submissively at home. She must not mind that he wore fine lace and rare emeralds. She must not question his expenditures or the whereabouts of her wealth which he had claimed as his own, or wonder about his supposed fortune. She must obey his every command, accept his every dictate. His word was law, and he did not want Pilar in his house.

It was in the past year that Pilar had received word her mother was ill with a wasting sickness. Pilar had written, begging to be allowed to come home, but silence was her answer. She had appealed to her only other relative, her dead father's sister who lived in Cordoba, in the hope that her aunt could intervene. Her father's sister had made inquiries, but it had done no good; Don Esteban assured the lady all was well and that Pilar was only trying to make trouble. Pilar had then written to her mother's confessor, Father Domingo, but could receive no satisfactory answer to what was happening, no permission for her release from the convent.

Then her mother had died. It was Father Domingo who had finally prevailed upon Don Esteban to allow Pilar to pray at the funeral bier for the repose of her mother's soul. People would think it odd, the priest said, if the dead lady's daughter was not there. They might begin to wonder why she was being kept away, wonder what it was Don Esteban was trying to hide. Father Domingo was no longer welcome in Don Esteban Iturbide's house, but an escort had been sent to bring Pilar to Seville.

The house where Pilar's mother had been kept a prisoner and where she had died had been in Pilar's father's family for more than five hundred years, since Ferdinand the Saint had driven the Moors from Seville. Pilar hardly recognized it when she returned. Where once the Sandoval family arms had been emblazoned above the door, there was a great, ugly Iturbide crest. Supercilious servants had taken the places of the retainers who had been with the Sandovals for countless years; Pilar could find not a single familiar face. The rooms and halls had been stripped of their fine old furnishings, their carved furniture, tapestries, and gold and silver plate. Her mother's clothing, her icons, her few pieces of fine gold jewelry were gone.

Everything had been looted to fill Don Esteban's purse, or else to further his ambitions at court. He had apparently achieved the success he wanted, for he had been given a position as *pena de camara*, or keeper of fines, one of the *regidores* of the Cabildo, the governing body of the city of New Orleans in the Spanish colony of Louisiana. Since he would wield considerable power, as well as retaining ten percent of the fines collected, the post promised to return to him far more in bribes than he had expended in gaining it. There were some who whispered that the position itself was a bribe meant to rid the king of Don Esteban and his ceaseless conniving for favor. If Don Esteban saw it in that light, he hid it well; he preened himself as if he had gained the highest of honors.

Pilar's mother, ill for many months, had died the day after Don Esteban had returned from Madrid with the news of his appointment. It had seemed a convenient coincidence, for a sickly wife could neither be taken to Louisiana nor left behind without it appearing that she had been deserted. Then Pilar had learned from her duenna, Don Esteban's sister, that Don Esteban had, some months before, brought a special tonic from Madrid for his wife. He had ordered her to take it, and issued strict rules that it be brought to her every day. On the morning of her death he had administered it to her with his own hands. Immediately after the death rites, he had returned to the house and commenced his packing for the voyage to Louisiana.

The night air of the patio garden swirled around Pilar as she came to a halt in mid-stride with her fists clenched in the cloth of her shawl. Had that shadow moved, there where the giant ceramic olla caught the water from the rooftop? She could not tell; it might have been the wind swaying the oleander shrub which grew behind it. Or it could be only her imagination and the waiting. She had waited the night before and the night before that, and El Leon had not come. If he did not come soon, tonight or the night after, it would be too late.

Deliberately, in defiance of the fear she would not acknowledge, Pilar turned her back on the shadowed corner and began to walk again. Somewhere a cat yowled, and from the street beyond the garden wall came the sound of low voices as two men carried on a murmured conversation while walking homeward. The sounds ceased and all was quiet once more. Too quiet.

Pilar shivered. In an assumption of self-control, she directed her thoughts to other things.

She had kept her suspicions about her mother's death to herself during the funeral rituals. It had been such a strain to hold her bitter grief and anger inside, however, that afterward she allowed herself to be drawn into a quarrel with Don Esteban over the looting of her father's house. It was his right to sell what he pleased, he said; the house had come to her mother on the death of her husband, Pilar's father, since there were no male heirs, and these same belongings became Don Esteban's on their wedding day by the wedding contract. But what did it matter? he inquired. Pilar would have no use for furnishings and jewels in the convent.

Pilar, retreating into caution, had questioned why she must return. She was told that she could not stay in the house alone while Don Esteban was in Louisiana, and there was nowhere else for her to go, no one to see to her welfare. She had no prospects for marriage, and was indeed an old maid at two-and-twenty. The convent would be a refuge for her, and Don Esteban would himself provide an endowment for the church in her name, a chest of gold worth several thousand pesos. This gold, to be sent with her on her return, would assure her comfort and gain for her the position within the convent hierarchy to which she was entitled by breeding and birth.

Pilar was not impressed by either the spurious concern for her welfare or the possible endowment that was less than a fraction of the estate that should have been hers on her mother's death. She declared firmly that she had no intention of returning to the convent, and that, moreover, she had a place to go and someone to look after her. She would take refuge with her aunt in Cordoba. A shouting match had followed. At the end of it, Don Esteban had shouted for his majordomo, and the two men had picked Pilar up bodily and carried her to her room. She had been thrust inside and the door locked behind her.

Two nights later she had awakened at the sound of a key in the lock. The door had swung open and a man had crept inside. She had sat up in bed, calling out, but he had not answered. He moved to the side of the bed and grasped her leg. She wrenched from his hold and slid from the bed. He caught her and they grappled in the darkness. It was then that her stepfather had burst into the room. He was holding a candlestick, and with him were several men and women, as if he had been having guests for dinner. The candlelight had revealed the man who had attacked her to be a lackey of her stepfather's, a loose-lipped and pimpled young man named Carlos.

The wrath of her stepfather had not fallen on Carlos, however, but on Pilar. She had lured the lackey to her bedchamber, he shouted in outrage. She was depraved, a disgrace to his house. She must marry Carlos or he, Don Esteban Iturbide, would send her back to the convent that very night, before she brought further shame upon both him and herself.

It was a trick and Pilar knew it; still, she was compromised beyond hope of recovery. Her stepfather's guests, standing behind him and staring with avid eyes, did not appear likely to believe her side of the story. If she married Carlos, she would gain nothing except a fumbling, lasciviously grinning nonentity for a husband, one who would have legal right to her body as well as everything she might own. Carlos was so much under Don Esteban's thumb that any portion of her mother's estate that might come to her legally on her marriage would be turned over to her stepfather at once. On the other hand, she might at least buy a little time with an agreement to return to the convent. With the last in mind, she had made herself appear crushed and contrite. She pretended to sob as she begged tearfully to return to her little cell with its single bed, where she would be surrounded by the gentle sisters and everything she had come to know and love. So appealing had she made it sound that for an instant Don Esteban had appeared reluctant to give his permission.

It had not been easy to maintain that air of drooping defeat while her heart corroded inside her with bitter rage, but Pilar had managed it. Her reward had been permission to go to Father Domingo's church for morning mass each day until her departure. There she had accosted the priest, pouring out her tale. The good father had only sighed and shook his head, counseling obedience and submission to her fate. Don Esteban could not be so black as she painted him; hadn't the grieving husband pledged himself to erect a stained-glass window in the church in memory of his wife? The ways of God were mysterious. Perhaps Pilar was meant to be a bride of Christ and this was His way of telling her so?

Pilar had no vocation, and she knew it well. She was

much too fond of the pleasures and luxuries of the world, had missed them too intensely during her incarceration to ever give them up willingly. There was no thought of submission in her mind, but rather a teeming multitude of plans for vengeance and wild possibilities for escape.

One of the last had been triggered by the sight of a young man named Vicente de Carranza y Leon. He was a theology student at the university who in better days had lived in the neighborhood and still returned there every morning for mass. Vicente was a stalwart young man with a kind and attractive face, but one who seldom smiled. He had little to smile about. His family had been ruined by Don Esteban Iturbide some years before, shortly after the don's marriage to Pilar's mother.

The Carranzas and the Iturbides were hereditary enemies in a feud that had been going on for four generations. Don Esteban, it was said, had hired assassins to kill Vicente's father. More, Don Esteban's son, the young man who was to have wed Pilar, had abducted and violated Vicente's sister, after which the girl had committed suicide. When Vicente's older brother, Refugio, had challenged Don Esteban's son to a duel for the crime against their sister, then spitted him on his sword during the fight, Don Esteban had used his recently gained court connections to have Refugio charged with murder. Refugio's refusal to surrender to the men sent with the guardia civil by Don Esteban for his arrest had resulted in a fight in which three of Don Esteban's hirelings were killed. Refugio had become an outcast, a brigand with a stronghold in the mountains who was called El Leon, the lion, after the big and deadly wildcats that roamed the hills, and also for his mother's surname, which meant the same. The hatred of Refugio de Carranza y Leon for Don Esteban at least equaled Pilar's own.

The next time Pilar saw Vicente standing outside the church, she walked quickly toward him. She outdistanced the duenna who hurried after her through the early morning crowds. As Pilar neared Vicente de Carranza, she looked into his thin, earnest face then let her shawl slip from her shoulders and slide to the ground. Vicente knelt to pick it up. She did the same. She murmured a few words as she took the shawl he offered. He gave her a sharp look from dark, expressive eyes before he inclined his head in a bow, but the young man made no answer. Pilar turned away as her duenna joined her, and walked into the church.

Had Vicente understood her? There had been so little time and no chance to be certain. Did he know who she was, know anything about her? Or if he did not know, would he trouble to find out? If he found out, would he do as she asked, or would he shrug off the incident as being of no importance? So much depended on that one short encounter.

Of course, even supposing Vicente passed on her plea to his brother to meet her in the garden of Don Esteban's house in the midnight hours, there was no guarantee that El Leon would come. It would take a rare combination of hatred, curiosity, and daring to bring him.

The hours of darkness were slipping past. Pilar's footsteps dragged. She was weary from her three-night vigil, yes, but it was the waning of hope that pressed hardest upon her shoulders. She had been so sure she could evade Don Esteban's plans for her, so positive she could best him. She would do it yet, with or without El Leon; still, she had placed so much dependence on the aid of Refugio de Carranza that it was disheartening to think she must find another way.

How she wished that she were a man! She would defy her stepfather with sword in hand, then demand an accounting for her mother's death and the looting of her heritage. What a pleasure it would be to run Don Esteban through with a steel blade and watch the sneer on his features give way to shocked surprise. Odious, strutting, vicious little man! To be forced to bow to his dictates would be beyond endurance. She would do anything, anything at all, to escape it.

A soft sound came from behind her, like the rustle of cloth. She started to turn. There was a single, swift movement, and she was caught from behind in a firm grasp, with an arm clamped like a band of Toledo steel around her ribs and a hand sealing her mouth. She drew in her breath, instinctively thrusting backward with an elbow. She connected with the folds of a cloak and, under it, a belly like a wall of stone. The hold upon her tightened abruptly, driving the air from her lungs. Her back was pressed tight against a hard male form while the warmth of his body and the soft wool of his cloak enveloped her.

"Be still," came a voice quiet and deep against her hair. "As much satisfaction as it might give me to defile a woman of Don Esteban's house on his own patio tiles, I'm not at present in the mood. Provoke me, and that may well change."

It was El Leon; it could be no one else. Anger for his distrust and his close, hard hold burgeoned inside Pilar, banishing fear. She shook her head, trying to dislodge his hand from her mouth.

"You want to speak, do you? Now that's encouraging, for I want nothing more than to hear you. But I would advise that the words be as soft and dulcet as the dove."

The hand on her mouth was lifted by degrees. She waited until it had been completely removed before she spoke, and the words were low and scathing. "Let me go. You're breaking my ribs."

"And shall I also lay my life at your feet all tied up with ribbons and faded roses? Thank you, no. Besides, I'm still entertaining the idea of reprisal. Intimate, of course."

"You wouldn't!"

"Tell me why I should not," he said, his voice suddenly

losing its soft tone, becoming harsh. "The last rape was by an Iturbide upon a Carranza. It must be our turn."

"I'm not an Iturbide, nor do I have anything to do with your quarrel!"

"You are in the house of Iturbide, and therefore of it." The words were uncompromising.

"Not of my own will. Besides, it was once my father's house." Pilar could feel the firm beat of El Leon's heart against her back. His implacable strength, his scent compounded of wool and horse, of fresh night air and his own maleness, crept in upon her senses. She wanted to turn to look at him, but could not move.

"I am aware of that, just as I know your name and station and recent history. I have made it my business to know, being neither an idiot nor a quixotic fool. What I don't know is what you want of me."

He released her waist in a sudden movement, then caught her wrist, spinning her around to face him. Pilar, off balance, put out a hand, bracing against his chest. She could feel the bands of muscle that sheathed it, sense the overpowering solidity of his presence. She stared up at him with her voice caught somewhere in her throat, stifled by doubt.

He was tall and broad, his shape exaggerated by the length and fullness of his black wool cloak. The features of his face were firm and regular and precisely molded, sunbronzed even in the moonlight, but his eyes were no more than dark sockets shadowed by the wide brim of his hat. There was about him an air of stringent control coupled with an edge of danger. There was not a shred of sympathy.

Refugio de Carranza looked at the woman he held, and felt as if a hand had squeezed his heart inside his chest. He had come to this rendezvous out of purest wanton curiosity, to see what manner of woman could rouse Vicente from his studies and persuade him to use methods of communication that were reserved, usually, for direst emergencies. He saw.

She was beautiful, with the fair skin and hair that spoke of the blood of Visigoth invaders in her veins, coloring that was common in northern Spain where he was born, but more rare here in the Andalus. There was pride in the tilt of her head and the set of her shoulders, and also determined bravery. Remembering the softness of her, the fragrance of her skin and silkiness of her hair against his cheek, he found it necessary to subdue a strong need to gather her close once more. He had thought himself invulnerable to the allure of her kind. It was incensing to be proven wrong.

"Well?" he said when she made no sound. "Did you have a purpose, or is it a game? Shall I seek to relieve your tedium, or would it be best if I guard my back?"

"I—I would never betray you."

"Your assurance eases my mind. That, and my inspection of this fine garden. I can only suppose that if there's an assassin present, it must be you."

"No!"

"It's a tryst, then. And here I am a laggard lover, behind in my embraces. Come and let me taste your sweet lips."

She gave an abrupt shake of her head, resisting the pull on her wrist that he still held. "It pleases you to make fun of me, though why it should I have no idea."

"Why not? There's little enough fun in the world for me and mine. But it would please me more to be told why I was bid to come."

"I want—" She stopped, horribly uncertain of the wisdom of what she meant to say.

"Yes, you want . . . ? Everyone wants something. Shall I complete what you are too bashful to say?"

"No!" she said in haste. "I want you—"

"I knew it."

She glared at him in annoyance and embarrassment. Then she saw, projecting over one shoulder, the neck of a guitar that he carried slung across his back by its shoulder strap. It came to her abruptly that he was the serenader she had heard; the timbre of the voice, its soft power, was the same. The knowledge eased the doubts inside her, though she could not have explained why. She drew a shallow breath and spoke quickly and a little too loudly.

"I want you to abduct me."

His grasp slackened. Pilar twisted her wrist free and stepped back. That she had surprised him gave her a fleeting satisfaction.

It was premature.

"By all means," he said, sweeping his hat from his head as he bowed with consummate grace. "I am at your service. Shall it be now?"

"I wish it might, but I have no means to pay you at this minute. If you will wait and take me as I am being escorted back to the convent, there will be a chest of gold, the endowment to be paid in my name. You may have it as your reward."

His stillness was complete, like that of a stalking cat before it strikes. When he spoke, the words had a slicing edge. "I am to be rewarded? Surely to have you would be enough?"

Angry confusion washed over her in a wave of heat. "You—You won't have me," she said. "You will deliver me at once to my aunt in Cordoba."

"Will I?" The question was softly suggestive.

The man in front of her had once been a grandee of wealth and title, with all the instincts and manners of his class. Now he was a bandit, an outcast who made his way by preying on his fellow men. He was El Leon, a leader of thieves and outlaws who could only have gained his position by being stronger and harder than the men he led. How could she trust him?

How could she not?

"You must help me, Refugio de Carranza!" she cried, stepping toward him and clutching the edges of his cloak in her hands. "I'm saying this all wrong, but I had no idea how it would be. I meant no insult; I only thought that you would have use for gold. I don't doubt that if you agree to do as I ask, it will be for the sake of striking a blow against Don Esteban. It would be a great injury to his pride to have his stepdaughter abducted from under his nose. And if it happens in the open countryside, as the caravan takes me to the convent, there will be no way he can hide it, no way he can deny it."

He said nothing for a long moment. Finally, he spoke. "Don Esteban himself will be with the caravan?"

"So I understand. He wants to make certain that I am safely locked away again."

"You realize," he said, lifting his hands to close them on her clutching fists and loosen their hold, clasping them with impersonal firmness, "that what you ask will mean your ruin? There isn't a person in Spain who will believe that your chastity survived this abduction, no matter how short the span of time you remain in my company. The enmity between my family and that of your stepfather is too well known for it to be otherwise."

She lifted her chin as she met the dark glitter of his eyes. "I don't care, if you don't. I have already been compromised, so more talk can't harm me." She told him quickly of her stepfather's scheme.

Refugio listened to the young woman in front of him with only half his attention. He had heard something of what she was saying already, and knew enough of Don Esteban to guess the rest. He was much more aware of the clear sound of her voice, of the translucent purity of her skin in the moonlight and the flashing life in her night-black eyes. The feel of her slender hands in his, the memory of her curves against him, clouded his thoughts, creating inside him a slow-growing need to know more of her. Aligned with it, however, was compunction as uncomfortable as it was inevitable.

"That may be how it was," he said, "but will your aunt believe what you say and take you in?"

"I believe she will, pray she will."

"Even if she should give you shelter, will she protect you from whatever Don Esteban may do afterward?"

"I can only trust that she may. There's no one else."

"Not even the church, the convent?"

The tenor of his questions, the evidence they gave of his swift consideration of her plight, gave Pilar hope. Her voice rang as she answered. "Never. I was not born to be a nun, and refuse to be forced to become one at Don Esteban's bidding."

"And will you be content to be a spinster, a dowerless female spurned by men who want a wife they can be certain is chaste?"

"If they are fools enough to want me only for my money or judge me from no more than rumor, then I have no use for them."

"Proudly spoken, but pride won't keep your feet warm on a long winter's night."

The doubts he expressed were more than familiar to Pilar. However, she had counted the cost of what she was about to do already and would not turn back. She lifted her chin, staring him straight in the face. "Will you take me or not?"

"Oh, yes," Refugio Carranza y Leon said softly as he watched her there in the moonlit stillness. "I'll take you."

CHAPTER 2

The caravan taking Pilar to the convent was not a large one. It consisted of the old and cumbersome carriage in which she was shut up with her duenna, Don Esteban cantering alongside upon an Arabian stallion, and eight lackeys riding guard, four before and four behind. It would have been even smaller, Pilar was sure, but for considerations of safety. Don Esteban was not a coward, but neither was he a fool. He muttered about the thieves and brigands who prowled the roads and his fears for the gold, in its chest strapped on the back of the carriage beside the trunk holding Pilar's meager possessions. Regardless, she suspected that the outriders had been hired against his enemy, Refugio de Carranza, for there was no safety from El Leon once they began to climb into the hills. Her stepfather's vigilance troubled Pilar, but there was nothing she could do about it. She could only trust that Refugio knew Don Esteban's habits and would take them into consideration as he made his plan of attack.

Don Esteban had insisted on an early start and permitted few stops along the way. He wanted to get this journey behind him. If they made good time, they would reach the hill village where the convent was located before dark. Then, after a night spent at the village inn, he could return the following day to Seville. Even if he had not been wary of trespassing overlong on El Leon's territory, he had no time to waste. He had received orders from the king's minister to proceed immediately to Cadiz, where a ship for Louisiana was making ready to sail.

The carriage jolted and bounced along the dusty, rutted roads. The countryside around them, which in summer was a soft green highlighted by the red of poppies and the yellow of wattle, lay brown and barren under the winter sky. Now and then there were the gray shapes of olive trees or a patch of silver-green weeds, but the only other color was in the hills that spread in long sweeps of blue and lavender against the horizon. Now and then they passed a farmer plodding along, leading a donkey piled high with sticks for firewood, or else a boy herding a few sheep or goats. Scarcely anything else moved except the wind blowing over plowed fields and stirring up the little whirlwinds of loose soil known as dust devils.

The afternoon was waning. They had turned off the main road some time ago to follow a track winding into the hills. Soon the spires of the village church would appear, the church that sat beside the convent. Where was El Leon?

He had given his word he would come. Pilar dared not let herself think he might fail her, but she could not prevent herself from drawing aside the leather carriage curtain every few minutes to peer out the window.

"What is it, señorita?" the duenna asked at last. "Is something amiss?"

Pilar let the curtain fall. "Not at all. I'm just . . . anxious to catch sight of the convent."

"You will see enough of it, I'm sure," the woman answered with an edge of irritation in her voice.

"Only the inside," Pilar said, her own tone subdued.

Her role of quiet submissiveness was beginning to wear on Pilar. She longed to shout her defiance and announce her approaching freedom to the woman who had been set to watch over her. She could not permit herself that luxury. She must bear with the restraint a little longer before she could escape Don Esteban. How surprised he would be. His ego was so great that he could not conceive of her finding the will, much less the means, to do so. How she would love to see his face when he realized he could not bend her to his will.

She had done everything she could think of to ensure that all went well. The day gown she wore was of wool in a gray-blue color without stripes or figures, ruffles or lace to attract attention, and her cape was chestnut-brown, trimmed only with a bit of braiding. Both were such as befitted a novice, but they were also warm. More than that, she had left off her *cul de Paris*, the crinolined bustle used to add fullness to skirts, since it might make riding horseback awkward. Her shoes were of sturdy leather and without buckles, in case she had to walk over rough ground. Her hair was perfectly innocent of a hairdresser's skill since there had been no opportunity to have the services of one either in the convent or in Don Esteban's house. She had done no more than draw it back into a neat knot at the crown of her head. At least it would not be a bother if she had to move hastily.

The caravan rounded a bend. Directly in front of it was a flock of sheep. The coachman shouted and swore, applying the brake as he sawed on the lines. The animals leaped here and there, bawling in alarm as the carriage rocked to a stop in the middle of the flock. A dog of uncertain breed nipped at the heels of the milling sheep, barking in excitement and throwing looks at his master, the shepherd. This last was an old man, bent and hobbling and carrying a crook, and dressed in faded rags and a hooded cloak. He crept along in the midst of the sea of dirty wool, but seemed to pay no heed to sheep or dog. He appeared not to hear the shouts of the coachman nor the commands of Don Esteban that he clear the way. In truth, there was no place for him to move his flock, for the hillsides rose steep on either side.

The carriage horses reared and whinnied, jerking the carriage back and forth. Don Esteban screamed out an order to his guards, who had fallen back beside the stranded vehicle, and they moved to the heads of the carriage horses to calm them. Pilar's stepfather then plowed through the sheep toward the old man. For a moment Pilar thought he meant to ride the shepherd down, but instead he lifted the short whip of braided leather he always carried and slashed it across the bent shoulders. The old man cringed, ducking his head as he turned. Don Esteban raised the whip again.

The braided leather came whistling down once more, but it never struck. The shepherd straightened, catching the slashing thong and whirling it around his wrist. He gave a hard jerk, and Pilar's stepfather was dragged half out of the saddle. At the same time the old shepherd's hood fell back, revealing a harshly handsome face set in lines of aversion, and dark, windblown hair.

"Carranza!" Don Esteban cried. He cast the whip from him, staring wild-eyed down at the shepherd. Abruptly, he called back over his shoulder. "Kill the girl! Kill her, I say! At once!"

"El Leon! El Leon!"

The cry came from Don Esteban's guards, but it was picked up by men in the hillsides above the carriage. Pilar heard the full-throated shouts that seemed to ring from the skies themselves, saw the the men of Refugio de Carranza's band appear as from nowhere, calling their leader's name. Her heart leaped with sickening force inside her. Her hand trembled as she clutched the curtain. It was here, the time of her abduction. It had come. It was now.

There was one of her stepfather's guards moving toward the carriage door. He was drawing his sword, though he was hampered by the frightened sheep eddying back and forth under his horse's feet. It was the lackey Carlos, Pilar saw, the man who had invaded her bedchamber on Don Esteban's order. As she stared at him, the words Don Esteban had called out took on meaning. Her stepfather had ordered her death. He meant to see her killed rather than allowing her to fall into the hands of his enemy.

She looked around her in frantic haste, searching for something, anything, to use to defend herself. There was nothing. Across from her, on the other seat, her duenna was gabbling her prayers, her eyes wide in a face gone colorless.

Her stepfather cried out again in strident outrage, a cry that was suddenly broken off. There was no time to look. The lackey Carlos was surging through the sheep, leaping his horse over a large ram. He reached out with his sword, thrusting through the window. Pilar flung herself backward as the blade slashed through the leather curtain. She snatched up a fat carriage cushion, and as the sword came slicing inside again, deflected the sharp blade with the thick, soft weight. Down feathers erupted into the air, swirling, drifting in a white cloud.

The sword did not penetrate the carriage again. Outside, there came the clang and scrape of steel on steel. A man with a hooded cloak hanging down his back blocked the view with his broad shoulders. In an instant there was a gasping grunt, then the body of the lackey Carlos tumbled from his horse as El Leon whirled away.

There were shouts and yells from every quarter now, followed by the sound of hoofbeats as a number of the lackeys in escort raced away in retreat. The carriage rocked as a man clambered up its side. At the same time there came the sound of a heavy weight falling on the roof, as if one of Refugio's band had leaped from the rocks above. Blows thudded from the direction of the coachman's box. Sheep bleated and the dog barked. Men cursed. Shots rang out. The duenna screeched and clutched her rosary as the carriage jerked back and forth with the plunging of the team. As Pilar reached for the carriage door, the duenna snatched at her arm.

"Where are you going?" she cried, clutching Pilar's wrist. "Come back. You'll be killed, or worse!"

Pilar shook off the woman's hold. She pushed the door panel open and eased outside, using the iron step as a viewing platform as she clung tightly to the swinging door.

The noise had begun to quieten. The coachman was being held at pistol point. Four of the eight guards were being trussed up, seated with their backs together. Carlos lay still and unmoving with a splotch of blood darkening his ripped coat, while the other three had apparently taken to their heels and were nowhere to be seen. Don Esteban was face down in the road in front of the carriage, with the sheep dog sniffing with wrinkled nose at his beard.

There was no time to see more. There came the thud of hoofs behind her. As she turned her head, a man mounted on horseback swept down on her. El Leon caught her waist in a hard grip and heaved her from her perch. Surprise drove a cry from her as she was lifted across the horse's neck and settled in front of her captor.

"This wasn't necessary!" she gasped. "I would have joined you."

"It must appear an abduction indeed, for your sake. Your duenna will be your witness."

The words were hard-edged with irony. She turned her head to look up into the face of El Leon. Its strong planes were set and stern, giving nothing away. His eyes, she saw, were a bright-faceted gray and burned with clear intelligence and fierce, exacting determination. A wave of doubt moved over her, one swiftly followed by dismay. To hide the last, she quickly turned her head.

Before her on the ground was the sprawled form of Don Esteban. She moistened her lips before asking, "Is he . . . dead?"

"No, thanks to Satan's own luck," Refugio answered. "He's unconscious, since he fell on his head when I pulled him from the saddle."

"You hate him so much, but failed to kill him because he wasn't conscious?"

"I prefer him to know who strikes the blow."

The horse under them was restive, sidling, tossing its head. Refugio de Carranza controlled it with iron muscles that she could feel in his thighs under her and in the hard arms clasped around her. Her voice was tight as she said, "It's a courtesy that could mean your death."

"Shall I let you down to finish him?"

"I have no weapon."

"I'll lend you my sword."

The temptation was great, but she knew the deed was beyond her. "Thank you, but no."

"Courtesy or fault, you share it, then," he pointed out.

"Yes."

"Shall we go?"

The question was grave, without haste, as if they would linger as long as it was her wish, as if he was giving her the chance to draw back, to return to the carriage if she so desired.

She did not dare put the matter to the test. Quite suddenly she could not bear to tarry an instant longer.

"Yes," she said with a breathless feeling in her chest, "let us go."

He wheeled the horse with a shouted order to his men. There were only three of them, though before she would have sworn there was a dozen. They leaped to their leader's bidding, one tying down the last strap on the pack saddle of a mule loaded with Pilar's trunk and the money chest, another gathering the reins of the extra horses, while the last jerked the final knot tight on the rope holding the captured guards. In an instant the three had mounted and they were all thundering away from the stranded carriage. The duenna, putting her head out the window, screamed invective mixed with shrill, despairing pleas after them. They did not look back.

They rode in grim silence for mile upon mile, threading intricate, branching paths through the hills and avoiding all habitation. At first Pilar expected them to regain the main road to Cordoba, the fastest way to reach her aunt. She soon realized that the caution of their passage forbade it. She began, instead, to make calculations of distance and time in her head, wondering how late in the night it would be before she was with her aunt. She knew that it was a two-day journey from Seville to Cordoba by carriage under the best of conditions. Horseback would be considerably faster, but she had no real idea how much the winding hill roads would add to the journey. She finally came to the conclusion that it would be dawn at best before she reached her destination.

The track they were on seemed to be getting rougher and steeper, as if they were heading into the mountains instead of making their way back toward the valley of the Guadalquivir River and the Cordoba road which followed it. Moreover, with the overcast sky and lateness of the evening, she could not tell whether they were even traveling in the right direction. The doubt and dismay she had felt earlier returned to plague her. What had she done? The refrain beat in her mind with the rhythm of the horse's hoofs. What had she done?

The arms of the man who held her were warm, but their

enclosing strength felt like a hold that might well be unbreakable. She was aware of warring instincts inside her; one
bid her to fight free, while the other urged her to accept his
protection. She could not understand her own ambivalence.
What was El Leon doing, except what she had asked? There
was nothing wrong in that. In addition, he had slain the man
who was trying to kill her, and for this she must be grateful.
If it seemed in retrospect that he had agreed too readily to
what she proposed, there was the chest of gold bouncing
along on the mule with them for an explanation. She was
safe; how could it be otherwise? What possible reason
would he have for betraying her trust?

There could be no reason, and yet she could not relax.
To permit herself to accept his support, to lean against his
body, was far too intimate a gesture. She did not know him,
nor he her. He seemed too hard and uncompromising, too
formidable a man, for such a thing to even be possible. The
miles passed and her muscles burned and ached with the
effort of remaining erect within his grasp, yet she still
refused to yield.

To distract herself she turned her attention to the men
who rode with them. The communication between them
had been brief, the caustic comments of men who knew each
other and their duties too well to need long speeches. There
had been enough banter, however, to give Pilar some idea
of their names. The one on her left had been called Enrique,
she thought. He appeared in his early thirties and his hair
was light brown and wildly curling. His eyes were the
brown that was near black, the chocolate eyes of Andalusia,
like her own. He had no great height, being hardly more
than two inches taller than she was herself, and his form was
slight. His mouth was outlined by a thin mustache that he
touched often, almost like a talisman, and as he caught her
glance he gave her a smile that was drolly cheerful. Of them
all, he seemed most approachable.

On the right was an older man addressed as Baltasar, who was bearlike in size and gruff in manner. His face was craggy, with a deep line between his brows and a series of pitted scars in his face, perhaps from smallpox. His eyes had the weary, faded look of a man who had seen much, experienced much, and most of it out in the weather. The gaze he turned on her as she rode with Refugio was shrewd yet troubled.

Following in the rear, leading the extra mounts, was a tall and lanky young man in his twenties who rode with his hat bouncing on his back, held by a thong around his neck, so that his dark hair flopped onto his forehead. His saddle was odd, with a high pommel and decorations of silver medallions in a style Pilar had never seen before; still, he sat upon his horse as if he had been born at a gallop. Of an age with Refugio, just over thirty, his light blue eyes were clear and watchful, though he carried with him an air of recklessness that verged on bravado. He was called Charro, if she had caught the word correctly, one signifying some kind of horseman, apparently not his real name.

Refugio had not troubled to introduce Pilar to these men. She doubted it was an oversight, since she was beginning to know something of him. It was more likely that he thought the less she knew, the less she could tell. She tried to convince herself that it didn't matter, that she would never see any of them again after today. Regardless, she found the precaution annoying.

It was a relief when Refugio called a halt. It appeared, from the way the men instantly began to transfer the saddles from the spent horses to the fresh mounts, one of them her stepfather's white Arabian, that the respite would not be long. Pilar had done more than appraise El Leon's followers: she was ready with a suggestion for her own satisfaction.

As Refugio lowered her to the ground and swung down to stand beside her, she gestured toward one of the extra mounts. "I can ride now, and relieve you and your horse of my weight."

"You're far from heavy. Besides, there's no ladies' saddle, and these brutes are likely to shy at flapping skirts."

"I'm sure I can manage," she insisted.

"How could I face your aunt if you were thrown? No, I can't allow it; I have my reputation to consider."

She glanced at him from under her lashes, wondering at the undercurrents she sensed in his answer. There was stringency in it, and also deft reassurance for her that could only be deliberate. Added to those things was an alertness, as if he stood ready to deal with any resistance she might raise.

"Really, I'll be quite safe," she said.

He was quiet a moment before he smiled. "Have you been so uncomfortable?"

"Not at all, but surely you were?"

"How can you think it? Maidens who fail to kick and scream don't come my way every day."

There was that flick of irony again. He had felt her apprehension. He was a man of acute perceptions; she must remember that. Being perceptive did not, of course, make him trustworthy. This she would also remember.

"You would not—" she began, then stopped.

Refugio, studying the pure lines of Don Esteban's step-daughter's features and the grave look in her large, lash-fringed dark eyes, watching the wind tease at a strand of her hair the color of old gold coins, felt an unaccustomed qualm. It had been years since he had traded banter with a woman, or at least a woman such as Pilar Sandoval y Serna. She was beautiful and intriguingly willful and had more than her share of courage. There had been a time when he might have approached her with gallantry and wit, serenades and a touch of reverence. Perhaps she would have responded with smiles. But that was long ago, and he had no time for regrets.

"I would not what?" he said abruptly. "Betray you? I could make you a pretty speech full of solemn oaths and protests of honor, but why should you believe it? Brigands have been known to lie. Besides, you are right to be on your guard. We are not headed toward Cordoba."

"What?" Her eyes widened as shock rippled along her nerves. "But my aunt will expect to see me by late this evening, or at least by an hour or two past midnight. I—I would not like to disappoint her, since she went to great effort to send word of my welcome when Father Domingo contacted her on my behalf."

"I believe Don Esteban knows that you once intended to seek refuge with your aunt?" At her nod, Refugio went on. "He will also know and fear the influence such a respected lady may bring to bear to have an inquiry made into the circumstances of your mother's death and your own disinheritance. There's little that he won't do to prevent you from persuading your aunt to that course. Assuming he regains his senses as expected, he will no doubt ride at once to Cordoba to intercept you. It will be best if you tarry along the way long enough for him to think you may have found other sanctuary."

"You mean, I should stay with you? Overnight?"

"Or longer. Don't tell me you are concerned for your good name? I thought you abandoned that in Seville."

"I did not leave behind my common sense!"

"Your common sense tells you that I mean you harm?"

There was a sting in the softness of his tone, one that sounded a warning in Pilar's mind. At the same time, she sensed the close attention Refugio's men were paying to the confrontation. The three maintained attitudes of indifference as, their tasks completed, they lounged against a tree or leaned with a shoulder propped on a horse's flank. Yet they made no unnecessary sound to draw attention to themselves, had nothing to say to each other.

Pilar met Refugio's gaze, her own unwavering though her heartbeat inside her chest was uneven. "The fact is," she said, "it was you yourself who mentioned the possibility."

He lifted a brow, his features relaxing a fraction. "So I did. I didn't think it made an impression."

"You thought wrong."

"My mistake. I believe I also explained why I refrained. My mood is the same as in Don Esteban's garden, which is to say, disinclined. I'll tell you if it changes."

His gaze swung to his men, hardening as he saw their suspended interest. "What?" he said, his voice like a soft lash. "Are you so bored you're reduced to eavesdropping? I have a remedy. Mount up!"

The others groaned and muttered as they obeyed, but there was none who was slow in moving. Pilar stood still. She had not agreed to go with El Leon, and was incensed that her consent was taken for granted. But what else could she do? To wander these hills alone, without means of protection or transportation, would be more dangerous than the alternative. Besides, her predicament was something she had brought on her own head.

Refugio de Carranza swung into the saddle of the white Arabian, then walked it to where Pilar stood. He leaned down to offer her his hand. She gazed up at him for long seconds with mutinous eyes, then she put out her hand and lifted her foot to place it on his boot. He clasped her wrist and drew her up before him in one smooth, effortless motion. His arms closed around her once more. As she settled into place they moved off down the track with the others following behind them.

Dark came, closing around them as if they had ridden

into a dense black fog. There was neither a moon nor starshine to guide them, due to the overcast heavens. A fitful wind arose, whipping into their faces. After a short while it began to rain. It was hardly more than a mist, but it was steady and had a windblown chill. The droplets swept into their eyes and dripped from their chins. Pilar huddled into her cape, holding it at the neck with her arms inside to keep the wet from seeping to her skin. It made it difficult to balance, and now and then she was jostled back against Refugio. However, she always struggled bolt upright again.

Finally he breathed a soft imprecation and caught her waist, dragging her under his heavy cloak and against his chest. As she stiffened and tried to pull away, he spoke with impatience in her ear. "Be still, before we both get soaked."

It was only practical to obey. She sank her teeth into her lower lip as muscles, cramped for hours in her unnatural position, relaxed. A tremor, totally involuntary, ran along her thighs.

His arm tightened at her waist. "To mortify the flesh for the sake of an idea is the act of a fanatic. Are you sure you shouldn't be a nun, counting beads while kneeling on beans and thinking of glory? It isn't too late to repent of this momentary madness."

"Oh, I think it is," she answered. "Anyway, I don't repent."

"Then forget pride and lean on me. I promise I'll not take advantage of it."

"I never thought you would," she said, turning her head slightly as if to look at him, though she could not see him in the darkness. She could not think how he followed the track ahead of them, unless he could see in the dark or else knew it as a peasant knew his tiny piece of land.

"Didn't you? Possibly it's true you have no vocation."

"What do you mean?" she demanded.

"Nuns shouldn't lie."

She was silent a moment, then said, "Are you always so quick to accuse?"

"You think me unjust?"

"There could be other reasons for keeping some distance between us."

"Such as?"

"A disinclination to burden you."

"You are all consideration."

Stung by the dryness of his tone, she went on, "Or it might be the lingering smell of sheep."

Somewhere nearby, Pilar heard the snort of a muffled laugh.

"I make you my apologies," Refugio said, "but some things are inescapable."

The sound of his voice, matter-of-fact, even shaded with humor, was oddly calming. She put her arm along his, which was clamped around her, easing back a degree more against him as she agreed. "So it seems."

"Precisely. Sleep if you can."

She gave a faint nod.

She did not sleep, however, did not feel even the slightest drowsiness. She was still painfully alert and on edge when they rode into the yard of a small stone house built into a hillside.

Yellow lamplight spilled out as the door was opened, shafting through the swirling mist of rain, outlining the shape of a young woman. The older man of the group, Baltasar, called out to the woman and she answered, though both kept their voices low. Refugio swung from the saddle, then reached to catch Pilar's waist, lifting her down. She slid into his arms, gripping his shoulders with convulsive fingers until the cramps eased from her legs. She thought of asking where he had taken her, but was too doubtful of a satisfactory answer, and too weary and miserably wet to make the effort.

Refugio turned her toward the doorway. The other woman, young and with anxious eyes, stepped back to let her pass inside. There was a call from outside for Refugio. He released Pilar and moved back into the yard again.

"I'm Isabel," the young woman said to Pilar in soft, hesitant tones. "You must be worn to the bone. Come to the fire and dry yourself."

Gratitude for the consideration behind the offer welled up inside Pilar. She moved toward the blaze on the blackened stone hearth that took up the back wall of the one-room house, holding out her hands to the warmth. Over her shoulder she gave her name and murmured her appreciation.

"I have some soup," Isabel said. She closed the open door and moved with light steps to swing a caldron over the fireplace flames. The soup sloshed over, sizzling on the coals. Isabel seemed not to notice. Giving Pilar a glance from the corners of her eyes, she went on, "It will be hot soon."

"That sounds wonderful." Pilar was ravenous, she realized, though she had not known it until that moment.

The two women smiled at each other, though with constraint. Isabel was slight of figure and attractive in a piquant, gamine fashion without being actually pretty. Her hair was a soft, dark brown cloud caught back with a worn ribbon just behind her ears, and her eyes, the color of spring grass, were tilted at the corners. With her quick, impulsive movements and tentative manner, she seemed somehow kittenish and vulnerable.

The stone house, perhaps once a shepherd's hut, was older and larger than it appeared from the outside. Though there was only one main room, there were curtained alcoves on either side of the fireplace which seemed to serve as sleeping quarters. The floor of earth was packed to stone hardness by generations of feet. The ceiling was black with the smoke of countless fires, and from the exposed rafters hung strings of dried onions and garlic and also small hams dry-cured, with the pig's hair still upon them. The smells of these things hung in the air, blending with the aroma of ham and bean soup. The furnishings were meager, only a table in the center of the room under a hanging lantern and a pair of crude, handmade bench seats on either side of the fireplace.

Isabel stirred the soup with an iron ladle. The two women did not speak again, though Isabel's gaze, wide and speculative, returned more than once to Pilar.

Behind them the door sprang open again to crash against the wall. Isabel gave a cry and swung around. Pilar turned from the fire to see Refugio striding inside carrying the brass-bound chest holding the endowment to the convent. He set it down on the rough, handmade table and flung back the lid, then tipped the chest so that the contents spilled across the tabletop. With his hands braced on either side, he stared across the room at Pilar.

The chest was three-quarters empty. The coins it contained were not gold at all, but thinnest silver.

"Pledges are cheap," Refugio said, his eyes glittering as he stared at her above the chest, "and I should have been warned, considering that I knew from where you came, Pilar Sandoval y Serna. Still, if this is the recompense you promised, it may be I prefer to exact my own."

CHAPTER 3

I didn't know! I swear I didn't know."

Pilar moved slowly to face Refugio across the center table. She spoke the truth, yet felt as guilty as if she had deliberately set out to cheat the brigand leader. She should have known, she thought, should have guessed that the generosity of Don Esteban's offer was not in his nature. No doubt he had meant to present the meager endowment to the mother superior of the convent in private, representing himself as acting for Pilar's dead mother to remove all blame from himself. Pilar would naturally have been left in ignorance of his parsimony until it was too late.

"I might believe you if there was moonlight and a dark garden," Refugio said, "but unfortunately for you, there's neither."

"Why should I lie? There was never a chance that I would have the gold for my own."

"But the promise of it was such a powerful incentive, or so you seemed to think."

The words had a slicing edge of sarcasm under the accusation. His face, enameled blue and yellow by the flickering firelight, was like an image carved in bronze, impenetrable, unrelenting. Rainwater trickled from his hair, tracking slowly down the frown lines between his eyes.

Pilar moistened her lips. The followers of El Leon—
Enrique, Charro, and Baltasar, who had entered the hut
behind him—avoided her gaze, staring at the floor, at the
ceiling, everywhere except at her and their leader. They
eased around the two of them there at the table, heading
toward the fire, where they held their hands to the flames
and pretended great interest in the warming soup. The only
person who watched them was Isabel, whose eyes were wide
and staring in her pale face. Pilar's voice was strained as she
spoke. "It would have been stupid to promise something
that I could not supply."

"Yes, unless you didn't expect to be found out until you
were safely with your aunt."

"I wouldn't stoop to so base a trick!"

"You are of Don Esteban's house. Why should you
not?"

"And you are a noble outcast to whom gold is an
insult," she returned with heat. "Why should you care so
much?"

"Though your charms are considerable, I did not risk
the lives of the men who ride with me for their sake, nor
for a few paltry pieces of silver. We require gold for horses,
for food and shelter, and for the bribes which can, at carefully chosen times, unlock prison doors."

"I'm sorry if you were disappointed, but I tell you I had
nothing to do with it! There's nothing, not a single thing,
that I can do to change what happened."

He watched her for a long instant. When he spoke, his
words were edged with feathery quiet. "Perhaps there's
something I can do."

Isabel took a step forward. "Refugio," she whispered,
"don't."

The leader of the brigands did not even look at the
other girl. "I wonder," he said to Pilar, "what your aunt

would pay to have you delivered to her, healthy, happy, and, oh yes, untouched?"

Pilar could feel her heart jarring inside her chest. "You mean to hold me for ransom? How sordid."

"Isn't it? And ignoble. But I never pretended to be otherwise. It's you who took me for a figure of tragedy, a righter of wrongs."

Isabel's face turned red and tears rose to shimmer in her eyes. "Oh, Refugio, don't say such things," she cried in dismay. "Why are you doing this? Why?"

Pilar, distracted by the other girl's distress, spoke baldly to the man in front of her. "Apparently I made a mistake. As for my aunt, I have no idea what she will or will not do for my sake. You will have to ask her."

"My next objective, I assure you."

He broke off as Isabel moved closer to clutch his arm with white-tipped fingers, drawing his attention. The girl spoke on a quick, indrawn breath. "You're doing this because you want this woman here. You want her, instead of me."

Refugio looked at the other girl and not a muscle moved in his face, nor was there a trace of emotion on the silvery surface of his eyes. Holding her piteous, beseeching gaze, he spoke a single word over his shoulder. "Baltasar?"

The older man was already moving to Isabel, putting his arm around her. "Come away, my love," he murmured. "It will be all right."

"Oh, Baltasar," Isabel said as she spun around and caught the big man's shoulders in a convulsive grip. "Make him stop. Refugio doesn't care about the gold; he'll only give it away. It's her, I know it is. He'll do something terrible because of her."

"Hush," was the only reply as the burly outlaw turned her and walked her back toward the fire. "Hush now."

Refugio swung with deliberation back toward Pilar. She met his gaze without flinching, but could see nothing except her own reflection in its wintry surface.

He said, "You were, I believe, anxious to be united with your aunt. That is now my dearest desire. Isn't it wonderful how these things work themselves out?"

She had not realized she was holding her breath until she heard his brisk tone. It was an effort to control the rise and fall of her chest without being obvious. Her voice was tight as she agreed, "Yes, isn't it?"

"I would tell you it's my sole desire—but that would be to assume you are concerned. You are not, of course." There was a grating edge of mockery in his voice.

"No," Pilar said.

He pushed away from the table. "I thought not. You had better eat something and try to sleep. We ride for Cordoba at mid-morning."

"Morning! But I thought—"

He swung back on her so quickly that the hem of his wet cloak made a pattern of water droplets on the floor. "Yes? You thought?"

"Haven't things changed? Aren't you . . . anxious to see my aunt, to arrange matters?"

"It will wait."

His attitude of barely contained impatience shaded with menace grated on her nerves, but she refused to be cowed. "I couldn't sleep. I would as soon ride on."

"Into possible danger from your stepfather's hirelings?"

"It seems no less dangerous here to me."

Light seeped into his eyes, making them shine with cool amusement. "You *are* concerned, then."

"It seems to me that that's what you want," she said tightly. "I don't know you well, hardly at all in fact, but I'm beginning to think that you usually have a reason for what you do. That being so, I have a right to be wary until I discover what you intend toward me."

"In light of what Isabel just said?"

She lifted her chin, her eyes steady on his. "And your own threats, yes."

"And do you think," he said pleasantly as he rounded the end of the table and moved toward her, "that your wariness would stop me if I decided to approach you?"

It was a test of nerve, that slow advance. She would not move, Pilar thought, as he came nearer and nearer, walking with the long-limbed grace of perfect physical condition and muscles oiled with constant effort. She didn't care if he walked over her, she would not move. Her mind sought here and there for an answer to the question he had asked. She could not find one, but no matter, she would not move. Behind her, the clink of dishes stopped. Isabel's soft murmurs of distress died away. The only sounds were the crackle of the fire and the light drumming of the rain overhead.

Pilar had little defense against the bandit leader. She could fight, but given his superior strength, he would overpower her in short order. She was surrounded by his friends and companions, men trained to do his bidding without question and who, equally without question, would stand aside while he took his chosen pleasures. Of her own free will she had placed herself in the power of El Leon. It would take an extraordinary combination of wit and luck to escape from the lair of this lion, unless he chose to let her go.

He stopped in front of her, standing so close that the ragged edges of his cloak swung against her damp skirts. He reached out his hand to cup the tender curve of her cheek in his strong, long-fingered hand. She flinched, a movement instantly stilled as she felt the heat of his touch, the hard ridges of the calluses that lined his palm and toughened his fingertips, and the jolting sensation of that deliberate contact. She drew a quick breath, her lips parting with the intake. His gaze narrowed upon their smooth surfaces and delicate curves, and he brushed his thumb across them in a movement of gentle and absorbed exploration that left them tingling. She shivered, her jaw trembling a little under his hold, while she lowered her lashes to hide her startled confusion.

He released her with an abrupt gesture, lowering his hand to his side. When he spoke, his voice was low and derisive. "Vigilant and valiant, and wet to the skin—what makes you think I'm so desperate for a bedmate that I would take one who is wild-eyed with aversion and has chattering teeth? Or that I have so little acumen as to lower the value of a hostage by a quick tumble?"

She swallowed hard, so chilled inside herself that she felt the ripple of gooseflesh at the removal of his warm caress. "Then the things you said were merely to frighten me."

"To encourage quick and clear answers to pertinent questions. I admit it was crude."

"But successful. Or should I worry that what you're saying now is yet another effort, one to make me biddable while you and your men rest?"

"Would you prefer it that way?"

"I would prefer that you abide by our agreement without detours and threats." She had begun to tremble in every muscle from purest reaction, and hid her knotted fists among the folds of her skirts in the attempt to hide it.

"There was nothing in our agreement that said I had to die for you, señorita. That's leaving aside the question of the vanished gold. You keep your bargains, and you'll find that I keep mine."

"There are some things we can't control."

He stood looking down at her for a long moment before he swung away. "Or escape," he said in tight acceptance. "I believe we are in agreement on that. But come to the fire. If you mean to count these uncontrollable and inescapable things, let us at least do it in comfort."

His tone did not encourage either refusal or delay. If he were resigned to taking no more than the silver for the service he had performed for her, he gave no outward sign. He had himself arranged their close quarters of the next few hours, and had also proposed that he face her aunt. What else was there?

There was the accusation Isabel had made, that Refugio had brought her to the stone hut for his own purpose. But no, Pilar could not believe it. There had been little in his manner to suggest he was attracted to her, much less that he meant to keep her against her will. She was no more than a means to an end to him, a way of striking at Don Esteban while gaining the wherewithal to keep his band of men alive. If there was some plan in which she played a part, forming behind the opaque gray of his eyes, it had nothing to do with her as a woman. The girl Isabel had upset herself for no reason, none whatever.

Pilar told herself these things, and yet it almost seemed that Refugio intended to prove her wrong. He drew up a chair for her next to his own and, going to one knee, ladled out a bowl of soup for her and passed it to her with his own hands. The smile he gave her, as her hands brushed his upon the crude earthenware bowl, held a sudden concentrated warmth that was disturbing. Before she began to eat, he reached out and unfastened her cape, drawing it from her shoulders. Then taking off his own cloak, which had begun to steam in the heat of the fire, he hung them both side by side on pegs set into the stones of the great chimney.

Isabel choked on her soup. Baltasar thumped her on the

back, but she thrust her bowl into his rough hands and jumped to her feet. Her eyes filled with hurt tears, she whirled from them all to plunge behind the curtain of one of the alcoves.

The men looked at one another, then away again. Refugio, for all the attention he paid, might not have noticed. He ladled soup into a bowl for himself with apparent unconcern. Still, as a stifled sob was heard, he checked. The knuckles of his hand tightened to whiteness, then relaxed once more. Face impassive, he finished filling his bowl and sat down to eat.

Pilar's appetite had fled. She swallowed a few mouthfuls of the savory concoction in her bowl, but used the piece of earthenware mainly to warm her hands. She was still shaken now and then by a shiver of combined chill and tension, but suppressed each one with valiant effort. Rainwater oozed slowly from the hem of her skirt, soaking into the earthen floor around her feet.

She felt Refugio's gaze on her from time to time but refused to look at him, staring instead either into her soup or else at the pulsing red heart of the fire. Her nerves leaped when he got suddenly to his feet, but he only swung away and disappeared into the alcove on the opposite side of the fireplace from the one where Isabel had disappeared. He returned a moment later, however, and in his hand was a man's dressing gown of quilted velvet.

"Here," he said abruptly, holding it out to her. "Take off your wet things and put this on."

She looked at the dressing gown in his hand, then slowly lifted her gaze to his face.

His expression did not alter, and yet soft weariness crept into his voice. "Not publicly, unless that's your whim."

"No," she said, her voice husky. "I . . . thank you."

"We'll leave you while you change." He sent a look

toward his men that brought them hastily to their feet.

"There's no need; I can go in there." She gestured toward the alcove he had just left.

"You'll find it warmer before the fire. But I make you free of the bed you'll find behind the curtain. I'll have no need of it, since it will be late when we return."

Pilar stared at him, heeding the unspoken reassurance he was extending even as he gave her other news. Finally, she said, "I thought you were going to rest."

"I have rested. We have rested."

"But surely—"

"Don Esteban's recovery interests me greatly. Don't fret. I'll leave Baltasar to watch over you. And if you are disturbed by my return, I will forfeit the silver."

Did he mean that he intended to disturb her so little he had no fear of having to give up his hard-won payment? Or was it that, if he decided to join her in his bed later, he would renounce his claim to the contents of the chest in return for her favors? By the time she had, with great irritability for the effort, concluded he meant the first, he was gone.

Baltasar left the hut with the others, muttering something about checking outside. Pilar waited until the sound of hoofbeats had died away, then got stiffly to her feet. The cold, combined with her tense, overstrained muscles, made movement an effort as she struggled out of her damp clothes. She hung her things on the drying pegs then picked up the dressing gown. The velvet was of fine quality in a rich maroon worked around the lapels with gold thread. It was hardly worn at all, as if it had been kept as a memento of another, better time, perhaps when Refugio's father had been alive. It smelled faintly of the tobacco leaves used to preserve it from moths, with also a whiff of chocolate, as if it had once been favored breakfast attire.

It was soft and warm against her skin. The sleeves were far too long, and the hem dragged the floor; still, its enveloping folds carried an odd sense of security. It was only as she wrapped the velvet around her, hugging it close, that she realized how cold she was, both on the surface and deep inside.

There was a movement of the curtain across the other alcove. Isabel pushed it aside and stepped into the room. She hesitated as her gaze fell on Pilar in her enveloping dressing gown, and a spasm of grieved recognition crossed her features. A moment later she dropped the alcove curtain behind her and came forward.

"Have they all gone?"

"All except Baltasar," Pilar answered the other girl, though she was certain Isabel could not have helped hearing every word that had been spoken in the room.

"I wish they had stayed. I don't like it."

"El Leon must know what he is doing."

She gave a slow nod. "He's always on his guard, which is why he is still alive. But I've never seen him quite so—so distant and hard." The other girl gave a shiver. Her face was puffy and her eyes red from weeping. There was something forlorn about her, like a child scolded unfairly.

"He is rather formidable."

Isabel's lips tightened. "Not always, not with me. He's a man of deep feelings, deeper than most. He receives the pain of others and makes it his. It isn't good for him to do this, but he knows no other way. Sometimes to protect himself he pretends to be unaffected, but it isn't so. It's never so."

"It seems you know him well." It was a leading statement, Pilar knew, but it stemmed from self-protection rather than curiosity. The more she knew of the man who held her, the better.

"I know him," the other girl said with a touch of pride. "He is the son of a hidalgo, a man who owned the most famous *finca* in Andalusia, one dedicated to raising the brave bulls of the arena. Refugio used to play at being a matador, a game for which his father punished him, since it was not only dangerous, it taught the bulls more than they should know about the bull ring. Refugio came to watch me once, when I danced the flamenco with the Gypsies of Seville. He sang a serenade for me and gave me a rose with a pearl inside. Later, years later, he killed a man for me, a man who beat me and sold my body on street corners. For a short time I was El Leon's woman and slept in his bed, though now I belong to Baltasar."

The simplicity of the confession robbed it of offense and even of most of its horror. Before she could stop herself, Pilar said, "You love El Leon."

"How could I not?" the other girl said, her smile soft. "But I wish I had not told him. He put me from him then, said he had made a mistake. Refugio doesn't want women to love him. He avoids it when possible, for he cannot, in honor, offer love in return."

"Because he has nothing to give them except—this?" Pilar gestured at the rough room around her.

"So he says. But I think he has such love hidden deep inside him that the woman who can release it will hold his soul in her hands. He fears this as a weakness, and so allows only women whom he cannot possibly love near him, those who will not be hurt by the lack."

"Except for you," Pilar said.

The other girl lowered her lashes, looking at the floor. "It's what he meant by a mistake. I needed someone so badly, and he could not refuse me without causing more pain than he thought I could bear. I knew that, so the fault was also mine."

Guilt for drawing the other girl out when she had been so upset crowded in upon Pilar. She said, "I'm sorry, I didn't mean to pry."

"Don't be sorry. I miss having another woman here in the hills. Baltasar is kind beyond words, and he listens when I talk, but he doesn't know how to ask the little questions that go to the heart of things the way women do. As for the others . . ." Isabel shrugged.

"Have you all been together long?"

"All? There are many more beside Baltasar and Enrique and Charro who ride with Refugio in his band. These three are only the ones he trusts most, his *compadres* who sometimes pass his orders to the others. But yes, it's been more than two years that we've all been together."

Isabel moved to swing the still simmering soup caldron from over the fire, then added a chunk of wood. As the flames leaped up again, Pilar settled herself onto the chair Refugio had deserted. It seemed unkind to get up and leave the girl after what she had just said. In any case, Pilar was not sleepy.

"These others you spoke of, they don't stay here?"

Isabel smiled. "No, no, there would be no room. There are other places for them, some in the mountains, some in the towns."

"I hadn't realized there were so many."

"But haven't you heard the songs, the legends?" Isabel asked it with a puzzled frown between her brows.

"I thought—I suppose I thought they were just tales somebody made up."

Even in the convent Pilar had heard the songs that were sung about the way El Leon had united the hill bandits, the petty thieves and crooks and those who had run afoul of the law through no fault of their own, how he had forged them into a force that could strike fear into the hearts of the venal and corrupt. It was said he barred those who had committed murders or rapes, or who had harmed children or used violence to take what was not theirs. But for those caught between starving and stealing, those accused unjustly or punished without cause, he had provided refuge and leadership and, sometimes, retribution.

"Enrique wrote some of the songs, yes, but they would not be sung in the taverns and whispered in the churches if they weren't true."

"The smaller man?"

"The one with the narrow mustache. How proud he is of it, that mustache, and how vain of its effect on women! But he is so droll that he makes me laugh. He's Refugio's friend because he makes him laugh also, and because they both have a passion for words, one to write, the other to say."

"It's hard to think that Enrique's a criminal."

"But he isn't!" Isabel said indignantly.

"But—why else is he here?"

"Enrique was with a traveling fair. He was part of a team of tumblers and also sometimes pretended to be a Gypsy in order to tell fortunes. It was a way, you understand, to hold the hands of the ladies. But he told the wrong fortune to the wrong lady. He said she would be robbed and her husband killed. The lady told everyone what the Gypsy had said. Then, when that very thing came to pass, she wept and lamented until everyone thought the Gypsy had foretold only what he meant to do. Enrique had to flee for his life. What Enrique didn't know was that the lady had a lover and wanted to be a widow."

"And Baltasar, is he also innocent?"

Isabel pursed her lips. "Not exactly. He was once a sailor on a treasure ship running between Cartagena and Spain. The ship's captain was a man who enjoyed watching other men flogged. Baltasar caused a mutiny, which was bad enough, but he also took a large portion of the king's gold with him when he left the ship. He lost it in a pirate's den in the Caribbean and found his way back to Spain, but the price on his head is high."

"I would imagine it might be."

"You want to know about Charro, too? His name is really Miguel, Miguel Huerta y Cisneros, but he talks so much about the *charros*, the riders who herd the cattle on his father's *estancia* in the Tejas country of New Spain, that everyone calls him by that name. He was sent here to Old Spain by his father for education and polish, and to end an unsuitable attachment to an Indian girl. He only found trouble."

"Naturally," Pilar said.

Isabel smiled her agreement. "Poor Charro had the misfortune to attract the attention of a countess who liked unusual young men. Her husband found out and challenged Charro to a duel. Charro should have allowed himself to be sliced here and there to satisfy the man's honor, but was too new to the game to follow the code. He killed the husband. The countess, not to mention the count's relatives, was not pleased; someone sent an assassin. Charro was nearly killed, and would have been if Refugio had not been there to prevent it. By the time Charro's wounds healed, he decided he could learn more with Refugio than at the university, and be safer than in Seville's society."

"Did Charro perhaps know Vicente at the university?"

"I don't think so, though Refugio had been to see Vicente the night he fought off Charro's attacker. He keeps close watch over his brother. Vicente is studying for the priesthood. I think Refugio feels it may be an atonement."

"Vicente regrets his brother's way of life so much?"

Isabel shook her head, her green gaze troubled. "It's more that he worries about him, and would join him if

Refugio would permit it. Since he won't, it's as if Vicente would strike a bargain with God, would offer his life to the church in return for his brother's safety."

"Some would find that admirable," Pilar suggested.

"It troubles Refugio that Vicente might be sacrificing himself for his, Refugio's, sins. Refugio prefers to make his own atonements."

"By sacrificing himself, you mean?"

"Not at all! He is not so—so—"

"So mystic?" Pilar supplied the word with certainty though she made it sound like a question.

Isabel nodded. "As you say. Refugio atones every day by the good deeds he does for others—the poor, the sick and hungry, and those who have no one else, no other way, to right the wrongs done to them."

"He is, in fact, a paragon." The other girl was obviously besotted with the brigand leader still, even if he had cast her off.

"Yes," Isabel said simply.

There seemed nothing to say to that. Outside, the wind moaned around the eaves of the cabin and rain spattered against the door. Pilar thought of Refugio and the others riding through the wet darkness once more after their long hours in the saddle during the day, and knew an unwilling sympathy. The life of a brigand, it seemed, was not an easy one. Baltasar was also out there somewhere, making sure they were all safe. He should be coming back inside soon. She would rather not have to sit and make awkward conversation with him also. Anyway, she was finally beginning to feel warm again, and with that returning warmth she could feel the slow creep of exhaustion.

She feigned a yawn that turned, suddenly, into the real thing. Smothering it with her fingers, she said, "I think maybe I should find that bed someone mentioned."

Isabel gave a slow assent. "You don't have to worry. Even if Refugio returns, he will take a blanket by the fire with the others."

"So he gave me to understand." Pilar's words were dry.

"Oh, Refugio says a great many things, mainly to see how people will take them, to see what they are made of; he doesn't mean half of it."

"It's the half he does mean that worries me," Pilar said.

"What?"

Pilar only smiled with a shake of her head, as if she had been making a poor joke. Struggling to her feet, stretching cramped, sore muscles, she said good night.

The bed inside the alcove was neat and clean and monk-like in its simplicity. It was also unexpectedly comfortable, with its horse-hair mattress covered by linen sheets which were worn to silken softness and a coverlet of sheepskins sewn together with leather thongs. Pilar lay for long moments listening to the rain pattering on the low roof and watching the flickering of the firelight coming through the thin curtain as it played on the ceiling.

She thought of her mother lying alone night after night, accepting the life of an imprisoned invalid, slowly dying. She wondered what Don Esteban had told his wife about her daughter's absence, what excuse he had given. Pilar doubted it was the truth. That her mother might have felt herself neglected, deserted in her last days, filled Pilar with such helpless frustration, such renewed pain and grief, that she could not contain the slow seep of tears from the corners of her eyes.

All her mother's dreams of court life had come to nothing. What a shock it must have been when she realized her husband meant to deprive her of that boon he sought so eagerly for himself with her money. How horrified she must have been when she recognized the nature of the man she had married. Had she guessed she was being poisoned? Had she tried at all to escape? Had she clung desperately to the hope that her husband was not evil, or had she lain hour after hour, lost in the apathy of despair, wondering how soon death would come?

Don Esteban had ordered Pilar's death. He had screamed out for his men to kill her. If ever she had entertained the least doubt of his guilt in the death of her mother, she had none now. But she had not been killed. It was a fact Don Esteban would learn to regret. She, Pilar Sandoval y Serna, would see to that personally.

She wiped at the tear tracks on her cheeks, scrubbing their wetness into her hair, swallowing their saltiness as she fought with heaving chest for the control on which she so prided herself. She owed her life to Refugio de Carranza. He was an infuriating man, high-handed and devious and confusing in his sudden shifts between hostility and concern, threats and magnanimity; still, she must not forget that debt. She had not thanked him properly, an error that should be remedied.

She thought of El Leon lying where she lay now, his long form filling the narrow bed. There was an uncomfortable intimacy in the idea, one she felt in her pores. She tried to decide what she would do if he should return and sweep the curtain aside to reclaim his sleeping place. She would protect herself, of course, but how? Before she could settle the question, her eyes began to burn. She closed them for an instant, just to soothe them.

It was sometime later that a soft, rustling sound penetrated the haze of sleep. She shifted in the bed, aware of the disturbance, yet too deep in layered darkness to respond further. Warm comfort surrounded her. She was safe. She sighed and slept on.

CHAPTER 4

She came awake with every sense tingling in alertness. Her eyelids sprang open. The light in the room was gray and dim. In it she saw the matching gray gleam of Refugio's eyes as he lay propped on one elbow, staring down at her. There was appreciation in his gaze and a faint, bemused smile on his firm lips.

"Good morning," he said, the words quiet, yet insouciant. "I took a rain bath to remove the sheep taint. You can now have no reason for complaint."

Pilar waited until she was certain her voice would be steady before she answered. "You're mistaken."

"What is it, my soul? I was certain sleep would sweeten your outlook, if not your disposition."

"There's nothing wrong with my disposition! You promised—"

"On pain of forfeiture. And have I deceived you?"

She stared up at him with an odd breathless sensation in her chest. She could feel the hard musculature of his body against her, pressed close in the narrow bed. His left arm was draped across her waist in a casual hold that might be for balance and accommodation to the narrow width of the bed, but felt like an embrace. He wore a shirt; that much she could see. What else he wore, and whether he lay under the covers or on top of them, she could not tell. She would have liked to know, but refused to look for fear of showing her trepidation. Instead she concentrated on the dark centers of his eyes, on his lashes which grew so long they tangled together as they curled down to touch the skin, on the individual wiry hairs of his brows.

"You know very well that you said I might have this bed for my use, mine alone."

"How was I to know that I would meet a round score of men who required a dry spot to roll up in their blankets? There's not space for a newborn pup in the outer room, I swear it. Besides, I required to be certain that you remained as undisturbed as I had sworn, regardless of the new arrivals. It was a matter of pride, overweening and my own, of course. This seemed the best way of assuring it."

"No doubt you think I should be grateful."

"No, no, only understanding."

She considered it. "That may just be possible since I'm now wealthier by a chest half full of silver."

"Half empty. But the pledge was to leave you undisturbed, not necessarily alone. Tell me at what time I joined you—and also why you allowed it—and you may claim the silver."

It was irritating how quickly and casually he could create his word traps. With a terse phrase or two he had made it impossible for her to say when he had arrived. She thought she knew, but if she had been truly roused, she would not have permitted him to stay. To claim otherwise would be to leave herself open to the question of why she had not protested, and how much more she might accept from him. She had been exhausted; that was the answer, though it was far from satisfactory. If she could hardly accept that explanation herself, how could she expect it of him?

"You are the most—" she began, then stopped as she remembered that this man had saved her life and, moreover, had not touched her during the night hours he had spent beside her. Or at least she thought he had not.

"Oh, come, don't be shy. I'm a collector of personal epithets, preferably unusual. Give me one I haven't heard."

Refugio watched her there in the semidarkness as she held back what she had meant to say by compressing her lips. The urge to lean and touch his own to hers was so sudden and violent that he was startled, and also annoyed by the heart-pounding effort it took to refrain.

She was beautiful as she lay there with her hair spread in shining abundance over the pillow and the soft morning light reflected in the dark mirrors of her eyes, but he had seen many nearly as beautiful. The situation between them at the moment was provocative, but he had weathered others more compelling without the stirring of flagrant desire. It was true that she had more refinement of manner and features than the women he had known these past few years, but what recommendation was there in that?

His motives for being there beside her were exactly as he said. He could have left before she woke, indeed had meant to do just that. Then had come the impulse to see what manner of steel she had inside her. So now he knew that she was stalwart and honest and not given to screaming. But had that been all? Might he not also have wanted to see how she would react to being close to him in a more private setting than the back of a horse or in a roomful of people? It was true, but unfair. It was also time to call enough. There were times when an analytical tendency could be inconvenient.

He threw back the cloak that covered him there on top of the sheepskin coverlet. Rising to his feet with lithe ease, he reached to catch her hand. "Up with you. The sun would be shining on Cordoba, if there was a sun, and it's time you were placed with your aunt."

Pilar was pulled upward so quickly that the sheepskin

coverlet fell back and the over-large dressing gown of stiff quilted velvet she wore gaped open to the waist. Feeling the waft of cool air on her bare flesh, she jerked back against his strong grasp, a movement that threw her so off balance she toppled over the edge of the bed. He caught her, his hands sliding inside the dressing gown, skimming over her warm and fragrant curves to clasp her against him. For a stunned instant they were still, while he slowly spread his fingers wide over the satin skin of her back and flattened his palm upon the smooth expanse of her lower spine. His gaze flickered downward over the blue-veined paleness of the small, perfectly formed globes of her breasts with their peach crests burrowing into the soft linen of his shirt, over the silken swath of her hair which trailed along his arm. A tinge of dull color appeared under his sun-darkened skin. Pilar, watching it, slowly closed her hands on the taut muscles that ridged his arms while every drop of blood in her veins mounted swiftly, frighteningly, to her head. Her heart jarred against her ribs and she could sense deep inside the slow rise of something unwarranted, unwanted.

She drew a ragged breath, wrenching backward as she gasped in accusation, "You—"

"No!" he said, the word harsh with the violence of his denial. "I never meant this. Clumsy I may be, but not entirely venal. I pledge you this much on my word of honor."

His hold, unbreakable until that instant, slackened, allowing Pilar to sink back onto the bed. She drew away, clutching the edges of the dressing gown together at her throat. She met his gaze, brown eyes clashing with gray, and saw the fleeting bafflement followed by self-derision mirrored there, saw the squaring of his shoulders, as if he was bracing himself for either her screams of outrage or her scorn.

It came to Pilar that he spoke the truth, that he had not intended that brief embrace. She lifted her chin, her eyes steady upon his hard features. "I accept your pledge."

"You accept it?" he said, the words tentative as he watched her.

"I can do no less," she said with dignity.

"But why?"

"I have benefited from your . . . hospitality. A Carranza would not, I think, press his attentions upon a woman under his own roof."

"Ah. My hospitality."

The current of understanding between them was strong. She was conceding to him full right to the honor inherent in his proud name and former station as a grandee, along with the manifold obligations of the code of conduct that went with it. He must, in return, remain bound by that code.

He inclined his head with a shadow of admiration lurking in his eyes. "Accept my gratitude, and my apologies."

"Not at all," she said, lowering her lashes before she continued. "You were speaking of leaving here, I believe. No one could be happier to be on the road than I, but my clothes are in there by the hearth. I doubt your men will want to have their sleep interrupted for the sake of a petticoat."

"What they want matters not at all. But don't stir; I'll bring both your clothes and your trunk. While I'm at it, do you take your chocolate strong or milky?"

"There's no need for you to trouble," she said as she swung her feet from the bed. "Maybe Isabel—"

"She's asleep, and it's my whim, taken this moment, to have you share my morning repast, and my privacy."

She glanced around the alcove. "Oh, I'm keeping you from your retreat. I'll get up and leave you to it."

"By no means," he said over his shoulder as he swung to brush aside the privacy curtain, "unless you prefer the odds on the other side of this barrier?" As she did not answer, he gave a nod. "I thought not. Be patient, and I'll bring what you need."

It was possible she might be safer in the other room, Pilar told herself as he ducked under the curtain and dropped it behind him, closing her into the alcove. Other men might be less trustworthy, but were not so disconcerting in their speech and their attitudes. The idea of his serving her while she waited in bed made her acutely uncomfortable, especially in light of what had just happened; a man of finer sensibilities and less confidence would have left her to recover in private. Joining her in his quarters was in essence a protective gesture, or so he implied, yet there was something almost possessive in it, with a hint of testing the trust she professed. She didn't like it, but there was little she could do. At least she need not endure the situation for long. A few hours more and she would be with her aunt. Once safely established in Cordoba, there was no reason she should ever see Refugio de Carranza again. None. That would make her extremely happy. Of course it would.

She was combing her hair with her fingers when he returned a few minutes later. Hurriedly bundling the thick, waving mass into a knot, she pinned it at her nape, then reached to take the cup of chocolate he held out to her. As he seated himself on the foot of the bed, she pushed backward to lean against the wall behind the bed's head. He gave her a look of sardonic amusement, as if he suspected her of putting as much distance between them as possible, but made no comment.

It was possible he was not entirely wrong. He seemed so large there in the tiny alcove, such an overpowering presence. To be shut away with him again behind the curtain, separate from the others, was unexpectedly provocative, as well as uncomfortable. That he felt the constraint also seemed evident from the stiffness of his movements and his comparative silence.

His manner was neutral as he handed her a piece of the bread he had brought wrapped in a napkin and balanced on top of his own cup. She took it with a murmur of thanks, adding in an attempt at light conversation, "I didn't know banditry allowed such luxuries as this."

"We live well enough, though the bread is made with coarse grains and the chocolate with goat's milk."

"You seem to manage better than most."

"Why do you say that?"

She gave a brief shrug. "I've heard the stories."

"You shouldn't believe them."

"If I had not," she said, her gaze on the piece of bread, "I would never have sent for you, never have escaped my stepfather. I am grateful, in spite of everything."

He stared at her a long moment. When he spoke, the words were soft. "I would have done it without the promise of gold, you know. It's just that I object to being taken for a fool."

"I would never do that."

"At least no more often than necessary," he answered dryly.

"No, really," she protested.

"I will try to believe you. How can I not?"

She met his gaze in brief acknowledgment of that tenuous pact. A slow smile lighted his eyes, warming their gray color with rich humor and creasing the hard planes of his face. It also brought a degree of ease to the atmosphere between them.

They ate in silence a few moments before Pilar spoke again. "Did you discover what became of Don Esteban?"

"He was gone from the place of attack. He apparently recovered enough to be taken away in the carriage, or so it appeared from the signs."

She nodded her understanding, her expression grim. "You don't seem surprised."

"I knew he could not be dead; that would be too fortunate."

"So bloodthirsty," he said with a droll shake of his head.

Her answering smile was brief. "It comes from a long association with Don Esteban. Things just seem to always go his way."

"Not always, but too often for comfort."

There was in the comment a reminder of how much he had also lost. Recognizing it, Pilar hastily changed the subject. "I've been thinking. If my mother had not married Don Esteban, he would not have had the means to pursue his ambitions—or his feud with your family. It's possible you have reason to distrust me."

Refugio watched her with a faint curve at one corner of his mouth before he spoke. "If the Carranzas had not inspired such hatred and need for revenge in your stepfather, he might never have pursued and married your mother, never have caused her death or sent you into exile. This sword has a double edge."

"That may be, but there is more. If you had not killed Don Esteban's son, I might have been forced to marry him. I owe you a great deal."

"You might, if I had killed the son for your sake. Since I did not, you owe me nothing. Nor is there any real question of blame. Shall we call that much settled?"

She inclined her head in uneasy acquiescence. "If you like."

"I do."

Pilar from under her lashes looked at the man sitting so near. His shoulders were broad, straining against the worn material of his shirt. His hair lay in dark, soft waves against his head, and his gaze from under thick brows was steady yet had rapier-sharp perception in its depths. His features were perfectly balanced, and there was strength and grace in the shape of his hands as he held the crude earthenware cup. Despite his guise as a bandit and the edge of danger it gave him, there was also a sense of breeding, of ancient lineage about him. For a fleeting instant she wished things were different, wished it were possible for her to continue her acquaintance with Refugio de Carranza y Leon under other, more proper conditions. She looked away, disturbed by the tenor of her thoughts.

The silence between them stretched. In the next room a man coughed and rose from his blankets with a muttered imprecation. The quiet crackle of the fire could be heard as someone placed more wood on the coals.

Refugio drained the last of his chocolate. "As pleasant as this is, it's time we began to plan in earnest for Cordoba, to think of a ruse to get you inside the gates."

"A ruse?"

"What did you expect? A grand procession with a gilded carriage, outriders, and the town fathers waiting to greet you?"

"Hardly," she answered, her tone tart.

"Good. Then you won't be disappointed."

She entered the ancient, walled city in a two-wheeled cart. If she had been traveling alone, she could have ridden through the great carved gates without worry or hindrance beyond giving her name to the guards. But she was not traveling alone; Refugio had agreed to see her to the house of her aunt, and he intended to do exactly that. Pilar had not considered, when she made her proposal to him, how El Leon would be able to keep his bargain. She knew that folk tales had sprung up crediting him with the powers of a ghost to pass where he would without being seen. She had also heard rumors about his many friends and sympathizers in the countryside and smaller towns who helped him come and go, and the bribes that were sometimes passed to allow him to enter and leave Seville at will. What other shifts he might be forced to use had never occurred to her; certainly she had never expected to become a part of one of them.

The cart was old and worn out, so that its tall wheels of solid wood squealed on their axles with nerve-shattering regularity. Its load of firewood, the sticks and stumps and odd-shaped branches of deadwood carefully scavenged from the forest, was almost too much for the ancient donkey plodding between the shafts. Pilar rode on the seat while Refugio walked to one side, with the donkey's lead rein in one hand and a staff that was stouter than it looked in the other.

They had found their dubious transportation at a farm well outside the city. The farmer's wife had also supplied the rebozo of black wool that covered Pilar's head and shoulders, and the piece of charcoal that had been used to make the dark, aging circles under her eyes and the hollows in her cheeks. Where Refugio had found the peculiar conical hat that he wore pulled low over his eyes, and the short, ragged breeches and rough shoes that made him look the part of a peasant, Pilar did not ask. She only stared at him from time to time, wondering in amazement tinged with respect at his attire, and also at the rough thatch he had made of his hair and the look of a dullard in his eyes.

It was early morning of the third day, a market day, before they made their attempt to enter the city. They joined a stream of carts, barrows, and donkeys headed toward the gates, all of them loaded with something to sell, from cured leather to jars of olive oil, fresh cabbage to trussed and squawking geese. Behind them, at some distance, trailed Baltasar, Enrique, and Charro amidst a herd of goats.

Pilar and Refugio, with the other three, had lain for what was left of the second night at the farmer's house, sharing its one room with the man and his wife, their nine children, five dogs, a black hen, and a liberal supply of fleas. After such a night, Pilar thought, they surely looked as slovenly and unlike themselves as anyone could wish. Refugio still wasn't satisfied, however. He insisted she carry the latest addition to the farmer's family in her arms, a fine boy of seven weeks who had protested at the top of his lungs at being removed from his mother's arms. The child had not ceased to scream since they left the farm, and had made three wet spots on Pilar's lap in spite of several changes of the rags that served for diapers. His mother, trailing with her husband behind the herd of goats, had come forward once to nurse the baby. He had quieted only a few minutes, beginning to cry again the instant he was given back to Pilar. He sensed her inexperience with him, she thought, and her fear of what was going to happen.

Ahead of them lay the Guadalquivir River. The water flowed greenish-brown and placid around its islands that were dotted with oleanders, before gliding through the great arches of the old Roman bridge that gave access to the city. The cart trundled past the tower fortress of Calahorra and began to cross the bridge. Before them Pilar could see the stone-pillared, Romanesque *puerta del puente*. There were two guards at the gate. One was talking with an attractive and vivacious young girl with a goose under each arm. The other stood watching their approach with his hands clasped behind his back and a look of dyspeptic gloom on his face.

The cart drew closer, its wheels shrieking as if in alarm. The guard stirred and released his hands to place them on his hips. A frown drew his brows together. Nearer the cart came, and nearer still. The guard took a step forward. Pilar sent Refugio a swift glance. The brigand leader seemed oblivious of their danger, only plodding onward with his gaze straight ahead.

"Stop!"

Refugio gave no sign he heard. Pilar ran her tongue over her lips, at the same time joggling the crying baby in the hope that he would be quieted.

The guard moved in front of them with his hand upheld. "I mean you, oaf! Stop!"

A species of panic ran over Refugio's blank features. He hauled on the lead he held, nearly jerking the donkey off its feet. As the animal halted, Refugio snatched off his hat and stood with bowed head, almost visibly trembling.

"That's better," the guard said, thrusting his chest out. "You're making a racket fit to wake the nobles in their beds. For the love of God, get some grease for your wheels. And you, woman, put that child to the breast!"

"Yes, your honor, but yes. Instantly, your honor," Refugio replied in servile tones. He bent himself almost double bowing, at the same time making frantic motions toward Pilar. The actions flapped the lead in his hand and caused the donkey to start forward again. The guard stepped back out of the way, though he stared so hard at Pilar that she flushed and lowered her gaze, fumbling at the front of her dress under the ends of her rebozo. Mercifully, the baby found the action and the way he was being held familiar, and lowered the volume of his cries.

They rolled onward, mingling with the crowd. Pilar sat stiff and straight, expecting at any minute to be called back, or else to hear Baltasar and the others behind them challenged. It did not happen. They were inside the city walls; they had reached Cordoba.

They moved along the street, past the walls of the

ancient mosque that had been built by the Moorish ruler of Cordoba over a thousand years ago and turned into a cathedral some four and a half centuries later with the conquest of the Catholic king. Its majestic arches towered above them, solid and enduring and harmonious in their symmetry. Refugio and Pilar scarcely looked up. The baby howled without ceasing. Refugio, plodding along beside the cart, sent her a quick slanting look. His voice shaded with quiet amusement, he said, "I see you're not maternal."

"Being maternal has nothing to do with it," she snapped. "The poor little thing knows something isn't right, and he wants his mother."

"No more than I want her to have him."

"You don't like children?" she asked pointedly.

"I dote on the little treasures, but not when they are attracting attention."

"Bringing him was your choice," she reminded him.

"Yes, well, he adds a certain validity to my image as a lack-wit with a scolding wife, don't you think?"

Pilar scowled at him. "I'm not your wife."

"Wonderful playacting!" he congratulated her. "The world can see you have a proper regard for your mate."

"I told you—"

"So you did. And tell me this, why is it you have so little concern for propriety. Why did you refuse to be made the wife of this Carlos?"

"I don't know what you mean," Pilar said, jiggling the baby vigorously, but with no effect.

"Most women in your place would be yelling for a priest and demanding the security of a man's name, any man's name."

She gave him a sharp look. "I have enough problems already."

"The purpose is to solve them, not make them, or at least to pretend that a ring has that power, that marriage is an estate to be longed for by a woman."

"It can also be a snare," Pilar said, thinking of her mother.

"Such heresy will see you hounded from the society of those who have made that bargain and have no choice except to celebrate it."

"You sound no more ready for marriage than I," she told him.

"It appears a blessed estate for those who love; I remember how it was with my mother and father, you see. It's only that love is rare."

"Yes," she said, her voice low. "Anyway, I'm not sure that a ring and a vow could restore me to respectability."

"Therefore you scorn them?"

A reluctant smile touched her mouth. "I see. You are doubtless thinking of sour grapes and foxes."

"No, no," he answered, "only honey and bees."

"What?" she asked, but he was looking behind them for signs of pursuit, and made no answer.

They wound through the old town, past wrought-iron gates that revealed glimpses of green and secluded patios, under geranium-hung balconies and along streets planted on either side with the pointed and dark green shapes of evergreen cypresses. On a side street in the shadow of the Alcazar, the old palace where Ferdinand and Isabelle had seen Columbus off on his voyage to the Americas and where the Holy Inquisition was housed, they stopped. Across the way lay a narrow house made of stone with a tiled roof, projecting balconies railed with iron, and a heavy, blue-painted door. It was a comfortable house rather than an imposing one. It was also extremely quiet.

Baltasar, with Enrique and Charro behind him, caught

up with them. They all stood looking at the house. Pilar gathered up her skirts and prepared to get down from the cart. Refugio put out his hand and touched her arm.

"Wait," he said.

Pilar hesitated. Refugio had discarded his dullness as if it were a piece of worn out clothing. His manner was alert, poised for instant action. His gaze, under the ridiculous conical hat, moved over the face of the house, searching every window and door, then traveled on to its neighbors'. A stray cat, ambling down the street, saw them and stopped. It hissed, bowing up its back, then fled.

"Stay here," Refugio said.

He did not wait for a reply, but strode away, crossing the street and angling for an alleyway. He glanced both ways, then glided into the dim passage. Pilar waited only until he was out of sight, then she motioned toward the baby's mother, who had trailed up behind the goats, and handed her the baby. Jumping down from the two-wheeled vehicle, she followed Refugio. The house before her belonged to her aunt, her only real relative. Pilar was prepared to take all necessary precautions, but the endless delays had been maddening. There was no sign of either Don Esteban or the authorities, and she could not wait to see her father's sister a moment longer.

There was a second alleyway leading off the first, one that meandered past the back of her aunt's house. Halfway along its length was a wooden gate set into a wall, a servant's entrance from all appearances. Pilar saw Refugio pause at the gate and push on it, saw it give under his hand to swing silently inward. He stood listening a long moment, then stepped through in a single swift movement before spinning instantly to one side.

He was inside a patio, for through the open gate Pilar could see the branches of shrubs and a stretch of stone tiles.

Somewhere a bird sang, a shrill, discordant sound at this season.

She moved forward, easing through the patio gate. Inside, the garden had a dank, dispirited air. The fountain was still, so that the long reflecting pool that caught the overflow lay as dark and glassy as a steel mirror in the gray light of the overcast day. The patio was deserted.

Pilar stood in the shadows, watching as Refugio crossed to the house and tried a back door. It was locked. He moved away, out of her sight, and there came the tinkle of breaking glass. She waited a moment longer, then followed in the direction he had taken. A long window set with small circles of stained glass stood swinging open. She crossed to it with quick footsteps and climbed over the sill, slipping inside.

She was in some kind of reception room, one of impressive size and stultifying formality. Gilt and red velvet chairs lined the walls beneath dark and formal portraits. The light coming through the colored glass of the windows made blue and green stains on the stone floor. The air was chill and smelled of cold fires, cracked leather, and ancient dust.

There was a stair hall through double doors, with a stairway winding upward into the shadows. Moving toward it, Pilar heard the faint creak of a step and thought that was the way Refugio had gone. She picked up her skirts, climbing after him.

The body was around the first bend of the stairs. It was an elderly servant, or so it appeared from the rough cloth of his night shirt, perhaps her aunt's majordomo. He was icy cold and his eyes were wide and staring, while blood from a stab wound splotched his nightshirt. He had died at night, for in addition to the nightshirt as indicator, the candle he had been holding had gone rolling as he fell, scorching a lower stair tread before burning itself out.

Pilar swayed a little as she hovered over the dead man. The apprehension inside her blossomed into horror mixed with dread, while something cold and hard closed around her heart. What had happened here? Where was her aunt?

Hearing another soft footfall above her, she made the sign of the cross over the man, then stepped gingerly over the sprawled form. Moving with care, staying close to the wall, she mounted upward.

The upper floor was a maze of sitting rooms and bed-chambers opening into each other. Pilar could not tell which way Refugio had gone. She opened her mouth to call out to him, then closed it again, since to disturb the silence seemed wrong as well as unwise.

She moved in and out of one suite and then another, coming finally to a set of doors that were larger and more ornately carved and fitted than the others. She penetrated an antechamber to reach a small salon dominated by a massive stove of Flanders tiles, then passed through a doorway hung with sea-green portieres. Inside was a bedchamber holding a bed raised upon a dais. The bed had a gilded and painted headboard and posts topped by gently waving ostrich plumes.

On the floor beside the dais lay a maid with a shawl over her nightgown and her gray hair trailing down her back. The maid, like the majordomo, had been stabbed.

Pilar's aunt was propped in the great bed, sitting up against a pair of pillows with a bible across her lap. She wore on her head a beautiful nightcap of Alençon lace trimmed with pink ribbon. A red ribbon of blood circled her neck where her throat had been cut. Standing over her with his hand across her face was Refugio.

Pilar gave a soft, gasping cry of shock.

Refugio whirled. He swore vividly, fluently, and without repetition. In an instant he had sprung from the dais, striding down upon her. He wheeled her around with his hand grasping her upper arm, thrusting her from the room.

Pilar caught the doorjamb, digging in her heels. "No, don't! I want to know. I have to know if she's—"

"Alive? No, positively not. She's dead, and has been for at least ten hours, possibly longer. Can you help? No. I closed her eyes. It's all we can afford to do."

"You think Don Esteban did this?" she asked, her voice faint.

"His hirelings, at a guess. Either that or else the fates are on his side. I prefer to think the first."

She shook her head, not in disbelief but in an attempt at negation. "How could he? How did he dare?"

"How? Easily. It comes from thinking that his wishes, his needs, and his will are supreme. As for daring, why not? He has served so many with their death notices that it's far from being a novelty."

There was a corrosive edge to his voice that struck through her horror. "I'm sorry," she said. "This must be a reminder for you."

His face there in the dim light of the shuttered room was shadowed with self-contempt. "It's a failure."

"Why? There was nothing you could have done."

"Oh, but there was, if I had taken thought. Instead, I ran prancing in circles around a chimera, yearning after an impossible consummation. I should be flayed, as a beginning."

"This was not of your arranging," she said, her voice stark. "If I had not involved my aunt, she would be alive."

He watched her for long seconds with a suspended look in his eyes. "Would you rob me of my self-immolation, or only share it? Either way may not be a kindness; I need something to drive me."

"I thought you had hatred enough for that."

His facial muscles did not change, yet his expression became merely polite. "Yes," he said, "though there are inducements of equal value and greater pleasure. To discuss them could be stimulating, but not just now. Deathbeds require more circumspection, as a general rule, and this one more than most."

The hint was delicate, but she took it. "I know you cannot be found here, but there are things that I should do. Someone must inform the police, send for a priest, arrange for the death notices and the vestments, so many things."

"For you to be found here with me could also have grim consequences."

"Then you must leave me now, before someone comes. I—I'll be all right, really I will."

"What makes you think so? What if the person who comes is the assassin? Or your stepfather?"

"I can't just leave," she protested with a glance back toward the silent bed.

"You can't stay. Do you really think that Don Esteban, having gone this far, will let you live? Linger here, and there will be another body with knife wounds by morning."

"It isn't your responsibility. I'm sure the authorities—"

"The authorities are conscientious, those not too intimately acquainted with Don Esteban, but they could not protect your aunt."

"But I can't just go with you back into the mountains!"

"Why not? Your aunt must have had other relatives, other friends who will see that the necessary things are done. You can't afford to let the guilt you feel become a trap."

"It isn't just that. What will I do if I go with you? What will become of me?"

"Isn't it too late for such worries? Whatever contamination you are going to suffer has been done already."

"I didn't mean it like that," she said, her eyes dark with worry. "Regardless, you must see how impossible—"

The words were cut off as he gestured for silence with a swift, slicing movement of one hand. He stood still, listening. Pilar could hear nothing, though she held her head up, barely breathing. Then she caught it, the quiet shrilling of a warning whistle from the street outside.

Refugio reached to clamp an arm of steel around her waist, swinging her toward the opposite end of the house. He swept her with him through the silent, dusty rooms. Their footsteps clattered on the stone steps of a back staircase, then they were dodging among the tables of a scullery and kitchen. A great wooden door loomed before them. Refugio put both hands on the wide iron bar that held it closed, leaning his right shoulder into it. In an instant the bar was raised, the portal easing inward, letting in the light from the back patio.

They paused at the edge of the reflecting pool. From the streets all around the house could be heard the drumming of horses' hoofs. There was a shouted order that was immediately repeated from somewhere near the back patio gate.

"Is it the police?" Pilar whispered.

"The good God alone knows, for I don't." Refugio did not look at her as he answered, but swept the trees near the patio garden wall with his narrow gaze.

"Where are the others?"

"Taking care of themselves, as we must." He touched her shoulder, then pointed toward a jacaranda tree that grew against the wall, reaching upward along the side of the house next door. Just beyond its highest branches was a flat rooftop in the Moorish style, one that in summer was used for taking the evening air. Refugio's meaning could not be plainer; this was their escape route.

She couldn't do it, she knew she couldn't. Before she could make that clear, she was being boosted among the tree branches. She grasped a limb and pulled herself upward in purest self-defense, then reached for the next limb as she sought a foothold out of the need to make room for Refugio, who was climbing up after her. A moment later he was swinging past her around the tree trunk, then passing hand over hand along the largest tree limb. He dangled a second over the rooftop, then let go. He plummeted downward, landing in a crouch. Straightening at once, he motioned for her to follow his example.

It had to be done; there was nothing else for it, no time to think, no time for doubts. Behind her she could hear the pounding of booted feet in the rooms of her aunt's house. In a moment she would be seen. If the men had been sent by her uncle, that could mean death for both Refugio and herself. But even if it was only the police, even if there was no danger for her, she must not set them on Refugio's trail. She could not be the cause of El Leon being captured, not after what he had done for her.

She swung herself out along the tree limb. Setting her teeth together, she let herself fall. Refugio caught her, absorbing the shock of her weight without apparent effort, holding her a moment until she caught her breath. Then they set off at a run.

They skimmed over the flat roof to the next, where they climbed a jointed clay drainpipe and clambered across a series of steep slants on their hands and knees. At the edge of the last they swung over the side to reach a narrow balcony. A quick glance inside showed that the balcony opened into a ladies' bedchamber and the lady was still abed, fast asleep. Refugio sacrificed his coat for a makeshift rope, and shortly afterward they were strolling away down an alley.

They found Baltasar and Enrique waiting in a side street a few blocks away, though Charro, and also the farmer and his wife with their squalling child and squeaking cart, were nowhere to be seen. They moved swiftly toward the city gate where they had entered, each of them on guard lest there had been a general alarm given and all gates closed.

The gate stood open. The sight of it standing wide, with the same dyspeptic guard on duty to wave them through, was disturbing to Pilar. It meant that the men at her aunt's house this morning must have been sent by her stepfather. It meant that their purpose in being there could only have been to kill her. That being the case, she had no alternative except to go with Refugio, to join him in his mountain stronghold. None at all.

Less than a mile outside the gates they met Charro on the road leading the horses they had stabled nearby against an emergency. They mounted up and swung back toward the mountains.

The small band reached the stone hut again in the small hours of the following morning. The journey had been fast and unrelenting. To Pilar it was a blur of rough trails, snatched bites of food taken at the gallop, and brief stops for changes of horses in lonely places. She was so weary she seemed to be moving in a fog. How she stayed in her saddle, she did not know, for her muscles had gone from aching cramp to numbness so complete she felt paralyzed. She swayed, clutching the horse's mane, but did not fall. At the hut she could not get down by herself, but had to be lifted bodily from her horse. As she took a step and the feeling began to return, she stumbled and would have fallen if Refugio had not caught her.

Pilar saw Isabel standing in the doorway holding a lantern, saw the look of consternation that crossed the girl's pale, agitated face as she saw her in the bandit's arms, but could not seem to find the will to be concerned or to feel anything other than gratitude for his support. All she wanted was a place to lie down, a solid place that did not move.

Isabel hurried toward them. Her voice seemed to come from far away as she spoke, and it was a moment before the sense of what she was saying penetrated. It was Refugio's sudden stillness that pierced Pilar's exhaustion so that suddenly, unbelievably, she understood.

"Oh, Refugio!" the girl cried, then faltered. "It's Vicente. I'm sorry, so sorry."

"What is it?" Refugio's voice was quiet, yet carried the crack of a whip.

Isabel wrapped one hand in her apron so tightly the cloth split. "The message was brought this evening from Seville, from Don Esteban. He sent word that he—he has abducted Vicente, taken him as he walked on the street. He says that he has branded your brother as his slave and means to take him with him when he sails for Louisiana. And if you ever want to see Vicente alive, then you must make sure that the woman you hold, his stepdaughter Pilar, causes no trouble until he returns."

CHAPTER 5

*S*ilence closed in upon them. Refugio's face hardened, his features taking on the sharp edges of an image cast in metal. The tremulous light from the lantern Isabel held caught in his eyes with a silver-gold reflection of virulent pain. His grip on Pilar's arm tightened, becoming a vise capable of crushing bone. The night wind that drifted around the eaves of the stone hut made a soft sighing sound and died away.

Behind him, Refugio's men stood in arrested movement: Baltasar holding the saddle that he had just taken from his horse, Enrique wiping the dust from his face with the tail of his cloak, Charro rubbing his mount down with a handful of straw. Isabel pressed one hand to her mouth with a sick look in her eyes, as if the message she had spoken had been a blow she had taken herself. At the same time, there was fear in her face as she watched the bandit leader.

They were all watching him, waiting, and they were all wary if not actively afraid. But of what? What did they expect of him? Did they look for some violent act of rage against them? Did they fear he would do something that might draw them all into a confrontation that would destroy them? Or was their concern that he might turn his destructive urge upon himself? Whatever it was, they made no move to deflect what might come. Nor did they show so much as a hint of the compassion that must surely be the first impulse of long-time companions.

Pilar put her free hand on Refugio's fingers where he grasped her arm. Her voice low, she said, "I'm sorry."

Slowly, he turned his head to look at her. "Are you?" he said, his voice no louder then the night wind. "Are you indeed? And are you sorry enough?"

Pilar flinched, not only at the raw lash of the words, but also at the barely contained ferocity she glimpsed in the depths of his eyes. She drew her hand back as though she had been burned. She could feel the sickening thud of her heart in her chest and the rasp of the air in her lungs.

Abruptly, he released her. Swinging away, he moved with long, swift strides into the darkness.

Pilar drew a gasping breath. One of the three men sighed and swore. Baltasar dropped the saddle he held to the ground, then moved to take the lantern from Isabel's trembling hand. Isabel began to cry with the quiet, hopeless sound of a lost kitten. The others gathered close together, not quite looking at each other.

"What is he going to do?" Pilar asked, her gaze going from one to the other.

It was the tall and rangy one known as Charro who answered. "Who can say?"

"He will kill Don Esteban," Enrique said, giving a shrug of one shoulder which said that the answer was obvious.

"Or die in the attempt." Isabel gasped the words on a fresh sob.

"I mean now, this moment," Pilar said. "You can't just let him go."

"How do you suggest we stop him?" Enrique watched her with an ironic lift of his brows.

"You could go after him, be with him."

"Yes, if we did not so love life."

Pilar eyed the one-time acrobat with irritation for that

hint of melodrama. "He's a man like any other. It can't be that bad."

"If you think so, then you are free to offer him comfort."

"I hardly know him, but you are his friends, his *compadres*."

"If you hardly know him, señorita," Baltasar said with slow reason, "why this concern?"

"I'm not—" she began, then stopped. She lifted her chin before she continued. "Maybe because I feel to blame."

"Yes," Baltasar said with a nod of his massive head.

"Don Esteban protects himself from all angles, or so it seems," Enrique agreed. "He kills the lady, your aunt, to prevent you from enlisting her aid and influence against him, then seizes Vicente as hostage against Refugio's good behavior, ensuring that El Leon will do nothing to further your claims before Don Esteban departs Spain or while he is out of the country. At the same time, Don Esteban has avenged himself against both Vicente and Refugio for their interference in his private affairs. He has, in fact, injured El Leon and effectively caged him at the same time. He has won. Tell us how we are to solace Refugio for this defeat?"

There was accusation in every face turned toward her. Pilar felt the heat of guilt rising to her cheekbones. "I didn't mean it to happen this way. You must know that."

"We know," Baltasar answered.

The words were flat. The sound of them made Pilar wonder at his meaning, wonder if perhaps they all doubted her innocence in the affair. It seemed beyond belief that they could think she might have conspired with her stepfather to place Refugio in his present position. Such an elaborate charade could hardly have been necessary, even without the danger from Refugio's retaliation as a deterrent.

She glanced away from them, staring in the direction

Refugio had taken. If his followers believed the worst of her, what must El Leon think? He had suspected her of enticing him into a trap at their first meeting. It could well appear that the trap had closed.

Lifting her skirts, she took a step into the darkness. Charro straightened from where he slouched against the doorframe. "Wait, señorita," he said, an urgent sound in his voice. "You don't know what you're doing. You'd fare better facing a band of Tejas country Apache in war paint than going out there."

"That may be," she said over her shoulder, "but I have to go." Without looking back, she moved away into the night.

She couldn't find him. She circled the hut, moving a few yards at a time before stopping to listen, then taking another few steps and listening again. Returning to the place she had started, some hundred yards from the front of the hut, she turned in a slow circle, her every sense alert for movement. She probed the shadows under the scattered trees and scanned the rocks silhouetted against the night sky. She even breathed the soft night breeze for a scent. There was nothing. Nothing moved, not a night creature, not a tree branch. The very light of the stars in the velvet-lined dome overhead seemed stationary and unblinking.

Long moments passed. Finally, Pilar began to walk again, straight ahead. She penetrated farther and farther into the darkness, until she began to wonder if she could find her way back to the hut. But as she paced, the first inkling of a suspicion came to her. It grew inside her, formed partly of instinct and partly of acquired knowledge of the man she sought. She walked on another step, and another. She slowed, stopped.

She stood unmoving, almost without breathing. When the silence had stretched to its greatest depth, when the stillness around her was near unbearable and the darkness seemed to be closing in, ready to smother her, she knew.

"If you touch me I may well scream," she said. "Not, you understand, from surprise or even fear, but from sheer vexation."

"Who would hear? Or hearing, come?" he answered from so close behind her that his warm breath disturbed the hairs on the back of her neck.

"No one, of course. But I would hate to waste the energy when I have so little left."

"You have my sympathy. But that was what you came to offer me, wasn't it?"

"In part. For the rest, I wanted to explain about Vicente."

The choice of words was wrong; she knew it the instant they left her tongue. She expected violence, an explosion of wrath and denial. Instead, she felt him receding from her, leaving her.

She swung around, crying out, "Wait! I know I've involved you in something far bigger than I expected, but I give you my word I didn't intend it. And I swear that I never meant that Vicente should be caught in it. Please believe me."

"I believe you. If it were otherwise, you would never have been left at my mercy. Assuming that Don Esteban would value you as an accomplice, of course. There is the possibility that you have merely been deserted."

"I assure you—"

"There is also the chance that I am meant to use you for my retaliation, meant to injure you, brand you, ravish you in the wildness of my rage. The temptation to return the transgression committed against my sister must be strong, must it not? More than that, it would serve to blacken the polish on the country legends, so that there would be less hue and cry if my body were to be found hanging at some remote crossroad."

The even, expressionless sound of his voice as he laid the potential in the situation bare sent a chill to the core of Pilar's being. She opened her mouth to refute it, but his words continued without pause, relentless in their logic.

"The situation is not quite the same. My sister was seduced away from her home by a mad attraction to Don Esteban's son, in addition to a head full of romantic ideals inspired by Shakespeare's tragedies and a family inclination toward self-sacrifice. She meant to heal the rift, you see? When she discovered the depths of her error, she was extinguished inside; to take her life was only a small added sin. You, I think, are made of stronger stuff. You would never permit yourself to love an unsuitable man, never allow your spirit to be violated along with your body."

"Is that what you think of me?"

"It is, though it's not possible to be sure. Shall we see?"

He had moved nearer again as he spoke. There was no warning of what he meant to do, no prelude to his last words. He stopped speaking, and abruptly she was whirling, falling. The breath was jarred from her as she struck the ground, though the stony earth was cushioned by a long, hard form. Strong arms closed around her and she was rolled to her back. His mouth descended on hers, its molded firmness seeking, burning its imprint into her memory. White heat flared in Pilar's mind. She made a convulsive movement, as if she would break free, then forced herself to stillness by an act of stringent will. She would not give him the satisfaction of overcoming her resistance, would not encourage him in his experiment by even a fraction of response.

And yet his kiss was tantalizing as its pressure eased. His lips upon hers were warm and smooth, subtly inviting. The touch of his tongue on the tender surfaces of her own mouth was sweet, its invasion one of infinite grace rather than demand. Pilar felt the surge of the blood in her veins, heard it begin to pound in her head. Her lower body grew heated and heavy. Her breasts, pressed against the hard planes of his chest, tingled with exquisite sensitivity, so that it seemed she could feel the weave of the rough peasant's shirt he still wore and the interlocking bands of the muscles that lay underneath. His thighs were rigid against her own. His weight was constricting so that she felt incredibly vulnerable, as if somewhere deep inside there was a place where she was defenseless, where if touched just so she might be enticed to yield.

Alarm, silent but strident, swept through her. She drew a deep, gasping breath and pushed him violently away from her. He let her go. In the same movement he rose to one knee, bracing his forearm across it as he hovered above her where she supported herself on one elbow. He gave a short, breathless laugh. "You see?" he said. "Stalwart and inviolate inside yourself. How could it be otherwise?"

It was a long moment before she could trust the steadiness of her voice enough to speak, before she could force her mind to function. She wanted to roll away from him, but refused to give him the satisfaction of that retreat. "How indeed?" she answered finally in husky tones. "There must be another reason, then, for this display. If it's the price to be paid for daring to pity you, I must tell you it's too high."

"On the contrary, it's wonderfully low, a decision taken in deliberation. Unlike some, I have no desire for a branded hostage."

"I'm not your hostage."

"Aren't you?" He reached to catch her hands. Rising in a single swift movement, he pulled her to her feet with such force that she was catapulted into his arms. Holding her palms pressed against his chest, he said, "Tell me, how long do you think it will take me to exchange you for my brother?"

If he returned her to Don Esteban, there was little doubt that her stepfather would kill her. With the blood slowly congealing in her veins, she whispered, "You—You wouldn't."

"You don't deny that I could. Does that mean you accept that I hold you, or only that you perceive me as capable of any iniquity?"

Anger stirred at having the knowledge of her position forced upon her with such unremitting intention. "Neither. It's only that I had not thought you would surrender so tamely to Don Esteban's manipulations."

"It's a question of a life. My brother's."

"And what of mine?"

"The choice, I admit, is difficult. Tell me why I should preserve you instead of the fruit of my mother's womb, a sibling who venerates and trusts me, and who waits even now, uncomplaining and burned like crisp beef, for me to come for him."

"You are asking for payment?" She could not keep the shock from her voice.

"If the form can guarantee forgetfulness, it will be considered."

His voice was clear and cool, yet there was buried inside it a crackling edge that caught at her attention. She was silent as she listened to its echoes in her mind. It was, she thought, the sound of denied pain.

"No, you won't do that," she said with certainty. "You will do something, I don't doubt, but not that. After all, you are El Leon, the bandit leader they sing about in the mountains. How difficult can it be for you to defeat Don Esteban? I expect that if you exert yourself, you can preserve me and Vicente at the same time!"

A sound like a dry laugh left him. "Who knows?" he said in slow acquiescence. "It might even be worth the effort."

Refugio, staring down at the woman he held, seeing no more than the pale curve of her cheek in the darkness, wanted suddenly to strip her bare. He wanted to see not her body, but her mind, wanted to know what she thought and felt and believed, and how he was placed in her view. He could do it with force and sharp, double-edged wit, but what would be the purpose? The act itself would cause change. Therefore, he must wait, must accomplish what he wanted by stealth. He would ply her with words and sweet possibilities until she revealed herself. And when his curiosity was satisfied, then he would, must, dismiss her.

She was different. She didn't cling with lovesick entreaties, nor did she lure him with crude gestures and promises; she wanted nothing to do with him, in fact. On the other hand, she didn't shrink from him or act the coy, retiring maiden. She had strength of purpose, more than his band, it seemed, or she would not be there. She could not be bullied, and if she was frightened, refused to show it. She met his more outrageous sallies with wit and flashes of understanding that were disconcerting.

He thought she was exactly as she had said, but could not be sure. She intrigued him, and was therefore dangerous. It was imperative that he discover everything there was to know about her. Always before, that had brought boredom and satiety. It would, pray God, again.

When she made no answer to his taunt, he stepped back, gesturing toward the faint light that shone from the hut as an indication that they should return to its shelter. The movement was exaggerated in its gallantry, but no less sincere for that.

Pilar moved ahead of him toward the hut. There should have been satisfaction in the fact that she had distracted him from his worry about Vicente, but she could not feel it. It seemed, instead, that she had gained not a concession, but a reprieve.

There was to be no rest. Refugio, brisk with orders and exhortations, waxing acerbic and dulcet by turns and with neither mood safe to question, got them all up on their feet again and back in the saddle. Pilar thought she would be left behind, until she was directed to her horse with a stinging rebuke. They took the small chest of silver because, she surmised, their leader felt it might prove useful, and took Isabel because the young woman refused in near hysteria to remain behind again. They were far along the road, with the sun climbing ladders of pink cloud into a sky of purest cerulean, before anyone thought, or dared, to ask where they were going.

Cadiz was their destination. Cadiz of a thousand years and ten thousand ships, where Phoenician merchants once dreamed of Tyre, where Carthaginians and Romans had saluted their dancing girls in the wine of Jerez, and where the yellow wealth of Aztec gods had been dragged ashore with grunts. Cadiz, where the sea surrounded the Alameda and the Alameda edged the houses of the town, and all was guarded by the rocky headlands of Los Cochinos and Las Puercas.

They were headed for Cadiz, where Don Esteban was to take ship for Louisiana.

No one asked what they would do when they got there. They failed to ask because there was no leisure for it, no breath or will. Pilar thought they had traveled fast before; she had been mistaken. They careened along the mountain roads, crowding less desperate travelers into the ditches, trampling chickens and geese under their horses' hoofs and sending curs yipping. They rode tough hill ponies into heaving, windbroken nags; they ate and drank with one foot in the stirrup, and they did not close their eyes for fear the caked grit of the road dirt would blind them.

Shadowy figures gave them food, led away their exhausted mounts and brought fresh ones. These men talked to Refugio in low voices, pointing south, explaining, absolving. Sometimes there was silver passed, sometimes not.

The leagues fell away behind them. The day waned and night came again, and still they rode on. Pilar, tired before they started, felt for a long time as if she were on a rack. Gradually she was overcome by a blessed daze through which she could hear and see but no longer feel. Her fingers were claws made to hold reins, and there were patches on her thighs and hips that might never grow skin again. Unlike the others, particularly Baltasar, who snored with closed eyes as he rode, she could not sleep in the saddle. She remained upright on her horse by sheer strength of will, that and a carefully nurtured hostility.

It was Refugio who was the focus of her wrath, El Leon, the man who rode with unflagging strength, who never swayed, never stumbled on the dismount, who continued alert and watchful and endlessly enduring. It was he who drove them, who would not let them tarry or dawdle, not let them stop to sleep, hardly let them breathe. She refused to complain, and bit back every moan of pain and weariness. But in her mind she castigated the man who galloped ahead as inhuman and unfeeling, a monster of arrogance. And she kept her mind half alert by plotting her vengeance.

They came to Cadiz late on the second day from when they had begun. The town walls were in such disrepair that they were falling down, and there was no one at the single landward gate. They threaded their way through the streets until they reached the outer edge of the docks of the bay. They drew up before a low tavern with a creaking sign showing a rooster riding a dolphin. Inside it smelled of sweat and brine, stale tobacco and sour wine. The proprietor was huge, a grossly fat behemoth who sat behind a table swatting flies and the backsides of any barmaid in reach with equal impartiality. He laughed when he heard the name of the ship they were inquiring after. His body shook with his amusement, rolling in waves, cresting here and there like a bilious sea.

There had been a great hustle and bustle about the loading of the ship, he said, for it carried a man who thought himself important and made sure Cadiz had the same opinion. The dock grapevine said he was quick to order the whip and mean with his money; he not only laid stripes on the backs of the stevedores hired to load his carriage, but also on a young manservant he had with him whom he called Vicente. Besides that, he had cheated the dock men out of their reward of a ration of grog. The mighty had their weaknesses, however. The nobleman's carriage had mysteriously been dropped into the sea as it was being loaded on the ship. It had been dragged out again, but the gilt trim and velvet cushions had been ruined. The young manservant was whipped over the incident, but he didn't seem to mind.

Was the ship still in the bay? By all the saints, did they see it? The vessel had cleared the harbor with the morning tide. By now it was far out to sea, well on its way to the West Indies!

The tavern was not designed to accommodate overnight guests. There was a single room under the eaves, but it was used by the barmaids to entertain the customers who wanted something more stimulating than a drink. The tavern keeper did not want to let them have it, and seemed inclined to question why they did not go to an inn. That was until Refugio leaned close and asked in gently satirical tones about the incidence of smuggling in and around the harbor. The fat man choked and and wheezed and looked closer at his customer. "El Leon," he muttered, his eyes goggling as he turned blue about the mouth, "El Leon."

The room was theirs. There was an offer to clear the taproom of the tavern, but it was refused since it might cause questions. Food was brought: a half of a roast pig, a dish of paella the size of a cart's wheel, several beehive shaped loaves of bread, and two pitchers of wine. A fire was made on the smoke-blackened hearth of the fireplace at one end of the room, a few tallow candles appeared. When all was prepared, they were left alone.

Pilar ate a sliver or two of the roast pork and drank a cup of wine, but was too tired for more. The heat of the fire was so soporific in combination with the sour drink that she felt dazed, disoriented. She was uncomfortably aware of a strong need for a bath, but since it didn't seem possible to arrange one in their present cramped quarters, she made no mention of it.

There were four beds in the room. They sagged here and there, and the single sheet that covered each was less than clean. Pilar, after inspecting the bed on the far wall away from the fire, grimaced, then stripped off the dirty sheet and threw it into a corner. Picking up the coverlet, she wrapped it around her and sat down on the side of the hair mattress.

For the four available beds, there were six people. It was obvious that two people would have to share a bed with someone else. Who it would be depended on a number of factors, none of which seemed terribly important at the moment. If no one objected to the bed she had chosen in the next five seconds, Pilar was going to fall into it. After that she didn't really care who joined her.

Isabel was already asleep, sitting upright in a chair with her mouth open in a way that should have looked ridiculous but merely made her appear frail. Enrique, his ebullience dimmed, was blinking sleepily at the fire. Charro was re-braiding a raveling leather lariat with lip-pursed concentration. Baltasar sat forward on a stool with his elbows on his knees and his chin in his hands. The brigand leader had stayed below, talking to the tavern keeper for some time before he rejoined them. Now he leaned back in an armchair with his long legs stretched out toward the fire and crossed at the ankle. He rested his head on the chair back, gazing up at the ceiling.

Refugio had been drinking; his cup had been refilled times without number. The planes of his face were a little slack and his eyes had a blind, inward-searching look. Regardless, there was not a tremor in his hands as he carried the cup to his lips, and his manner was as commanding as ever. His voice, when he broke the somnolent stillness, was as clear and commanding as a convent bell.

"What say you, my *compadres*," he said, "to a sea journey?"

"No," Baltasar said. "You don't mean—" The big peasant stopped as Refugio turned his head, impaling him with a steel-gray glance.

"Why not?" their leader asked gently. "What is there here that you can't live without? What joy that can't be replaced? Or is it that you relish being hunted?"

"If you mean to follow Don Esteban, we must have money to pay our passage. Then we would need something more for the voyage than the clothes on our backs."

"We have the silver, and the horses have value even in a quick sale."

"A ship's a small place," Baltasar argued, "one where it would be easy to be cornered if some fool discovers who you are."

"Fools are distressingly common, but are seldom dangerous unless someone is careless. We will not be. Other than that, not everyone knows my face, and names can be changed." The voice of their leader was patient, yet held a firmness that would not be denied. It was plain that the time would soon come when a choice must be made.

"It may be a year or more before any of us can return, if then. There are people who depend on El Leon. Would you leave the band to fend for itself?"

"How would they fare if I were captured this evening and hanged at daybreak? Our calling has no guarantees, either of allegiance or a leader. And you must know that those who require these things don't last long in it."

Baltasar stared at Refugio a long moment, then gave a deliberate nod. "It looks as if you're set on it. So be it, then."

Refugio turned his gaze to Charro. The young man grinned with a slow creasing of the lean sides of his face. "I smell a wind from the Tejas country, and it's calling me home. Try to keep me in Spain."

"Enrique?"

The slight man gave an elaborate shrug, smoothing his mustache. "It will be different. The women will be different. You speak of changed names, and I have a desire to be a grandee and have people address me as Don Enrique. Promise me this, and I am, as always, your man."

Refugio smiled with the bright flicker of firelight in his eyes. "Done."

Pilar rose to her feet. Holding the coverlet around her shoulders, she moved toward the others, deliberately pushing into their circle. Her voice calm, she said, "What of me?"

"You?" Refugio shifted his shoulders so he could turn to face her.

"Yes, me! I have an interest in tracking down the man who killed both my mother and my aunt and who cheated me of all I own."

"Except the chest of silver."

"A paltry amount."

"But I thought you were claiming it."

There was something in Refugio's gaze upon her that sent a ripple of wariness along her skin; still, she could see no reason to withdraw her request. She answered, "True, but Don Esteban took so much more."

"Then you won't mind playing the Venus de la Torre in order to try to reclaim it? Naked, if need be?"

The Venus de la Torre, Pilar knew, was a famous sculpture, the representation of a woman totally unclothed and imprisoned inside an ivory tower. The model was said to be the mistress of Count Gonzalvo of Cordoba, a beautiful woman who had been kept a prisoner for years by the eccentric nobleman. So perfect was her form that the count had hired an obscure marble cutter to make a life-sized statue of her. The poor artist had fallen in love with the mistress, however. When his commission was done, he had gone away to make a copy of the original work from memory, a masterpiece that had been purchased and displayed by King Carlos III.

Pilar drew herself up as well as she was able in her ragged coverlet. Her voice scathing, she said, "Don't be absurd!"

"There is no absurdity, only necessity."

Refugio's gaze was stern, though there was a glint in its depths that might have been caused by either satisfaction or wine. Of one thing there was no doubt, he meant what he said. If his manner had not told her so, Pilar would have been warned by the swiftness with which he had answered her proposal. He had known she would ask to go with his band, and he had been ready. It was galling to be so maneuvered, but there was nothing she could do.

"I suppose you will be the count?" she said in chill tones.

His face was bland as he inclined his head. "I mean to go as Count Gonzalvo, a man heard of by many, but seen by few. To complete this masquerade, I require a Venus. You will travel as my imprisoned mistress, keeper of my heart, señorita, or you will not go at all."

CHAPTER 6

She went as the Venus de la Torre; there was no other choice. She did not go naked, but in silk and velvet and a plumed hat, and with her bare throat draped with faux pearls, though they were fine quality of their kind. She went as the inamorata—incomparable in beauty, of course—of a nobleman of great wealth, unstable disposition, and flamboyant habits, Don Gonzalvo, whose name and crest were recognized instantly, though not his visage. She traveled with a maid named Isabel to carry her jewel box, a manservant called Baltasar to hold the cushion for her feet and perform the other tasks that might add to her comfort, and with a pair of gallants known as Don Enrique and Don Miguel, friends of Don Gonzalvo who could be trusted to amuse her without encroaching, and also to keep other men at bay.

Pilar was the touchstone, the key, the one who justified the disguises of them all. She accepted the position, but the knowledge was incensing. It angered her, not because of the invidious position in which she had been placed, but because it was further proof that she need never have asked to join Refugio and his men. The scheming bandit had never intended anything else, but had used her appeal as a lever to persuade her to an impersonation she might not otherwise have assumed. More than that, her role was a constant reminder that she was his hostage.

If she had thought that the imposture they were all undertaking would be conducted with some degree of moderation, she soon learned her error. Moderation played no part in Refugio's plans. He wanted her, and the nobleman at her side, to be the focus of all eyes, the subject of such surprise and amazed conjecture that no one would have the time to consider that they might not be who they seemed.

It was Enrique and Baltasar who proved most capable at creating interest in the tale of Count Gonzalvo and his mistress. With guile and competence and strong heads for wine, they spread the story of how the count was taking his Venus away to the Caribbean to remove her from the notoriety surrounding their love affair, and also from the importuning of the men who were enraptured by her loveliness, both in marble and in the flesh. They spoke of the terrible jealousy of the count and whispered of the men slain in duels for the sake of his Venus. They hinted at wealth beyond the dreams of mortals, wealth that gave ample license for his violent temper and odd whims, such as bathing every day, eating no fruit other than pomegranates, and commanding the manservant Baltasar to act as his food taster on the odd occasion.

It was also Enrique who, with Refugio, visited a discreet Moorish Jew who dealt in ersatz jewels and clothing cast off by the rich due to ennui or death. It was there that the entire party had been outfitted, and at minimal expense. The greater part of the cost had been applied to Pilar's wardrobe. Neither man could understand why she was not more grateful for that fact, or so they pretended.

There was no ship embarking for Louisiana from the Cadiz harbor, and would not be for at least a month, possibly longer. There was, however, a vessel called the *Celestina* which was bound for Mexico by way of the island of Cuba. If they landed at Havana harbor, they might then find passage to Louisiana aboard a coastal trader plying between the island and the ports of Mobile and New Orleans. It would be a roundabout way of reaching their destination, but could well be faster than waiting for the later ship. Moreover, it was a safer alternative for Refugio and the others than remaining in Cadiz. The chance that one of them might be recognized by the authorities was always with them. The sooner they took up their new identities, the sooner they were out of Spain, the better it would be.

It was Charro who provided the carriage for their arrival at the docks. He had borrowed it, in a phrase, from its owner, an invalid who seldom left his sick room and would not miss it for a few hours. There was a crest painted on the doors, but it was so artfully splattered with mud as to be undecipherable. The coachman and footmen who accompanied it wore livery of burgundy velvet laced with gold. If their faces were suspiciously red with the effects of strong drink and there was a jingle of silver in their pockets, no one came close enough to notice.

The gaze of the five or six other passengers already on board the ship, as well as that of the greatest portion of the crew and every drunken seaman and waterfront lounger in Cadiz, was on Refugio as he descended from the carriage. He moved with animal grace, yet there was about him the hauteur of a prince. He was splendidly visible in a jacket of red velvet piped in burgundy and set with silver buttons the size of apples. With it he wore golden-yellow breeches, gray stockings, and black shoes with silver buckles. His tricorne hat, set on lightly powdered hair, had a burgundy plume, and his cane of polished malacca was as long as the average man was tall and had a head formed of gold filigree. His cloak was embellished by a multitude of capes, each fuller than the next, so that his wide shoulders appeared broader still.

With magnificent indifference for his audience, he

brushed aside the aid of a footman and, turning, gave his hand to Pilar to help her alight. She was his match in demure splendor, outfitted in a traveling gown of gray velvet lined with pink satin, and wearing a wide-brimmed hat of gray felt tied with a wide pink gauze ribbon under her chin. The faux pearls gleamed on her bosom with an opalescent sheen that made her skin appear luminous—and there was a great deal of it to be viewed. The gown was low cut, with a pink-lace edging at the neckline that acted as a frame for the display. Pilar kept her eyes lowered, though she sent Refugio a fulminating glance from under her lashes as he bent over her hand in a gesture nicely calculated to indicate homage and adoration. She felt he was making a spectacle of her, turning her into something she was not. At the same time it seemed he was laughing at her, though it could just as easily have been himself he mocked.

They swept up the gangplank. Behind them came Isabel, simply dressed and carrying what had every appearance of a jewel chest but was actually the last pitiful remnants of the silver. Enrique strolled after the girl, a refined courtier in a blue vest and breeches worn with a pale gray coat, a diamond in his sky-blue cravat and his hair white with powder and with its back length caught in a silk bag.

Baltasar was perfection as the manservant. His raiment was sober, even a little rough; his hair was natural, his expression stolid, and he carried the first of a number of boxes being decanted from the carriage. Charro wore a short black riding jacket that matched his shadow-striped black vest and also his breeches, which were tucked into gloveleather boots. With his flat-crowned hat and lariat of braided leather coiled around his shoulder, he appeared the consummate horseman. The quality of his attire hinted, perhaps, at some hacienda devoted to the breeding of Arabians, or of bulls for the arena; still, his role was so nearly his own identity that he seemed natural in it.

The captain of the ship came forward to welcome them. He bent himself in half, his face wreathed in ingratiating smiles.

"To have you traveling with us is an unexpected pleasure, Don Gonzalvo," the ship's officer said. "You do us great honor. We will do our utmost to make your journey comfortable, and memorable."

The captain would have presented the other passengers, but Refugio waved the suggestion away with a languid hand. Later, perhaps. The señorita was fatigued, he said, and he wished to personally inspect his cabin for cleanliness before the ship sailed.

Pilar had never been on a ship before. The few pictures that had come her way had failed entirely to prepare her for the small size of the one she was on, or for the cramped quarters allotted to passengers. The cabin she and Refugio were shown contained a narrow berth, a corner washstand with a basin set into the top, and a minuscule table with two chairs. There was hardly space for a full step between any of the furnishings, and this was the most lavish accommodation on the ship, next to that of the captain himself.

The space allotted to the others was apparently on a lower level, for Baltasar set down the box he carried, then with Enrique, Charro, and Isabel, followed after the sailor who had been detailed to see them all installed. Pilar would have trailed after the others, but Refugio put his hand on her arm.

"One moment, my dove," he said with a melting smile, then closed the door behind the others. Turning, he leaned his shoulders against it.

Pilar looked at him, at the lingering elation underlined by gaiety in his eyes. She tilted her head. "You're enjoying this, aren't you? This playing of parts and running risks?"

"It's bearable."

"More than that, I think."

He inclined his head, as if in recognition of her insight. "To be restricted to the hills of Spain and to the places that have been made safe by money or loyalty is a kind of imprisonment. Prisons are notoriously dreary. To break free even for a day is gratifying."

"But dangerous."

"The prospect of weeks, even months, at large is a gift from the gods. Such gifts are best accepted without counting the cost."

"That's all very well," she said, her brown eyes cool with condemnation, "but there are some of us who don't enjoy fear. Or walking into possible traps."

He tilted his head. "Such as?"

"This room. I have the strangest feeling that you are waiting with anticipation for the moment when I must concede that a man's mistress usually shares his quarters."

"Hardly anticipation. More like considered interest. What took you so long?"

She gave him a tight smile. "I thought you usually slept alone and preferred it that way. I thought that the supposed eccentricity of your nobleman would surely extend to separate cabins. Failing either, I thought sharing accommodations with all your followers might be so ingrained a habit that you would not think of doing otherwise. I thought a great many things, none of them, it seems, quite correct."

"You have nothing to fear from me," he said softly.

"You have held me against my will, threatened me, and forced your attentions on me. Tell me why I should believe you."

"My attentions," he repeated, the words musing.

"Do you deny it?"

"By no means. But you might realize that the attentions

you mention were an exercise in restraint compared to what I could have done."

It was true, that much she would admit. She transferred her gaze to the wood grain of the door behind his right shoulder. "That doesn't make them acceptable."

"I repeat, you have nothing to fear. All that's required is the appearance of intimacy."

"I don't like it." The statement was bold with strain.

"Why? Even if those for whom the masquerade is being played out found out who you are, it could not harm a name already damaged beyond reckoning. As it is, why should a new-made Venus care?"

"Don't call me that," she snapped.

"Then trust me," he returned, the reasonable quality dying out of his tone to be replaced by light acerbity. "If I were breathing prayers and pleas to taste your sweet favors, you might have reason for complaint. I am not."

"For the moment."

"Oh, agreed. Is that the objection?"

"Not at all!" She could feel the heat of the hot flush that made its way to her hairline. It was sheer rage that caused it, and not the mental images his words conjured up in her mind.

"Proving that you are not pining to nestle at my side with gentle cooing and soft, intrepid explorations? If there is neither dread nor yearning between us, what can trouble our slumbers?"

"We are forced to travel together. We are not forced to sleep together!"

His gaze narrowed and his voice grew quieter, both warning signs. "Oh, but we are. Unless you prefer to change places with Enrique. Charro I refuse to have for a berth-mate; he wears his spurs to bed."

"You mean—"

"That's the choice."

"What of Isabel?"

"Baltasar is unlikely to agree to her leaving him alone. She might exchange places with you, however, and Baltasar might permit it, but the question is whether you would find the arrangement an improvement."

"You think I should prefer you?" There was derision in the challenge. It hid the sudden flutter near her heart that the words brought.

"Oh, I'm sure of it," he answered in unimpaired self-esteem. "You see, I don't snore."

"I am not proposing to sleep with Baltasar!"

"No? Neither am I."

She swung away from him, moving to stand at the porthole with its small, thick, salt-smeared panes of glass. From that position in the stern of the ship, she could see the stretch of the dock with its milling activity and, beyond that, the curve of land that would be her last view of Spain for a long time, possibly forever.

"You think it's easy," she said over her shoulder in a voice that was uneven with weariness and the anxiety she was trying valiantly to hide. "You don't mind setting out for a colony on the other side of the world. You are used to being thrown together with Baltasar and Enrique and the others. The prospect of being crammed together with an-other person in a space hardly bigger than a nun's single cell for weeks on end is, to you, only an inconvenience. I can't be that way."

"You misjudge me. I have never shared a space this small with another human being, and the thought affects me with doubt amounting to terror. I am aware, you see, that this cabin is not, and never will be, a nun's cell."

His choice of words was odd. For Refugio, the oddity could only be deliberate. She swung to face him.

There was no one there. The door panel was just closing. It shut with a brittle snap.

They sailed within the hour. The backs of the men who bent to the oars of the boats that pulled them from the bay glistened in the sun. Drops of water, dripping from the straining ropes, fell glittering like lost diamonds. Cadiz receded in the glare, shimmering above the water as if dancing a farewell bolero. The ocean beyond the harbor greeted them with swells. The sea birds following, crying above the ship's topmost sails, tipped their wings and glided back shoreward with the tender boats. The ocher and gray-green of the land that nestled gently against the pure blue of the sky turned misty. It faded into purple, became a gray haze, then vanished in an instant. The turquoise of the sea deepened and darkened and became the color of new-made ink. Twilight approached from behind them and became night.

Pilar was reluctant to leave the cabin. She deplored the apprehension that held her there, but could not deny it. The small room had become a refuge where she was safe from weighing, judging eyes. She felt the urge to gather them all, Isabel and Baltasar, Enrique and Charro, and especially Refugio, inside, as if that would protect them. The consequences if Refugio or any of his men were recognized seemed too dire to risk moving around, exposing themselves to passengers and crew. For herself, she had little concern. The likelihood that she would see anyone who knew her was remote; she had been shut away in the convent too long for that. And yet, her safety depended on the others remaining safe also.

She knew the sense of security in the room was false, knew that to remain hidden would be the surest way of attracting attention. She couldn't help it. She needed time to adjust to this new danger and to her new position.

It felt strange, knowing that people thought she was Refugio's woman. The idea aroused such a host of feelings inside her that she could not separate them all. That she had not objected more strongly was peculiar, even to herself. The reason, she thought, was that somewhere inside herself she trusted that it was merely a subterfuge. Added to that was the need to belong. She had no one, neither father nor mother, relative nor friend. She would grow used to that fact given time, but for now there was comfort in being a part of Refugio's band, in sharing the warmth and the jokes as well as the hardships. She need not be alone. Moreover, there was someone else who understood her aims, needs, and enmities, someone who would come to her aid if need be. She might resent the fact that Refugio meant to keep her with him against her will, might be incensed that he would use her for his ends, but she depended on the strength of his intention. That she also resented that dependence was natural.

The way Refugio made her feel, her sheer physical reaction to him as a man, troubled her. She could not seem to control it, which distressed her even more. No good could come of succumbing to an infatuation with a brigand, a man whose most likely future was an ignoble death. Whatever he might once have been, that much was clear. Added to it was his own resolve to avoid all entanglements except those without emotional complications. To love such a man could only bring pain. Her own future was uncertain enough without that burden.

Pilar did not join the others for dinner, but pleaded exhaustion as an excuse to keep to the cabin. Refugio dined with pomp and affectations of grandeur, and with Baltasar standing behind his chair to taste each morsel on command. Enrique was voluble and charming, talking of his jaunts about Europe, though without mention of the acrobat troupe. Charro spoke a great deal about the Tejas country and his father's holdings there near the northern capital of New Spain known as San Antonio de Bexar. He held forth in particular about the men who worked the cattle, roping, throwing them by twisting their great long horns, branding these beasts descended from Spanish ancestors.

Isabel, when she brought Pilar her evening meal on a tray, told her about the ordeal. Pilar was just as happy not to have been there. Inviting Isabel to share her dessert, she plied the girl with questions about the other passengers.

They were five in number, Isabel said. They included a young and handsome priest going to report to his bishop in Mexico City, a merchant who owned a tannery in Havana and was traveling home with his giddy new wife, just fifteen years old, and also his wife's mother. There was, in addition, a wealthy young widow who, like themselves, was en route to Louisiana.

The last lady seemed to have earned Isabel's dislike. The woman dressed herself in silk and lace, though it was colored the black of mourning. She had intended to depart on the ship taken by Don Esteban, but had been prevented from making the sailing by an accident on the road from Madrid. The widow was going out to oversee the dissolving of an estate left her by her late husband. She had married him, an older man, some five years before while he was in Spain, and had intended to join him in the colony. She had, she said, been prevented from this aim by a long string of difficulties too tedius to mention. Isabel, however, thought the whole tale less than truthful. The widow was a poser of the first order, Isabel declared, a frivolous woman most likely delayed in joining her husband by parties and other amusements at court. Why, the widow had taken off her black veil for the sole purpose of flirting with Refugio across the table. She was shameless!

Refugio was late returning to the cabin. He did not

light the lantern swinging from its hook overhead, but disrobed in the darkness. Pilar shut her eyes as she saw what he was doing; though the cabin was dim, there was the glow of moonlight on the sea coming through the porthole. She could tell from the soft rustling and quiet thuds when he removed his coat and tossed it aside, when he took off his shirt and removed his boots. As the sounds faded she clenched her teeth, waiting for him to approach the berth.

There was only silence. She opened her eyes by degrees to see him at the porthole. He was silhouetted against the glass while shifting silver gleams outlined the width of his bare shoulders and slid along the muscles of his arms and downward over his lightly furred chest to the narrow flatness of his belly. He had retained his breeches, for the gleam of his skin ended at the waist.

He thought himself unobserved, it appeared. Lifting a hand, he pressed it to the glass and, spreading the fingers, slowly bent his head to rest it on his wrist. He pressed his eyelids tightly together, his breathing even, noiseless though compressed, as if it was an effort to keep it that way.

The minutes ticked away. Pilar fought an urge to sit up, to ask if he was in pain, to offer help, consolation, something. However, it would be an intrusion upon an intensely private moment, she knew, and so lay still.

At last Refugio moved. He stepped to one of the boxes and, going to one knee, lifted the lid. He reached inside and took out a bottle; after drawing its cork, he raised it to his lips. He drank again, then replaced the bottle and took out a blanket. Wrapping this around him, he lay down against the wall.

Pilar had thought Refugio de Carranza invulnerable, his strength and endurance endless. It was not so. Everyone, it seemed, carried around with them their pains and their griefs. Some allowed theirs to be seen, others didn't. If they chose the latter course, it didn't mean they felt less, perhaps even the opposite.

It was sometime later when Pilar finally closed her eyes, later still when she slept.

The widow was present on the afterdeck when Refugio, rejuvenated and gorgeous in lime-green, escorted Pilar up to take the air. He introduced the two of them with all courtliness. The widow was Luisa Elguezabal. She was in her early thirties, with red-brown hair and eyes of bright hazel that saw everything and were avid for more. Short in stature, rounded in form, she carried herself in a manner that thrust her bosom outward like a pigeon. Her gaze as it rested on Refugio was hungry and amused and slyly arch. She had no attention to spare for Pilar, but smiled up at the brigand in his gentleman's clothing.

"I've been waiting for you," she said, her voice low but lilting.

Refugio's bow was polite, though Pilar thought she saw a flicker of wariness in his eyes. He said, "This is a boon, one surely undeserved. Had we known you would display such graciousness, my companion and I would have made haste to join you."

The other woman ignored that reference to his semiattached state. Her voice low, she said, "How very gallant a sentiment, my brave man. And a total lie. You knew I would be waiting. The truth is, you knew me the instant you saw me last night, Refugio de Carranza. Admit it, you did. How could you think I would not know you, or that I would let our meeting pass unacknowledged?"

"There must be some mistake."

"No, none. It isn't every day that I discover an old lover I thought never to see again—or that I am presented with the opportunity to beard a lion, the great El Leon."

Refugio remained the unperturbed grandee. His face

was still, a mask for the cogent thought passing behind it. Pilar inhaled the scent of musk and hyacinths that wafted from the other woman and felt the rise of sick, baffling dislike inside her. She wanted to slap the widow for putting them in jeopardy, though she was sure she need not exert herself. Refugio was not surprised; he must have recognized the woman, also. Pilar waited with confidence for his annihilation of the widow. It would be swift and complete, and verbal, of course. Regrettably.

Refugio laughed, a sound of rich amusement and rueful pleasure. "Was there ever such felicity as this meeting? I feared you meant to deny me, Doña Luisa. Puerile romance can be forgotten, and ours was long ago."

"Not so long."

"And you look as nubile now as then, in spite of the widow's trappings." The compliment rose easily, without apparent effort, to his lips.

"What a charmer you were," the widow said, fingering her black veil as she sighed.

"May I charm you now?" Refugio offered his arm to Luisa Elguezabal, his dark gray gaze sweeping sightlessly over Pilar as he deserted her.

It was a surrender, a capitulation without skirmish or defense and under the most vulgar of terms. There were reasons for it. If Doña Luisa recognized Refugio, then she could harm them all, and he must prevent that if he could. The lady had, apparently, decided on the price she required for her silence. Refugio had no choice except to pay it.

Pilar watched the other two walk away, watched Refugio bend his head toward the widow with a guileless and gentle smile. She watched, and accepted the necessity, and even understood it.

Understanding did not prevent the desolation that assailed her. Or explain it.

CHAPTER 7

The narrow room where the passengers, as well as the captain and officers of the *Celestina*, took their meals was used between times as a salon. Toward afternoon of their third day at sea, Pilar found the widow Elguezabal ensconced there. Doña Luisa had every appearance of a lady ready to receive visitors; her hair was elaborately coiffed and covered by a fine muslin cap edged with black lace, her day gown as fresh as if she had just changed. There was a plate of bonbons at her elbow, and in her hands was a piece of embroidery to while away the time. She was, however, alone.

Pilar's first impulse was to go away at once. She overcame it with an effort. Her manner casual, she moved to take a seat near the woman. She essayed a pleasantry, and it was answered with a comment both bland and banal. She tried again.

"Please accept my sympathy on the death of your husband. His loss before you had the time to know him must have been a great blow."

The widow smiled piously with lashes lowered. "Indeed, yes. So sad."

"What an irony it is that you must now travel out to the Louisiana to attend his affairs when you could not before."

"These things happen," came the answer, though it was accompanied by a sharp glance.

"But to have such a choice forced upon you at this time is terrible. I wonder you support it so well."

"We do what we must," the widow agreed, her tone acid. "There was, you see, an unexpected encumbrance upon the estate, the matter of my husband's mulatto mistress and her two daughters, quadroons, of course."

Pilar felt the rise of a flush. A part of it was embarrassment, but a part was also annoyance, for she knew very well that the widow meant her to be nonplussed. "How unfortunate," was all she could find to say.

"Isn't it? The daughters are twelve and fourteen. One feels sorry for them, of course, but they can't be allowed to interfere with what should be mine."

"I see. The arrangement seems to have predated your marriage. Did you not know of it?" Since Doña Luisa had introduced the subject, there could be nothing wrong in pursuing it.

"Of course I knew. It would be folly to contract an alliance without inquiring into the circumstances of the prospective groom."

The words were blandly condescending, while the look in the woman's hazel eyes mocked Pilar's delicate attempt to discomfort her. Pilar pretended not to notice. The hostility she felt toward the woman had good cause, she thought. Doña Luisa seemed to be enjoying her position of power among them. She had taken to ordering Isabel about when the girl was present, and had appropriated Enrique and Charro for her amusement, keeping them in attendance upon her with demands that they play at cards with her, or regale her with tales of El Leon couched as fables.

"You married the man, regardless," Pilar pointed out.

"I did not require to be loved, at least by a husband, but

only to be kept in reasonable wealth. It seemed a fair bargain."

"And was it?"

Doña Luisa stared at Pilar a long moment, unsmiling. Finally she said, "You know that Refugio and I were once betrothed?"

Pilar had not known. Her gaze deliberately clear and undisturbed, she said, "Were you?"

"It was arranged between our fathers, though we two were not opposed. Oh, no, far from opposed. He used to come and sing beneath my window in a voice to rend the heart. He would have climbed up to me, I know, with the least encouragement. His passions were so violent in those days, yet so tender. Now that's all done. It ended when he had to flee after the death of Don Esteban's son in the duel between them."

"He didn't try to see you again?"

"If you think he would, you don't know him. Pride kept him away."

"And responsibility. And, perhaps, caring?"

"What was that?"

"Nothing," Pilar said. "You didn't contact him?"

"I couldn't, any more than I could invite him to climb to my bedchamber, though sometimes I have wished that I— But never mind. I had not seen him since then, not until he came on board this ship. Still, I knew him at once. How could I not?"

The woman's voice was too loud for such confidences. Pilar lowered her own in an attempt at compensation. "You are keeping your own counsel now out of—affection, then?"

The woman smiled. "That, and the prospect of, shall we say, diversion? It's a long and tedious way to Louisiana."

"You aren't afraid that the diversion might prove hazardous?"

The other woman drew back. "My dear girl, are you daring to threaten me?"

"Not at all," Pilar said with acerbity. "I was thinking of what might happen if someone else learned what you know."

"I shall denounce Refugio at once, and vow that I was deceived."

An odd distress rose inside Pilar. "Would you really do that? Perhaps he should be warned."

"What a child you are, my dear; Refugio knows this very well. He would expect nothing else."

"And is that a good bargain?"

Doña Luisa gave her a placid smile. "So long as I am pleased."

The cloying smell of the woman's perfume was in Pilar's nostrils, threatening to choke her. She rose to her feet. "There is a man you may have seen at court, Don Esteban Iturbide. Do you know him?"

"Indeed, yes," the widow said, a spark of interest in her eyes, as if she saw further opportunities for diversion.

"I thought you might."

Pilar turned and would have walked from the salon, but her way was blocked. Isabel stood just inside the room. Hovering behind her in the doorway with a troubled look on his craggy features was Baltasar.

"Did I hear right?" the girl said to Pilar, her face pale. "Does this woman know—does she know that—"

Isabel had trouble with the new cognomen that Refugio had taken. She could seldom remember what it was, and found it difficult to address him by it. "It's all right," Pilar said quickly. "Everything is all right."

"But she said he sang to her."

"So he did," the widow said with a lifted brow.

"He sang to me," Isabel declared, "when I was a lace maker in Cordoba. He used to watch me with the bobbins, and play tunes that would make the rhythm of weaving them in and out and over each other easier."

Pilar, touched by the softness in Isabel's face, spoke almost at random. "I thought you were a dancer?"

"What? Yes. Yes, he sang then, too. That was before he saved me from being sold to a Moor and taken to Algiers."

Puzzlement surfaced in Pilar's eyes, but before she could express it, Doña Luisa said, "You seem to have had an interesting life, for a maidservant."

"And you, too." Isabel scowled at the widow. "Unless you're lying. Are you sure your husband is dead? Are you sure you ever had a husband?"

"Good heavens!" Doña Luisa exclaimed, before turning to Pilar. "The creature is touched in the head, I do believe. She's your maid; have you no control over her?"

Baltasar, fidgeting in the doorway, made a lunge inside, catching Isabel's elbow. "Come sweeting, I told you there are things to be done. Come and help me."

Isabel gave him a distracted look. "What is it?"

"I'll show you," the older man said, his voice soothing. He tugged gently at her arm. Isabel went with him obediently enough. Throwing Pilar a look of apology, Baltasar led Isabel away.

"Well!" the widow said in dudgeon.

Pilar returned no answer to the comment, only staring after the departing couple with a frown between her eyes. She had not heard Isabel speak quite so vaguely before. She was, apparently, distraught with fear for Refugio. With a murmured request to be excused, she moved from the salon, following after the other two members of Refugio's band.

Baltasar was walking too quickly for Pilar to catch up with him and Isabel, especially since she didn't want it to appear that she was chasing them. He led Isabel to the cubicle they shared. By the time Pilar reached it, he had dropped the curtain that closed it off, and from behind it came the deep rumble of his voice in censure and Isabel's tearful protests. Pilar could not intrude, even if she was concerned for the other girl; it would be too much like interfering in a squabble between husband and wife. Turning aside, Pilar made her way back up toward the deck again.

The open air was cold and damp and left the taste of brine on the lips, but it was fresh. Pilar stood holding the rail, facing into it, until the disturbance of her mind had blown away and she was calm again. She could not quite understand why she had permitted herself to be so upset. It was not as if Doña Luisa and Isabel, or their relationships with Refugio, had anything to do with her.

She was growing used to the rise and fall of the ship, to the constant noises of creaking timbers and snapping sails and the bass song of the winds in the sheets. There was something hypnotic about the lift and surge of the ship as it pointed its bow toward the horizon and strained to reach it. It was fascinating to know that somewhere ahead lay the Canary Islands off the African coast, that they would land there for fresh water and fruit and vegetables before heading out across the sea to the new world.

Pilar had been afraid she would not like sea travel, afraid she would be homesick for Spain, that she would be ill, or that the vast reaches of water would make her feel puny and afloat in nothingness. She had been wrong. The far-stretching emptiness and the open sky suited her. Somehow, this discovery about herself was satisfying. It was just as well, since little else pleased her in her present situation.

Borne on the wind came the faint sound of music. She looked around, expecting to see a sailor with a squeeze box, or perhaps a mouth organ. She caught a glimpse of a flapping cloak half hidden behind the forward mast. It had a familiar look. Clasping her arms around her against the damp chill, she moved in that direction.

Refugio stood with his back to the mast, leaning against it as he cradled a guitar in his arms. He looked up as Pilar appeared beside him, but did not stop playing. The melody he plucked from the strings was slow and sweet. She had heard it before, though she could not quite remember where.

"I understand," she said in clipped tones, "that you are known for your serenades."

He looked at her, squinting a little against the wind that ruffled his hair and flapped the ends of his cravat. "Who says so?"

"The widow, for one. Isabel, for another."

"It's a fine thing to have fame, no matter how undeserved."

"Are you denying it?" To press the matter was a mistake, nearly as much of one as opening the question in the first place. She knew it, but knew also that it was too late to draw back. More than that, there was an ache inside her that needed the assuagement of an answer.

The tune he was playing was a counterpoint to his words. "I sang Isabel to sleep once."

"I'm sure." Her lips tugged at the corners in a wry smile. "After which rescue?"

He kept his gaze on his intricate fingering. "Do you suspect me of concocting her daydreams? Or only of taking advantage of them?"

"Are you saying that the stories she tells aren't true, that you never kept her from being sold on a street corner, or being taken to Algiers by a Moor?"

The first mate, somewhere behind them, bawled an order. Seamen scampered past, leaping into the shrouds like monkeys, swaying as they swarmed upward to bend on sail.

Refugio turned his attention to the climbing men, assessing their progress as he answered.

"I found her shivering and bruised in an alley one rainy night. How she came to be there, she never said. I'm not sure she knows."

"But why—"

He stopped playing with a twanging discord. "Why not? Why shouldn't she change her past to suit herself? Are your memories all so fair you would not make a substitute or two? If so, then be glad."

Pilar ignored the question, since she knew that he was aware of the answer. "The changes Isabel has made involve you. Doesn't that trouble you?"

"My past is not so spotless that another stain or two can matter."

"You might have tried to convince her that you were not her heroic savior, her El Cid who vanquishes all her demons."

"Oh, but I tried. I supplanted her with another rescued maiden."

Her eyes widened as she accepted his meaning. At the same time, she remembered Isabel's distress on the night she had arrived at the hut in the mountains. Reasons, there were always reasons for what he did.

She stared up at him, at the dark hair that was ruffled by the wind, the chiseled planes of his face, the width of his shoulders under his flapping cloak. His scent came to her, one made up of clean linen and masculinity and the fresh tang of salt air. The force of his presence brought the blood beating up in her throat and caused a flood of warmth in her lower body that she was helpless to prevent. And yet, there was more to him than handsome features and wide shoulders and mere animal attraction. There was the swift, sharp shifting of his mind to be reckoned with, and the

febrile intensity of his will. Armored in intelligence, in
fierce competence and superior intentions, he was formidable. Therefore, the question presented itself: If he had reasons for what he did, why had he let her know his purpose
in taking her to his mountain retreat? The probable answer
made asking too daunting a prospect to contemplate.

Her voice compressed, Pilar said, "I see."

"Yes," he agreed, his eyes somber, "I thought you
might. Tell me, was it cruel, or kind?"

"To whom?"

"To Isabel, of course. It seems unlikely that I figure as
your savior, heroic or otherwise."

"No," she answered, glancing away out over the heaving sea. Finally, she answered, "I suppose it was meant as
a kindness." After a moment she swallowed, then looked
back at him. "But what of the widow? She seems to think
that you are the lover of her youth returned."

"You suspect her of daydreaming, too? Never mind, I
will attend to Doña Luisa. Her dreams have nothing to do
with you."

His eyes as she met them were opaque, no more to be
read than if he were made of stone.

Pilar decided, with painful acknowledgment of the risk,
to persevere. "You should be aware that she knows Don
Esteban."

"Many do."

"Don't you think it's strange?"

"No," he said, a note of irritation rising in his voice.
"I think it's unfortunate and wearisome and damnably inop-
portune. But Luisa is a creature of the court at Madrid, as
was your stepfather, so no, I don't think it's strange. Why?
Do you dislike her?"

She had known she was making a mistake. There were
ways, however, to deflect questions. She gave him a wry

smile, meeting his gaze with every assumption of frankness. "Oh, the lady is amiable and worldly-wise, and as free with her gossip as she is with her bonbons. More than that, she knew you when you were tender. How can I dislike her?"

He watched her for long moments with speculation and reluctant amusement rising in his eyes. Finally, he said, "She smells good, too."

"Doesn't she?" Pilar's answer was given with unimpaired composure.

He made a sound that might have been a smothered laugh, then bent his head, beginning to strum the strings of his guitar again.

Pilar, finding it possible to retreat without feeling that she had been rebuffed, turned and walked away. As she went, the melody that followed her was the same that he had been playing minutes before. It was a haunting tune, mellow and yearning. It raised an image in her mind of a garden and darkness, and the close presence of a man.

She stopped, standing still with her skirts blowing around her. That was it. The song was the serenade she had heard on the night Refugio had come to her, one sung in the street outside while she waited. How like him it was, she knew now, to deliberately draw attention to himself in that way. At the same time, remembering that rich, warm voice filling the night with yearning and pathos, she was oddly disconcerted by the message it seemed to hold now.

She walked on again more slowly.

There were a great many things that she had heard and seen in the past few days without comprehending. She had been so immersed in her own problems and worries that there had been little time to consider what might be taking place with the rest of the band. In addition, she had assumed that the time she would spend with them was limited, that they would soon part company and never see each other again. Under such circumstances, people seldom become personally involved.

Matters had changed. Long weeks of close association stretched before them all. They were, in their present quest, dependent on each other for support and companionship and, most of all, for safety. A slip of the tongue made by any one of them could mean death for some, imprisonment for the rest. In this Pilar had no illusion; she would, after this escapade into false identities, be considered one of the band and treated accordingly.

She realized that she was traveling with a group of people of whom she knew next to nothing. More than that, what little she did know had been told to her by a woman who appeared to be at best unreliable, and at worst unbalanced. Or was she? Either way, it made her own position extremely precarious. There must be something that could be done about it, some way to learn more. The knowledge of who and what each one of them were had suddenly become vital.

Of them all, Baltasar seemed closest to Refugio. He was not a man given to talking, however, and it was probable that his tight-lipped manner and close-held loyalties would make it difficult to learn much of value from him. He was also shut away with Isabel for the time being, or had been the last time she saw him. That left Enrique and Charro. Neither of them was likely to tell her anything of real import; still, they were far easier to approach than Refugio. From him she could expect nothing except what he wanted her to know.

She found the two men playing at cards, a respectable game of Reversi with the Havana merchant and one of the ship's officers in a corner of the salon. Doña Luisa was still there also, and was holding the merchant's childish wife and his mother-in-law enthralled with the gossip concerning the dissolute behavior of Maria Luisa, the Neapolitan princess who was married to the heir to the throne. With the ladies was the young priest who sipped a glass of wine with an impervious air while he listened.

Pilar did not want to attract too much attention, nor give her questions too great an emphasis by dragging either of the men she sought from their game. She found a book lying on a table, a copy of Manrique's poems, including his *Coplas on the Death of his Father*. She settled down with it in a chair that was made from half a wine barrel.

She sat patiently reading for some time, all the while listening to Enrique and Charro exchange comic quips, slurs on each other's playing, and other assorted insults. Her reward came perhaps an hour and a half later, when another officer took Enrique's place. The acrobat, his face a study in disgust, came and flung himself down at her feet. Drawing up his knees, he clasped his arms around them.

"The luck of some people is enough to make the Pope himself suspicious," he growled with a backward glance at Charro and the first officer.

Pilar, who had gained a strong suspicion in the time she had been watching that Enrique and Charro were busily fleecing the others, gave him a smile without replying.

Enrique reached and took her book from her hand. Scanning the contents, he flipped it aside. His beatific smile was emphasized by the narrow line of his mustache. "Mediocre where it isn't morbid," was his comment on her choice of literature, "though I grant you the man writes a good poem on death. But the poet is dead also, and I am alive. Talk to me."

"Are you bored already?" she asked, more willing than he knew.

"Why not? There is the widow who sees only our Refugio, and the young wife with whom it would be unwise to meddle. You are left, our Venus, to receive the benefit of my charms."

"I'm honored."

"No, you are diverted, you are entertained, you are even amused, but you are not honored." He lowered his voice. "Therefore I am safe."

"Safe? From entanglements? But I thought the absence of those is what you were deploring?"

"Yes," he said, and sighed. "But I am also safe from Refugio's wrath, so long as I can talk to you and you only laugh."

"He requires that you be circumspect?"

He gave her a long look with a lifted brow that might have meant anything. "It seems wise, if not necessary."

"For us all," she agreed. "But do you think Refugio would really mind if Doña Luisa was charmed by you also?"

He glanced over his shoulder at the lady with a speculative light in his eyes. With one finger he scratched at his mustache, then smoothed its thin dark line. "Do you think she might be?"

"How can she fail?" Pilar grinned down at him.

"Cruel, cruel female!" he accused. "You are playing with my affections, raising dreams that the lady over there would rend like the rind of an orange. If Refugio doesn't rend my body first."

"Surely he wouldn't?"

"We were warned last night, all of us, Charro, Baltasar, and I."

It was fitting, perhaps, that the answer she received to a question so far from her real purpose should be oblique. "Don't tell me he fears being supplanted?"

"I think he is more concerned with discretion. Intimate moments have a way of bringing out the truth, don't you find?"

"I wouldn't know," she said, the words a trifle stiff. She would have to be more careful; it seemed she was also being measured.

"Endearing, if true." He tilted his head with its powdered and tightly curled wig to one side, watching her with bright brown eyes.

She smiled, holding his gaze. "Isabel tells me you were an acrobat with a traveling fair."

"A tumbler, to be accurate. But I have been many things." The last admission was expansive.

"Among them, a Gypsy fortune teller. I would think you would be good at that."

He put a finger to his lips, looking around him, then leaned forward. "I am," he said, and gave a modest flutter of his lashes.

Keeping her voice as low and conspiratorial as his own, she bent toward him. "And you are also a good grandee, though I should tell you that most I've met think too much of their dignity to sit on the floor."

A frown drew his brows together over his nose. "Is this really so?"

"I give you my word."

He nodded, then pursed his mouth. He sent a glance toward the corner where Doña Luisa held court, then shifted his sidelong gaze to the card players. He looked back to Pilar. A lithe flexing of muscles, made without touching so much as a finger to the floor, and he was on his feet and moving to draw a chair next to the one where she was seated.

"There," he said, lowering himself into it, crossing his legs at the knee and smoothing his breeches. "How is this?"

"Excellent," she answered, her voice grave.

"Dignity. I must remember that. And if I make any other errors, I will trust you to point them out."

"I'll do that, though, as I said, you are doing very well.

Charro also, though his part is not so difficult since he has only to play himself."

"I doubt he could do anything else. You've noticed his speech?"

"You mean the way he sometimes forgets the Castilian lisp?"

"Exactly. The oaf refuses to admit the elegance of it, says it comes hard to his tongue."

"They don't use it in the Tejas country?"

He shook his head. "It's a barbaric place."

"The polish his father wanted for him seems to have been a failure."

"Not precisely. He discovered a few things about the company of older women, and I have taught him a little about the younger ones, among other things."

"I'm sure he's grateful."

"He isn't grateful at all! In fact, he accuses me of stealing his women away from him while displaying my technique. It isn't true, and you must not believe him."

"No, I won't," she said solemnly.

But neither could she believe what Enrique said. His answers to her questions were given easily enough, and seemed to bear out most of what Isabel had told her; still, he was not as simple a man as he pretended, none of Refugio's followers were. Enrique might well mislead her for the fun of it, or else might tell her what he thought she wanted to hear out of courtesy. He was also, she thought, capable of clouding the issue for purposes of his own or on Refugio's orders, or else for what he conceived to be the good of the group. She would have to talk to Charro. Perhaps she could then compare what each man had to say and arrive at something near the truth.

With these things churning in her mind, she said softly, "Do you think Refugio is still enamored of the widow?"

"Still? She's a ravishing creature, but I've never heard her name pass his lips before this voyage. More than that, though an indolent attitude and a fund of idle chitchat have an irresistible appeal for some, I would have said these things would drive our leader mad in less than an hour."

The niggling gladness his words brought was quickly repressed. Pilar pursed her lips. "Still, she is his lost love."

"A fatal allure, yes. Doña Luisa also has the goad for his ox held firmly in her little white hand."

"But is he a man to accept the goad? I think not, unless it pleases him."

Enrique gave a swift shake of his head, his brown eyes grave. "You think he would choose a noose about his neck instead of a woman's arms? He might, out of a grandee's precious dignity, except for one thing. He would not hang alone."

It was a point. Refugio's care for those who rode with him was legendary. He had, more than once, risked his life to save one of his own from the noose or firing squad.

Pilar had no chance to answer. There came a quiet footfall from the direction of the door behind them, then Refugio bent over them with a hand on the backs of each of their chairs. "Clacking like two crones over the chocolate pot," he said. "How gratifying it is that you have found a common interest. I am, of course, all fluttery delight to be chosen. What a pity if you should run out of subject matter. Never fear, I will not fail you."

Straightening, he walked to where the widow sat and took a place beside her. And for the next few hours the company was entertained by as fine a display of accomplished flirtation as was ever presented for public viewing. There were compliments of sonorous grace and gestures of delicate homage; there were glances and sighs and looks of languishing and improper intent. The widow coyly re-

treated before the courtly advance; the brigand, withdraw-
ing, enticed her to be bold. He took her fan and, spreading
it, fanned her flushed cheeks. She retrieved it and rapped his
shoulder, then drew the furled lace along the strong jut of
his chin with its dark shadow of beard. Doña Luisa fed
Refugio a bonbon, and he chewed it slowly, savoring the
taste, before running his tongue along the inside edges of
his lips.

Pilar refused to watch. She laughed and joked and
allowed herself to be drawn into the card game, and only
glanced now and then at the performance going forward at
the other end of the room. Somehow the evening passed,
dinner was consumed, and the hour came when she could
reasonably excuse herself and go off to bed.

Sleep was slow to come. Her head ached, the cabin
seemed close and airless, and the rolling of the ship more
pronounced, as if somewhere on the ocean there was a storm
brewing. As the night deepened and the ship grew quieter,
she wondered where Refugio was and what he was doing.
Delighting himself, probably, she thought with sour cyni-
cism. Punching her pillow in an attempt to make it softer,
she closed her eyes with determination.

It was after midnight when Refugio entered the cabin.
He closed the door behind him with noiseless care and stood
listening. The night had grown overcast; there was neither
moonglow nor starshine beyond the cross-hatching of panes
at the porthole. He moved by instinct in the sea-black
darkness to the single berth. Going to one knee, he leaned
over the woman who was lying in it.

Pilar's breathing was even and nearly without sound.
She was, he saw, quite safe, and deeply asleep. She lay in
trusting repose, wearing nothing more than a thin shift, for
he could see the pale edge of the neckline across her breasts.
He put out his hand to touch the silk of her hair spread over

the pillow. It was warm, vibrantly alive under his fingertips. He drew back, closing his fingers slowly into a fist.

He was, ten times ten, the fool. This evening he had allowed irritation and despair and a species of jealousy to spur him into a crass exhibition of a passion he did not feel. He had thought that if he was to be damned, then he might as well be damned completely. He had not known how much the condemnation in another person's eyes could hurt. Or how easily the sickness in his mind could reach his heart.

The impulse to lie down beside Pilar, to curl his length around her and wait for sleep or the morning, whichever came first, was like a grinding pain in the top of his head. She was so sweet and innocent and beautiful that it would only be natural.

She might, if he were patient, wake and turn to him. One touch and he would be lost. He would taste the rosy smoothness of her mouth, and learn the gentle curves of her body with delicate, wandering care. Blind and deaf, mute and without memory, he would seek in her his private salvation. With diligence and rigorously held desire, he would lead her in the dance of love until she felt the music, until she joined him in its passionate rhythm and the melting wonder of its finale.

It was impossible. Even if she would permit it, he was not innocent and certainly not sweet. He moved, in fact, in a fugue of sweat and secondhand perfume with a scent of decaying hyacinths, both manured with generous ladling of self-pity and regret. He could not afford, or abide, for Pilar to catch a whiff of any of it.

A saltwater bath at dawn would cleanse him of the smell of this night's work, and the self-pity would vanish with the early light, of this he had no doubt. For the regret, however, there was no remedy.

CHAPTER 8

The corsair caravel appeared at first light, lifting silently out of the night mist. It might have been a Portuguese ship from its lines, but was lanteen rigged with a single square sail on the foremast in the style of the African Mediterranean. By the time the ship was sighted by the lookout of the *Celestina*, it was so close upon them it was possible to see the turbaned heads and dully winking weapons of the men who lined the rails, perched on the crosstrees, and swarmed upon the ratlines as thick as lice in a beggar's blanket. From the mainmast flew a green banner with a crescent, the symbol of the sons of Islam known as the Barbary pirates.

The overcast sky of the day before had become blue-black, and there was a sprinkling of cold rain in the rising wind. The Spanish captain was a cautious and somewhat indolent man; his ship was riding the waves with sails reefed for the coming storm, and had been for hours. Roused from his comfortable berth and apprised of the danger, he dithered and called on his saints, and stared over the quarterdeck rail at the other ship. He discussed the situation with his officers in high-pitched tones, but rejected all suggestion that he stand and fight. He could not quite decide if there was time to make an escape, however; Spanish ships were notorious for their sluggish maneuvering, though they rode well in heavy seas. In the meantime the eager, babbling cries of the pirates began to be heard across the water.

The captain, in a frenzy of fearful anger, called an order. A brass trumpet squawked and died away. There was a flurry of secondary commands, followed by shouts and curses and the thud of feet as men pounded up to the decks. Seamen ran here and there with pale faces and eyes bulging with excitement. They leaped into the rigging and sails flapped and boomed, blooming white against the sky. The ship floundered, wallowing as it came about under a confusion of contradictory commands. Then with ponderous deliberation it caught the rising wind. A salvo was ordered by the captain to slow the pirates. A single shot was all that could be got off. The report thundered. The smoke of it drifted in a pall over the ship while the ball skipped uselessly across the sea like a stone over a mill pond. Raising its figurehead above the waves, the Spanish ship began to surge forward in a desperate bid for escape.

It was too late. The pirate ship was closing. Nearer it came, and nearer still. Arrows whistled like an endless flight of thin and vicious birds. Booming fire from muskets spat down on the decks. There were yells and screams in a half-dozen languages. The blue-water gap between the two ships grew more narrow. Grappling hooks were brought out by the pirates and set whirling. They whined through the air, rattling and skidding as they fell to the *Celestina*'s deck, biting into the wood with a screeching crackle.

The pirates hurled themselves upward and over the rails, tumbling onto the Spanish ship with knives and swords in their hands and blood lust in their eyes. In a moment the decks were clogged with the fight. Men struggled, grunting and cursing, heaving and slashing before sinking in gurgling death. Swords whipped the air to clang and scrape in engagement. Blood splattered, spread, gathered into trails that crept along the deck seams and seeped into the scuppers.

Pilar, on deck when the Barbary corsair was sighted, had been ordered below to her cabin. She had gone at first, but the confinement had been too close, the dread of being cornered there too great; she had stayed only a moment. She ventured first into the passageway, then to the salon. The young priest was there, kneeling beside a chair with head bent over his clasped hands and his low voice droning in fervent prayer. She thought he was alone, until she saw the merchant cowering under a table with his eyes squeezed shut and his hands over his ears. Pilar stood staring at them for a moment, then picked up an empty wine bottle by its neck and made for the hatch that led to the deck.

She had no idea what she meant to do with the bottle; it was just that she felt the need for a weapon of some kind and that was all that lay to hand. She had scant idea of being much help in the melee above, but could not bear to remain shivering below like a rabbit in a hole, or like the Havana merchant. The Barbary pirates sometimes took captured ships back to port, but more often they took passengers and crew captive then set fire to the vessels. She could not bear the thought of perhaps being trapped in the flames, and if she was going to become a slave in the house of some Muslim, it would at least not be without resistance.

As she emerged on deck, she heard the shouting that rose above the tumult, strong, exultant voices crying a name over and over like some benison of faith. "Gonzalvo!" they cried. "Gonzalvo! Gonzalvo!"

It was a magnet, that sound. It drew her forward, though she kept in the lea of the poop deck with her back flattened against it. There on the larboard quarter where the grappling hooks were thickest and the pirates swarmed like flies on a carcass, she saw a phalanx of men, a fighting wedge with Charro and Baltasar and Enrique at its triangular core and Refugio at its head. Their calls had brought others running, strengthening the human plow they pushed forward. With savage tenacity and vicious force they were holding their place and slowly, irreversibly, pushing the turbaned pirates back. At the same time, Refugio's voice, incisive and carrying, rang out with an order that brought the ship's scattered contingent of musketeers clambering to the poop, where they formed ranks. A moment later there came the crash of a murderous volley, then another, and another.

There was a stretch of breathless time when it seemed that nothing could end the fighting except death to all, that the ferocity and the prodigal spending of strength and will and blood would go on until none were left alive. Then came a sway in the line of turbaned attackers. A man fell back, then another. A bearded Levantine threw down his broken sword with a curse. He whirled and fled. A half-dozen more followed. The Spanish surged forward with redoubled effort.

Aboard the pirate ship the watching corsair captain, marked by the feather held in his turban by a winking jewel, cried out an order. Nubian giants stationed on the decks drew sword and began to slash the grappling lines free. Suddenly it was a rout of yelling, scrambling men. They leaped from the *Celestina*, swinging on cut sheets, springing from the railing, diving into waves so that great fountains of blue water spouted. Surfacing, they swam toward trailing ropes as the two ships drew apart.

Refugio and his followers harried the retreat, wading into the thickest of the stragglers. The firing began to die away. The acrid smoke of gunpowder swirled about the masts, obscuring the wounded and the dying and the figures that still struggled here and there along the deck. Refugio, with sweat streaming from his hair, and his chest heaving with effort, began to drop back, to turn as he swept the deck with a comprehensive and vigilant glance. His questing gaze stopped, became fixed. Stillness touched his features. His lips parted as if he would call out.

A last muffled shot exploded. Refugio flinched, staggering back as bone splintered and muscle ruptured in a bright red decoration on his chest. He lowered the tip of his sword to the deck with slow grace. In the midst of the fulsome shouts for the Spanish victory, his eyes closed. He sank boneless and heavy toward the deck.

It was Baltasar who caught him, who lowered him to the planking. Enrique and Charro, their faces white, closed in with swords in their fists, uselessly protective as they blocked his body from view. The shouting died away. For a brief instant there was stunned and weary silence.

Pilar dropped the wine bottle she held. It rolled across the slanting deck and plunged into the sea. Along the deck the injured groaned and cried out. Spanish seamen, savage in the release of fear, moved here and there, kicking the bodies of the pirates over the side, and also those not yet dead. No one moved to help the injured Spanish seamen or tend the dying. No one moved to help Refugio.

Pilar felt as if her heart had burst. The burning pain erupted inside her, taking her breath, dimming her sight. She could not move, could not think. Her voice was trapped, suffocatingly, in her throat. The morning receded, so that the cries and groans around her grew distant, without meaning.

Abruptly, she shuddered, drawing air deep in her lungs. Her head cleared so that everything she saw and heard was sharp-edged, crystalline and bell-like in its clarity. Without conscious thought, she moved toward Refugio, then she was running to where he lay.

Enrique, his hands red to the wrist, was bending over him with a wadded sash pressed to the wound. The brigand leader lay unmoving, with shadows forming like bruises under his eyes.

"Is he—" Pilar began.

Enrique spared her a glance. "Alive, barely."

Warm energy pulsated along her veins. "Bring him below," she said, her voice firm and clear.

The band hovering around their leader looked at her, then at each other. Baltasar nodded. As one they bent to Refugio and began to lift him.

"Take care!" Pilar said.

They looked at her again, but made no comment.

In that instant the priest, emerging from below, moved to join them. In quiet helpfulness he aligned himself beside the other three men. Sliding their hands under Refugio, they formed a support with their linked arms. Moving as carefully as a young mother with a new babe, they started toward the hatchway.

There was no physician aboard the ship. The ship's officers and seamen took their illnesses and injuries to one of their number who had some experience with such things, or else treated themselves. Passengers were expected to do the same.

At the convent Pilar had attended there had been a nun who, in an attempt to ensure that Pilar had some degree of usefulness, and perhaps out of an impulse of kindliness, had taught her to tend wounds, and also the recognition and cultivation of healing herbs. Pilar was by no means sure that her sketchy knowledge was adequate for the situation confronting her, but could not think it greatly inferior to what was otherwise available.

She directed that Refugio be placed on the berth in the cabin they shared. Enrique she sent in search of brandy or rum, while she set Charro to tearing the single linen sheet into strips. She herself made a pad of Enrique's sash, holding it firmly in place. She had turned to ask Baltasar to go for a basin of seawater when from the door there came a thin and despairing scream.

It was Isabel. Her eyes were desolate and her mouth a circle of woe as she stared at Refugio on the berth. Starting forward with a throat-wrenching sob, she flung herself at the red-stained and still form.

Baltasar caught her before she reached the berth, dragging her up short so that her hair swung in a wild tangle around her red-splotched face. He gave her a hard shake. "Stop it, stop that noise! He isn't dead yet!"

Isabel gulped and tears streamed from her eyes. "Oh," she said, shivering. "Oh," she whispered again, then threw herself upon Baltasar's chest, crying in noisy sobs. He held her, soothing her with awkward pats on the back. In his eyes was a look of baffled and angry anguish.

For an instant Pilar felt the rise of tears, but she forced them back. There was no time to cry, no time to inspect the distress that poured like an endless stream through the recesses of her mind. Refugio was bleeding, the red tide soaking into the cloth she held, wetting her fingers with its warm flow. Something had to be done. She would do it.

Charro was the member of the band who was most useful to her. His father's hacienda, he said, was far from a town or other people. Everyone there, including his family, saw to their own injuries. He had helped his mother in her makeshift infirmary from the time he was small. Later he had performed rough and ready surgery on animals, and also on the men who rode for his father, the *charros* who had been gored by the longhorn cattle or torn by the wiry shrub growth known as mesquite, or who sometimes settled their differences with knives or musket fire.

Together, Charro and Pilar exposed the wound, examining the damage. They found the ball where it had come to rest, nestling against a lung after tearing a furrow from left to right across the chest and shattering two ribs. They extracted the piece of misshapen iron and cleaned the wound with brandy. Hoping that the welling blood had cleansed where they could not reach, they pressed a thick pad to Refugio's chest, strapped it tightly to him with strips of sheet, and let him be.

He had not regained consciousness. He lay with his chest rising and falling in so gentle a rhythm that it was necessary to stare hard to see it. His hands were lax upon the blanket that covered him, and his lashes made thick shadows on his cheeks. His lips were bloodless, their firm molding edged with blue.

No one wanted to leave the room. They sat watching, waiting. Isabel's tears had diminished to a few dismal sniffs. Now and then someone coughed or shifted in his seat with a rustle of clothing. Otherwise they made not a sound.

The impending storm swept over them with thunder and high seas and driving rain. A lantern was lighted against the gathering darkness and Refugio was wedged in the berth with rolled bedding to keep him still against the pitching and tossing. His wound, which had nearly stopped bleeding, opened again under the onslaught. There was a desperate hour while they wrapped him with thicker and thicker bandaging. Then the storm slowly eased off. The movement of the ship grew less violent. The bleeding finally stopped.

The day, marked by gray drizzle and rough seas, passed. Now and then intimation of a frown twitched Refugio's flaccid eyelids, or else his fingers cramped as if at the remembered heft of a sword. That was all.

The bright subtropical sun came out just at sunset, burning away the last of the clouds and mist. Its rose-red glow flooded the cabin, rousing them all. The men slipped out one at a time for food and drink and fresh air. Invariably they came back within a short time.

Those returning brought bits of news, of the mounting death toll among the injured seamen, the minor damage done to the ship, the hysterical demand of the merchant's young wife to be returned to Spain—and her virulent language and violent tantrum when denied.

Doña Luisa came to the cabin as the evening waned toward night. Her eyes were soft with pity and she held a handkerchief of lace in her hand as she stood staring down at Refugio. "I can't believe it," she said, her voice tremulous. "One would think he had had misfortune enough for one man. If he had not been so bold—but then he would not have been the lion, would he? Still, it's such a waste, such a terrible waste."

There was something in the woman's tone that disturbed Pilar, as if the widow counted Refugio already dead. Still, she was polite as she spoke. "Perhaps you would like to sit with him for a time? Since you and he knew each other well, it could be he will respond to you."

Alarm crossed the other woman's face. "Oh, no! I'm no good at all in sickrooms, really I am not. I never know what to do, and the sight of blood sends me swooning, while the odors—" She raised her handkerchief to her nose.

Isabel, sitting quietly in a corner, spoke up. "Never mind. We don't need you. Refugio doesn't need you."

"I'm sure that's perfectly true," Doña Luisa said with undisguised relief. "Perhaps later, when—when he is better, there will be something I can do. Perhaps I can amuse him then."

"Yes, later," Pilar agreed, and this time her voice was cool.

Isabel, for all her protectiveness and good intentions, was useless. She could not control her tendency to drip tears on their patient, and her hands as she touched him were so unsteady that once she nearly drenched his bandaging with a basin of dirty water. She would have choked him as she tried to make him drink, too, if Pilar had not whisked the glass out of the other girl's hand.

The presence of so many in the tiny cubicle made movement difficult if not impossible. Their recommendations, though meant to be helpful, were merely worrisome, since they made Pilar doubt her own instincts. The air, heavy with the smell of dried blood and brandy, grew hard to breathe in the cramped quarters. Finally, when she had tripped over Baltasar's long legs for the twentieth time, Pilar had had enough. Promising them each their allotted turn at watch, she begged them all to leave. They went away, but reluctantly.

It was just after midnight when the fever began. She wiped Refugio's dry lips with a cool cloth and bathed his face and arms; still, the heat of his body dried the cloth in her hand and his face grew flushed. She was brushing back his hair, laying her fingers along his hot cheek for the hundredth time to test its heat, when his lashes tightened, shivered, then lifted.

His gaze was bright and liquid with fever, but lucid and searching. Pilar saw him gathering himself, as if to speak. To forestall the necessity, she said quickly, "You've been shot, and you're in the cabin, our cabin."

"I know," he whispered, and closed his eyes again.

"Is there anything I can do? Would you like water, or more cover?"

He shook his head in slow negation.

Pilar bit her bottom lip as she tried to think what else to say to hold him with her. It would be stupid to ask if he was in pain; of course he was, but there was nothing she could do. If she ran to bring some of the others, he might slip away again while she was gone.

He opened his eyes with infinite effort. "You saw—"

She knew precisely what he was asking. How had he known? She had not realized he was even aware she was there on the deck during the fighting. "It was not a pirate who fired at you, that much I know. But I didn't see his face."

He sighed and his eyelids dropped as if weighted. Long moments later he whispered so softly that it might have been no more than a breath, "Stay. Don't leave. Don't leave the cabin."

"No," she said, "I won't."

There was nothing more. She thought that, after a time, he slept.

She sat watching in a chair beside the bed with her hands folded in her lap. Her neck ached, her back hurt and her eyes burned, but she was not sleepy. She sat bolt upright, staring at the wall, while fear ran through her veins like some pervasive poison. Over and over in her mind she saw the moment when from the knot of musketeers firing into the mob of retreating pirates there had come the shot that had felled Refugio. She had not seen who the man was, but Refugio had. He had seen, and he knew as he lay injured that the man who shot him had been neither pirate nor known enemy.

Somehow Don Esteban had hired a man to kill El Leon. Yet how could that be when her stepfather had gone on ahead? How was it possible when he could have no idea that they had sailed on the *Celestina*?

There were several potential explanations. The first was that Don Esteban's hirelings had followed after them, one or more of them picking up their trail in Cordoba at her aunt's house, then tracking them to Cadiz and taking passage on the ship to complete the task assigned. The second was that some hireling of the don, following after them as far as Cadiz, had paid one of the ship's seamen to do the deed. It was also possible that the hireling was a renegade from El Leon's band, perhaps a man who had provided horses on the ride to Cordoba, then contacted Don Esteban to offer himself for the job. Another alternative was that someone traveling on the ship was, by unfortunate coincidence, in the pay of the don, and had either taken up a musket himself when the opportunity arose or else hired a seaman to do it. A final possibility was that it was one of their party, Enrique, Charro, Baltasar, or Isabel, who had arranged to have the shot fired. Of the last two ideas, she did not know which was most unlikely.

She had felt so safe. The ship had seemed an oasis in a time where the fear of stealthy death need not trouble her mind. It was a shock to find it was not so.

Stay, Refugio had said, as if even in his extremity he was concerned for her safety. It was he, however, who had nearly died. Why should that be, if it was her stepfather who had sent the killer? She was the one he wanted dead.

Vengeance was the obvious answer, vengeance for the humiliation Refugio had heaped upon him, vengeance for thwarting his plans for Pilar. What else could it be? What other enemies could Refugio have who would go to such lengths to remove him?

But why had the killer not shot her also? Pilar asked herself. Why had he not knifed her in the passageway during the confusion, or even thrown her overboard in the dark of night as she walked the decks?

There was nothing to keep him from it, not now. There was an illusion of safety there in the cabin with Refugio, but nothing more than that. He could not protect her, nor could she protect him, though she stayed, as he had asked, for that purpose as much as any other.

She should go for one of the others. They could keep Refugio safe.

Or could they?

Soon one of them would come to relieve her, to sit beside Refugio in the dark hours toward the dawn when spirit and body were weakest and easiest to snuff out. How could she allow it when she had promised? Was there any way to stop it?

It was Charro who came, ducking his head as he entered, giving her a quiet grin. His hair was tousled and his eyes heavy with sleep. He seemed so normal and unthreatening as he smothered a yawn and shook himself that she felt the brush of guilt for the tenor of her thoughts.

He refused the chair she offered, waving her back into it. Placing his back to the wall beside the door, he lowered his lanky form to his heels, hunkering there with his hands dangling between his knees. His balance was rock steady in that position, one that seemed perfectly natural for him. His gaze on Refugio, he asked, "How's he been?"

"As you see. His fever is running high."

"There would be something wrong if he had no fever; it's nature's way."

"But still worrisome. He spoke a few words." She did not elaborate.

"A good sign." Charro surveyed her with the ghost of concern in his eyes. "You look tired. Why don't you sleep?"

"I'm not sure I could."

"You could try."

"Perhaps in a moment." To refuse would make her look overly concerned, as if she didn't trust Charro. It might also make it look as if she was forming an attachment to Refugio, and that would not do. If she only postponed her rest, there should be no cause for suspicion.

"Refugio is lucky to have you with him."

She sent him a swift look, but there was only approval in his face. The corner of her mouth tugged in a wry grimace. "I'm not sure he would agree with you. If it were not for me, his brother would not be a prisoner, he would undoubtedly not have been shot, and he would still be in Spain at the head of his band."

"It's all your fault, in fact. He had no choice about what happened, no will or reasons of his own."

"As to that, I don't know; I suppose he did. But you'll have to admit—"

"You did something that I've been trying to do for months, and that's persuade Refugio to leave Spain. There was no future for him there, no hope except that when death came it would be swift. Oh, he had his band and his troubadour to sing of his victories against injustice. But the man is a genius at organization, a fiend for work, and a wonder at bringing out the best in men. He is capable of so much more. He deserves so much more."

"There are laws and authority in Louisiana, and news from Spain comes often. What makes you think his past won't arrive with him, and be counted against him?"

"Who's talking about Louisiana? I speak of New Spain, the Tejas country. And yes, there are laws there, and authorities. But the road between there and Spain is long and slow. Letters and messages must travel overland to Mexico City and then to Vera Cruz on the coast of the Gulf of Mexico before being put on a ship for Spain. Answers and orders must make the journey in reverse. It can take a year, sometimes two, for a request to be sent from the town of San Antonio de Bexar near my home to Madrid, and an answer received. There is danger from Indians, wild animals, disease, accidents, storms, and pirates along every step of the way. The route across the land from Louisiana to San Antonio is even longer and more treacherous, mainly because of the Indian tribes known as the Apache. Much communication is lost, and even if it's not, it's possible for the answers that finally come to be ignored or forgotten."

"Ignored?"

"Why not? Spain cares little for her most distant outpost; she hardly feeds and clothes the handful of soldiers who guard its open spaces, and ignores the missions begun with such labor to convert the Indians, since they have, for the most part, failed. The men and women sent by the crown to settle and civilize the country have been as good as abandoned for a hundred years. They have all, soldiers and priests and colonizers alike, learned to make their own rules based on what people are and how they live, not who they are. The others who have come on their own are not grandees and not, truth to tell, without a stain or two on their own pasts. What matters is living well enough to make God frown, but not so well as to make the devil smile; the rest is nothing."

"And yet," she said, "you were sent all that long way to acquire the polish of Spain."

"My father still loves the idea of Seville and the life there. He believes in the benefits of a classical education and of rubbing shoulders with the sons of noblemen. It was a matter of pride to him to be able to send his son, though he himself would never leave New Spain. There are many, however, who even after three generations and more still plan and scheme and talk about returning. For most, it's only a dream. For me, it was a mistake."

"You weren't impressed?"

"Oh, yes, Seville is beautiful, and I have an affection for her. And my head is stuffed with knowledge that I'll be digesting for years. Still, I had never learned the knack of bowing my head to every passing hidalgo who felt the need for homage, nor of playing at love."

"Isabel mentioned your duchess. It seems she had taste, at least."

He stared at her, his eyes shadowed though the flickering lantern hung just above him. "You're very kind, señorita."

"Not at all. I suppose you will be traveling on to your home from Louisiana soon after we land, then?"

"As soon as I can persuade Refugio to go with me."

"He . . . will have other things on his mind."

Charro lifted his shoulders. "I'm in no great hurry."

They talked of other matters, of the flat country around his homeland with its mild, dry weather and waving grass watered by the San Antonio River; of the grapevines shading the walls of his home, which was built like a fortress against the raids of the Apaches; of the horses raised on the hacienda and the cattle herded by the *charros* which sometimes stood taller than a man at the shoulder and had great spreading horns that were sharp as spears; of the mission fathers and their irrigation ditches which had changed the land; and of the mission Indians who were docile and God-fearing and nothing like the Apaches of the wide open plains. Pilar listened and asked questions with bemused interest. To her the Tejas country was somehow unreal, like a place in a legend, one that was beautiful and magical yet troubled by demons.

They were still talking when the gray light of morning, seeping in at the porthole, made the lantern light unnecessary. Charro, in the midst of a tale of how his aunt, his father's sister, had been captured by the Indians as a child, and how his grandfather had been killed trying to get her back, stood and snuffed the light. He stretched, raising his arms above his head so that his fists brushed the ceiling. Clasping his hands behind his neck, he glanced at the berth. He stiffened.

Pilar followed his arrested gaze. Refugio was awake and watching them with quiet care.

It was one of his few moments of awareness.

Refugio did not rouse again, not in the day that followed, or the next, or the next. He wanted nothing, needed nothing, required only to be left alone. He lay with eyes closed for long periods, though it was not possible to tell if he was conscious or unconscious, asleep or awake. Sometimes he stared at the ceiling or gazed at whoever was talking, but seemed neither to see nor hear. It did not appear to matter who came and went, what was said or done. He did not respond to Isabel's pleas for him to drink or to Baltasar's gruff demands to know what he thought he was doing, starving himself. There was no sense that he did not know where he was or who was with him, only that he no longer cared enough to acknowledge these things. He had retreated somewhere inside himself and was entrenched there. Whether it was the result of fever and his injury in combination with years of upheaval, or only of his own inviolable will, they could not tell.

Doña Luisa, some forty-eight hours after her first visit, brought Refugio a posset. She had made it with her own hands, she said, an art she had learned from her mother. It was made of wine and spices and a few other ingredients that were guaranteed to give him rest. Pilar, who was alone with him at that moment, eyed the cup of dark and steaming liquid with distaste and more than a little suspicion.

"Rest," she said, "is something Refugio has had in plenty. What he needs is nourishment."

"What do you know of such things?" the other woman said, her eyes flashing in annoyed chagrin that someone would contradict her. "Under your care he fades away before our eyes!"

The strain of the long days had had its affect on Pilar's temper. "That may be, but I will not allow you to force your witch's brew on him."

"Witch's brew! How dare you! You forget yourself, my girl. You are only his woman, not his wife."

"And what are you, pray?"

"His friend!"

"Oh, yes, so long as his friendship provides you pleasure and the price isn't too high."

"Why, you little—I would know what to call you if I were not too much the lady. He can't go on like this, or he will die. He will die and you will be to blame, if you will let no one help him."

Pilar was suddenly tired, as if she carried a great weight that none could remove. "Just go away," she said. "Take your posset and drink it yourself, use it for a mouth refresher or hair restorer or anything you please, only go away."

She shut the door in the other woman's face. After a moment there came a most unladylike exclamation from the other side of the door panel, then the clack of heeled slippers in withdrawal. Pilar stood listening a moment. She almost wished that she had taken the posset, if only in order to dispose of it herself. It was always possible for another one to be made, of course, so it was unlikely to make a difference. This constant vigilance was wearing. It would be nice to be certain that it had a purpose.

She turned from the door, glancing at the berth in what had become a fixed habit. Refugio lay watching her. His face, though flushed with fever and shaded with the stubble of his dark beard, was set in stolid composure. Yet for an instant she thought she saw the sheen of amusement in his eyes.

She moved to the berth and knelt beside it in a billow of skirts. Reaching for the cloth lying in a pan of water left close to hand, she moistened his dry lips. His regard was focused on her face but was lifeless once more, as though the direction of his gaze was no more than an accident.

Putting down the cloth, she took up a cup of water and held it to his mouth, tipping it a little so that a small amount ran between his teeth. He swallowed once, twice, his strong brown throat moving with difficulty but plainly, though it was hard to say if the action was from thirst or simple reflex.

She straightened, considering him. She put the water

cup aside, then turned back. Her voice quiet, almost reflective, she said, "What is it? What's wrong. I know you're hurt and weak, but I can't believe a man of your strength can't mend. I refuse to believe that you want to die."

There was no answer, no recognition that he had heard. She went on. "You can't die, I won't let you. We all need you. Without you, what hope does Vicente have of being freed? What chance is there that Charro will ever reach his home again, or that he and Baltasar and Isabel and Enrique will not be taken up by the police the minute they reach Havana? And what chance do I have of catching up to Don Esteban or getting back even a portion of what he has taken from me? And if I don't get it back, how will I live? What will become of me?"

The reply she waited for did not come. After a time she closed her eyes. She was so tired, so very tired. She felt as if she were moving in a fog of fatigue, and her nerves jangled with what seemed like endless eons of being unable to sleep. More than that, she was angry, yes, angry, at Refugio for his continued lack of response to all they had done and were doing for him. But most of all she was angry at his desertion of them.

He was so strong, so vital. It did not seem possible that he would simply give up, no matter how extensive his injuries. What could his passive behavior mean, then, except a deliberate withdrawal? That he had a reason, she could not doubt, and yet she was not sure that his body could sustain the effort he was requiring of it, the lack of real nourishment or movement. She did not care what he was doing; he must be made to abandon it.

It seemed as if there must be something she could do to reach him, some words or act she could use to startle him into an awareness of his danger, some way she could seduce him from the course he had set himself. So much depended on it that it seemed, in the confusion of her exhaustion, that whatever she might try would be worth the cost.

She reached for the cloth again, squeezing some of the water from it but leaving it fairly sodden. Drawing down the blanket that covered Refugio, she began to bathe his face and neck as she had done a thousand times over in the past days in the constant attempt to contain his fever. As she worked she spoke, almost to herself.

"It's possible, I think, that your lying here like this has a deeper reason than just the attempt to kill you. I sometimes think that it may be because you know who did it, or think you know. Maybe you saw something, heard something, that gave away the identity of whoever paid your assailant. Possibly you are so soul-sick at the knowledge that you have no will to be well."

Was that a fleeting shadow of response behind his eyes? Had she, somehow, gained his attention?

She drew the cooling cloth down his neck and over his shoulders with slow care, her gaze resting on his face. There was nothing there. A thoughtful frown between her eyes, she returned to what she was doing.

She turned the cloth over, then dipped it into the hollows at his collarbones. Her movements smooth yet lingering, she trailed over the broad, hard-muscled planes of his chest on either side of his breastbone. She brushed down first one arm, then the other, and holding his wrists, wiped his hands, the broad backs and callused palms and each separate, well-formed finger.

Bending, she swished her cloth in the cooling water and squeezed it out, then returned to her task.

"What is it you want?" she asked in quiet contemplation as she circled his bandaging with care, then brushed across his abdomen underneath. "Are you making a target of yourself, is that it? Do you think that you can draw whoever tried to kill you here? Do you think your weakness will encourage them to try again?"

There was an extra wet corner on the cloth. It left a trail of water across his abdomen that trickled to puddle in his navel. It was wetting the waistband of his linen underbreeches. Noticing it, Pilar swiped at the water but could not quite reach his navel, for the waistband covered it. Dropping the cloth back in the pan, she began to unbutton the waist of his underbreeches.

He drew a soft, hissing breath.

Pilar's movement stilled as she realized what she was doing and his consciousness of it. For a long moment she gazed at the area of flesh she had exposed, an area paler in color than his chest and marked by a line of tightly curling dark hair that disappeared under his last breeches buttons, an area that was board-hard with taut muscles. The slow beat of seconds passing seemed to sound with her heart's throbbing in her ears.

Quickly, before she lost her courage, she raised her lashes to stare at him. There was sentient warmth in the dark gray of his eyes, and accusation.

She drew a shaky breath and let it out slowly. "I really think that's it," she said. "I think that this weakness of yours is feigned, a deliberate pose designed to entice whoever wants you dead to this cabin."

The dark centers of his eyes expanded, but still he made no answer.

She moistened her lips, which had a tendency to tremble at the corners. Her voice no more than a whisper, she said, "I think that's it, but I can't be sure. There must be a way to make certain. All I have to do is find it."

CHAPTER 9

She waited for most of another week. She delayed until Refugio's followers had had several turns at watching with her through the long night hours, until they had each tried with useless pleas and commands, attempts at humor and even anger to rouse him. She waited until her weariness became so dense that she seemed to be walking in a dream, until she was certain there was nothing else to be done, or else that she would go mad from weighing the decision if she did not act. She waited until she could wait no longer.

She almost abandoned the idea out of the misguided hope that it would not be necessary. On the morning after her confrontation with Refugio, his fever broke. Perspiration made a wet sheen on his bronze skin. It trickled from his hairline and pooled under his eyes and in the hollows of his collarbones. The dangerous flush faded from his face. His eyes became calmer. He took a little broth as nourishment and permitted himself to be bathed and shaved and changed into a fresh pair of underbreeches, since he had no nightshirt in his wardrobe. Still, his acceptance of these attentions was listless. He was as detached from them as if they had nothing to do with him. And he did not speak.

It was his silence, the loss of that bantering, caustic, vigorous voice, that troubled Pilar the most. It was as if the most vital part of him had been extinguished, for that voice was the reflection of the complex operation of his mind. That it might be stilled by his own will was infuriating; that it might not was insupportable. The strain of not knowing which was more than she could bear. It was that loss, finally, that compelled her to go forward.

It was late evening of what had been a perfect day. They had spent the best part of forty-eight hours in port in the Canary Islands, loading fruit and wine and Turkey carpets, plus another passenger or two. Then they had sailed with that morning's tide. The seas had been calm, the air balmy, and the breezes from the right quarter. There had been a red sunset that splashed rose and carmine, lilac and violet-blue and orange-gold across the western sky, and stained the water with opaline reflections. The last lingering flares of color shone through the open porthole of the cabin. They made pink gleams on the walls and dappled Pilar's arms and face with the iridescence of mother-of-pearl as she sat finishing her dinner, which had been brought on a tray. Refugio, who had already been fed the small amount of gruel he would take, lay propped on pillows, watching her. The refracted light, catching in his eyes, gave him a deceptive look of dazzled appreciation.

The light began to fade with the swift fall of night common to these latitudes. As shadows gathered in the cabin, Pilar rose from the table, picked up her tray and set it outside the door. Shutting the door panel, she locked it. As she turned away she began to take the pins from her hair. It uncoiled in a thick rope that slowly loosened, becoming a dark gold swath across her shoulders and down her back to well past her waist. Loosening it with her fingers, she moved to the corner washbasin.

She poured water from the can sitting ready into the basin, then washed her hands. Taking up a cloth, she wet it and squeezed it out, then ran it over her face and neck with slow care. Tossing back her hair, she put down the cloth, then began to unlace the bodice of her soft green silk gown with its open-fronted skirt.

There was a polished-steel looking glass above the basin, small but adequate for the purpose. Pilar kept her gaze on it as she spread the laces of her whaleboned bodice wide, then slipped her arms from the sleeves and lifted the gown off over her head. She tossed the gown onto a chair. Next came her decorative top petticoat of yellow silk embroidered in forest-green. She kicked off her shoes and peeled the stockings from her legs, then untied the tapes of her under petticoats before letting them fall to billow around her ankles. She stepped out of them with swift grace and draped them on the chair also. Clad only in her shift with its low neck, three-quarter length sleeves, and short length which barely covered her knees, she took up her washing cloth again.

Pilar had grown accustomed to making her toilette in front of Refugio; there had been no help for it since his injury. She had always preserved her modesty by taking care to draw one piece of clothing off only under the protective covering of another. She had also chosen times when she thought her patient slept, though sometimes she thought she heard a change in his breathing, which drew her attention, or else turned to find that he had shifted positions. When she looked, however, his eyes were always closed. Gradually, she had become used to his presence. Almost.

She didn't know if Refugio was watching now. He had not been asleep when she began, of that much she was certain. She felt exposed, as if her shift was transparent. The breeze from the open porthole blew the thin material against her so it outlined every curve. It dried the moisture left on her skin as the cloth passed over it, causing goose flesh from the coolness and the prickling of her nerves in anticipation of the moment to come.

Finally it was upon her.

Her heart swelled inside her, pulsing with a heavy, jarring beat. Her hands shook, and she could feel the slow burning rise of a flush making its way to her hairline. She swallowed hard. Quickly, before she could change her mind, she opened the neckline of her shift, slid it from her shoulders and let it drop to the floor.

She closed her eyes tightly, as if shutting out her own view would hide her nakedness. Doubt about the wisdom of what she was doing swept over her. If she stopped now, if she picked up her shift and skimmed back into it, she could pretend that letting it fall had been an accident. She could go on just as before; everything would be the same.

But what would that help, what would it prove? No. She had discovered the one small weakness in Refugio's armor, and she must pursue it. She must, or they might all be lost.

She bent her head so that the shining curtain of her hair slid forward, offering a degree of concealment. Behind it she reached to squeeze out the cloth once more. She ran it with minute care over her breasts and down her sides to her abdomen and thighs, which under their slender turns shimmered with dampness like palest alabaster. Moving in self-conscious grace, she lifted each leg, smoothing over the calves and ankles, bending to wipe even the soles of her feet. Her ablutions completed, she dropped the cloth and picked up her hairbrush. With lashes lowered, faintly quivering, she began to draw it through her tresses, removing the tangles, polishing the thick strands so they glowed with the sheen of old gold coins there in the gathering dusk.

When she was done, she put the brush down. She breathed slowly once, twice, then turned with precision and care. Lifting her chin, she walked toward the berth where Refugio lay.

He was awake, and he was watching.

Pilar, seeing his gaze upon her, faltered, with the blood draining from her face. There was rage and frustration in his eyes, and something more that had the look of hunger. It was the last that gave her the courage to take the step that brought her to the edge of the berth. She refused to look at him again, however, as she sat down beside him.

He recoiled from her in haste, retreating until his shoulders were against the bulkhead. His movement left her more room. She took it, because it seemed that if she did not lie down, she might well slide off the edge of the berth to the floor. Trembling in every fiber, she lowered herself to recline on the mattress. She turned toward him, supporting herself on one elbow, then swung her legs up and stretched out beside him.

For long moments neither of them moved or spoke. The breeze from the window flowed over them, ruffling the sheet that covered Refugio to the waist, lifting tendrils of Pilar's long hair so that they drifted toward him like delicately searching fingers. The bunk was so narrow that their legs touched from the thigh downward. The movement of the ship rocked them closer still, easing them together with a slow, plunging rhythm.

His breathing was harsh, the rise and fall of his chest under his bandaging rapid. Concern touched Pilar. With a frown gathering between her eyes, she reached out toward him, placing her cool fingertips on the pulse at the strong hollow of his throat.

He shot out his hand to catch her wrist in a bone-wrenching grip. His voice hoarse, grating with anger, he demanded, "Why?"

Triumph moved deep inside her, a counterpoint to the strained terror that gripped her. She had to moisten her lips before she could speak. "Vanity, what else?" she answered with more bravado than she felt. "What woman could resist the possibility of bringing a man back to life?"

"Try again. Try maudlin self-sacrifice brought on by pity in barrels, topped off with a layer of compassion."

"Oh, no, I've discovered the price for pitying you already. As for the rest, I wouldn't dream of trespassing on your territory."

His eyes narrowed. "I have my reasons for what I'm doing. They have nothing to do with self-sacrifice or compassion. Or with you."

"But they must if I'm required to play handmaiden and nursing drudge, not to mention sleeping on the floor."

"The floor is hard, as I have reason to know, but that doesn't explain what you're doing here beside me."

"Will you accept curiosity?"

"You are here to try whether what you guessed the other night was right? You could have done that from across the room just now, if you had cared to look. Perhaps you are concerned for your safety? Surely you know that my men will protect you. Indeed, after watching and listening to them with you these last few days, I'm not sure they wouldn't protect you before me."

"Maybe I object to being set up as bait with you?"

"In that case you should go elsewhere."

"And leave you defenseless? How could I? Besides, you are supposed to be my protector."

"So you play at being the mistress, all hovering concern and sympathy, while plotting to undermine whatever I might be doing out of sheer interference and juvenile revenge."

She met his gaze without flinching, though the pounding of her blood in her veins made her feel ill. "You are trying to insult me so I will leave you alone. What is it you're afraid of? Is it what I might do, or is it just me?"

"Take care, *cara*. There may be more life than you

bargain for left in me, and less judgment. I warn you that I have a headache like a Norse god's own hammer beating in my head, and inclinations that if turned to wind could blow this ship to Havana by morning. And I have never been more your protector than at this moment."

"I'll take care," she said, her voice low and soft, "if you'll rejoin the living."

Refugio stared at her for long moments, while inside he felt the slow loosening of the bindings of his will. This sweet temptation was more than a man should be expected to resist. That he had scant strength to try was not due to his injury so much as to the long days of living close to Pilar. It had been purgatory to be so close, to watch her dress her hair while the movements stretched her bodice across the fullness of her breasts, to catch her delicate female scent as she brushed past him, to lie and listen to her soft breathing as she slept and know that to touch her was forbidden to him by every rule of decency.

She had breached those rules, deliberately discarding them. He understood the reasons she gave, but though he doubted they were the only ones, did not dare ask for more. What she was doing was not lightly undertaken, of this much he was certain. Nor could it be lightly dismissed, not without causing her great humiliation. She might be able to bear that; he could not.

It was possible he was weaker than he knew, else surrender would not have so potent an allure.

He was defeated. He had known it from the moment she turned and walked toward him, the moment he realized that she had not forgotten he was there. Dear God, but the imprint of that moment would be burned forever into his mind.

She was magnificent in her determined seduction, lying there with conquered fear and some strange exultation in the dark and mysterious depths of her eyes. Her skin was like rare pink marble in the dying light of the day, her breasts as perfect as small sweet melons, her waist slender and sculpted as if to fit his hands, her hips gently curving with their own delicious symmetry, beckoning with every rise and fall of the ship. The rich, wild silk of her hair gleamed, enticing where it lay over her shoulder, shimmering with the quick beat of her heart. So enticing.

He drew a ragged breath, letting it out on a slow, soft sigh. Lifting a hand, he closed his fingers in the skein of her hair, winding the silken strands about his fist.

"Is it stalemate, then?" he whispered in aching tenderness as he drew her nearer. "I could also protect you by holding you naked in my arms. I could say it was to improve both our disguises, could I not? Did I warn you about my impaired judgment? I'm awash in sophistry and excuses and passionate good intentions, or else good, passionate intentions—"

The last word was smothered against her mouth. The touch of his lips was warm and a little dry from the fever, sweet and tender and rigorously restrained. He molded her mouth to his, tasting the moist honey, tracing the tender curves with the tip of his tongue while he released her hair and encircled her with his arms. With soft hesitation her lips parted under his. His grasp tightened and a shudder ran over him. Raising himself on the pillows, he shifted so she was rolled to her back. Delicately invading, he touched the small, sharp edges of her teeth with the tip of his tongue, then pressed deeper as if seeking the source of her sweetness.

Pilar strained against him, sliding her arms upward to clasp them around the strong column of his neck. Her breasts pressed against his chest, flattened on the hard planes and the rough swath of his bandaging. Fueled by urgent need and vestiges of the self-sacrifice she had denied, she felt the swift rise of ardor. It burned along her veins so that her skin seemed heated from the inside, glowing with awakening sensitivity. She curled her fingers into the dark waves of his hair with a soft murmur in her throat of confused and flustered desire.

She accepted his tongue, twining it with her own in sinuous exploration. Then, in growing boldness, she followed his retreat to taste the smooth inner surfaces of his lips. Lost in a wondrous blossoming of the senses, she felt time and place recede. All that was left was the descending darkness and the man who cradled her to him.

His hold loosened. For an instant she knew a fluttering disappointment, then her breath caught in her throat as she felt the open palm of his hand on the skin of her abdomen. He spanned its flatness, smoothing the firm, fine-grained skin in gentle circles before trailing his fingers inexorably downward toward the soft triangle at the apex of her thighs. At the same time, he bent his head and pressed the wet heat of his mouth to her breast.

The nipple tightened under his circling, smoothing tongue. Her breast swelled toward that ravishing caress. The tingling pleasure spread through her in waves. Her heartbeat quickened, throbbing in her chest. The lower part of her body grew suffused and heavy. Then she felt the first shock of his intimate touch.

Her abdomen muscles contracted in spasms and she caught her breath, but did not move, did not draw away. Inside she could sense the unleashing of incalculable impulses. She wanted him, wanted to know what it was to make love with this man. Had she fooled herself with her reasons and causes and sacrifices? Did it matter?

His shoulders under her clasping hands were wide and strong, the muscles supple as they glided with his movements. The aura of power he carried with him, unquenchable even in injury, surrounded her. It affected her with an odd weakness, a languor that urged her toward a surrender of inescapable completeness. There was more than the loss of her virginity at stake, and well she knew it.

She was not the kind to forget, neither was she the kind for half measures. Whispering his name, she touched his face. As he took her lips once more, she gave herself in fervent and silent offering, a gift without encumbrance.

Tenderly marauding, Refugio explored the curves and hollows of her body, always returning to the seat of her utmost delight. She drew her hand down his chest, touching the flat nipple of one pap tentatively with just her fingertips. His rib cage swelled with his indrawn breath, and he adjusted his position to allow greater access. She spread her fingers wide, feeling the strong beat of his heart, the bands of muscle that encased his ribs, skipping lightly over his bandaging to the flat expanse of his waist. Greatly daring, equally dexterous, she unfastened his underbreeches.

He skimmed from the hampering garment, tossing it aside. As he drew her to him once more, he spread his hand over her hip, drawing her against his hard length.

She was beguiled, and suffused with moist, pulsating heat. But she was not quite without concern. She whispered against his neck, a catch in her voice. "Is it—will it be all right?"

"It will be glorious," he said with shivers of laughter in his voice. "It will stupendous, a bright reflection of heaven, but it won't be all right, ever."

"I mean—can you . . .?"

"Who can say? But I must try, or else give you leave to take my guts for leading strings for the idiot I must become, and bid you be a gentle keeper—"

"There is no danger," she said.

"And yet," he went on as if she had not spoken, his

voice low and not quite controlled, "bid me cease, and I will. I promise I will."

She did not doubt it. "It's I who need a gentle keeper," she said.

"Why," he said, "when I am here?"

And he was gentle. He was also firm and springing and resilient. There was hardly an instant of pain at his entry, and it was eased by myriad caresses and the free flowing of beatitude. She held her pent breath while the core of her dissolved, coalescing around him. She drew him to her with a hand at his waist, pulling him deep and deep and deep and even deeper, as if there was no end to her depths.

He whispered her name, brushing her eyelids with his lips, then he lifted himself higher above her, preparing for the deepest plunge.

It came, and she cried out his name. In rising and falling tumult he gathered her close and swept her with him into rapture. With tightly closed eyes she reveled in the closeness of the union, felt the mounting ecstasy of it vibrating through her, recognized her own sensual joy in his desire for her. There was no fastness left unbreached. She gave herself without stint, enclosing him in vibrant heat. So intense was the ecstasy that the sudden spiraling pinnacle of it caught her by surprise. She cried out again, and his hold tensed while he filled her, prolonging the pleasure to the edge of infinity.

Then, dynamic and elemental, they soared, locked together in promised grandeur. Vivid with perception, they plumbed sensation and found it immense enough to fill the world. There was only the two of them, unclothed, splendid in their communion, unheeding, unneeding, sufficient in their glory.

Pilar felt the rise of tears. In the midst of their liquid heat he plunged into her once more, twice, then gathered her to him, holding the bond as he rolled to his side and was still, deathly still.

Their chests heaved, their hearts thudded together in double time. The ship under them seemed to plunge with them in remembered rhythm, rocking them in soothing reassurance. Refugio, his hand unsteady, brushed her hair from her face so she could breathe more easily. She clenched and unclenched her hand on his arm. Then slowly, by minute degrees, they began to subside.

Concern shifted inside Pilar. With a small exclamation she lifted her hand, reaching to press it to his brow as if testing for fever. He closed his fingers about hers and brought them to his lips. His mouth warm against them, he said, "I'm as peaceful as a twice-shriven monk and blithesome as a petted puppy, with good reason. And you, *cara*?"

"The same," she said, her lips curving in a hidden smile.

"Then sleep while I watch for a change."

She did as she was bid, and did not wake until Enrique came pounding on the door and shouting about breakfast.

They arrived in Havana on the island of Santiago de Cuba some three weeks later. The remainder of the crossing had been without incident and blessed with unusually fair weather. Under the endless parade of sunny skies and days of brisk salt-laden winds, Refugio had made rapid improvement. He had abandoned his near catatonic state without apparent effort and with little explanation. His manner casual and his dress neat and even lordly, he had sauntered into the salon in mid-afternoon of the day following his night with Pilar.

"My dear count!" Doña Luisa said, rising to her feet and hastening to take his arm. "Welcome, welcome, how we have missed you! Tell us, if you please, to what we owe this miraculous recovery?"

"Why, what else except sea air and the solicitude of friends, and that sovereign remedy for all ills of the flesh, the care of a beautiful woman."

"You were certainly in my prayers," the widow said, "but I fear you flatter me."

"Not at all," he answered, and as he bowed, turned his gaze to exchange a long and faintly smiling glance with Pilar.

He entertained the company with stories of cunning and wit, with music from his guitar and soft songs that flowed in endless succession far into the evening. If the unaccustomed exertion tired him or pained his wound, there was no sign. The following morning he changed his bandaging himself, then spent the hours before noon strolling the deck with Doña Luisa on one arm and the merchant's young wife on the other. By the end of the week he was exercising with swords with his men on deck while entertaining the watchers with caustic quips.

His temper had not mended with his body. There were times when nothing seemed to suit him. On such occasions his words and phrases had an edge that sliced to the bone. Small things irritated him beyond bearing: a sloppily fastened line, the way the cook had with beans, the scent of Doña Luisa's handkerchief as she flapped it in his face, the sight of Pilar playing at cards with Charro and Enrique. He could not be satisfied until he had tied the line again, decreased the amount of grease in the beans, thrown the widow's handkerchief overboard, and broken up the card party with a spate of orders that sent Charro to one end of the ship and Enrique to the other. The result was that there were long hours when both passengers and crew left him alone. That, at least, suited him.

A certain amount of restlessness was natural for a man like Refugio, one used to action and broad spaces, not only cooped up on a vessel at sea, but haunted by fear for his brother. There was also the specter of his failed duties, the strain of the masquerade, and the constant arch comments and calls upon his person and his patience of Doña Luisa. Another reason, Pilar thought, was the headaches which remained with him. She learned to recognize their symptoms, the heavy-lidded eyes, the tightness at the corners of his mouth. She learned also that it was possible to withstand both his cold manner and his cutting words. All she had to do was ignore them, she found; there was seldom anger behind them, and they were never personal. At least with her.

His followers realized that she had less to fear from him than others; still, they rallied around her, deflecting as many of his barbed comments as possible. Sometimes they even protested at what they felt to be his cavalier treatment. They meant to help, but Pilar thought it only made matters worse. He accused her, in his more savage moods, of beguiling them. It smacked of jealousy, these comments. She would have liked to believe it. It would have been so much more satisfactory than supposing they stemmed from mere irritation of the nerves.

Sometimes at night she massaged his temples and the taut muscles of the back of his neck; it seemed to help. He swore it made it better, also, to have her sleeping beside him. Once when he had made her angry by some comment about her propensity for the company of Charro, she had moved her blankets back to the corner of the cabin. By the time he returned from a late tête-à-tête with the widow, she had finally managed to drop into restless slumber. She was awakened, however, by a sudden jolt as she was lifted against his chest. Carrying her to the bed, he sat down with her in his arms and set himself to cajole her with honeyed words and beguiling caresses until she joined him once more on the mattress.

Afterward, as he lay holding her in the hard circle of his arms, he said, "Count Gonzalvo was a wise man."

"Was he? How so?" Somnolent with content, she smoothed the dark, curling hair on his chest with one finger to keep it from tickling her nose.

"He kept his Venus safe, and his own mind at ease."

"But what of her?"

"He worshiped her, or so they say, and provided everything she could desire for her amusement."

"Is that supposed to be enough?"

He bent his head, trying to see her face. "Do you think it's not?"

"To be loved and left free seems better." She kept her eyes lowered, refusing to meet his gaze.

"What, no purdah for you, no harem with high walls? Have you no desire for safety?"

"If I did, I wouldn't be here. I would be in the convent where my stepfather wanted me."

"True."

"Besides, if women can't keep men in towers, why should men be allowed the privilege of keeping women there?"

"Why, indeed? Would you like to keep a man in a tower?"

A smile curled her lips. "It sounds dangerous to me, though there is a certain appeal."

"You would, then," he said, his voice low and deep. "Shall we go in search of a tower and keep each other there?"

She raised her eyes to meet his then, expecting to see the light of laughter. Instead she saw herself reflected in their gray darkness. There was also a line between his brows, one etched by pain. She lifted her fingers to smooth it, then trailed them down the contour of his cheek to the rigid turn of his jaw. He reached to catch her fingers, carrying them to his lips.

"No?" he said, his breath soft and warm against their sensitive tips. "Then I will make a wall of kisses around you and let it keep us safe for now, if not forever."

It was a task she was willing to aid.

Pilar didn't know whether Refugio was also sharing the bed of the widow. She didn't think so, but not caring to be proven wrong, didn't ask. She liked to think that he must lack the strength, and certainly the inclination, after leaving her bed. She was aware, however, that this was not necessarily so.

In any case, she had no right to complain. She had thrown herself at him, after all. Regardless of her reasons, this could not be denied. He owed her no fidelity, even if the safety of them all did not dictate his continued acquiescence to the wishes of the widow.

There was no question of love between her and El Leon. Of course there was not. Their union was based on proximity and a virulent attraction of the senses. And self-protection; she must not forget that. If she ever allowed herself to think otherwise, she had only to recall what Isabel had said—that Refugio would never involve himself with a woman for whom he cared deeply. There was comfort, in an odd way, in that memory, since his attendance upon Doña Luisa could be viewed in the same light.

Havana was stifling. The sun had a yellow-white, metallic glare as it reflected from the shore-bound waves, the shelving beaches, the hard green fronds of the palm trees. The deck of the *Celestina* soaked up the heat and sent it radiating upward around the party of government officials, the representative of the custom house, the harbor master, tax collector, notary, and a petty clerk, who came aboard as soon as the ship had dropped anchor.

There was a moment when Pilar, watching the men stride along the deck toward where she stood with Refugio and the captain, felt the brush of alarm. It faded as the officials came to a halt with stiff bows and the round of presentations and obsequies began.

Refugio was polite but distant, as became a supposed aristocrat with vast holdings in Spain. The officials were deferential; their welcomes, particularly to Pilar, were fulsome. No one tried to stop Refugio as he turned from them with languid inattention and strolled away with Pilar on his arm.

If he had thought to avoid people, however, he soon discovered his error. It was not every day that a grandee arrived in sleepy Havana-town, and news of it quickly spread. By nightfall a dozen invitations had been delivered offering everything from breakfast with a wealthy planter known to have five daughters of marriageable age to a ride about the island with the governor. The breakfast could be graciously declined without suspicion, but not so the ride. Returning from it some time later, Refugio pronounced it pleasant enough. It had resulted in yet another invitation, however. This one was to a masked ball at the governor's palace.

The invitation was not for Refugio alone, but also included as many of his entourage as he might care to bring. It was assumed this extended to Pilar, since it was well known that Count Gonzalvo attended no function from which his Venus was excluded. It was, in part, this attitude that had made him so reclusive. The invitation could also be accounted for by the fact that it was a masquerade ball for carnival; conventions were never as strict on such occasions. As for the danger of going among so many who might have known either Refugio de Carranza or the count, it was slight, for they would all wear costumes and masks for the greatest part of the evening. Some excuse for leaving could always be found before the unmasking.

Doña Luisa was delighted at the prospect of society, no matter how provincial; she had received a separate invitation through the offices of a friend of her late husband's, a gentleman once a member of the municipal council of New Orleans and who now served in some similar post in Havana. Señor Manuel Guevara, most unexpectedly, had met the ship and extended a request for her presence under his roof until the cramped coastal vessel to which they would all be transferring was ready to sail, a matter of a few days. He would be delighted to extend the invitation to Refugio and the others. She had told the thoughtful soul they would all accept.

"You manage things so beautifully, Doña Luisa," Refugio said, inclining his head in ironic compliance. "Such efficiency must give you immense satisfaction."

If the woman felt the sting of the irony, she gave no sign. With a smile tilting her hazel eyes, she answered, "It does, on occasion."

"What do you think will happen if this gentlemen is acquainted with the count? Or if he may have seen Refugio de Carranza, or Enrique, or Charro, in passing?"

"Or if he was once the lover of your Venus? One seems as unlikely as the other; he has been out of Spain for years."

His face bland, Refugio gave a shrug. "Ah, well, no need to trouble ourselves. If he should dredge up recollections uncomfortable to any of us, we can always dispatch him and his household down to the last crawling babe and scullery girl."

"What a cruel desperado you are," the widow cried with a trill of laughter.

"And wicked, too. What a spectacle I should make as the hangman fits me with my hood. Or perhaps you prefer an auto-da-fé; the Holy Inquisition has no monopoly on consigning men to the flames. Anything, my lady, so long as you are entertained."

"Fires are exciting, don't you think?" the widow said, her eyes shining.

Pilar, watching them, following their brittle banter, shivered with the sudden awareness of a chill around her heart.

CHAPTER 10

The house of Señor Guevara was built of blocks of white coral limestone, a solid and foursquare structure designed to withstand the tropical storms that roared in during the fall season of gales. Its many floor-length windows on all sides were protected by galleries which shaded them from the hot sun as well as allowing them to be thrown wide for air during lighter rains and to catch the full benefit of the constant trade winds. Standing isolated on a headland, it enjoyed magnificent views of the turquoise sea rolling toward it, and was surrounded by fruit trees with exotic names which shaded garden paths laid out in geometric patterns and edged with bright, bold flowers. Some few hundred yards distance behind it was a waving green sea of sugarcane, for Señor Guevara was also a planter.

The hospitality of the official could not be faulted; Pilar and Refugio had been given the best of the guest rooms, with the others nearby, and had been plied with food and wine and regaled with songs by the daughters of the house. The need of the señor and his large family for news of Spain, any news, was so great that it seemed they would have entertained a blind beggar to get it. The questions they asked were endless, particularly those of the planter's older son Philip, who fancied himself something of a rake with a need for larger fields of conquest. The ladies wanted to know about fashions and colors and which of the women at court was setting the styles. Señor Guevara was curious about various scandals among the court ministers. Everyone wanted to know about the latest dances and music.

Count Gonzalvo's supposed reclusive habits proved their value since any lack of knowledge could be blamed upon them. Refugio made up for this deficiency, however, by sitting down at the jangling harpsichord one night and playing a medley of the newest airs with such verve and grace that there were cries for more. He obliged with a series of old ballads and nursery songs of such nostalgic sweetness that the entire company dissolved in tears of homesickness.

It fell primarily to Doña Luisa to satisfy the thirst for the latest tidbits and gossip, though she had a surprising amount of support from Enrique in his role as a grandee. It had been his part to gather intelligence for Refugio, it seemed. In the process of moving around Spain on this assignment, he had learned much else. The two of them, the widow and the Gypsy acrobat, were wicked, and often hilarious, in their assassinations of character and descriptions of sartorial folly.

Costume balls were a favored pastime on the island, and clothing for them was plentiful in the Guevara household. The party from the *Celestina* had only to make their choices from among the plenitude, if they so desired. They did.

For Refugio it was easy; the robes of a Moorish prince suited him perfectly. However, Pilar refused to go as a Moorish princess, wrapped to the eyes in stifling draperies, or as a dancing girl in considerably less veiling. The habit of a nun did not please her at all. She consented at last to the enormously wide panniers covered by midnight-blue silk, whaleboned stomacher trimmed with rows of pale blue bows, and the stiff-neck ruff of a court lady of the previous century.

Refugio put on his snow-white robes and headdress

with gold cord, then left Pilar and Isabel in possession of the bedchamber. His purpose was to give them room for the difficult business of getting Pilar into the basketlike panniers, a courteous gesture that was not uncommon for him. Pilar watched him go in the looking glass over the dressing table while Isabel dressed her hair in a high pile of pomaded curls ready for the powder. He looked restless and on edge, she thought, and also incredibly foreign. In his flowing costume he appeared some desert chieftain ready for revelry if it presented itself, but just as ready for destruction if it became necessary.

Pilar emerged from the bedchamber onto the gallery a short while later, moving through the door with an awkward sidle. Turning in a sweep of wide-held skirts, she sailed, billowing, toward where Refugio stood at the far end of the covered promenade.

As she neared, there rose sudden loud wails of grief. The noise came from the opposite direction, around the far corner of the house. Refugio turned in that direction, then moved away out of sight. As Pilar came to the corner, she saw him going to his knees in front of a child, a small boy no more than three years old whose face was screwed up in an expression of woe. It was the official's youngest son, the last of his large family. The boy wore a tiny pair of knee breeches and a shirt that was coming out at the waist. There were buckles on his small shoes, and his fine silky hair was pulled back in a minute club. He was holding out his finger on which was a tiny bead of blood. Behind the boy, following him in stolid, pigeon-toed determination, was a yellow-headed green parrot.

"He bited me!" the boy sobbed. "He bited me!"

"Who did?" Refugio asked as he took the small pink finger between his own rough, brown ones and wiped the blood away with the corner of his robe.

The boy swung to point with his other hand at the parrot. "That mean bird. He bited me finger!"

"Yes, I see," Refugio said in grave tones. "And what did you do to him?"

"I only play with he."

"Maybe he doesn't want to play."

The boy said nothing, only giving a mighty sniff and scrubbing at the tears on his cheeks. The parrot, reaching the boy and the man, began to circle around them.

"Is he your parrot?" Refugio asked.

The boy shook his head. *"Madre's."*

"Shall we tell her about this and let her punish him?"

"Won't."

"I see," Refugio said. "This has happened before, then."

The boy looked at the floor without answering. The parrot, tilting his head to one side, said with cheery hoarseness, *"Hola,* Mateo."

"Is that you? Mateo?"

The boy nodded and ducked his head again.

"Well, what does this mean bird deserve for biting you? Shall we cut off his head and put him in a stew pot?"

Alarm appeared on the boy's face. "No!"

"No? Maybe we should tie up his beak?"

The boy shook his head, cutting his eyes to where the parrot had found a convenient fold of Refugio's robe and was climbing up it toward his shoulder.

"Would you like to bite his finger, then?"

"Doesn't have a finger."

"He has a claw. Two of them."

A smile dimpled the boy's cheek. He gave a little crow of laughter. "No! Too dirty."

Refugio heaved a sigh. "Then I don't know what to do."

"I do!" the boy shouted. Reaching out, he held his arm

in front of the parrot. The bird hopped on with practiced ease and walked up to the boy's shoulder. Mateo whirled around and ran away with the parrot wildly flapping as if in flight.

Refugio got to his feet. His face as he stared after the boy was softer, less harried than it had been in a long time. Watching him, Pilar was aware of an ache somewhere deep inside, and also an odd emptiness.

Refugio turned. He surveyed her, his gaze moving leisurely from the powdered crown of her hair, down over the square bodice which exposed the rounded tops of her breasts and the corsetted narrowness of her waist, to the panniers which jutted out to the ridiculous width of a full yard on either side. He smiled, with slow enjoyment rising in his eyes. "You look majestic," he said at last. "And beautiful, of course. I thought I preferred the nun's habit for you, but I believe this one is better after all."

The compliment was unexpected and intriguing. Keeping her voice light with an effort, she said, "Why is that?"

He extended his hand and she reached out the full length of her arm in order to take it. Turning, he promenaded with her back down the gallery, still with their arms at full length out over the width of her skirts. "Because," he said, "with what you have on, no man can get close enough to you to matter."

"Unless I help him." She gave him a quick glance from under her lashes.

"There is that chance, but I don't think, given your soft heart, that you will extend unwise encouragement."

"What has my heart to do with it?"

"You would not like to be the cause of a death."

She held his intent gaze a long moment before she looked away. "What would be one more?"

"What?" His voice was sharp.

"After my aunt's, I meant."

"That's another matter entirely. You aren't to blame for a madman's decisions."

"No? Nor are you, then," she replied in quiet tones.

He stared at her as she moved beside him with the gold of the sunset in her hair and calm in her eyes, but he did not answer.

Dinner was served in state. It was apparent that the official's wife, having acquired the presence of what she thought was a member of the Spanish nobility, intended to impress her neighbors. A large number of them had been invited to fill the table, along with the older members of her family. Every piece of silver in the house had been polished to a glassy sheen and set out in the dining room. The Venetian crystal glittered, the English china gleamed, and there were so many candles down the long board that their heat had made the short-lived tropical flowers wilt in their Sèvres vases. There was such an excess of people, utensils, and candelabra, in fact, that the table was far too crowded for the elegance the lady had obviously hoped to achieve.

Refugio was seated to the right of the hostess, and Doña Luisa to the right of the host. Pilar was down the table from Refugio, between an elderly man in rusty black on one side and the elder son of the house on the other. The older man applied himself to his food with noisy appreciation and little inclination to talk. Philip Guevara was not at all interested in food.

"Señorita," he said in tones low enough to be covered by the hum of conversation and rattle and clink of dishes around them, "I feel such a fool. I pray you will forgive my ignorance, but I had not realized who you are. To think that the famous Venus de la Torre has been under the same roof for two days, and I not aware."

The young man beside her was handsome in a refined Castilian manner. He seemed also to be rather spoiled, with a more rakish and experienced manner toward women than he should have at his age. Pilar said, with exact truth, "Please, I would rather not speak of it."

"I should have known; why did I not guess? Your form, your shape, so beyond compare. It's not to be wondered at that the count keeps you shut away, for I would do the same if you were mine."

"I should remind you that the reason is the count's extreme jealousy." Pilar nodded in the direction of Refugio, who was watching them over the rim of his wineglass.

The young man barely glanced in the direction she indicated. His dark eyes glowing, he said, "Do you fear him? Shall I save you?"

"Certainly not! You will not think of anything so foolish."

"Foolish? You speak as if you think me incapable of it."

Pilar, recognizing the affronted vanity in his voice, made her voice as soothing as possible. "Not at all. I simply have no need for a champion since I am quite content."

"You are afraid, rather, I think. Do I dare hope that your concern is for me?"

"I hardly know you," she protested.

"Men and women have loved in less time, from a glance shared in the promenade, a brief word exchanged at morning mass." His face was flushed. The look he gave her was meant to convey passion.

She was a challenge to him, a mystery to be possessed; she could see that. To him she was a courtesan whose charms had enslaved a nobleman as surely as the nobleman had imprisoned her. It appeared that merely speaking to her excited the young man. The attempt to seduce her could well be irresistible.

"Not I," she said coldly. "I have no use for love."

"A woman who looks as you do cannot mean such harsh words."

"I assure you, I can."

"You prefer to be adored, as in the past with the count; I understand perfectly. It would be my extreme pleasure to kneel at your feet."

"Thank you, but it won't be necessary."

"If it's wealth you want, I have it."

"Your father has it, you mean. And what of a title?"

"It pleases you to be cruel, but that will make it all the sweeter when you surrender."

She was wasting her breath and, probably, her consideration. Feigning a shrug of indifference, she turned away. Her gaze caught that of Charro just down the table. He must have been following the exchange, for he grinned at her, his blue eyes bright with amused sympathy.

It was well into the night by the time the last course of the enormous dinner was finished and the guests had refreshed themselves and gathered to be transported to the ball. The younger men would ride on horseback, carrying torches to light their way. The older men and the ladies would travel more sedately in the carriages that were arranged in a line.

Refugio elected to cover the short distance on horseback, as did Enrique and Charro. Baltasar, in the guise of a manservant, would ride on a perch on the back of one of the carriages. Señora Guevara, with her eldest daughter and the girl's duenna, a cousin of some degree, were to ride in the family carriage. The woman was about to assign the fourth place to Pilar, or so Pilar thought, when the widow Elguezabal joined the group with a mask in her hand and a mantilla over her plump shoulders.

"Do you go, Doña Luisa?" the older woman inquired in surprise.

"Assuredly," the widow answered in the same tone, then went on. "Oh, you are thinking of my widow's weeds. I will not dance, of course, but I must have gaiety to keep my mind from my loss. My dear husband would have wished it, I know; he was a most unselfish man."

Enrique, standing nearby, said *sotto voce*, "He was, without doubt, a saint."

"So he was," Doña Luisa said.

"Was that why you could not abide him or abide with him?"

The widow turned a plump shoulder to the acrobat, paying him no more attention than if he had been a fly. Nodding at the empty carriage seat, she said to her hostess, "I see you have left a place for me."

"If it pleases you." There was a trace of censure in the voice of Señora Guevara.

Pilar was entertained by the widow's single-minded pursuit of her own desires, and also by Enrique's baiting the woman about them; still, she was disturbed at the same time. She herself was not even wearing mourning for her dead aunt, much less preparing to forego the pleasures of the evening. The situation was difficult, it was true, but there might have been some way to show her respect.

Señora Guevara was speaking to Pilar, though her manner was no less stiff than that shown to Doña Luisa. "I am sorry for the imposition, señorita, but I fear I must ask you to ride with my good friends, our neighbors, the—"

Her son spoke then. "Your pardon, Mother, but I will drive the lady. It will only take a moment to have the horses put to my calèche."

The woman frowned at her son before glancing around at her guests, who were watching the proceedings with avid interest and varying degrees of disapproval. Her face reflecting her chagrin, she said to Pilar, "This is satisfactory to you?"

Pilar was aware of Refugio's gaze on her from where he was already mounted on a dancing, sidling black stallion. It seemed, in truth, that half those in earshot were waiting for her reply. Her voice composed, she said, "Perfectly. I had thought to take my maid Isabel in case of problems with my costume. This way will be more comfortable for her than riding on top with the coachman."

Philip appeared somewhat discomfited, but did not withdraw his offer. He was definitely not pleased, however, when Refugio, Charro, and Enrique closed in on either side of the small carriage, riding escort.

The drive to the governor's palace was pleasant. It took them along the edge of the harbor, in view of the old citadel of La Fuerza, with its watchtower crowned by a weather-vane in the form of an Indian maiden that was known as "La Habana," and past the two fortresses that guarded the harbor entrance, Morro Castle and La Punta. The fortifica-tions, including that of La Cabana behind Morro Castle and the city walls, had been built, so Philip informed Pilar, to discourage pirates and also to confound the English. They had served well for the first, not so well for the last. Havana had been captured by the English a little over twenty-five years before, during the Seven Years' War. It had been returned a year later, at the war's end, in exchange for the territories of the Floridas.

The governor's palace was an imposing pile of baroque splendor located on the eastern side of the town center which was known, as usual in Spanish colonial cities, as the Plaza de Armas. It was newly built, and parts of it were still under construction. Its rooms were large and richly fur-nished, in keeping with the consequence of the man who had final jurisdiction over all Spanish officialdom in the new world.

The ball at the governor's palace was a gala affair, for Mardi Gras was a day of revelry and mirth just prior to the abstinence of the lenten season. The ballroom was long and narrow, with a cavernous ceiling enlivened by a religious fresco touched with gilt, and French doors on two sides which were thrown open to the night air. The lusters of enormous crystal chandeliers tinkled in the draft from the doors. The music of violins and guitars, a flute, harpsichord, drums and castanets, was spritely, with an edge of passion that seemed to vibrate in the air. The guests, gleaming with jewels and shimmering with costly silks and velvets, danced constantly, crowding the floor as if they craved the abandon of movement in time to the music. Men bowed, women plied their fans and smiled with flashing glances from behind their masks.

Regardless, propriety was firmly in place, with duennas and anxious mothers fanning themselves as they sat along the walls, and stern husbands on guard. The repressed nature of the passions only added to the air of licentiousness hovering over the gathering, increasing the hint of barely restrained impulses and only half-spurned temptations.

Pilar danced first with Señor Guevara. It was, she thought, both a duty dance from her host and an attempt by the señor to establish for her a degree of respectability. His manner was stiff with decorum, scrupulous in its adherence to the rules of formal conduct. Immediately afterward Philip insisted on leading Pilar onto the floor for a quadrille. It seemed impossible to refuse after his father's gesture, and especially since he had taken the trouble to drive her. She regretted her agreement immediately, however. His attitude was of someone showing off a prize. His costume was the velvet doublet with the hose, breastplate, and helmet of a conquistador. It was fitting, since it seemed he was intent on conquest. Though Pilar had felt a little self-conscious from time to time on the ship with her role as the count's Venus, she had never until that moment felt demeaned by it. The burning looks Philip gave her, the lingering touch of his hands as he guided her through the dance, were like a public declaration of the kind of woman he thought her to be, and of his desire and intent to possess her.

"If you do not stop looking at me in that idiotic way," she said to him through her teeth, "I'm going to slap you."

"I don't know what you mean." The gleam in his eyes belied his words.

"I think you do. I am not some silly maiden to fall swooning at your feet. The game you are playing is dangerous, I tell you."

"Are you sure? I think you may place too high a value on yourself. I don't see your protector leaping to your side to take you away."

"Because he would prefer not to make a public spectacle of himself, or of me."

"Or else he doesn't care. Men do tire of their mistresses."

It was, of course, a possibility, but she refused to consider it. "I'm amazed you would be interested in discarded goods."

"To me you would be fresh and new, besides being far more beautiful than any lady of the night Havana has to offer."

Her face congealed in anger, she said, "You flatter me, I'm sure."

"Impossible."

"You are the one who is impossible!" she said in a chill undertone, and refused to speak again.

The music came to an end. Charro, by accident or design, was beside her. He bowed to Philip and offered Pilar his arm to lead her away. For a moment it appeared Philip would refuse to release his grip upon her hand. He scowled as he squared up to Charro, staring into his eyes. Something he saw there, however, gave him pause, for he executed the briefest of bows and turned away.

Pilar, curtsying to her new partner as the music began, gave him a warm smile. "The rescue was timely. Thank you."

"He's making a pest of himself, that one?"

"It's no great matter. He's merely young and full of himself."

"I can send him home, if you like."

"I'd rather not attract attention."

He laughed, his narrow face creasing with amusement as he moved with her into the country dance just beginning. "It's too late for that."

Charro was dressed as a Knight Templar, a medieval Christian warrior from the monklike order based on the island of Malta. His militant appearance, with the red cross on his tunic, suited him somehow. His comments on the other guests were apt and funny; his manner was admiring yet carefully, perhaps too carefully, impersonal. His bow as his dance was ended carried that extra degree of depth and duration that lifted it above mere politeness. His light blue eyes seen through the slits of his half mask, as he gave her into Refugio's keeping, held dedication tinged with regret.

Refugio, watching the byplay, was disturbed but not surprised. For the effect Pilar had had on his followers, there was no one to blame except himself. She was beautiful, persecuted, and alone in the world; the result was inevitable. He himself felt the warring instincts of protectiveness and exploitation. Why should he expect the men of his band to be any different?

What did Pilar feel? He wished he knew. She was flushed from heat and the exertion of the dance; her skin was moist and warm and her breathing quick. He took her hand

and curled the fingers into the crook of his arm as he moved to stand in an open doorway. He gave her a little time before he finally spoke in bland warning.

"Devotion from admirers improves the complexion and warms the heart, but has a way of exacting its price."

Pilar glanced after Charro, knowing it was to him Refugio referred. She was aware of the way the other man sought her out, but felt sure it was only the close association of the long voyage that caused it. Refugio's attendance on Doña Luisa, however, was not quite so innocent. Her tone was cool as she answered.

"You speak, of course, from experience."

"Of course."

"And what form does this price usually take?"

"The devoted require bits and pieces of you, chosen at random."

The words were exact and astringent. He was not speaking in general terms. Could he be thinking of the past days with the fiancée he had lost? She said, "Can't a person defend themselves?"

"It requires a strong stomach and an aptitude for giving pain."

"The alternative could be total acceptance?"

"Yes, there is that, if you have a taste for martyrdom."

"Or if martyrdom is forced on you?" she asked, her gaze on the hard planes of his face, though her thoughts were elsewhere.

"There is usually a choice."

"Except when others are involved."

"Even then. Clean wounds heal and babes weaned in season don't cry after the breast, and a fast death carefully selected is better than a stinking progression to the same end."

He was telling her a great many things, none of which she was sure she understood. Slowly she said, "I see why you don't want to be loved."

"Who was speaking of love?" he answered. "That's another subject altogether."

Dancing with Refugio was an exercise in precision and the glory of perfect timing. There was knowledge and guidance in it, but most of all there was untrammeled instinct and limitless grace. He enjoyed it. The music was an exultation inside him which he translated into movement, taking his partner with him.

Pilar, making these discoveries, felt her own pleasure rise triplefold. She had her instincts and they met his and mated with them. That she could, with some small effort, match his exacting pace was a private triumph. She looked into his silver-gray eyes as they advanced and retreated with the steps, and what she saw there, half hidden by his lashes, made her fingers tighten in his grasp. He might not wish to take love or to return it, but he was not indifferent to her. It was a potent consolation.

The evening progressed toward midnight, the hour that would bring the ending of Mardi Gras and the beginning of Ash Wednesday. Then would come the unmasking, also, though there would be few surprises. Shortly before that hour there was served a last supper of meats and pastries and all the rich comestibles that would be forbidden during lent. The governor of the island, resplendent in silver lace, a full wig of white silk, and shoes with red heels, led the way into the dining room. He was flanked by scarlet-clad guards carrying silver maces. Laughing, joking, in fine appetite considering the short period of time that had elapsed since dinner, his guests trooped behind him.

Refugio took Pilar in to supper and found a chair for her. By the time he turned to go in search of food for them both, Philip was there proffering a filled plate. Not far behind him was Charro, also bearing a selection of delicacies, and behind him came Enrique with an extra glass of wine. To be surrounded by men was gratifying, even if the intentions of several of them were more protective than amorous. It was also ludicrous, for there was far more food than she could eat. The only way to prevent hurt feelings was to taste something from each offering. It did not help that it must be done under Refugio's sardonic gaze. Still, she nibbled first one confection and then another, and sipped at the wine, all the while making pleasant chatter designed to alleviate the awkwardness between the men.

Enrique and Charro did not seem to care for Philip or his presence. They made a number of sly comments, only half joking, about the provincialism of the island, the blandness of its food, and the complexions of its women. In a final closing of ranks, they disparaged the island-bred horses, the horsemanship of the riders, and even cast doubt on the local level of expertise with a sword. Philip, at first inclined to agree with them and to long for the excitement and adventure of a sojourn in Spain, began to grow pink in the face.

Pilar looked to Refugio, expecting him to put an end to the baiting. It would be unwise to start an imbroglio at the governor's palace, especially with the son of their host in the middle of it. The bandit leader, however, seemed to have found something of supreme interest in the bottom of his wineglass; his concentration upon it was total.

The comments continued. Pilar herself attempted to redirect them, but to no avail. As Philip's voice in defense grew hotter and his face redder, she sent Refugio a fierce frown.

It was then, during a temporary lull, that an elderly woman nearby spoke, her tone querulous and positive.

"The man is an impostor, this I tell you! He is far too

handsome, for one thing; for the rest, he lacks fire. If he were Count Gonzalvo, there would not be this cluster of men around his Venus, oh no! If he were the count, there would have been swordplay by now."

Refugio stiffened, then turned slowly to face his detractor. There was about him, in that moment, the unyielding pride of generations of grandees, with also the chill hauteur of the Moorish prince that he was portraying for the evening. His face behind his mask was dark with anger.

Around them the spreading silence grew, broken only by the soft sibilance of whispers. Those guests who were nearest turned to look, pausing with their supper plates in their hands.

The apprehension that rose inside Pilar was as much for how Refugio intended to answer the woman as for the danger that had suddenly caught up with them. An angry defense, or one of cold and formidable formality, would be wrong, she thought; it would give the old woman's idle words far too much weight.

She moistened her lips, gathering her courage. "Ah, my love," she said to Refugio in a tone of low, humor-tinged intimacy, "how little the lady knows you."

He swung his head to look at her in surprise, then he smiled, a realignment of the features that brought the light of impatient desire to his eyes and curved his mouth with sensual remembrance, caressing promise. He answered softly, "Or you, *cara*."

Returning his attention to the elderly woman with what appeared to be an effort, he inclined his head. "I would not seek to justify my conduct to you, señora, for there is nothing that compels it. However, I would not have you think I value my Venus less now than in the first days of my love. Think you that it is impossible to trust a woman? You would be wrong. But there is more. Show me which of these men around her is worthy of her smiles. You cannot, for she is too far above them, just as she is too far above me. Slaying them would be as sensible as trying to slay every man who gazes with longing upon the moon."

"If you were Count Gonzalvo, you would try," the old woman said, though there was a certain approval in her faded eyes.

"How can I?" Refugio asked, all rueful frankness. "To spill the blood of the son of my host would be an intolerable breach of conduct, nor can I think that the governor would appreciate a gory ending for his ball."

Behind Refugio, Philip uttered a sharp exclamation. "The blood spilled might well be yours."

"It might, if your skill was equal to the task," Refugio replied politely.

"I also have strength and youth. What would you wager on the chance?" The young man's face was purplish red, his stance belligerent. His gaze flicked to his mother and father, who stood chatting on the far side of the room, then moved away again.

"Do you expect me to place my Venus as a prize? A vulgar notion, one she would doubtless refuse."

"I would," Pilar said as the two men looked to her in speculation.

"You need have no fear of paying the forfeit, I assure you," Refugio said, his tone light, before his gaze moved above her head to where Charro and Enrique stood.

Some communication passed between the three, Pilar thought, some semblance of an order given and received.

A frisson of purest alarm ran along her nerves. Refugio was up to something, but what was it? She wished she knew, wished she could tell whether she was meant to indulge him by agreeing or aid him by opposing him. She thought the latter, though she despaired of ever being certain of the convolutions of his reasoning. Her voice low with her indecision, she said, "I have no fear."

"How very gratifying."

"Not to me!" Philip Guevara declared. "I demand a meeting."

"I also," Charro said suddenly.

"And I," Enrique added, drawing himself up in imitation of Refugio's rigid stance. "The honor of us all has been besmirched, as well as that of the men of Santiago de Cuba. We require redress."

"No," Pilar said, her eyes widening as she saw the direction that was being taken. "I will not be a part of such madness."

"But yes," Enrique declared with fervor. "Have I not been insulted, along with the horses and the women of this island?"

"Horses?" the old woman who had begun the incident said in puzzlement.

Refugio shook his head. "This grows ridiculous. It would be repetitious to fight you all. Besides, what would it prove, the private and deadly settlement of this issue? No, no, I will not be guilty of such disregard for hospitality."

"You must," Philip said. "It would be infamous to refuse now."

Refugio heaved a mock sigh. "I have no need for further infamy. But should the governor and his guests not gain some further entertainment from the contention? What say you to a public trial, one more nearly equal? What's needed is a tournament, the splendor of a passage at arms, a contest pitting men against each other."

"A tournament?" Philip said in disgust.

"Precisely. Doesn't it please you to think of demonstrating your skill before all, particularly the ladies?"

A speculative gleam appeared in the young man's eyes,

then he shook his head. "That might be, but it would take too long to arrange. Now, a duel—"

"What arrangements are necessary? We have a night and clear sand at the edge of the sea. We have horses and men and swords, and even a moon to light the field. The prospect is perfection. Unless you have no stomach for it."

"You mean—tonight?"

"What better time? After the governor's ball is over, of course. I would not want to offend him."

"But what honor can there be in this?"

"The same as in battle, the defeat of a worthy foe."

"You will participate?"

"It will be my pleasure." The gold cord of Refugio's headdress gleamed as he inclined his head.

Charro spoke then. "What shall be demonstrated, skill at swordplay or horsemanship?"

"Need it be one or the other? The ancient tournament was a test of skill in both, a mock war."

A murmur rose from those listening. In it was intrigued interest, and also admiration. From the phrases that emerged, it appeared that most thought the exercise was a wonderfully concocted excuse by the count, one designed to supply him an audience for the drubbing he meant to give the admirer of his Venus.

"I don't like this," Pilar said, propelled to her feet by burgeoning fear.

"But I do," Refugio said, his eyes bright with challenge. "And you shall be judge, if not also the prize. What could be better than a veritable moon goddess, fairest of the fair, impartial, incorruptible, and also endlessly accommodating."

"Stop this!" she demanded. "It can't be necessary."

"But it is, I promise you. Proof is required, don't you see? Proof that I value my Venus, and am, therefore, who

I say. Proof for them all. And for me."

Who had heard those last soft words? No one, she thought, except herself. Her voice equally quiet, she said, "I'll have nothing to do with it. Nothing."

"No? The loss will be felt; how could it be otherwise? We require watching and favors, as well as judging. And you, my sweet Venus, unlike the goddess of justice, are not blind."

CHAPTER 11

The news of the contest flashed around the ballroom as swiftly as the reflected light of a looking glass. Señora Guevara cried out in alarm as she heard, but for the most part the prospect was greeted with delight for its novelty. So great was the preoccupation of the governor's guests that the midnight unmasking became a perfunctory rite, a signal for the beginning of the entertainment instead of its end. That was, doubtless, Refugio's intention, though not his only one.

Refugio and his men, with Philip and a number of his friends, left immediately after dropping their half masks. They were closely followed; few felt inclined to miss the spectacle.

The ball guests flowed down the steps of the governor's palace and, calling their servants from their private party, mounted to their horses, their carts, and carriages and galloped after the contestants. They headed for the seashore beyond the neck of the harbor. Their passage through the town attracted the attention of others, the late revelers of lesser rank and station, mulatto servants, street vendors and musicians, seamen and stevedores from the docks. These followed on foot, laughing and drinking and shouting back and forth to find out the reason for the frolic.

Pilar found a ride with Señora Guevara, piling in ahead

of Doña Luisa without waiting for an invitation. Her welcome was chilly. The older woman's gaze as it rested on her in the light of the carriage lantern was sharp, as if she knew Pilar was at the center of the affair, but she made no accusation. Requesting that Doña Luisa stop dithering about the possibility of her gown becoming crushed in the overcrowded vehicle and get in if she wanted to go, the official's wife gave the order for the carriage to start.

Somehow, Pilar had thought Refugio and his men meant only to spar among themselves, with Philip as one of their number. By the time she reached the beach, however, the scheme had changed. Philip had brought three of his friends into it. Among them, they had collected enough mounts and swords and makeshift shields for all eight of the contestants. Two of them were helping Charro outfit the horses with blankets by way of protection, while Philip aided Baltasar and Enrique to blunt the swords.

Pilar leaped down from the carriage and pushed her way through the laughing, chattering crowd toward where Refugio stood. He had removed his Moorish robe and headdress, retaining the sleeveless tunic over breeches and boots. He was checking the bit of the horse he was to ride, calming the animal, which was excited by the noise of the gathering crowd and the flaring, windblown light of the long torches that had been thrust into the sand at both ends of the designated field.

He saw her coming, but continued with what he was doing until she stopped in front of him. "You decided to bring us your denied blessing?" he said, his voice light. "Or is it mere morbid curiosity?"

"The last, of course," she snapped. "Will you please tell me what you think you are doing?"

"Why, yes, *cara*, I will, since you hold some right to demand answers. What do you want to know?"

His irony carried a sting that made her lips tighten. "It's my life you're endangering as well as your own. Why? Why are you doing this?"

"I had in mind to escape mingling after the unmasking, but it seems to have gone awry. Never mind. The field will be dark when the torches are put out."

"Is that supposed to reassure me? You could be killed, and so could the others!"

"And you would weep and ride off with the victor."

"That's the most ridiculous thing I've ever heard you say. What use have I for Philip Guevara?"

"I did wonder that myself."

The words were pensive, and a deliberate incitement to mayhem. She controlled the impulse with an effort. "You're enjoying this. You can't wait to hack and slash at somebody."

"Not having had my quota of blood for the day?"

"Having no one to vent your bad temper on since Don Esteban eluded you, except your own men, who now need some outlet for their own violent impulses."

"I did say you weren't blind." His tone was dry.

"Oh, I understand you very well, if that's what you mean. You might have wanted to leave the ball, and you may have decided to present your men with a use for their energies, but more than these you wanted to prevent the bloodletting of a duel while teaching the son of our host a lesson."

"In swordplay and horsemanship? I have it on the best authority, his own, that he is the champion at both on the island."

"I would have said the lesson was to be in discretion."

"Now there's a thought. And if in defeat he learns to curb his tongue and his amorous penchant, will he not be a better man? And will there not be cause for rejoicing if, afterward, we find ourselves homeless but safer?"

She stared at him while the wind blew her skirts about them both and tore at the elaborate curled structure of her hair. It was probable, as he was suggesting, that they would not be welcome in Señor Guevara's house after tonight. No doubt lodgings elsewhere would be better, since a question had been raised about his identity and the Guevara family would be watching them more closely. It was the widow who had procured them their current place, however.

Pilar said, "What about Doña Luisa?"

"She must do as she pleases."

"And what if it's you who are defeated?"

"It's been agreed that the winners have leave to kiss all the loveliest ladies."

"That isn't what I meant." Her eyes were shadowed as she watched him.

He smiled with slow and singular sweetness. "I know, having eyes. And ears. You have ribbons to spare; I claim one for a favor."

The ribbon, one of a row forming bows and nestling between her breasts at the top of her stomacher, was untied and slipped free of its fastening before she could form an answer. She felt the warm touch of his fingers, then the loosening of her bodice. She brought her hand up quickly to cover the bare space, giving him a tight-lipped stare for his tactics of evasion.

He met her gaze and, still smiling, wrapped the ribbon around his arm and tied it, leaving the ends fluttering. He took her hand then, and led her to a place that had been made for her at the edge of the sand. It was a chair placed on a blanket on the ledge of scrub-covered land overlooking the field. He seated her, then bowed and moved away. Watching him go, Pilar realized that the seat had been made ready before she arrived, that he had known she would come in spite of her denials.

The other contestants, taking their cue from Refugio, began to move among the crowd, seeking favors. Young Havana ladies blushed and hid smiles as they gave away their scarves and ribbons to their gallants. Baltasar took a sash from Isabel's dress. Enrique, with comic courtliness, sought out Doña Luisa with a plea for the ribbon from her widow's cap. Perhaps because she was pleased to be a part of the proceeding, or perhaps only to put an end to a supplication that was embarrassing to her, the widow gave it up with a careless gesture.

Pilar, turning from watching that encounter, found Charro on one knee before her. There was daring in his eyes and a certain bravado in the set of his shoulders as he importuned her. "A ribbon also, my lady, to increase my honor?"

How could she refuse? This was playacting at chivalry, for the most part, with no deeper meaning, no obligation, attached. She slipped another ribbon bow free and tied it to his shield, a round piece of wood covered with bull hide of the kind used for practice in soldiers' barracks. He knelt there, watching her, until she was done. He reached then and caught her hand, carrying it to his lips. His mouth was warm and lingering on her skin, and the look in his eyes one of reverence.

At last he released her. "I will make you proud," he said as he sprang to his feet. A moment later he was gone.

The combatants moved up and down, pacing off the field and marking it, testing the ground and their equipment. They discussed strategy in low voices in groups of two and three. The crowd grew thicker behind Pilar. Not far from where she sat, the governor and his lady were made comfortable in chairs. The musicians from the ball, augmented by a few street hawkers with mouth harps and concertinas, struck up a lively tune. Orange sellers and pie men plied their wares, all the while insisting with menda-

cious vehemence that Ash Wednesday with its lenten abstinence actually began at dawn. There was a brisk traffic in
the stools brought by an enterprising carpenter, and on the
outskirts of the gathering an even more lively trade in the
wares of certain women. Still, the most frenzied activity
was in the betting, with the odds running strongly in favor
of the island men.

That was until the crowd saw what was happening.

Refugio and his group had gathered at one end, hud-
dling in a circle. When they turned, their shirts and tunics
had been removed, and their faces, arms, and upper bodies
had been blackened with grease and soot. They would fight
nearly unprotected from the blows of their opponents, but
they would blend with the dark, making it harder to find
them to strike.

Pilar was grimly amused, though she could not shake
her apprehension. The soot was for disguise, as well as
weighing in the favor of Refugio's team. At the same time,
the removal of his tunic exposed the purplish scar of
Refugio's injury as a dark streak across his chest, a reminder
of his past weakness. What if he was struck there again? She
could not bear to think of it, was not sure she could stand
to watch. That the rest of his audience had no such qualms,
and that they approved of the tactic, was plain from the
sudden shift in the betting.

Philip and his force did not take it so lightly. They
protested, only to be offered grease and soot. Grandly, the
younger man declined. He would not so demean himself as
to take refuge behind dirt. What Refugio replied was lost
in the shouting of the others, but Philip turned and stalked
away to join his friends. He sent Pilar a look compounded
of anger and hunger and baffled suspicion, but made no
move to approach her.

Refugio stepped forward, facing the gathering like a

gladiator about to take the field. His feet spread wide, his sword held as lightly as a dance master's baton in one hand and his shield in the other, he addressed them.

"Greetings, my wanderers of the night, dwellers of these enchanted isles!" he called. "We welcome you to this last revel of a carnival season that is speeding from us. In token of our esteem for your hospitality, we pledge you a contest of skill and strength and equine command. Let all those who have ever dreamed of daring deeds and knightly honor join us. And if you will not fight at our sides, then cheer friend and foe alike. For we come not to spill blood, but only conceit; not to take life, but to salute it!"

He continued with the rules of the game. It was a tourney in the truest sense, a war to the finish. The swords were blunted but could still inflict damage. There would be slashing blows in plenty, but no thrusting allowed. A man who was bloodied was presumed dead and must retire from the field. A man who was disarmed could be taken prisoner and held for ransom. A man rendered unconscious could either be removed by his friends or taken prisoner by his opponents, whoever reached him first. There was no obligation for a man who unhorsed another to dismount to fight. A man unhorsed was permitted to steal the mount of another, if he could. The last man or team left standing were the winners, though the fight could be ended at any time by the surrender of the opposing team. It could also be stopped by the judge, who in this case was a fair lady, the Venus de la Torre. She would give the signal to begin.

It was simple yet grandiose, proud yet plain. Refugio, in clear, incisive tones, invited the participation of the audience while setting the limits of what they might expect. The crowd was entranced by his presentation and the scent of a rare treat, and roared its approval.

What Refugio did not say, but which had become

obvious to Pilar as he talked, was that the stripping away of the outer garments of his men and himself had been done for one last reason. In a real sense, it evened the odds for Philip and his friends. Refugio knew his men to be superior in age and experience and the kind of skill learned by vicious drilling and scant praise and honed by fights that could lead to bloody death or hanging. He was a fair man, and so he had given away an advantage. To make him and his men bleed would be easier since they lacked the protection of clothing against the blunted blades. Recognizing what he had done, Pilar felt her heart jar in her chest, then begin a slow, sickening throb.

Refugio sketched a brief bow, then turned and leaped to the back of his mount with lithe, accustomed ease. He sat it in the center of the field as one by one the others came forward to be introduced and to make their obeisance to judge and spectators. That done, the combatants swung their horses and moved back into place behind the lines drawn at either end of the field. The tall torches were upended in the sand to extinguish them, and darkness descended.

In the sudden quiet there could be heard the murmurous sound of the sea and the whisper of blowing sand. A horse snorted and a bit jingled. Somewhere far away a dog barked. Nearer at hand, a man sneezed and a woman smothered a laugh.

In the dimness could be seen the double line of horsemen, dark shapes like shadows in the pale light of the moon. The wind ruffled the manes of the horses and also fluttered the full sleeves of the shirts, whitely gleaming, of the four men lined up on the right. Beyond them the sea rolled endlessly shoreward, glistening with the moon's faint track on its gently shifting breast.

Pilar had not been told beforehand that she must signal, had no idea how it should be done. Somewhere behind her a drummer had begun a light roll that slowly grew in volume. She glanced around her for something to make a loud noise, for some final light to extinguish, for a scarf or a hat to be thrown. There was nothing that could be seen in the darkness. Abruptly she noticed the gleam of the pale ribbons on her dress. There was one more that could be sacrificed. Quickly she stripped it free, untied it. Rising to her feet, she lifted it high above her head so that it caught the sheen of moonlight and the lift of the offshore wind. Then with a wide gesture she tossed it toward the center of the field.

It floated, gliding, shining, collapsing earthward. As it touched the sand the drumming stopped with a final booming thud.

The night exploded with shouts and yells and pounding hoofs. The men came together with a shock that threw half of their mounts back on their haunches. Swords clanged and grated. There were grunts and cries and curses. The thump and crash of blows caught on shields was a dull undertone. A horse reared. Another broke from the fray and was hauled back again. It was every man for himself, a hacking, cutting melee.

The crowd, finding its voice, began to scream and call encouragement and to shift this way and that for a better view. Men pummeled each other in excitement. A few women shrieked and jumped up and down while others turned their heads, unable to watch. Pilar did not resume her seat, but stood with her hands clenched into fists in front of her. She could hardly bear to see, but neither could she bring herself to look away.

A horse went down. The rider jumped free, then scrambled out of the way of the others. It was Enrique from his size and the sheen of dark grease on his torso. There was a moment when he scurried this way and that, trying to catch his panicked mount as he was pursued by a mounted man from the other team. His horse galloped away down the beach and he turned back toward his attacker. He dodged and ducked, sword firmly grasped in his hand. Then swiftly he tumbled, rolling under the belly of his opponent's horse, coming up on the other side to drag the man from the saddle. There was the flash of a blade in the moonlight and a dark streak appeared on the man's shirt. Enrique pulled himself into the fallen man's saddle and sent the horse back into the fray.

The drum beat a quick tattoo. The injured man stumbled to the edge of the field, where his friends stripped off his shirt in order to patch the wound. The fighters were reduced to seven.

Pilar, straining to follow the movements of the shifting phantoms, thought she saw a blow aimed and caught on a shield that had not been between friend and foe, but between two of Refugio's men. It must have been an accident, a mistimed hit as the men shifted at speed; still, it made her catch her breath. Anything could happen out there in that twisting, turning morass of blows and hoofs and unprotected flesh. Anything at all.

Now there could be heard, beneath the harsh gasps for breath and the explosive exclamations that marked a hit, the rise of a calm, objective voice approving, disdaining, correcting, explaining every move, every cut and parry, every error. It was Refugio, harrying the enemy in his own way and also giving them free instruction which they could put to use or not, as they chose, and whose value they might not recognize until a later time. The gathered throng, hearing it, laughed and cheered. The engagement took on a different, slower tempo. The combatants became more wary, the blows more deliberate as anger and blood lust seeped away to be replaced by grim endurance.

Then the moon began to go behind a cloud. The field grew slowly darker, then darker still. The moonlight was extinguished. All that was left was the gleam of starshine on shining leather tackle and silver bits, and on the pale shirts of Philip's three men. Refugio's followers became mere wraiths that advanced and retreated and struck from nowhere. The blades of their swords were like flails, in constant movement, spewing arcs of orange sparks as they scraped and clanged. The island horses, fine-hearted beasts but not trained for such fighting or conditions, became more and more nervous, rearing and screaming as they caught slashes meant for their riders. Then Charro was out.

Pilar did not see it happen. One moment he was in the thick of a savage hacking match, the next, Refugio was rapping out an order that caused Charro to lower his shield and wrench his mount from amidst the struggle. The man from the Tejas country slid from the saddle and stood gentling the animal before slowly walking the horse up the incline to where Pilar stood. As he came nearer, she saw the trickle of blood along his jaw from the dark line of a cut across his cheekbone. She put out her hand as if she would touch it, but he turned his head quickly and stepped back out of her reach. He did not speak, but stood watching the fight with narrow and intent eyes.

Pilar wondered briefly if he blamed her for the contest going forth and for his injury. It was, in a way, her fault. If Philip had not been attracted to her, the protective instincts of Refugio's men would not have been aroused and the whole thing would not have started. She could not think what she might have done to make things turn out differently, still she felt somehow at fault.

It was possible, of course, that Charro's behavior had nothing to do with her, but rather was caused by his embarrassment at being eliminated from the tournament. His pride would not permit him to easily accept defeat or to acknowledge the injury that caused it as anything more than a trifle.

On the field the knowledge of men and arms of Refugio's followers was being brought to bear. Matched man per man, the shirtless ones were pushing back the others, forcing them to retreat step by step, to break and regroup. Their superior skill and unflagging strength carried them forward inexorably. Philip and his two men fought well, but it was easy to see they were outclassed.

"Twice damned devil," Charro said, adding a short, sharp epithet without taking his gaze from the action.

"What is it?" Pilar asked as she felt the brush of alarm.

"I just realized who put me out of the game."

She stared at the twisted frustration on his face and the way he followed Refugio with his hard gaze. "You don't mean . . . ?"

"Who else? It appears he meant to even the odds before inflicting his punishment." He touched his fingers to his face. "Or maybe this was a part of the rest."

"But I don't see why."

Charro looked at her, his gaze bleak. "Don't you?" he said.

She refused to accept it. She stared at him for long seconds. She was still looking at him when the tumult of screams and shouts rang out around her.

She swung back with her heart pulsing in her throat. Three, no, four horses were down. They thrashed and kicked in a mad tangle of saddles and riders. It appeared that one had injured his knee and fallen, taking the others with him. There was a white-shirted rider lying to the side, with one leg twitching. The other men were ducking among the plunging horses, tugging at bridles as they tried to get them to their feet, dodging flying hoofs, bending, searching for and retrieving swords dropped or thrown down in the fall. And then the moon came out.

In its light Pilar saw Philip rise from the ground with a sword in his hand, almost from under Refugio's feet. The blade glittered, the light running along the edge from hilt to tip with a wicked, honed gleam. The whine of the slash he aimed at the brigand leader was a malicious sound in the night.

Refugio caught the stroke on his shield, and the tough leather that coated the wood split like rotten silk. Then he was parrying, retreating before a hail of blows driven by rash fury and sudden confidence. The edges of the two men's swords rang together with a bell-like tolling, hissing and shrilling as they whirled around each other, then clanking like two iron pots thrown together as they locked hilt to hilt.

The two men faced each other with inches between their faces. Refugio spoke, a low-voiced warning. Philip laughed, then sprang back with his sword poised and ready. An instant later he attacked.

The crowd drew a collective breath. There was not a person there who had failed to see that the sword Philip held must be unblunted, who could not guess that Refugio had told Philip and that the young man had refused to acknowledge it.

And suddenly the pace of the fight between the two men shifted while around them horses struggled to their feet unaided and the other combatants stood staring with their sword tips trailing on the ground.

Refugio met Philip's assault with controlled force and spare movements executed with blinding speed. It was plain to see that he had released some internal restraint and was calling on reserves of art and proficiency that had been held in abeyance until this moment. His movements dictated by hard and potent justice made deadly by rage, Refugio began a slow and steady advance. He dominated his opponent, giving him no room for error. Philip stumbled backward, desperately defending, his face as white as his shirt.

Pilar's eyes burned as she strained to see. She became aware of a woman praying. It was Señora Guevara. Beside her was Doña Luisa, her eyes shining with horrified excitement. The crowd was calling, warning, yelling, while somewhere in the rear frenzied bets were being placed. Charro was standing with his hands clamped on his sword. As he felt Pilar's gaze, he turned his head.

"He'll kill him," he said. "Before God, Refugio will kill him."

Philip was backing among the trampling, jostling horses. Sweat poured down his face, his breath rasped in his throat. His ripostes had become leaden, his parries perfunctory. He was demoralized by the cold fury of the offensive that had been unleashed against him, his skill and training forgotten. The only thing that prevented his defeat, that had held it off for long moments, was the whim of the man who faced him. And then that whim settled, congealed, and moved in for the end.

The moonlight skated on the whispering blade as it swirled in Refugio's hand, catching on that of the other man, skimming with a blue diamond sparkle toward Philip's heart.

Pilar saw the moment approaching and knew terror. Refugio must be stopped, he must, but how? Then she saw it. She was the judge. She had been given the right to put an end to this appalling trial. "Stop," she said in a hoarse whisper. Then she jerked taut muscles into movement, running forward. "Stop! Stop it! Now!"

Refugio never wavered. Sooty black and glistening with oil and sweat, he continued in his drive. His final thrust was perfectly launched and as precisely timed and directed as it was lethal. Philip twisted, trying to parry, trying to slip past the vicious sighing steel. It was too late.

Philip cried out, sagged to his knees. Refugio stepped back. His face set, expressionless, he pushed his sword into the ground. With deliberation, he turned and walked toward where Pilar stood. She watched him come while pain engulfed her in a bitter tide, rising like blackest gall to force tears into her eyes.

Then, behind Refugio, Philip staggered to his feet with a friend on either side. On his shirt, directly over his heart, were ragged tears caused by a sword point, tears in lines that were stained dark red and formed in the sign of a cross.

Pilar looked from Philip to Refugio as he came to a halt in front of her. She met his heated gray gaze, her own vulnerable, troubled, and yet glad.

He reached out to grasp her arms, drawing her against him. He bent his head and touched her mouth with his in a kiss that was fleeting, yet fiery.

His voice soft and deep, he said, "I have stopped, my lady, and I claim the forfeit. The game is over."

CHAPTER 12

They arrived in New Orleans four days before Easter, after a voyage of stultifying boredom. The last leg was the hardest to bear, the journey up the Mississippi River with its endless leagues of rolling, yellow-brown water, its progression of curves and unbroken vistas of trees and mud. There was some novelty, at first, in the humid landscape, the marsh birds and snakes, frogs and alligators, and the myriad varieties of vicious insects. It was also a relief to enter calmer waters on the sluggish, wallowing vessel in which they had taken passage. Still, they were all anxious to reach their destination, to be released from the confines of the cramped common quarters where they had been sleeping practically on top of each other, and to come within grasping distance, finally, of their quarry.

One reason they were so heartily sick of the coastal ship was that they had spent the last three days of their sojourn in Havana under its sweltering decks. They had quitted the Guevara house directly after the midnight escapade on the beach, pausing only to gather up their belongings. This was what Refugio had intended, of course; the surprise was that Doña Luisa went with them. She did not intend to stay behind, she said, and have the recriminations of Señora Guevara heaped on her head alone. Philip's mother was in a hideous rage over the incident, which had not only come close to killing her son, but had stained his honor as well.

But the accommodations, a single cabin lined with berths stacked one on top of the other with only a greasy curtain dividing the section for ladies from that for the men, had not suited Doña Luisa's notions of comfort or her consequence. She had demanded the use of the captain's cabin, only to be refused. The details of the acrimonious quarrel that ensued, along with the insults the captain had spoken, his disgusting appearance and personal habits, comprised the bulk of her conversation for the rest of the voyage.

The other recurring subject was the tournament. It was worried between them all like a particularly juicy bone by a litter of bored puppies. Conclusions were scant. No one could say where the sharp sword Philip had acquired had come from, whether it was a blade that had somehow missed being blunted in the darkness and confusion of the swift preparation—one in use by one of Philip's friends all along—or if it had been secreted in the accoutrements of one of the riders. If the first, it seemed unlikely that the man using it had not noticed, for the islanders chosen to participate had been experienced in defending themselves in the not infrequent duels of their class. For the man with it to have noticed and kept quiet was not impossible, but was conduct outside the code of honor. In addition, if the sword had been present the full time, the swordsman who had wielded it had been most inept, for there had been no sign left by a sharp blade on any of the shields of the band, nor had they felt its effects on their swords.

It appeared, then, that the sword had surfaced during the melee with the downed horses. The first animal to fall had had a cut knee. It could be claimed that the injury was deliberate, but strange things happened in battle, and it could just as easily have been caused by a wild downswing.

If it had been planned, however, it could have been for the purpose of bringing out the sharp weapon.

Philip claimed to have found the sword close to his hand after his own was knocked from his grasp. Was that a lie? Had he planned and made the exchange himself? Had he provided himself with the sword for later use as a means of evening the odds should the game go against him?

Charro tended to believe Philip innocent of murderous intent. But who else was there? One of his friends could have acted from the same motive of angry pride, but placed the sword near Philip's hand to save his own honor. He could also have been paid by someone acting for Don Esteban. The question was, who?

As with the shot that felled Refugio, it seemed that there must have been an agent of the don on the ship with them, someone who had followed them from Spain. That there had been no other attempt on Refugio's life since they sailed from Havana might indicate that this person had been left behind on the island, or only that there had not been another convenient opportunity.

The nature of the attacks thus far was suggestive. It seemed that the agent was too cowardly to perform the deed himself, but preferred to pay someone else. It could also mean that the person was too weak to go against Refugio in a personal encounter, perhaps an older person, someone unfamiliar with firearms or swords, such as a clerk or merchant—or, possibly, a woman.

Refugio seldom participated in the discussions of the two attempts. Whatever opinions he had of them he kept to himself, nor could he be drawn. He did not hold himself aloof; he played cards with them, gave them music, told stories of pointed hilarity, made extravagantly gallant gestures to the ladies and chivied his men to exhibitions of wrestling and swordplay on the decks as well as leading them scampering like monkeys about the masts and cross-trees. Still, when the subject of the attacks came up, he either gave the conversation an adroit turn or found reason to be elsewhere.

And he slept alone.

The narrow bunks in the open sleeping cabin made anything else difficult, but Pilar was not certain he would have chosen to have it otherwise. His manner in private toward her since the tournament was polite yet distant, though she sometimes caught him watching her with a speculative light in his eyes that was intensely disturbing. There was some satisfaction in the fact that his manner toward Doña Luisa appeared no warmer. Pilar wondered if he was not just as satisfied to have an excuse to avoid private sessions with the widow also. That may, of course, have been her own wishful interpretation.

The ship dropped anchor in the crescent bend of the Mississippi River before the town of New Orleans just before midday. It was late afternoon by the time the customs officials had made their cursory inspection and issued landing permits. The band disembarked as a group, leaving the city as night fell. Their destination was Doña Luisa's holdings, located some distance outside the city, along a waterway called Bayou Saint Jean.

The house the widow had inherited on the death of her husband was a rambling, whitewashed structure in the French West Indies style. It had two floors with six rooms each, and a hip roof that projected out over upper and lower galleries on all four sides. There was also a connecting wing known as a *garçonniere*, which was usually used for the older boys in a family, or else for indigent relatives or visitors. The walls were of vertical logs with the interstices filled with *bousillage*, a plaster of mud thickened with moss and animal hair.

There was a mulatto housekeeper and her two teenage children installed in one of the downstairs rooms of the wing. They appeared not to understand Spanish, but Doña Luisa, using her court French, soon made her husband's former mistress understand who she was and why she was there. The mulatress was inclined to be sullen, but soon accepted the fact that bedchambers must be made up, bath-water heated, and a meal prepared.

Doña Luisa made a circuit of her new abode, walking quickly through the interconnecting rooms. Immediately afterward she began to assign bedchambers. For herself she chose one of the corner rooms at the rear of the main house. Refugio she directed to the front corner bedchamber which connected to her own, while she gave Pilar the other front bedchamber, one separated from that of Refugio by a sitting room. Baltasar and Isabel she sent to the upper floor of the *garçonniere*, with Enrique and Charro in the remaining rooms of the wing. Having arranged everything to her satisfaction, she turned and began to order the mulatress and her children to carry the pieces of hand baggage stacked on the front gallery to the various chambers.

"No."

The objection, simple but firm, came from Refugio.

"I beg your pardon?" Doña Luisa's brows were raised to her hairline as she faced him.

"Forgive me, but no. You have been everything that is kind, and have earned our gratitude for offering hospitality at this time. I am desolate at being forced to countermand your arrangements; still, I have a greater duty to protect those who have come so far with me."

Doña Luisa brushed away the politeness with an impatient gesture. "You prefer to sleep elsewhere?"

"I prefer to have those who are dependent upon me sleep closer."

"Such as?" Their hostess's voice was harsh.

"Pilar will share my quarters."

"Oh, but really—"

"Nothing else is acceptable. It will also be more convenient if the others are in the main house. I suggest Enrique occupy the chamber next to your own, Doña Luisa, with Baltasar and Isabel on the opposite corner. Charro can then have the other front chamber."

"What impertinence! I'm not sure I can allow it. Next you will be telling me when I may come and go."

"Not at all. You are free to do as you will. If our presence displeases you, we will of course find other accommodations."

The two of them stared at each other across the dusty, candlelit room while the others shuffled their feet and gazed around at the rough walls and shuttered windows, the handmade furniture and the few pieces of pewter and faience that served as decoration. Pilar did not look away, but divided her glances between Refugio's expectant features and the pale face of the widow. She was the cause of the contention between them, but she could not see Refugio's reason for making an issue of it.

Abruptly, the widow threw up her hands. "Have it your way, as usual! I don't remember you being so hard all those years ago, Refugio, and the change is not for the better."

"Am I to blame for the inevitable? You wound me." The words were laced with mournful humor.

The widow eyed him with disfavor. "I wish I might think so, but I doubt it!"

They retired to their respective rooms soon after dinner; there was something about reaching the end of their journey that was wearisome, and they all knew they must begin early the next morning on the mission they had come so far to accomplish.

Pilar was standing in the middle of the bedchamber she

was to share with Refugio, staring at the plain bed of cypress wood with its gauzelike curtains of mosquito netting when he entered. He paused on the threshold, then came slowly into the room and closed the door behind him.

She turned her head to look at him, and her voice was cool as she spoke. "You angered our hostess over these sleeping arrangements. Was that wise?"

"No, only necessary."

"But you have been at such pains to keep her happy."

"And so I should have waited here, panting like a lapdog for the joy of receiving her caresses? Doña Luisa has given us shelter; that fact does not carry extraordinary privileges."

"Only ordinary ones?"

He inclined his head in agreement. "There are limits. She can command me, she cannot command you."

"That's a privilege you prefer to retain for yourself."

He moved closer, his body loose-limbed and powerful, his gaze dark gray and intent. Softly he said, "You object to my protection?"

"Is that what it is?" she asked in mock surprise as she held her ground. "Are you sure I'm not protecting you?"

"Occasionally, though not often enough."

There was the shadow of a smile in the words. It was enough to bring heat to her face as she remembered her frenzied attempt to stop the tournament. "You know I didn't mean that!"

"Didn't you? But you must have, or else I'm left to believe that your vexation is from pique, or worse."

The implication was that she was jealous. It had been a mistake to challenge him on this matter of the rooms when she was so uncertain herself what she wanted. There was only one way to retrieve the situation. She lifted her chin, her gaze steady upon his as she spoke. "I have no claim upon you."

"And would scorn to make one. I understand perfectly."

"I don't think so. I'm trying to say that whatever may happen to me, it won't be your fault. I asked you to take me with you that night in the garden, and regardless of where that request may finally lead, I would do the same again."

The angles of his face were still, impassive, but there was a flicker of something bright and vital in the depths of his eyes. "Endearing," he said, "but while you are busily absolving me, you might consider that there are more recent obligations between us."

"You mean my attempt to rouse you from your self-imposed paralysis?"

"Rather, your success."

She kept her voice even in spite of the images his words conjured up in her mind. "Either way, the situation is the same. It was my choice."

"And mine. Do you think I could not have refused your tender sacrifice? It might have imperiled sanity and soul, but was a possibility."

"I am aware, now. Why didn't you?"

"Courtesy, fatalism, and intemperate logic. They can all be vices."

"Intemperate," she murmured.

"Violent, and for my own ends. Does that make it more acceptable, or less?"

"What?" Her gaze was focused somewhere beyond his left shoulder, her thoughts elsewhere.

"My protection. Are you inclined to accept it?"

She met his gray gaze, taking careful note of the derision half buried there, and the purpose. "You ask so courteously; why do I feel that I have no choice?"

"You are a lady of some discernment."

"Then why pretend?"

"Illusions can be comforting."

Holding courage close, she said, "Who do you think has need of them?"

"I do, of course," he said without hesitation as he reached to cup her face in his hands. "Will you allow me this one, that you care?"

Once more he thought to spare her. In the face of such generosity, how could she refuse his protection or the desire cloaked within it? It was far too late for maidenly scruples, and in any case she lacked the will to invoke them.

This could not last. In his world, women were fleeting distractions; he had no time, no wish for more, and was too steeped in notions of honor to follow a different inclination. One day soon, perhaps tomorrow, he would either kill Don Esteban or be killed by him. Whichever happened, he would be gone. This moment they held between them, then, might well be their last together.

"I will do more," she said quietly, "I will share it."

She heard him inhale, a sharp breath of surprise. Unable to meet his eyes for fear of what she might see, she let her lashes flutter downward. He lowered his head, and his lips, warm and sweetly rewarding, touched hers. Her sigh wafted over his cheek, and she moved nearer, pressing her firm curves against him. He caught her to him for a long, aching moment so she felt the hard beat of his heart and the cool steel of his coat buttons. Then he bent swiftly to put his arm under her knees and lift her high in his arms.

She swung giddily, then felt the soft brush of mosquito netting about her. A feather mattress gave under her hips and shoulders. He lowered her to the surface, then stripped away coat and cravat, waistcoat, shirt, and breeches, before joining her there. His broad shoulders blocked the light of the single candle that burned on the table beside the bed. It gilded his skin, rimming his form in a glowing nimbus while leaving his face in shadow. He turned and stretched a long arm through the folds of netting to snuff the flame with his fingers. All was dark.

Pilar kicked off her slippers so they landed on the floor; there were no stockings to trouble with since she had not replaced them after her bath. She lifted her hands to fumble with the hooks of her boned bodice. He stilled her movements by clasping her wrists with his long, sword-callused fingers.

"Allow me," he said, his voice rich and deep.

The hooks gave way beneath his touch, and the bodice, which acted also as stays, was tossed aside. He untied the tapes that held her skirts and petticoats and drew them down her hips, pushing them lower until she could free her ankles. It took only a second to strip her shift off over her head. He lay propped on one elbow beside her for long moments afterward while he smoothed the small ridges and channels pressed into the skin of her waist by her stays, then slowly he lowered his head and began to follow them with soft kisses and the heated touch of his tongue.

He was a gentle marauder, but a relentless one. With flowing phrases and delicate guidance, he persuaded her to be the same. He cupped her breasts in his hands while he suckled the rosy crests. She trailed her fingernails through the silky mat on his chest, flicking and tasting the erect sweetness of his paps like sun-dried peach rounds, soothing the puckered scar between them with her tongue. He brushed the cream-smooth inner surfaces of her thighs with his lips, dipping toward their apex and the secret and fragile convolutions of fragrant skin there. She explored the warm and resilient length of him, measuring, cupping, saluting his indomitable firmness. Together upon the mattress they turned and twisted, matching hardness and softness, muscled curves and moist hollows, until the blood surged hot and throbbing in their veins and whispered in their ears and their rasping breaths were taken in plundering forays from each other's mouths. When finally the melding could no longer be postponed, was far beyond denial, he sank into her welcoming softness in a fit that was as wrenching as it was consuming. Together they moved, shuddering with pleasure, lost in untrammeled bliss.

Pilar's mind was on fire, her body dewed with moisture. There was nothing in the blackness of the night except the man who held her and the magic of their joining. She ached with fullness and her muscles quivered with the intensity of her need. His implacable rhythm sent her spiraling higher and higher into realms of feverish joy. She hovered, straining, clenching her hands on his shoulders while inside she felt the slow unfurling of her innermost self, the ultimate release of her being.

It came like the bursting of an internal dam, flowing in heated flood, carrying her with it on a tide of purest pleasure. Rising on its crest, she wrapped herself around him and took him with her, mightily striving, into oblivion.

Their bodies entwined, they lay as if they had been slain. Sleep overcame them while his hands were still entangled in the tarnished gold cloud of her hair.

They woke toward dawn and enjoyed each other again in slow, smooth communion. Their lips curved in smiles of gentle pleasure, though the light was a distraction. And as it grew brighter, pressing against the shutters, they used their lashes as shields for what lay hidden in their eyes.

CHAPTER 13

Immediately after breakfast on the following morning, Refugio and the other men went into the town of New Orleans. Their purpose was to seek the whereabouts of Don Esteban, to find out what kind of household he had established and where. At the same time, they would discover as much as possible about how the town was laid out and how it was policed, and how often the main streets were patrolled. All this could be important in what lay ahead.

The men had been gone no more than an hour when a message came from the colony's governor, Esteban Miro, ordering the widow Elguezabal and her guests to present themselves at the government house. The coastal vessel's captain had informed officialdom of their arrival. They must be questioned to determine if they were of suitable character to remain in Louisiana and had the means to settle any debts they might incur during their stay. If the examination was favorable, they would be issued a permit to remain for a specified period. It was a formality, but one that could not be omitted.

At Pilar's insistence, Doña Luisa sat down at once and wrote a note to the governor, setting a time when they would appear before him, subject to the governor's approval. It would not do to give the man reason to send soldiers after them. If Refugio did not care for the time the widow appointed for him, he could change it.

The band returned shortly before noon. New Orleans, they said, though it appeared to contain upward of six thousand souls, had the style of a French country village. It was a haphazard collection of dwellings of one and two stories, most of them of timber and *bousillage*, though there was a newer house here and there of plastered brick decorated with wrought iron imported from Spain and featuring arched doorways and enclosed courtyards. The residences were scattered over only half of the sixty-six blocks laid out for occupation within the palisaded town walls. They were, for the most part, to be found along the river or else set about the Plaza de Armas. It was on this square that the prison, or *calabozo*, and also the guardhouse were located, standing cheek by jowl with the church of St. Louis. On the other side of the church was the house of the Capuchin fathers, while the soldiers' barracks, built in a rather grand French baroque style, faced the square at right angles on either side.

New Orleans, like most tropical ports, was not known for being salubrious. There was a place outside the city walls called the Leper's Land where these unfortunates were isolated, and a Charity Hospital to take care of the many indigents who persisted in dying in the streets. These streets were standing in water because there were no drainage ditches, a possible contribution to the health problems. As additional drawbacks to public welfare, there was no arrangement for lighting the streets at night, no organized municipal services such as firefighting, and no regular patrols of the streets by police. At least two of these civic failures were seen by the band as possible benefits.

Don Esteban, they had discovered, had taken a house near that of the governor, on Chartres Street close to the square. His house was built in the French style, with the front door opening directly onto the street. The rooms used for entertaining were on the front and the bedchambers in the back, while the kitchen was a separate building lying at the rear edge of a large, open garden area. The whole was only lightly guarded; it was apparent the don did not expect visitors of a troublesome nature.

They had not been able to catch sight of Vicente, but they had heard a cook in the back calling out to a scullery lad, giving him the French form of that name. Casual conversation at a wine shop had gained the information that Don Esteban had a young bondsman who stood behind his chair at meals to serve him.

The order from the governor requesting their presence came as no surprise, for they had been warned by a shop-keeper about the need for a residency permit. They had heard that Governor Miro was a severe and exacting man, one who placed great store in rules and regulations and paternalistic gestures; on taking office he had proclaimed that the ladies of New Orleans must restrict the excessive ornament in their dress, and that women of color were forbidden jewelry and plumes and compelled to wear tur-bans known as *tignons* as a badge of their state. Answering such an official's questions might be awkward, but the danger of recognition was not high. The governor had served in this colonial outpost of Louisiana, in various capacities, for some years.

Still, with any luck, Refugio said, they would not have to trouble the governor for a permit. Doña Luisa must keep the appointment with him, but make the excuses of her guests. If she used her considerable charm, she could persuade the honored gentleman to accept another date for Refugio and his men. Before that date arrived, it was likely that their business in New Orleans would be concluded.

It would be interesting to know if Don Esteban had

made Vicente's presence known to the governor on his arrival, and in what capacity. Perhaps Doña Luisa could inquire, delicately of course.

There was much discussion over the luncheon table about ways and means of mounting the rescue. Baltasar was in favor of a full-scale frontal assault on the house, but the suggestion was set aside as being too dangerous for Vicente and too likely to cause official repercussions. Enrique wanted to sneak into the house by night, spiriting the boy away. The information gathered, however, seemed to indicate that Vicente was kept chained to the wall in the house at night. In addition, there was also a heavier guard posted at that time. Charro was for infiltrating the house, taking Don Esteban by surprise, perhaps at a meal where Vicente was serving. Refugio conceded the last as a possibility, but how, he asked, was it to be accomplished? How were they to approach the house without attracting the attention of Don Esteban's guards?

"We could pose as street entertainers," Enrique said, the words tentative. "We might beg the pleasure of playing for the don."

"Or bribe soldiers for the use of their uniforms for a few hours," Baltasar suggested. "Then we could demand to see Don Esteban's permit which everyone must have, claiming dangerous criminals had come into the colony by stealth."

Isabel, sitting playing with her dessert of bread pudding in a brandy-pecan sauce, spoke under her breath. "It all sounds so dangerous, too dangerous."

Refugio nodded at each suggestion but made no comment. His manner was withdrawn, as if his young brother's plight weighed heavily upon him. It almost appeared that his fear for Vicente made him reluctant to move with his usual decisiveness.

Silence crept in upon them. When Pilar spoke, her voice seemed loud. "Today, there was an old woman who came by the house here driving a cart. She was selling fresh greens for salads, and also herbs, parsley, and scallions, and something she called file for gumbo. When Doña Luisa's cook called out to her, the old woman drove her cart right up to the kitchen at the back of the house and stayed there drinking tafia for over an hour. She was only one of several who came by."

Baltasar and Enrique glanced at her, then looked at each other with lifted brows, as if her words made no sense. Charro kept his gaze on his plate, where he was using a tine of his fork to turn a piece of bread into crumbs. Isabel looked receptive but puzzled.

Doña Luisa turned around in her chair to face Pilar. "Really, my dear," she said, "I don't see—"

"Let her speak," Refugio said, his gaze intent on Pilar's face.

"I only thought, that is, it seems to me that street vendors make themselves very free of households. They come and go at all hours, selling all manner of things, eggs and milk and vegetables, hotcakes and pies; they collect rags and sharpen knives and scissors and mend pans. Some of them carry their wares on trays, of course, but others drive carts that are quite large, large enough to hold a man, or two men."

As she finished speaking, she met Refugio's gaze. He held it with his own for long seconds. A smile touched the firm curves of his mouth, then was gone. Speaking directly to her, he said, "This time, there is no crying babe for our use."

"No," she agreed, "but I might make a fine hag."

"No."

She had been afraid of his refusal. "Why not?" she asked

with mutiny rising in her eyes. "I was able to help at Cordoba."

"So you were, but this isn't Cordoba. Don Esteban will not give up Vicente easily, even if taken by surprise. It could be dangerous."

"There was danger in Cordoba."

"I remember it well, which is why I prefer not to have to divide my concern between you and my back. Or between you and Vicente."

"I don't ask you to protect me!"

"But if you are there, I must."

"Really, Pilar," Doña Luisa said. "You should not be so bold. Let the men attend to this."

"I have as much at stake as they," she said in a brief aside.

"Not quite," Refugio answered her. "Not yet. And I cannot allow there to be more."

"So I am to do nothing? Do you think that after you have taken Vincente from Don Esteban by force, my stepfather will welcome me with open arms when I go to ask for my dowry?"

"We will undertake to relieve Don Esteban of your dowry as well as Vicente."

"You're too kind. But I'm quite aware that gold will not be your first objective. Nor would I expect it to be. On the other hand, I could search for it while all of you are busy elsewhere."

"Impossible."

Charro cleared his throat. His face as he spoke was troubled but earnest. "Why should Pilar not come with us? She's proven her usefulness before."

Refugio turned slowly to face the other man. His voice as he spoke was softly savage. "Because it's my will as your leader, and that is reason enough. Unless you would like to take my place."

The silence was suddenly thick with unspoken warnings. Charro held his leader's gaze for long moments while the blood suffused his lean face. At last he looked away.

The difference between Refugio's tone to her and the one he used with Charro was an indication of his unusual forbearance toward her. She could not allow it to matter, however. She met the gray steel of his regard, her own gaze clear and steady though her blood thrummed in her veins and her hands were clenched on the arms of her chair. "You will understand, then," she said, "if I make my own arrangements."

"Before the arrival of the street vendor, of course?"

"It seems necessary."

"Realizing that any visit from you will put Don Esteban on his guard, that it will jeopardize our assault on his house?"

"What of mine? I have no way to live without the money owed to me by Don Esteban."

"You have been living for these many weeks without it."

"On your sufferance," she said tightly. "It can't last forever."

"Can't it?"

She refused to answer the quiet question. "Anyway, it isn't just the money. The don has taken everything I had, my home, my way of life, as well as the ones I loved. I refuse to let him keep what he has gained by his cruelty. It's mine and I want it."

"And you will put Vicente in danger to get it?" Refugio's voice was distant, immutable.

Down the table Isabel made a soft sound of distress, but no one else spoke or gave any sign that they noticed the disagreement. They avoided catching the eye of either Refugio or Pilar, and did their best to pretend that they were deaf.

"Of course not, not by choice," Pilar said with a tired

sigh. "But the alternative is obvious. You can take me with you."

Refugio's face was like hammered bronze in the afternoon light coming through the open floor-to-ceiling windows of the dining room. "I have given you my answer."

"And you have mine."

"It would be a pity," he said, "if it became necessary to prevent you by force."

Pilar got to her feet, pushing back her chair. "It would be worse than that; it would be criminal. But I should have expected no less."

If the taunt touched him, he did not flinch from it, but neither did he attempt to stop her as she turned and left the table.

She walked outside the house, moving along the side gallery to the far end, well away from the dining room. The day was warm, with a soft wind out of the south. A honeysuckle vine twining around one of the columns of the house was laden with small white and yellow blossoms that spread their perfume on the air. In the yard below was a red and brown hen surrounded by chicks like yellow puffballs that ran hither and yon among the decaying leaves of the previous winter and the clumps of dark green spring grass. She stood for long moments, breathing deep of the soft air as she tried to control the erratic pounding of her heart.

The peaceful scene before her turned suddenly grim as the long blade of shadow of a hawk came sweeping over the ground. The hen squawked and the baby chicks came running to shelter under her spread wings. The hen crouched low and motionless except for a faint trembling. The hawk flitted on past. It circled and passed again. Finally, it swept away. Pilar stood clenching the gallery railing, watching the flight of the hawk until it disappeared over the treetops. It was some time before she left the gallery and went to her room.

Refugio made no immediate effort to carry out his threat. He and the others remained in the dining room for hours; the sound of their voices could be heard, a low rumble, as they made their plans. As the time crept by, Pilar began to wish she had not been so impetuous. She was so used to being involved in all their discussions and plotting; she did not like feeling left out in this way.

Refugio was being so unreasonable. Why would he not permit her to lend her help? He pretended that it was concern for her that was at the bottom of his refusal, but was it? Or was it simply that he did not want her in his way?

She should not have spoken as she had, should not have suggested that he was a criminal. But his implacable attitude, his calm assumption that he had the right to dictate her actions, was infuriating. The fact that she had shared his bed did not make him her master. She was her own person, and must act for her own benefit. She could depend on no one else.

The men left the house again toward the middle of the afternoon. A short time later Pilar heard Isabel moving about in the next room and went to join her.

She had grown to like Isabel, in spite of the disjointed history of her past, and had done her best to befriend the girl on the long voyage. However, her purpose in seeking her out now was a shameless quest for information.

The other girl could tell her little. She had left the table shortly after Pilar to go and inspect the kitchen with Doña Luisa. She did say that Refugio had assigned Enrique the task of hanging around the taverns and drinking houses near the river levee in order to discover when the next ship would be sailing for Spain. Enrique was also to search out a contact with the smugglers said to operate among the bayous and bays of the gulf, importing goods into New Orleans without paying the official tariffs. These contacts could be important since it might be necessary to make a hasty departure once they had Vicente safe. Governor Miro could not be depended on to see the justice of their attack on his newest *regidor*, especially if the governor came to accept Don Esteban's word for Refugio's identity.

It was far into the night when Refugio and the others returned, and then they came with the squeak of cartwheels and the braying of mules. It gave Pilar a certain grim pleasure to realize that they had been out collecting the means to use her idea for entry to Don Esteban's house. She lay listening as they led the animals to a shed on the back of the property. A short time later they returned to the house.

The door of the bedchamber creaked a little as it swung open. Refugio carried no candle, but moved with soft, sure footsteps in the dark. There came the rustle of his clothing as he undressed, then the bed yielded to his weight as he settled upon it.

Pilar lay stiff and still and well on her side of the mattress. She kept her eyes tightly closed and breathed in a slow, steady rhythm, in and out, in and out. She need not have bothered. He made no move to reach for her. Within minutes his own breathing grew deep and regular. By degrees she allowed her muscles to relax. She was relieved. Of course she was. At last she slept.

When she awoke, he was gone.

It was difficult to realize that the holy season of Easter was upon them. The time spent at sea had drifted past, hardly seeming to count, and yet the winter was gone. It was Good Friday. Doña Luisa was going to morning mass at the church of St. Louis, after which she would see the governor as arranged. A rather worn cabriolet had been found in the back of the shed, and a horse had been discovered pastured behind the ramshackle building. She meant to have herself driven into town. Pilar, she said, might join her if she wished.

Pilar was delighted at the opportunity. She dressed circumspectly in a gown of gray with a white bodice and threw a white mantilla over her head. With her face set in lines of determination, she climbed into the two-wheeled carriage beside Doña Luisa.

There were no church bells ringing to draw the faithful to mass on this day; by hallowed custom, they were silent in reverence for its holiness. Pilar said her prayers with due devotion but could not concentrate on the sanctity of the occasion. She hardly heard the words of the service, scarcely noticed the rather primitive interior of the church except for the carved figures decorated in the French manner, which seemed too brightly colored, too overblown and worldly to her eyes.

As they left the church, Pilar parted from Doña Luisa. She had a few errands to take care of, she told her, and would see the other woman back at her house, in time for a late luncheon. Doña Luisa was inclined to protest, demanding to know precisely where Pilar was going. Pilar only shook her head and walked away with a cheerful wave.

It was good to be doing something, finally, about her stepfather. At the same time, it felt strange to be nearing the end of her quest after so long a time spent traveling toward it. It was peculiar, but she wasn't afraid to confront him. Don Esteban had committed many crimes and had ordered others done, but he had never offered her violence with his own hands. It was not that he was incapable of it, she thought, but merely that he was prudent. He preferred that someone else perform such chores requiring violence, and do it well away from him. He had no taste for physical danger to himself, but most of all, he meant to provide no evidence of his direct involvement in the crimes. The merest hint of such a thing could be ruinous to his chances for advancement; this was why he had been at such pains to remove Pilar and those who might help her prove the cause of her mother's death. Pilar trusted that such wariness would be her protection still.

His house, pointed out to her by a passerby, was much as Refugio had said, with whitewashed walls, a roof of weathered wood shingles, and shutters at the windows painted green. The street in front of it was a quagmire of mud, centered by a gutter filled with water in which floated kitchen refuse and the emptyings of chamber pots. There was no sign of Don Esteban, and the window shutters that were firmly closed against the fresh and balmy south wind seemed to indicate no one was at home.

Pilar walked slowly past the house along the raised wooden sidewalk as she considered what she must do. She must move with care for, in spite of what Refugio had said, she had no intention of endangering Vicente. Not again.

Just down from the house of the don she had to pause as a man emerged from a doorway. He was obviously a town official of some importance, for he not only bore himself with immense dignity, but carried in his hand the tall gold-headed cane that was his badge of office. He turned back to speak to a woman who must have been his wife, from her velvet dress, fine lace cap, and the rings on her fingers. Behind the plump housewife and to the right could be glimpsed the doorway leading to a small private chapel. Inside it, in honor of the holy day, the altar was laid with a cloth of lace. Tall wax candles in candelabras of silver burned there, while behind it was a fine crucifix of carved and painted wood framed on either side by lace curtains. This was plainly the more wealthy section of the town.

Regardless, just a little farther along the street was an apothecary shop with its mortar and pestles and bottles of odd mixtures. Beyond it Pilar skirted the tables that spilled out of a wine shop where bottles were ranked against a back wall that contained Catalonian wine, the Cuban brandy called *aguardiente*, and also the French brandy known as eau-de-vie. Next to the wine shop was the window of a jeweler.

She wandered inside to look at a tray displaying buttons in bone and gold and ivory, fans with ivory and gold sticks, rings and earrings with stones that the shopkeeper swore were from Thrace, and also point-lace veils and walking sticks with gold heads. Most of the shopkeepers lived either behind or above their businesses, for from these quarters came the cries of babies and raised voices of mothers calling to playing children. Between the buildings could just be seen the gardens in the rear, where trees lifted new green leaves to the sun and plots of flowers, herbs, and vegetables flourished in the dark, moist soil.

The language heard everywhere was French, with only a smattering of Spanish filtering through now and then. Shop signs were in French, the music that came from street musicians or drifted from open windows was French, and the food that could be smelled cooking for the noon meal had a distinctly French aroma. The reason for the lack of Spanish influence was not difficult to comprehend. Three-quarters of the population were, even after twenty-five years of Spanish dominion, still of French extraction. The majority of those of Spanish blood who had come to the colony were men, men who had since married French women; even the governor had a French wife. Children in their cradles were taught French, fed French food, sent to schools with French teachers. Added to this was the fact that the Spanish regime had begun with a revolution of the French populace that had been put down with bloody force. In order to prevent the same thing happening again, and to keep peace in this distant yet strategic outpost, the Spanish had adopted a policy of benevolence, going to unusual extremes to placate the people. The fiery residents descended from the original adventurers and malcontents who had settled Louisiana, feeling their French pride was at stake, had made little effort to adapt themselves to Spanish ways. The result was an entirely different kind of Spanish colonial town. Certainly New Orleans bore little resemblance to Havana.

As she came to the end of the street called Chartres, Pilar could see little ahead of her. In one direction was what she took to be the powder magazine, while in the other was the custom house. Directly opposite where she stood was the palisade, the thick pole walls that surrounded the town on three sides, but left the riverfront open. The street that she must cross to reach any of these other points was standing in muddy ooze. She tarried for a long moment, enjoying the warmth of the day and the strong south wind that caressed her face, fluttered her lashes, and tugged fine tendrils of hair loose from her tight chignon. It brought the smell of flowers blooming and green growing things, a fecund miasma straight from the swamps about the town, one that was foreign yet enticing. She breathed deep of it and felt an easing somewhere deep inside.

There was no point in going on, she decided; she had seen enough. She turned and began to retrace her steps.

As she neared the house of the town official again, she saw a familiar figure approaching. Her stepfather was dressed in black and wore a bag wig that shone with powder, and his coat buttons and shoe buckles gleamed silver in the sun. He strode along, giving way to none, his face set in grim and haughty lines.

He had not seen her, but he would at any moment.

An odd dismay gripped Pilar. She was not ready. She was assailed by a sudden doubt that she was doing the right thing, by a conviction that once she stood before her stepfather, she would find nothing to say to him and the whole interview would go wrong. So great was the feeling of impending disaster that she stopped where she stood. Ahead of her lay a cross street, the last before the block where Don Esteban's house was located. Forcing herself to move with normal strides, she walked toward that thoroughfare, then swung quickly to the left, crossing the muddy intersection and heading the opposite way from the house.

The relief at being out of sight was so great that she took several deep breaths and wiped at the perspiration on her forehead with the back of one hand. She could not linger, however. At any moment Don Esteban would reach the cross street also and might look down it in her direction. Picking up her skirts, she walked on at a faster pace. If she could reach the next street, or even an alleyway between the houses, she would be all right. There was one of the latter ahead of her.

She looked back over her shoulder at the intersection some yards behind her. Any moment now her stepfather would appear. There were only a few more steps to go. A few more. There he was!

Hard hands closed on her arm. She was whirled around and half dragged, half thrown into the alleyway between two houses. She came up against a plastered wall. The jolt scraped her shoulder blades and caused bright fragments of golden light to flare behind her closed eyelids. A cry rose in her throat but was trapped by a firm hand over her mouth. A man's body pressed against hers.

"Curse me quietly," Refugio said against her ear, "and I'll do the same for you."

CHAPTER 14

Anger surged up inside Pilar. She shoved at Refugio with both hands, bracing her shoulders against the building wall for purchase. He stepped back, but retained her wrists in a loose clasp, standing balanced and ready to forestall any attempt at escape.

"What do you think you're doing?" she cried. "You nearly frightened me to death."

"You had every appearance of trying to avoid Don Esteban, and I sought only to aid the cause. If I was wrong, I can withdraw."

"Oh, yes," she said bitterly, "you were aiding the cause. Your own! I was not quite ready to meet the don, but that doesn't mean that you can stop me from seeing him. My reasons are as compelling as yours, and you can't make me stand aside."

"Stand aside? Oh, no, I would not dream of asking that."

She stared at him with suspicion rising in her eyes. "What do you mean?"

"My hope, my dream, is that you see Don Esteban. Imagine my joy to find you still intend to do it."

"I am trying to do that," she said in heavy irony.

He released her, giving her a taut smile. "Never mind. Come let us put our heads together like a pair of thieves, and decide how you are to deliver yourself to our enemy."

She stared at him as comprehension seeped into her face. "You're going to let me help you?"

"Help me? No, no, my love, how could I be so unfair? It's I who am going to help you."

She raised her chin, never taking her gaze from his face. "Why?"

Why, indeed, Refugio asked himself. The decision had been sudden and instinctive, and caused by fear. He was afraid of what might happen to this woman if she were not with him. He had refused her help before because he wanted to keep her safe. Torn now between a desire to strangle her and the need to close her in his arms and banish the lingering fear behind her eyes, he recognized his defeat and dismissed it. Changing his plans and intentions toward Don Esteban at speed, he smiled.

"Why not?" he said.

The explanations did not take long. Within minutes Pilar was standing alone before the front door of Don Esteban's house. It opened to her knock, and a manservant, her stepfather's majordomo, appeared in the opening. The man's eyes widened as he saw her, but he invited her to step inside. From a room not too far away came the clink of silver and glassware and the murmur of familiar voices, as if her stepfather was at his noon meal. No doubt he had been returning home for that purpose.

She was shown into a salon, a room of some size laid with a Moroccan carpet. The chairs grouped here and there were cushioned in green velvet trimmed with gold cord. At the shuttered window were gathered and poufed taffeta draperies, and a chandelier of crystal and bronze hung from the ceiling. The embellishments were rather like lace on an everyday gown, however, for the walls were of plain whitewashed plaster and the floors of unpolished cypress.

The salon was the main room of a house built, in typical French fashion, much like that of Doña Luisa, with all the rooms opening into each other. Access to most of these other rooms appeared to be gained from this central salon, for a number of doors were set into the walls. Though the front door opened directly onto the street, the house appeared to have a gallery across the back that overlooked the garden. This outdoor area was open, without enclosing walls, and connected with the gardens of the houses on either side.

Pilar moved to the window. The casement was open for air, and she reached to push the shutters open also, in order to look out. Coming toward the house along the outside street, moving at a slow pace, was a cart piled high with the gray, curling moss known as Capuchin's beard, which grew on the trees along the river and was used for stuffing mattresses. The man on the seat, a hunched and pathetic figure, wailed a thin and quavering song: *"Fine moss, soft moss/Moss for bride's beds and accouchements/Moss fit for babies and dear old ones/Buy my moss, fine moss!"*

Footsteps were approaching at a hurried pace. Pilar pulled the shutter gently closed and turned to face the room. She moved to stand beside a chair with a tall back on which was carved the lions and castles of Spain. A tremor of dread ran over her. She put her hand on the chair arm, as if the lion's paw that formed it could give her courage.

Her stepfather appeared in the doorway, coming to a halt. He still held the napkin from his interrupted meal in his hand. He wiped his mouth with the cloth and handed it to the majordomo, who hovered behind him. Waving the man away in dismissal, he walked forward into the room. His face creased in a harsh frown as he spoke.

"So it is you. I could not believe it. How did you come to be here?"

"By ship, as you did."

"I am amazed."

"Yes, you thought me safely in Spain. Or safely dead."

"An unjust charge. How can you think such a thing?"

He was speaking at random, it seemed, as if trying to collect his wits. "I don't just think it, I know. I heard you order me killed."

"You must have misunderstood," he said, the words pompous, his manner overbearing. "You are my dear dead wife's daughter whom I was attempting to place safely with the nuns during my absence. Your kidnapping by the bandit El Leon must have left you confused in your mind. Where is he, by the way? How did you manage to escape him?"

"My mind is perfectly clear, I assure you," she said. "As for El Leon, I have nothing to say of him. I have come to talk to you about my mother's property which you took as your own."

"Your lack of trust, your lack of gratitude for my care of you, saddens me, but I am not surprised. It's of a piece with your attempt to seduce my man Carlos. You are a willful, irresponsible female, one doomed by the cravings of the flesh. I would wash my hands of you if it were not for the love I bore your mother. As it is, I will take you back into my household out of charity. If I do this, however, you must submit yourself to my wishes and to the discipline I will impose."

The words sent a chill along her spine, even though she knew she need not heed them. Her voice steady, tinged with sarcasm, she replied, "You are everything that is good and compassionate, as always, but I don't require a place in your household. I require what is mine."

"Ah." He turned away, circling a table on his short, stout legs before he faced her again. "Did you travel here alone?"

"I am not a fool."

"Who is with you and where are they?"

"That is no concern of yours. You will give me what I ask, now, this minute, or else I will go to Governor Miro and tell him that you are unfit for the position you hold. The governor, I understand, is an exacting official, one who likes to go by the book. He will not be pleased to learn of your activities before coming here."

"He won't listen to you. In the first place, you are a woman, and in the second, you have been disgraced and discredited by your time spent in the company of a notorious bandit. All I need do is let it be known."

There had been a time not too long ago when his assurance, along with his position and the recognition of his enmity, would have been enough to make her retreat. Now she thought of her mother and her aunt and the way they had died, and refused to be intimidated.

"You may be right, then again, you may not," she said. "It should be interesting to see, don't you think? But I don't believe you really want to make accusations. You have a weakness, you see, the presence of El Leon's brother in your house."

Don Esteban's smile showed too much teeth. "The young man indentured himself to me because of a debt. He changed his mind afterward, so has to be restrained."

"What kind of debt? One whose payment is in blood?"

Her stepfather's smile faded and purple color filtered into his face. "What do you know of it, of the pain and sorrow inflicted on my family by those whoresons, the Carranzas? They must and shall be exterminated, destroyed root and branch. In no other way can I live in peace."

"Exterminated," she repeated. "But not before you have the pleasure of inflicting pain and humiliation upon them, as you have done with Vicente."

"It's a right I have earned. But you are mightily concerned with the younger Carranza brother."

From somewhere to the rear of the house there came a dull thud. She ignored it. "Does it seem so?" she said, holding his gaze. "Perhaps it's because I feel to blame for his plight. I assume he is still with you?"

"Naturally. He is not so experienced in escape as his brother."

Nearer at hand, perhaps in the dining room, there was a strangled call followed by a crash. Pilar stepped forward in haste to catch her stepfather's arm, speaking in louder tones. "Never mind Vicente, I want my dowry! How can I live without it? You have left me nothing, no one of my own, no way to live. You have taken everything. I don't require much, just my rightful share. But I will have that, or else I will hound you to the last day you live!"

He shook her off, his look baleful before he strode toward the door, calling for his majordomo. "Alfonzo!" he shouted. "What is this disturbance?"

As no answer came, he swung back to her. "It's El Leon, isn't it? You've joined forces with him. He's come for his brother. That's it, I know it."

She must distract him, delay him, if only for a few seconds more. "What do I care for Vicente?" she said. "Or for El Leon, if it comes to that. But I want my gold. Where is it? Where have you hidden it?"

Don Esteban's face twisted with contempt. "I'll not give you a peso, not a livre or a piaster. We might have dealt well together, you and I, if you had been quiet and obedient, if you had kept your place. You chose instead to defy me. You cast your lot with a bandit and his band of cutthroats and whores. You went with them of your own will. Well, then, stay with them. That's where you belong!"

A smile curled her lips. "Oh, yes, I went with El Leon.

More than that, I sent for him. Now I have no other place, no other choice; you have seen to that. But where do you belong? What place is there on this whole wide earth for a killer of women?"

Don Esteban cursed her, a virulent sound that was nearly drowned by the sudden clash of arms in the next room. The look in his eyes was savage as he whirled away from her.

He did not reach the door. He was met by the sharp tip of a sword as Refugio rounded the frame of the opening in a smooth glide with his weapon in his hand.

"What a pity to interrupt this charming meeting," the bandit leader said, his gray eyes chill, "but I have an interest in any question of gold."

The blood drained from Don Esteban's face as he stared down at the sword point nudging under his chin. He held himself as stiffly erect as his paunchy body would permit. "How did you—"

"Easily. Annoying, isn't it, to be taken by surprise."

"I'll have somebody's ears for it!"

"Not," Refugio said succinctly, "if I cut your throat first."

Don Esteban swallowed visibly. "It isn't your way to kill an unarmed man, or I've heard that's your boast."

"You should never depend on gossip." The sword tip did not waver.

"If—If it's Vicente you want, take him and get out!"

"I have your permission? How gracious, but I have him already. My men are even now striking his chains and tying up your stalwart hirelings. What I want is the woman behind you, and your gold."

"I knew the bitch was with you, I knew it!"

The sword point sank into the fleshy neck of the don until a bright red drop welled. "What was the title you gave her? I don't believe I heard correctly."

"The—lady," the don said with a hoarse gasp.

"And the gold?" Refugio prodded him gently.

"I—If you want it, you'll have to let me show you where I have it hidden."

Refugio withdrew the sword point a short distance. "I have been waiting with hopeful patience for nothing else. But I'd advise you to move carefully. It would be a pity if there were an accident."

Sweat had appeared on Don Esteban's face, gathering at his hairline and caking in the powder that had sifted from his wig onto his skin. He wiped at it as he turned, leaving a white smear across his forehead. He stumbled in the direction of a side door leading out of the room with Refugio stepping softly beside him. Pilar followed close behind them.

They moved into a bedchamber at the rear of the house, the don's own if the size and richness of the furnishings were any indication. The older man pointed toward a massive armoire of French design. Refugio indicated with a brief jerk of his head that he was to open it. Don Esteban took a key from his waistcoat pocket and put it in the lock. Drawing the tall doors, he bent to delve inside. With a grunt of effort he lifted out a small brass-bound chest with a dangling lock. He staggered as he turned, then flicked a malevolent glance at Pilar.

"Look out!" she cried.

Don Esteban cursed and heaved the chest at Pilar.

Refugio reached to drag her aside, but she was already leaping back out of the way. The chest crashed to the floor at her feet, overturning with a dull rattle. She stumbled, off balance from Refugio's grasp.

In that instant Don Esteban thrust his hand into the armoire and snatched out a sword. The steel of the blade rang as he whipped it from its scabbard.

Refugio sprang in front of Pilar, engaging the sword

of the other man with a clang that vibrated through them both and brought echoes from the corners of the room. Their weapons slashed and rang in a flurry of blows as Don Esteban sought to profit from his moment of surprise. There was no advantage to be gained. Refugio's guard was impenetrable. Don Esteban wrenched himself back out of reach. The two men circled, stepping warily.

Refugio studied his opponent's eyes, his own narrowed and intent. Don Esteban's lips were drawn back in a grimace of effort and malice. Pilar, judging her moment, bent down and dragged the gold chest out of the way. Standing well back, her hands clenched into fists before her, she watched with sick hatred for swordplay in her heart.

Don Esteban was no untried young man such as Philip Guevara. He had experience on his side and a thousand tricks learned from the Italian masters who had their *salas de armas* in Madrid. In addition, he was cunning and unscrupulous. The languid pace and rich food of the Bourbon court had taken its toll, however, making him corpulent and short of wind.

Refugio had the advantage of reach because of his height, and also of the kind of strength gained by hard physical exertion. There was no doubt that his skill was equal to the other man's, if not superior. Regardless, it had been no great length of time since he was dangerously ill from his chest injury. Despite his heroics during the tournament in Havana, Pilar was afraid that a prolonged contest would tax his stamina. Protests, warnings, rose up inside her, but she stifled them. He did not need that kind of tax upon his concentration. All she could do was pray for a swift conclusion.

The two men feinted and parried, testing each other's striking ability, will, and resistance. Their feet scuffled back and forth on the rough boards of the floor. Their breathing grew deep. The muscles of their arms stood out in ridges under their coat sleeves while their wrists remained as pliant and supple as striking snakes.

Don Esteban tried a wily stratagem. Refugio parried it in seconde, laughing.

"That one has a beard on it," he said. "Try another, and while you're constructing it, tell me this: What made you move against my brother? He had been in Seville for months. Why turn on him after all that time?"

"He's a Carranza, which is reason enough. Besides, I had been watching him, saving him for the time when I might need a hostage."

"Holding my brother was supposed to prevent me from championing Pilar's cause?"

"I may have erred." The don's voice was breathless. "Besides, I suspected I had been duped by Pilar; she went with you so willingly, you see. Vicente was the most likely go-between, according to Pilar's duenna, my sister. For that he had to pay."

"You did err," Refugio said, and mounted an attack that drove the other man, panting, desperately parrying, from one end of the room to the other.

The bedchamber was long and narrow, with French doors opening out onto the back gallery. Don Esteban, with his back to the doors, wrenched up short with a defense that made Refugio skip back three quick steps. The two faced each other with sweat beading their faces. Refugio's breathing was fast, while Don Esteban's had a wheezing sound.

In the lull, there came the sound of quick footsteps from the direction of the salon. Vicente came bursting into the room. He was thin and dressed in rags. On the left cheek of his distraught face was the red scar of a brand, a letter G, for *guerra*, one usually reserved for captives during war.

"Refugio!" he cried. "Stop them! They have beaten

Alfonzo insensible, and now they are tearing the house apart!"

The distraction was brief, but Don Esteban abandoned honor to seize upon it. The handle of the French door was behind them. He shoved it down and whirled through the opening. Refugio caught the door before the other man could slam it shut. They pushed back and forth, then Refugio gave a shove that sent the don stumbling back.

As Refugio snatched at the door, Vicente caught his shoulder. "Let him go! He's an old man, and the killing can't go on forever!"

Refugio stared at his brother with blank surprise on his features, then he jerked his arm free. "I am not the killer, but it will end when Don Esteban is dead."

"Or when you are," his young brother answered.

"Don't be so retiring, my sibling. There will still be you to carry the name."

"Not if I'm a priest," Vicente said, but the words were spoken to empty air. Refugio leaped through the doorway with the ease of escaping smoke. The thud of his footsteps sounded, then he was gone.

Pilar touched the younger Carranza brother's arm. "Tell the others to stop. The gold they are after is in there, on the floor. You can take charge of it."

"I? But whose is it? What do they want with it?"

"Never mind," she said, already moving out the door. "Just keep it close to you, no matter what happens."

It was fear that drove her, that made her follow the two fighting men. Though the pitiless, ringing blows of the swords and the thought of the razor-sharp points sinking into flesh made her cringe inside, she had to be there. She could not bear not to be there.

She sprinted across the garden behind the house, which was planted with flowers and neat rows of vegetables. She searched the open area with her eyes, seeking among the ranks of houses and shops for some sign of men running or fighting. There was nothing.

Then came the scream. It reverberated from the house just down from where Pilar stood, on her right. She swung in that direction, stumbling a little as she began to run.

The back entrance door stood open, swaying on its hinges. She pushed inside and became aware of the chiming of blades even as she crossed a bedchamber and stepped into a salon much like that in Don Esteban's house. A woman stood in the middle of the floor with her hands clamped to her pale face. Pilar recognized in her plump and well-dressed figure the wife of the colony official whom she had seen earlier in her walk down Chartres. The woman's eyes were wide and glazed with her fear. She was staring at the entrance to the tiny private chapel that was attached to the house.

Inside, Don Esteban had his back to the altar. His sword tip darted in and out as he sought to keep his guard firm. Sweat ran in streams down his face, dripping from the tip of his nose. His cravat was askew, his coat was ripped in two places, and his breathing was a harsh gasping in the hallowed stillness of the chapel.

Refugio's coat was damp between his shoulder blades, and his hair had a wet sheen. His movements were still quick and forceful, but had lost that fine precision they had shown earlier. He was flagging. As Pilar watched, the quick shuffle of his booted feet in advance and retreat seemed to slow. His fierce concentration on his opponent's blade wavered as he became aware of Pilar.

Don Esteban smiled in triumph and sprang forward. Immediately he was thrown back, forced to defend against Refugio's vicious counterattack with an awkward frenzy of parrying maneuvers. He staggered backward in retreat, coming up against the altar. Rigorously defending, he slid along its edge, dragging the lace cloth with him. The candelabras rocked. The flames of the burning candles trembled on their wicks, and hot wax ran down in small rivers to congeal on the silver bases and puddle on the altar cloth. Don Esteban staggered again, going to one knee before wrenching himself upward again.

"You need not kneel," Refugio said, his voice deadly quiet. "There is no priest here to give you succor or unction, nor is there sanctuary."

"You can't kill me here," Don Esteban said on a panting breath.

"Why not?" Refugio said simply, and closed in, carrying his sword before him in a dazzling steel-blue whirl.

It had been a trick, a pretense, Refugio's moment of weakness. Annoyance and rich gladness ran together in Pilar's veins as she realized it. Her heart beat with a jarring thud inside her chest and the fear in her veins circulated with the cold ache of poison. She paid no attention to the lady of the house, who continued to scream behind her, nor to the murmur of the crowd beginning to gather on the street outside, attracted by the screaming of the official's wife and the clanging of the swordfight. Pilar could not breathe, could not think, could do nothing except strain to follow the shifting movements of the men before her.

They fought each other there before the altar while the sun's glow through the one high window sifted soft gold light down upon them. The candlelight ran in fiery gleams along their blades and tinted their damp faces with glassy shades of orange and blue and yellow. Their coarse striving in that place was profane, and yet carried also a trace of lofty purpose, as if the issue of life and death had its own ennoblement.

Don Esteban was harried and worn, with cruelty lingering in his eyes. Refugio's features reflected intent, pitiless patience. It was the patience of the stalking lion. He was El Leon. What reason was there to fear for him?

What reason, except that if he died, Pilar knew, a part of her would die with him? What reason, except love?

She loved him.

That truth of it hardly had time to penetrate before Don Esteban clenched his hand on the altar cloth and gave it a hard jerk. The candlesticks toppled. The candles spilled, rolling, falling to the floor. The don swirled the altar cloth like a matador's cape and tossed it at Refugio, trying to entangle his blade. In quick reflex, Refugio knocked it aside. He caught the end to drag it from the other man's grasp, tossing it in his turn. Don Esteban thrust at the soft white folds with a savage swipe that sent the cloth lofting back toward the altar and its flickering, smoldering candles. At the same time, he heaved himself around with his back to the end of the altar, then darted behind the heavy piece, setting the lace curtains that flanked the crucifix to swirling. Refugio dodged to the other end. The don scrambled to the reverse side once more, tearing the lace curtains down from their fastening and flinging them between himself and Refugio. As Refugio sidestepped the dragging mass, the other man dived along the wall, overturning chairs, circling toward the entrance doors, toward Pilar.

Refugio called out to her as he sprang after his opponent, but she had already seen her stepfather's murderous intention. She backed swiftly away, searching for a weapon. The nearest one was a tall candlestand of wrought iron, with unlighted candles on the spikes of its branched arms. She skimmed behind it and picked it up, using it like a pitchfork to ward off her stepfather. Don Esteban growled a curse, but ran past her. He caught the wrist of the official's portly wife, twisting it behind her back, then he pressed his sword point to her well-padded ribs.

"Stop there, Carranza!" he shouted.

Refugio skidded to a wrenching halt. Pilar put down the candlestand and stepped to his side. The four of them stood still. The breathing of the two men was ragged. The air whistled in Don Esteban's throat while his chest heaved. The official's wife bleated with every breath. Behind them came an ominous fluttering sound and the flare of light.

Fire!

The altar cloth had caught from the fallen candles. The flames had ignited the sagging lace curtains and they were flaring high, setting those still attached to the wall alight. There was a soft explosion of fire that leaped to the ceiling. As they stood there, the dry wooden boarding began to smoke while small tongues of flame licked along its edges.

As she turned back to Don Esteban, Pilar saw the sneer of satisfaction on his face. "You did it," she said. "You did it on purpose."

"Wasn't it clever of me?" he said, and gave the official's wife a hard push that sent her catapulting into Refugio's arms. Spinning around, he leaped for the door and flung it open.

"El Leon!" he shouted to those gathered outside. "It's the bandit, El Leon, scourge of Spain! He's robbed the house of Treasurer Nuñez and set it on fire!"

CHAPTER 15

$\mathcal{A}$n outburst of calls and yells followed Don Esteban's pronouncement. Cries of "Fire! Fire!" could be heard as one person after another picked it up and sent it on down the street with the accusation against Refugio. The noise rose like the angry buzzing of a disturbed beehive. A man appeared in the open doorway, and then another, and another.

"Out the back," Refugio said.

The words held rage and distaste for the retreat, but were spoken without hesitation. He was right, of course; there was no other way. For Refugio to force a fight on Don Esteban while a fire raged and his past rose to confront him was impossible. To try to battle his way out the front through the growing mass of people would be a dangerous incitement, and to remain behind suicidal. Don Esteban had won his freedom and also redeemed his life.

Refugio cast a harried, frowning glance at the chapel where the light of the burgeoning flames reflected on the walls.

"There's no time," Pilar said quietly.

"No," he answered in grudging agreement. He caught her hand as he swung toward the rear of the house.

Pilar plunged with him through the rooms at a run. They emerged from the back door and cleared the rear gallery with a few steps and a soaring leap. They raced across the open ground with their heads down, jumping across rows of beans and peppers, circling drainage ditches filled with scummed water. Behind them came the peculiar rumbling roar of a mob gathering for pursuit. The first of the men swarmed out of the treasurer's house. There came a shrill yell as Pilar and Refugio were sighted.

Charro, Enrique, and Baltasar dashed out to meet them as they neared Don Esteban's house. With drawn swords at the ready, the three closed in behind Pilar and Refugio as a rear guard as they dove inside. Orders, succinct and detailed, flowed from the lips of the brigand leader. By the time they passed through the house and spilled out the front door, Baltasar had been dispatched for Isabel, Enrique sent to find Doña Luisa, and Charro and Vicente assigned to remain, no matter the cost, at Pilar's side.

Refugio, vocal and incisive at their head only a moment before, was not with them when they reached the street. They did not pause to question why, but set out at a run in the direction of the river. They were far down the street when Pilar, over her shoulder, saw Refugio slide from the front door of Don Esteban's house, gesture behind him with a shout, then lope away in a different direction from that they had taken. A tight knot formed in her throat as she saw the angry mob pour out the door he had just left, swarming after him. He was leading the pursuit away from them.

All around them was clamor and confusion. Smoke rose in a dark cloud behind them. Minute by minute it grew darker, boiling higher. They could smell it as it was driven toward them in a haze along the streets, backed by the warm wind out of the south. Soldiers in uniform came running toward the smoke. They shouted orders and called for help, for buckets and water barrels, ladders and axes. The words were in Spanish, however, and the French shopkeepers and clerks and housewives running to view the commotion shrugged in incomprehension.

"The church bells! The priests must be told to ring the bells, to spread the alarm!" someone was yelling as they neared the church of St. Louis at the Plaza de Armas.

"They will not," came the answer. "It's Good Friday."

"They must! The town will burn!"

"It's Good Friday. The bells are silent on Good Friday. They will not ring the bells."

The bells did not ring. They did not ring while Pilar and the others pounded past the rickety stalls of the marketplace. They were not ringing while they raced alongside the walls of the convent of the Ursuline nuns. They still had not rung as they stepped up on the low and curving river levee and slowed to a walk. They did not ring as they reached the boats that would take them through the swamps.

Refugio was not there. The two boatmen who had been hired to guide them were standing on the levee, staring at the swirling column of dark gray smoke that rose into the sky above the houses. They asked quick, anxious questions of Pilar and the others, for they had relatives in the town. They seemed not to like the answers they got, because they drew off a few yards to talk it over between them.

Behind the men, at the foot of the levee, lay the two boats. They were hardly more than dugout canoes, but must have been cut from trees of enormous height, for they were at least thirty feet long. They appeared clumsily built, with the marks of the ax still on them, yet rode easily in the water. They provided no overhead protection from the elements, but the bulwarklike cross sections of wood left in three places to strengthen the boat made rudimentary seats.

Enrique joined them a short time later. Doña Luisa would not come, he said. She wished them a fond farewell, but could not leave her property claims in the colony unsettled, nor did she have any reason for, or intention of, braving the sea voyage again so soon.

Baltasar arrived just afterward with Isabel at his side. She had with her a number of bundles containing their clothes, and also a few sacks of provisions, since there was no way to tell how long they might have to wait before making contact with a privateer willing to take them to Havana. The other girl fell on Vicente with cries of joy, hugging him until he turned scarlet. She was full of exclamations about the fire and the way it was spreading, and asked every two minutes where Refugio was and why he was not with them.

The smoke grew thicker, becoming a pall that darkened the sky as it climbed into the heavens. It drifted out over the river in acrid, throat-burning rolls that hid the anchored ships and flatboats from sight. Above the rooftops could be glimpsed leaping orange arrows of flame. The sound of yells and shouts came on the wind, along with the muted crackle and roar of burning wood.

Refugio came walking out of the smoke from the opposite direction of that which they were watching. He had removed his coat, and his shirt was torn. His hair was tousled and his skin gray with soot. He looked at the provisions piled around Isabel's feet, and a frown creased his brow.

"Spectacles are enthralling," he said, "but hardly worth the risk of starving. If I am forced to load these wares, then everything not my own goes into the river."

They converged upon him, but before they could answer his unspoken charge of slothfulness, he spoke again. "Where is Doña Luisa?"

Enrique explained with a sad shake of his head. "I tried to tell her it was your order that she come with me. She still refused. She was not impressed with the reasons I gave her, and when I threatened to take her by force, she laughed. I could not harm her, so I left her."

Baltasar grunted. "Let her stay here, then."

"To die?" Refugio said quietly. "She has done nothing to warrant being left to Don Esteban's revenge."

"You think he would strike at her?" Pilar asked.

"Since he will be balked of striking at us, there is nothing more likely. More than that, Doña Luisa might find herself answering questions from the governor about her recent guests. Don Esteban's ruse is a great success. There's scarcely a person, child or crone, who isn't now watching for the fiendish bandit, El Leon. It makes for difficulties."

"The sooner we leave then, the better," Charro said in low tones, "and the more likely it is that we'll have our transportation."

Refugio glanced behind the other man at the boatmen near the water's edge. "There's a problem?"

"They seem to be having second thoughts," Charro answered.

"Let them go where they will," Refugio said after brief consideration, "but keep the largest of the boats at all costs."

"We need the men for guides," the other man said, though the words had a tentative ring.

"Only if we try to make our way through the swamps."

"If?" Baltasar growled in disbelief.

But there was no answer. Refugio had vanished into the smoke again.

"Where is he going?" Isabel demanded, her tone querulous.

"At a guess, after Doña Luisa." It was Enrique who answered in a voice heavy with disgust.

Charro agreed. "Ten to one he brings her back."

"I'm not so great a fool as to bet against a certainty," Enrique said.

"I don't see what he wants with her," Isabel complained.

"A conscience sop? A hair shirt?" Charro answered.

"Take your pick. Our Refugio collects both."

Vicente stepped forward, a frown on his thin face. "Who is this woman, Doña Luisa? What has she to do with my brother?"

It was Enrique who explained. Pilar hardly heard what he said. Charro was right, she was sure; Refugio was afraid to leave Doña Luisa behind for fear of what might happen to her. But was that all there was to it? The attachments formed early in life, especially those thwarted in some way, were often stronger and more enduring than those of later years. He had gone to Doña Luisa so readily that day on the ship, without a word of protest or a backward glance. That could mean that it had not been a totally distasteful sacrifice. To have refused would have caused danger for his men and for her, but did he have to go so easily, with such smiling charm?

What a terrible thing it was to love. It caused such doubts, such fears. She was suddenly jealous of the time Refugio had spent with Doña Luisa, but most of all she envied the other woman her knowledge of him when he was young and without care. What a charming young grandee he must have been, full of wit and laughter, music and uncomplicated sentiment. She would never know him like that. Never. It hurt.

How long had it been since she began to feel this way? Had it begun in the patio garden in Seville? Or was it in the mountains when Refugio discovered his brother had been taken by Don Esteban? There had been something there, some painful awareness, some current of attraction that she had tried to deny.

That night on the ship, when he lay injured and near death, or so she thought—how easily she had made the decision to offer herself, to use her body to rouse him from his reverie with death. She could not think of it without feeling her face burn. She should have known then. Perhaps she had known, but had kept the knowledge carefully hidden, even from herself. How else to explain it?

What point was there in thinking of it? He was a bandit, an outcast who was now wanted in the new world as well as the old. He had no future that he could share with a woman. He kept her with him, and Doña Luisa, because he felt responsible, but each was another burden, their safety a duty doggedly assumed. He might make love to them on occasion, but it was no more than a way to pass a pleasant hour, a means of forgetting, or else it was yet another duty.

She must not let him know. She was not quite certain what he would do. He might turn on her with scathing reminders that he had never intended to entice her, never meant to bed her. Or he might just as easily smile and pretend with sweet and aching tenderness that he returned what she felt. Either one would be more than she could bear.

Tears burned in her throat, rising to her eyes. She wiped them from under her lashes, hoping that anyone who saw would think they were caused by the smoke.

They well could be. New Orleans was burning. Driven by the wind, the flames were spreading in a wide swath. People were fleeing in panic, streaming out of the town gates carrying whatever they could salvage, or else taking to boats and paddling out to the safety of the middle of the river. It appeared that the house Don Esteban had been staying in must be on fire, along with most of the rest of Chartres Street above the Plaza de Armas. Several of the ships tied up at the levee near the square had caught fire also, the flames leaping into their crosstrees like so many torches.

Abruptly, somewhere near the far side of the palisade, an explosion erupted. The thunder of it boomed with a cracking roar that echoed back from across the river. Debris spouted into the air along with a great fountain of fire that lit up the sky with lurid orange and yellow.

Isabel gave a small scream, crying out. "What was that?"

"A cache of gunpowder, at a guess," Charro said.

"The powder magazine," Baltasar said.

Charro nodded. "It will spread the fire."

He was right. Nor was that the only explosion. Gunpowder was necessary for hunting, and hunting was a way of life in the colony. The shopkeepers who sold it, and the hunters who stockpiled it, provided stores that in their eruptions increased the consuming fury ten times over. It began to look as if the entire city might be engulfed.

There was a furtive movement behind them and a faint, lapping sound. The boatmen, under the cover of the explosions, were making ready to shove off their boats.

"Hey, you! Wait!" Charro yelled as he turned, leaping down the gently inclined side of the levee.

"Sorry, my friend," they called. "We can't waste our time here while there's money to be made ferrying people away from the fire!"

Charro's sword rasped as he drew it. Enrique and Baltasar whipped out their own as, seeing the problem, they took a running jump after him. Vicente, though unarmed, wasn't far behind them.

Charro reached the boats before the two other men, presenting the point of his sword so the boatmen jerked away from the dugouts, standing erect. However, Baltasar, holding his sword above his head, made no attempt to slow his progress, but slammed into the boatmen. They went sprawling. The big outlaw bent over one, catching the front of his shirt, smashing his sword hilt into the man's jaw. Enrique snatched his dagger from his belt and, reversing it, struck the other boatmen alongside the head. The bandits bent over the men on the ground, but they lay groaning with no fight left in them.

"Tardy but efficient," Refugio said, his breathless, acerbic voice coming from some yards down the levee as he approached at a lope. He leveled a finger at the largest of the crafts. "Everybody into that boat and shove off. Now!"

He was covered with a coat of gray ash, and sweat made wet tracks in the soot on his face. Doña Luisa was draped over his shoulder, sobbing and pounding his back with a dull and monotonous thudding. Behind him, just storming out of the smoke cloud, was a rabble of men carrying scythes and rakes and shouting in rage.

"Arsonist! Murderer! El Leon! Kill him! Kill him!"

Charro swung with his sword in his hand, calling, "The guides?"

"Leave them. Shove off!"

As amazement made them slow to obey, Refugio reproved them with imprecations that were inventive, virulent, and efficacious. They swung to fling themselves into the dugout even as Enrique bent in haste to toss aboard three or four of the most important bundles lying still unloaded. Baltasar used his great strength to free it of the muddy levee bank and push it out to float free. As it caught the current, Baltasar waded after it to leap aboard.

Refugio, never slackening his stride, scattered a few pieces of silver in the direction of the groggy boatmen as payment for their craft. He bounded down the incline and splashed into the river's flow, kicking water head high while Doña Luisa spluttered and choked and screamed in terror. He grasped the side of the boat with one hand and with the other heaved the widow up so that Enrique could catch her around the waist. The acrobat dragged her over the gunwale like a sack of wet flour, then dumped her in a heap at his feet. He would have helped her to sit up if she had not slapped him. Immediately afterward she burst into tears.

Refugio vaulted up with water streaming down his legs, then somersaulted over the side to land on his feet in the bottom. Baltasar and Charro, taking up the paddles, began to pull out into the race of the river. Behind them the shouting mob came to a halt ankle deep in the water and stood cursing and shaking their weapons after them. Refugio rose to a crouch. Keeping low, he made his way to the stern, where he took up the steering paddle.

The boat veered under his powerful strokes, leading away from the direction Baltasar had set. "What are you doing?" the big man called back to their leader. "You're pointing us upstream."

"What lies downstream?" Refugio replied, his voice carrying strained calm. "Spain is only a receding dream, and Havana will welcome us no more. We are wanted again, and not for joy. Can you think that—now Don Esteban has made us so well-known—Governor Miro will not set a watch for us at every ship, that our description will not resound around the West Indies? We are denied both passage and rest every direction we turn. Except one."

"What place is this?"

"A distant land of myth and magic, peopled by strange beasts and savages, made lovely by golden sunsets."

"The Tejas country," Charro breathed, his face lighting so that his eyes glowed bright blue.

"Oh, mother of God!" Doña Luisa groaned, rocking with sobs. "We'll all be killed. Or worse."

"Or saved," Enrique said.

"Or forgotten," Baltasar muttered.

"It will be a test," Vicente whispered to himself.

Isabel, her voice small, said, "But it's so far."

Pilar turned on her seat to stare at Refugio. She wondered what was in his mind, wondered if he was as certain as he seemed that he knew what he was doing.

He was looking back over his shoulder, staring at the burning town that was New Orleans. His grim-streaked face reflected the red of the flames, and the water that glittered on his lashes and lay beaded on the planes of his cheeks had the look of tears.

CHAPTER 16

Refugio sent his paddle plunging deep into the yellow-brown water of the river, steering the boat to the left to avoid a half-submerged tree trunk that was floating toward them. The boat responded well, the morning was bright and clear. The sun was warm and the wind at his back. There was relief in the hard physical labor of paddling, like a penance for the expiation of sin. The demands of the river, fighting the currents, watching for whirlpools and logs and staying alert for river pirates and Indians, required most of his attention. There was little time for thinking, for remembering. It was better that way.

He had gotten used to handling the boat the evening before. They had traveled late, making camp on the bank only when they were many miles upriver from New Orleans. They could have asked for a night's lodging from some planter along the waterway, and would probably have been made welcome, but it had not seemed worth the risk. The fewer people who knew which direction they had taken, the better it would be.

It had not been a comfortable night. For himself and his men it had not mattered that the ground was hard and damp and the mosquitoes like a hoard of tiny stinging devils. He regretted it for the women. They were not used to such rough living.

On the seat just ahead of him Pilar sat weaving hats for

them all from the palmetto palm branches she had picked
the evening before, only looking up now and then to watch
the shoreline slip past. Luisa slumped down between the
thwarts at Pilar's feet. In front of the two women were
Vicente and Baltasar, with Isabel perched on a bundle in the
hollowed-out section between the thwart on which they sat
and the next, where Enrique and Charro were in the prow.
The paddles wielded by the men rose and fell in a rhythm
that was both soothing and invigorating. Luisa had fallen
silent, apparently taking a nap, which was a merciful dispen-
sation. It was the first time she had ceased to complain since
he had hauled her on board. She was not a woman who was
at her best in difficult situations.

Pilar was such a woman. She had demanded a turn at
the paddles several times during the day, spelling Vicente.
She had tended the various injuries of them all the night
before, and lain beside Refugio on his coarse blanket
through the darkness hours, merely covering her face
against the marauding insects when she could stand them no
longer. She had even managed to sleep a little. She had sat
on the hard boat seat hour after hour, weaving with palmetto that pricked her fingers and helping watch for hazards. There had not been a word from her about the
discomfort or where they were going or how long it might
take them to get there. Her forbearance did not make him
feel less guilty at bringing her to this pass.

She deserved better. She deserved it, but it was unlikely
that he would ever be able to give it to her. It was possible,
even probable, that they might never see civilization again,
much less Spain. He had brought her on this wild quest for
a dozen reasons, most of them selfish if not actively base.
He had made an outcast of her, had endangered her along
with all the rest. The regret he felt was like a live coal in
his chest.

The sun gleamed in Pilar's hair, turning the strands to

filaments the color of old gold. Its rays caught the curve of her cheek, the turn of her neck, her slender forearm below her sleeve, touching them with a silken sheen. He thought of the way she had felt against him in the night, of the trust with which she had lain there with her back to his chest and her thighs alongside his. He dug his paddle deeper into the water.

She would be sunburned by mid-afternoon, earlier if the sun stopped retreating off and on behind the clouds that were drifting in from the southwest. They all would be burned. Perhaps the hats she was weaving would at least shade her face. His concern wasn't just the discomfort for her, but the danger of illness. For himself and his men, it didn't matter; they were used to the sun. Pilar was different. And Luisa and Isabel, of course.

Pilar turned her head to glance back at him. She said, "Is something wrong?"

Refugio realized he was frowning, and made his features relax with a conscious effort. "You see me as merry as a mule with a load of dry hay and nowhere to take it. What could be wrong?"

"A great many things," she answered, "but none that can be helped by worrying about them."

"But then, I have nothing better to do."

"If you're thinking of New Orleans, it wasn't your fault it burned."

"Now that's a possibility that had not occurred to me."

"I somehow doubt it."

"I see what it is. You're afraid that I'm going to lapse into a stupor again, and leave you to make your way alone."

She stared at him with cool eyes. "Not at all, since I doubt your will was ever beyond your control."

"You flatter me."

"I think not. But you underestimate me, I think. I feel

sure I could make my own way. Not totally unaided or in complete safety, perhaps, but one way or another."

An odd emotion he recognized as fear seeped into his mind. His voice was more slicing than he intended as he answered. "You are warning me of some substitute arrangement already made, I presume. Do you intend to tell me about it, or shall I guess?"

"Neither. Not everyone is as complicated as you; I was simply stating a fact."

"As you see it."

"How else? There is no other person who can speak for me."

"Meaning you will not be bound by my wishes."

"Meaning you are not bound by responsibility for me."

She was getting very good at picking up the tenor of his thoughts. He would have to watch that. "You are wrong. I have been responsible since I accepted your suggestion in a dark garden. Nothing you can say will absolve me."

"If you insist on being a martyr, I can't stop you."

"But I play the role so well, don't you think?" He heard the bitterness in the soft words, though he hoped she did not.

"Excellently, which is why I feel sure you think New Orleans is in ashes because of you."

"It seems logical." He pulled hard with the paddle.

She shook her head. "Because you think you should have stopped Don Esteban? I can't see how."

"I could have killed him as I would a snake, without giving him a chance to strike."

"You aren't made that way."

"No, and isn't that a fault?" He waited patiently to hear what she would say.

Her eyes were clear as they met his. "Some might think

so; it doesn't seem that way to me. To kill without thought would make you as as ruthless as Don Esteban. But I could always claim my portion of blame. If I had not been with you, you might have approached my stepfather's house differently, with more quietness and better luck."

"Or never have been able to approach at all? Never mind. The decision for how we went about it was mine."

"But I caused you danger by my presence and contributed to the fire as well. There might have been no crossing of swords with Don Esteban if I had not interfered, no fight in the chapel."

"That would have been a pity, since I required an excuse to kill him, especially after seeing Vicente. It wasn't your fault I failed."

"Will you rob me of the pleasures of guilt, as well as responsibility for myself?"

"It was never my intention to rob you of anything."

The words hung between them as their eyes, soft brown and cool gray, met and clung. Color that had nothing to do with sunburn rose slowly into her face.

"Intentions change," she said.

He gave a short nod. "And people."

"What are you two arguing about back there?" Vicente asked over his shoulder.

"Robbery and good intentions," Refugio answered in clipped tones.

"The box of gold? I looked inside, you know."

There was condemnation in the young voice. Refugio's reply was controlled, yet shaded with weariness. "Not exactly, no."

"I think we should speak of it. You might have given some thought to how I would feel about being made a party to theft." His brother's gaze was earnest, yet uneasy.

Refugio sighed. "I would have, if I had known they

had turned you into a self-righteous dolt at the university."

Vicente managed a grin. "That's right, take my head off. I'm used to it; Señorita Pilar isn't."

"Your address for the lady," Refugio said, "is informal for such recent acquaintance."

"I knew her before you, my brother."

"Did you?"

The words held that degree of politeness that could be translated as a warning. Vicente ignored it. "She came to me first."

"Then why did you not rescue her, bearing her off across your saddle like some gallant Moorish prince of legend?"

"She did not ask my help. Alas."

The implication in his voice was guileful. Refugio ignored it, inclining his head in Pilar's direction. "Felicitations. You seem to have acquired a champion. Another one."

"I'm honored," she said.

"I thought you might be," he answered bitingly before turning back to his brother. "But what of the gold? I haven't seen the casket."

Vicente's face clouded again. He gave a swift shake of his head. "I couldn't take it, of course, once I knew what was in it."

"You left it?"

Vicente gave a slow nod, his gaze caught by the amusement rising in his older brother's eyes.

"How brief is the reign of champions," Refugio said, his voice choked with the rise of rich laughter. "The gold belonged to the lady, my gallant, and she had use for it."

"You left it," Pilar asked in disbelief. "You left it behind in Don Esteban's house?"

"It—It seemed the right thing to do." Vicente squirmed

uncomfortably on the boat seat, looked to his brother for support. Refugio was unresponsive.

"And the house burned," Pilar said.

"I believe it did," Vicente agreed, his voice weak.

Pilar stared at him, then the frown between her eyes faded as her gaze narrowed to the scar on his cheek. She shook her head. "I suppose I have no right to complain. I injured you far more by involving you in my troubles. I . . . should apologize."

"There's no need. Refugio would never allow me to join him before, but now he can't deny me. I'm grateful to you."

"He wouldn't allow it?"

Vicente flashed his brother a glance both defiant and warm. "He seemed to think one bandit in the family was enough."

"It is," Refugio said shortly.

Pilar and Vicente exchanged a wry smile, then turned away, facing forward once more.

Refugio, thinking of what Pilar had said, watching the determined straightening of her backbone, felt compassion and something more shift inside him. He was sorry for her disappointment, but at the same time aware of a niggling, shameful triumph. She needed him still, and would for some time to come.

After a moment he lifted his voice in a chanson that set an easy, even pace for the paddle. His men picked it up, and they sent the boat skimming north and west, following the river.

It was dark once more when they made camp. Afterward, when they should have been sleeping, they sat around the glowing coals which were fingered by blue flames. It was pleasant to relax from the vigilance needed on the river, their hunger satisfied by a fish stew that Isabel had made

from two peculiar-looking fish with whiskers that Vicente
had caught using one of Pilar's hairpins. Besides that, the
smoke helped to keep the mosquitoes at bay. Around them
the night pulsed with the sounds of crickets and peeper frogs
and other night creatures. The blue-black sky overhead was
dusted with stars. The hunting cry of a swamp panther rang
out once or twice, a sound like a woman's scream.

They had passed by the village of Baton Rouge not
long after dawn that morning. In the hours since, they had
seen little sign of habitation. They knew they must watch
for the village and fort of Natchez on its high bluff, but for
now it seemed they must be the only humans in this vast
near-empty wilderness.

There was something intriguing in that thought for
Refugio. It was not like Spain, this land; it was too flat and
damp, the vegetation too abundant with its dense thickets
of trees and tangles of vines that cut and scratched. There
were too many strange animals, from alligators and snakes
to pointed-nose, scraggly-furred creatures that carried their
young in pouches in their stomachs. Yet the singing solitude
had an insidious appeal. He thought he could grow used to
the softness of the air and the dense quality of the nights.

Spain had had her day. For all the glitter of the court
at Madrid, all the ships that sailed the oceans and the colonies still held in far quarters of the globe, the golden moment of supremacy was past. His country had been in
decline for nearly a hundred years.

Spain had founded an empire based on being the best,
the bravest, the most intelligent, the most noble. Having
established it, the powers at the top had found it perfect.
They felt it to be so perfect, in fact, that they refused to
change, refused to accept new ideas. They had become
narrow in thought and action, suspicious of innovation and
bitterly protective of the old ways. The wealth gained in

the new world had slipped away, dissipated in wars, lost as colonies changed hands with the signing of treaties. Spain was dying, and men such as Don Esteban, like relatives gathered around a death bed, were feasting on its dwindling estate.

By contrast, this new country seemed rich with possibilities and wide enough to encompass any number of fresh ideas. For the first time in years Refugio felt little need to look over his shoulder or search the shadows in front of him. Here, for the moment, there was nothing except the night, no danger beyond that brought by nature.

Doña Luisa slapped at a mosquito on her arm. The sudden blow jarred the wooden bowl of cold stew she still held in her lap. It tipped over, pouring greasy gravy down her skirts. She jumped up with a wail, dropping the bowl, then kicking it with the sharp-pointed toe of her shoe so that it rolled into the fire.

"I hate this!" she cried. "I am being eaten alive, my skin is burned so that I could be mistaken for my husband's mulatto mistress. I have nothing to wear except what I stand in, and all I'm given to eat is swill not fit for swine. I demand that you take me back! I will give a thousand pesos, two thousand, to the man who will take me back to New Orleans."

Refugio bent swiftly to take a stick of kindling and knock the wooden bowl from the flames. He pushed it to one side, where it lay smoldering; they had only one bowl each and there was no way to tell when they would be able to get another.

"You have as much as any of us," he said to Luisa. "However, if you want to die, we can leave you here. It will be a great deal less trouble than returning to New Orleans."

"Here! That would be murder!" She gave him a look of angry hauteur.

"Maybe not," Enrique said, joining the conversation with a sly glance at the noblewoman. "You might be found by an Indian savage and taken into his bed. He would not work you overmuch, except for the daylight hours, nor trouble you for your favors after the first four or five little savages were born."

Doña Luisa looked at the acrobat under her lashes. "Disgusting."

"You may find it so at first, but I expect you would get used to it."

"You are an ignorant little man."

"And you are vain and spoiled, but I forgive you."

"I didn't ask your forgiveness!" she cried.

"Isn't it generous of me to give it to you anyway?"

Pilar, sitting with her elbows propped on her knees as she followed the exchange, sat up straight. "Your life is in danger, Doña Luisa, and will be so long as my stepfather remains in New Orleans. He is not a reasonable man in his vengeance."

"Your stepfather, yes," the other woman said, curling her lips. "I might have known this was your fault."

"Don't blame Pilar," Enrique said in stern tones. "You threw in your lot with us of your own choice aboard the *Celestina*. The reason was the thrill of flirting with danger. It's not our fault if things turned out more dangerous than you expected."

"Your Pilar might be used to the company of bandits, señor, but I am not."

"No?" Enrique inquired with irony. "You knew what we were on the ship. That was fine so long as no one else knew."

"Quarreling," Refugio said, "can be such sweet enmity. I give the two of you leave to enjoy it, but there is no one to spare to return you to New Orleans, Luisa. Pilar is right. I took you from there to spare you the revenge of Don

Esteban. There is no reason to think that the danger has passed."

She tossed her head. "I can't believe he would harm me."

"So my sister thought of his son. But come, you are a woman of valor. If it were not so, you would never have embarked for Louisiana. We have need of valor now."

"I hate being uncomfortable," Doña Luisa said, slapping at a mosquito. "I despise seeing only water and water and more water."

"We will leave the river soon enough, and then you may long for water. But you can bear whatever comes because you must, and because you have strength inside that has never been used."

"You think so?" she asked without looking at him.

"Naturally. It's in your blood, the strength of your ancestors who fought and died on the plains of Spain to oust the Moors and bring holiness to the land, who marched against the Indians of strange lands with their swords in their hands and a prayer on their lips and returned to their mother country with gold in their purses and thanksgiving in their hearts."

"Yes," Doña Luisa agreed, sitting down again, a faraway look in her eyes. "Do you know if there is gold in this Tejas country?"

Charro, who was sitting behind Doña Luisa, began to shake his head, opening his mouth to speak. Refugio stopped him with a small gesture of one hand. His expression calm, he said, "The illustrious Francisco Vasquez de Coronado marched across the western lands in search of the wealth of the Seven Cities of Cibola. He never found it, but does that mean it isn't there? Does it, when in the lands farther south the Indians once dressed themselves in sheets of beaten gold? There are also rumors of silver."

"That would be something, to return from this far

country with a fortune." Doña Luisa gave a small sigh.

"Wouldn't it?" Refugio murmured as Charro and Enrique exchanged a droll look.

Doña Luisa said no more, but there was a speculative gleam in her eyes.

"My father had gold," Isabel said, her voice soft, musing. "I used to play with it, stacking the coins in piles on the table. Then he gambled it all away, and we had nothing. We were thrown from our house and left to wander the street in rags. It was there that Refugio found me. He saved me from two cart drivers who were trying to carry me into a stable."

"Don't think about it, Isabel," Baltasar said, his voice rough with weary tenderness. "Don't talk about it, either. Let's go to bed."

Isabel looked at the big man a long moment, then gave him a sad and tender smile. "Yes," she said, "I'm ready."

Refugio watched them go, and his gray eyes narrowed with what might have been a defense against pain.

They all sought their blankets shortly afterward. Refugio lay for long hours, staring up into the night sky. A cynical smile curved his mouth as he thought of the gold he had spoken of to Luisa. Gold. Dear God. He sought in his mind for some hope for the future, much less wealth, and could find none. Ahead lay only the unknown.

Hope was not, of course, a commodity with which he was overly familiar. He had been resigned to a short life for some time. Or so he thought. Circumstances changed. Foolish aspirations were not restricted to dissatisfied widows.

For the moment, however, he was content. It was a sensation both foreign and unsettling. Wakeful, he lay beside Pilar and watched as she slept. He listened to the soft sound of her breathing and reached often to brush mosquitoes away from her face.

It was as they were getting into the boats again the next

morning that Doña Luisa looked at Pilar. "How does it happen that you have almost no welts from mosquito bites on your face. I have so many my face feels as swollen as a frog, and the itching is driving me mad."

Pilar touched her face. "I don't know."

"If you have some special cream or something that saves you, I think it's mean of you not to share it."

"It's nothing like that, I promise it isn't. Maybe they just don't like the way I taste."

Doña Luisa looked skeptical as she stepped into the boat and sat down.

"Really," Pilar said, "if I had anything to guard against the mosquitoes, I would share it."

Refugio turned away to hide his wry smile.

They reached the Red River a few days later and turned into this more westward-flowing tributary. On an afternoon just under two weeks from the time they had left New Orleans, they paddled up to the landing at the old military post known as Saint Jean de Baptiste de la Natchitoches.

A warm rain was falling as they pulled the boats up on the shore. It pocked the surface of the river and fell with a soft clatter through the brilliant new green leaves on the trees. The air had a green cast as the fresh, rich color was reflected from the prismatic raindrops. This was aided by the warm and watery sun that peered now and then through the clouds. Regardless of the heat, however, they were all miserable in their drenched clothing.

They were approached with caution, but with friendliness; any traveler with news from downriver was apparently welcome. Nevertheless, they kept the tale of the burning of New Orleans to themselves. They could give no idea of exact damage or loss of life, and to explain why it had been necessary for them to leave the city before this information became available would be sure to call up questions difficult to answer.

There was something seductive about the sleepy little town with its buildings that were rustic but inviting, its warm hospitality and gentle voices lilting in a patois that mingled French and Spanish, Indian and African words. It seemed that this outpost must surely be too far from New Orleans for interference, far enough for safety. Still, if they could reach it so easily, so could others.

They sold the boat for a goodly sum. They added that to the last of the silver, and with it bought horses—most of them cheap but fleet and sturdy plains ponies, though Vicente found a young stallion with an appearance of fine bloodlines which he insisted on having. They also bought flour and dried corn, dried beef, bacon and beans and peppers, plus another musket or two to increase their store and an additional supply of ammunition. Finally, they bought a pair of pack mules to carry everything.

Doña Luisa tried to insist that a change of clothing be bought for each of the women to replace those left behind in New Orleans. The only thing to be had, however, was a few lengths of cheap cloth suitable only for the Indian trade. It was Enrique who, disappearing in the afternoon, returned a short time later with a collection of blouses and shirts and even a day gown in Doña Luisa's size. He would not say where the items came from, but they were still damp, as if fresh from a washline. Nevertheless, he basked in the approval of the ladies, at least for a while.

At dawn two days after they had landed, they mounted up and rode their horses away from the post and along the trail that led to the Sabine River and the Tejas country beyond.

CHAPTER 17

They left the mosquitoes behind, for the most part, once they crossed the Sabine. They traveled for several more days through rolling hills covered with dense stands of pine and hickory, sweet gum and ash trees, and where wild plum bushes and haw trees were hung with small green fruit. Slowly the trees became more sparse and the pines and ash and gums gave way to scrub oak. The hills became flatter, more spreading. The winding waterways grew farther apart and narrower. The swampy bottomlands opened out to stretches of long grass blowing in the wind.

Charro became their guide, pointing them along the faintest of paths in a southwesterly direction. He did not pretend to know the way, however; this he told them plainly. He had only heard tales of the trail that was a part of the old El Camino Real, the king's highway, and could recall but a few landmarks mentioned during stories told of caravans that had disappeared and massacres by Indians at lonely way stops. He knew the route began at Natchez on the east bank of the Mississippi, crossed the river and passed overland to Natchitoches and through what had once been the mission settlements along the Sabine, including old Los Adaes near Natchitoches, and then continued on to Mexico City. There had been a time when there was much movement on it. In the days of the French in Louisiana, it had been a favorite contraband route for men bent on cheating the king of Spain of the silver from his mines in New Spain, or of the proceeds of the trade between the two colonies, a trade that was illegal under Spanish law. There had also been diplomatic missions between the French commandant at Natchitoches, St. Denis, and the Spanish settlements along the Rio Grande. During one of the latter St. Denis had been arrested for smuggling and imprisoned by a Spanish military commander, then had married the military commander's daughter. Since the closing of the Sabine missions some sixteen years earlier, after Louisiana became Spanish and the area ceased to be one of contention between France and Spain, traffic on the highway had slowed to a trickle and nearly ceased. Travel along it was dangerous for another of the reasons that the missions had closed—the depredations of the Indians of the Tejas plains.

The man in Natchitoches who had sold them the horses had thought they were crazy to be setting out on the El Camino Real alone. They should wait, he said, at least until another group came along heading in their direction. There were sometimes traders who moved among the Indian tribes, men who exchanged muskets and the *aguardiente*, known as firewater, for buffalo hides and other furs, men with knowledge and experience in the vast country through which they would be traveling. Such traders were not exactly persons of respect, but the larger the party, the less likely the Indians were to attack. There was a quartet of traders and their helpers who were due to leave in a week or so.

It was decided among the band that they must go on. The news of who they were and what had taken place in New Orleans might reach the town before the traders were ready to depart. In addition, the kind of men who would arm savages with muskets might well be more dangerous than the Indians. They did not need more trouble than they had already.

The men were glad to be on horseback again. They showed it by staging impromptu races and displays of horsemanship in which they did everything except make their mounts stand on their heads. Such high spirits soon waned, however, under the day-to-day tedium of the journey.

Pilar also enjoyed being back in the saddle. She had grown used to the hard pace Refugio set during her few days with the band in Spain, and though it was exhausting, the tiredness it brought was healthy. It was also welcome, since it prevented her from thinking.

Doña Luisa was shocked that she was expected to ride, something she had never done in her life. She had, at first, refused to go at all unless a carriage, or at least a cart, was found for her use. No arguments about the unsuitability of the country ahead for carriage traffic or the slowness of that mode of transportation moved her. Only Refugio's threat to tie her facedown across a saddle brought capitulation. It also added a bitter note to her ceaseless complaints.

The woman sat her horse like a bundle of soiled linen ready for the wash. She moaned through the first two days, cataloging her every sore muscle and bruise and rubbed section of skin, and castigating Refugio as a beast for dragging her along on his flight from prosecution. It took two men to help her onto her mount, and three to haul her down again, and she was so insecure in the saddle that their rate of travel was reduced by a third.

On the morning of the third day Enrique interrupted the woman's grumbling with a suggestion. Doña Luisa could ride pillion with him, he said; he rode light, so the two of them together would not overburden his mount. She refused, she protested, she cried and even cursed. Regardless, she was hoisted up behind the acrobat. Enrique kicked his horse into a gallop. The lady screamed and flung herself against him, wrapping her plump white arms around his narrow waist. Grinning like a dog with a new bone, Enrique wheeled in a wide circle, then came high-stepping back to rejoin the others.

Doña Luisa's endless cataloging of her grievances did not stop, but only found a new outlet. Enrique, unlike Refugio, did not ignore them, but took issue with every word she said. He questioned her reasons for grumbling, cracked jokes, ridiculed her lack of equine prowess, and generally goaded her into rage. The resulting quarrels and shouting matches seemed to give him vast satisfaction, and at the same time so wearied the lady that she ceased to rail at her circumstances.

Whether Refugio approved or deplored the arrangement, no one could tell. He was distant, preoccupied. He often ranged for miles ahead, bringing back information on diverging paths and watering holes and instructions on resting places. Sometimes he backtracked, circling around in a wide loop to watch the trail behind them.

It did not seem to trouble him that Charro had taken a position of leadership. The two of them consulted together often and long, holding midnight sessions in which Refugio went over everything the Tejas-born man knew about the country and its dangers. He extracted details concerning the route they were following that Charro was hardly aware he knew, the names and locations of rivers and distances between them, the detours for dry stretches and best ways to cross the open prairie lands, and the characteristics of prominent landmarks. He also delved into the nature, habits, and tricks of the different Indian tribes, from the forest-dwelling, sun-worshiping Caddo Hasinai to the cannibalistic Karankawa of the coastal areas; from the primitive Coahuiltecans of the southern desert and nonmalignant Tonkawas of the grasslands, to the warlike Apaches and hard-riding Comanches who had made the plains their own by driving all others from them. Of the last two tribes, it was difficult to say which was worse.

The Apaches, Charro said, feared nothing that breathed or walked. They were cunning and devious and renowned for their cruelty. All efforts to convert them to Christianity had failed. They had, during the two-hundred-odd years of Spanish occupation of the Tejas country, been the greatest single factor preventing the settlements from prospering.

The Comanches were more recent arrivals, sweeping down from the mountains to the north within the last hundred years. Incomparable horsemen, aggressive, swift, and deadly, they were competing with the Apaches for mastery of the plains, and so were their enemies. Caught between the Comanches on one side and the Spanish on the other, the Apaches had become more daring, more vicious, as they waged a campaign to the death against both. In retaliation, the Spanish had formulated their own policy of extermination of the Apaches. Toward that end they had attempted to create alliances with the other Indian tribes, but the rate of success was not impressive. Spanish expansion in the vast region bounded by the Sabine, the Rio Grande, and the western mountains had officially stopped; unofficially, it was in retreat.

Regardless of the Indian danger, the leagues slid past without a hint of trouble. The weather was dry and mild, a succession of perfect days. Birds called, bees hummed in the wildflowers and the clover, and the sun shone down with heat that slowly increased. Rabbits with tails as white and fluffy as cotton were flushed from the grass before them, and coveys of quail flew up sometimes from directly under the hoofs of their mounts. In the drowsy heat of the afternoon they watched the languid circling of sparrow hawks and buzzards, while dusk often brought the call of coyotes.

It did not seem possible that there could be savages some-where beyond the haze-shaded horizon, savages waiting for a chance to kill them or inflict the horrible tortures Charro described. Imperceptibly, the fears of the past weeks receded, as if they were being left behind as surely as the mountains of Spain and the Mississippi River which curled around New Orleans.

Vicente grew brown and healthy. The scar on his face faded to a pale design, one they all ceased to notice and which he ignored as if it weren't there. Gradually, the solemn introspection of the boy's manner gave way to interest in his surroundings. He seemed to take to life on the move, especially the changes in the countryside. Sometimes he rode with his brother, sometimes with one of the others, but often he sought out Pilar. She thought it was because she shared some of his growing fascination with the strange flowers and grasses, the birds and animals they came across.

Vicente was riding with her and Charro one afternoon when they topped a rise and saw before them an open plain. A shallow stream wandered through it and a few trees stood here and there, but it was the grass that made them draw up their mounts to look. It grew green and thick near the water and more sparse farther away, but mingling with it, like bits of fallen sky, were patches of low-growing wild-flowers of deepest blue. The color was so intense it hurt the eyes, yet at the same time it soothed the soul.

"Beautiful," Pilar said softly as she placed her hands on her pommel and eased her weight in the saddle.

"*El conejo*, we call it," Charro answered. Stepping down from his horse, he bent to pick a flower from the grass at their feet and hand it up to Pilar. "You see the white tip inside the blue? That's the rabbit's white tail, *el conejo*. You'll see acres of them from now on." He gestured toward the lower end of the plain. "And over there are wild cattle."

Pilar had been so bemused by the wildflowers that she had not even noticed the cattle. She raised a brow as she looked in the direction he indicated. "Is it my imagination, or are they larger than in Spain?"

"No, you're right. They're descended from animals that escaped from the herds that traveled with the great *entradas*, the expeditions and explorations into this country made by men such as Coronado. The land here was well-suited to cattle, but not without its hazards, so only the biggest, the toughest, and those with the longest and sharpest horns survived to breed. Now they are formidable."

They were indeed. The largest of the herd, a great dun-colored bull, appeared to stand as tall at the shoulder as a horse, and had horns with a span far wider than a man could reach with both arms outstretched. The twenty or thirty cows the bull watched over also had horns, and they were not much smaller.

"You say they're wild?" Vicente said.

Charro nodded as he remounted and gathered up his reins. "They have to be, out here so far from any settlement. All such cattle belong to the king, according to the law, but any man daring enough to put a brand on one can claim it with few questions asked."

"This is the kind of cattle your father raises?"

Again Charro agreed, with a trace of pride. "As you can see, they are not animals that could be herded by a man on foot, like sheep. They are mean and crafty, they run like horses, and they range for miles every day as they graze. It's these cattle that made the *charro*, the horsemen of the Tejas country, for only a man on horseback can handle them. And as the grandees of Spain have always known, putting a man on horseback makes him different. It makes him lordly, gives him courage—and creates in him the determination to ride any horse that lives. We have a saying: 'To be a *charro* is to be a hero; to be a *ranchero* is to be a king!' "

"That explains why you're so lordly, then," Pilar said, sending him a laughing glance.

"Am I?" A smile lighted his blue eyes as he turned his head to look at her, and in it was gratification at her personal notice.

"Only now and then," she answered, relenting.

Vicente said to Charro, "According to what you say, your father's *estancia* must be fairly large."

"Not really. His *mercedes*, his grant given at the king's mercy which he inherited from my grandfather, contains some twenty-square leagues. It stretches as far as the eye can see, but there are others that are larger."

"The cattle are raised for the hides?"

"As you say, and for the tallow. The meat's a bit stringy, but tastes like something out of paradise when sliced thin and cooked with peppers and onions. I'd give half my life to have a plate of it before me right now."

Pilar met his gaze with sympathy; she was also tired of their spartan diet. The thought came to them both at the same time. They blinked, then amusement rose into their faces. They turned their heads to stare at the herd.

"I feel such a fool," Charro said. "I should have thought of it at once, instead of sitting here talking."

"Will you wait for the others?" Pilar asked. The three of them had been riding ahead of everyone else. Refugio had left them to search their back trail and had not been seen for most of the morning. Doña Luisa had demanded a rest stop to attend the needs of nature, and asked Isabel to come with her a few yards off the trail to screen her from view. Baltasar and Enrique had remained behind on guard. It should not be long, however, before the others caught up.

Charro reached to pick up the braided leather lariat he always had with him. Loosening the coils, he said, "I can have a cow butchered before they get here. Besides, we're downwind. The herd is a little curious about us, but not disturbed. If the others come riding up, they may get spooked, take off. The time is right."

"I suppose you know what you're doing," she said.

"Can I help?" Vicente asked with a shading of eagerness in his voice.

Charro replaced the rope and took his musket from its saddle scabbard. As he attended to the weapon's priming, he shook his head at the boy, saying, "Stay here with Pilar."

The younger man obeyed, but watched with something close to envy as Charro nudged his horse into movement and rode at an oblique angle down the slope.

The bull watched him come, twitching his tail in a restive rhythm. A cow somewhat larger than the others also raised her head to eye the intruder. She snuffled, testing the wind. She did not seem unduly alarmed; still, she began to move. She made her way to the front of the herd, stopping between Charro and a calf that was separated from the others by a few feet of grass scattered with blue wildflowers.

Pilar, watching, hoped that Charro would not choose that cow and her calf. There was something indomitable, yet curiously vulnerable, about them there in the hot spring sunshine. Quite suddenly she was no longer so hungry for fresh meat.

Vicente's horse, the young roan stallion he had chosen in Natchitoches, had apparently never seen cattle before. It snorted and sidled, trying to rear. Pilar reined the mare she was riding to one side, out of the way. Vicente's roan whickered and fought the bit, plunging on stiff forelegs down into the flat valley as his rider clung to his back.

On the plain beyond, the bull bellowed and lowered its head. The cattle were beginning to mill, shifting in circles. They watched Charro but did not seem to identify him as a danger. Charro had dropped his horse to a walk, sitting his saddle with his musket across his thighs. He was closing in. A few feet more and he swung down from the saddle. Leaving his mount on a ground tether, he crept forward through the tall, waving grass. He dropped to one knee, then lifted his weapon to his shoulder.

The shot shattered the still morning air. A cow bellowed and dropped to her knees, then keeled slowly to the ground. The herd surged forward, the cows bounding and leaping, bellowing as they ran a few yards up the shallow valley toward Pilar and Vicente, before slowing down and milling to a walk. The great bull trotted after them, then stopped and threw up his head. He pawed the ground and bawled out his rage.

The explosion of the shot sent Vicente's roan into paroxysms of wild terror. The horse reared straight up, then came down on its front legs with its heels flying skyward. Vicente sailed over the horse's ears. He landed with a thud, rolling in the grass in a sprawl of arms and legs. He lay still.

Pilar cried out in concern as she swung down from her own horse. The mare danced at the end of her reins, her eyes blaring with nervousness as she tried to follow the roan that was galloping away back down the trail. Pilar spoke to the mare in soothing tones, dragging her toward Vicente. She went down on her knees beside him. Refugio's brother shuddered, then began to rock back and forth in agony. There was a twisted grimace on his features, and he was pale beneath the new tan of his face.

"What is it?" Pilar asked in urgent tones. "Where are you hurt?"

Vicente gave a sudden, wheezing gasp, then began to breathe in heaves. He stopped writhing. "Breath—knocked—out of me," he managed.

Relief brought a low laugh from Pilar's own throat.

She reach out her hand to help Vicente sit up. "Are you sure that's all?"

"I think—so. Feel stupid—getting thrown."

Pilar opened her mouth to reassure him, but was cut short by a shout. It was Charro. He was sprinting toward his horse, yelling as he ran. At first she thought it was the joy of triumph that moved him, then she saw it was fear.

The great long-horned bull was charging. It was charging, but not at Charro. Something about the rearing of Vicente's horse, or Pilar's being on foot, or perhaps even the flapping of her skirts in the wind, had attracted the enraged animal's attention. Now it was lumbering straight at them. Its hoofs made a dull thundering on the ground, throwing up clods of dirt and bits of grass and blue wildflowers behind it. Its horns shone in the sun, glinting at the needle-sharp tips. The muscles in its powerful shoulders bunched and rippled. It snorted with distended nostrils, and there was death in its blaring eyes.

Pilar jumped to her feet and caught Vicente's arm to drag him upright. She whirled to her mare, but the horse sidled, neighing in terror. It took both Pilar and Vicente to hold her steady. She motioned to him to go first. Vicente, recovering at speed under the impetus of necessity, pulled himself into the saddle, then reached down to Pilar. She looked over her shoulder as she was hauled up to the pillion. The bull was so close she could see the brindle hairs of his forelock. She had barely caught Vicente's waist when he swung the mare around and kicked her into a gallop back toward the crest of the rise.

It was too late. The bull slammed into the belly of the mare. The horse screamed. The jarring impact broke Pilar's grasp and sent her hurtling to the ground. She lay for a stunned instant with her cheek pillowed on stinging grass, then she whipped over, scrambling to her knees.

The mare was shrieking as the grunting bull harried her. The smell of blood was in the air, pouring from a gored place in the horse's side. Vicente was still in the saddle, trying to avoid the bull, trying to lead the maddened animal away from where Pilar lay. He threw her a frightened glance. "Run!" he yelled. "Run!"

"No, don't run!" Charro shouted as his horse bore down on her at a hard gallop. He was swinging his braided rope above his head so that an open loop was forming, growing larger. "Don't run! Don't move!"

There was nowhere to run, no shelter that she might reach before the bull could catch her. Pilar stood still, while vivid in her mind was the memory of that moment when she had felt the bull's long horn plunge into the soft belly of the mare like a thick, sharp spear.

Charro's rope whipped through the air. The wide loop settled over the bull's horns and was jerked tight around its neck. Charro gave the rope a swift turn about the horn of his Tejas saddle as his horse jolted to a halt and sat back on its haunches. Vicente, free of the bull, rode the stumbling mare a short distance away, where she crumpled slowly forward and fell onto her side. Vicente jumped free, then whirled to face Charro.

The bull was kicking and huffing and bellowing, fighting the rope while foam dripped from its mouth. The braided rope flapped and snapped taut again and again, twisting with the strain. Charro could not hold the animal for long, that much was plain. What was needed was another horseman, another rope.

The horseman came over the rise, riding fast, leading Vicente's young stallion behind him. It was Refugio. He took in the scene at a glance and swept forward, already loosening the lariat at his own saddle horn.

In that moment the braided rope holding the bull

snapped. The end flew back, wrapping around the head of Charro's mount. The horse reared with forefeet pawing the air. The bull staggered back as it was released, then gathered itself and wheeled away from the rearing horse and thundering hoofs of the approaching horseman. Lowering his head, the animal pawed the ground once, twice, then charged straight at Pilar.

Refugio loosed the reins of Vicente's young stallion and swerved away from his brother in the same smooth movement. Riding low, already reaching, he raced toward Pilar.

Man and beast, shoulder to shoulder, they bore down on her as in some fabled contest of right and wrong, carrying with them power and fury. Pilar watched them come and steeled herself to motionlessness while the sun caught gold gleams from the loosened tendrils of her hair and the wind fluttered her skirts like signal flags. The smell of trampled earth and grass, horses and blood, was in the air, and the pure blue of the wildflowers flowed at her feet. Behind her the cows bawled and shifted this way and that. Somewhere, as if from far away, she could hear Charro shouting, his voice cracking with strain.

Then Refugio was there. His arm caught her at the ribs with a grip of iron. She felt the tug as a horn ripped her skirt, then she was hoisted upward. She clung with her fingers clenched in the folds of Refugio's shirt and her face buried against his shoulder. He held her that way for a breathless instant before, merciless in his strength, he dragged her across the saddle in front of him. Controlling his mount with hard hands and rigid thigh muscles, he sent the horse wheeling around, leaping back the way he had come. They were joined by Charro and Vicente, and the four of them hurled themselves up the slope. At the top they looked back. The bull, still trailing the rope, had not stopped running. Gathering his cows, he was harrying them down the plain.

They drew up, letting the horses blow. "You could only have been more welcome just then, my friend," Charro said, "if you had been Jude, saint of lost causes himself. It was miraculous."

There was an edge of what might have been resentment or embarrassment to Charro's voice. Refugio's features stilled as he registered it, yet his voice was even as he answered. "There was no miracle. I was riding after you when I found Vicente's horse. Unless Vicente had become a pilgrim, doing penance on foot, it meant trouble."

"I was thrown," Vicente explained, "though it was no great matter. But I don't think Pilar's mare can live. Someone should go back and—and put her out of her pain."

"Someone?" Refugio's gaze was unsympathetic as it rested on his brother.

Vicente's face paled, but he said, "You were speaking of penances, I think? Yes, I will do it."

"I'll come with you," Charro said shortly. "I have to fetch our beef anyway."

They swung their mounts and rode back down toward the plain. Refugio did not move, but held his horse still in the middle of the track. Turning her head to look at him, Pilar found that he was staring sightlessly after his brother and his friend. His face was rigid, the skin drawn tightly over the bones so they stood out in relief. The veins rose in ropelike blue-gray prominence across his hand where he held the reins, though his grasp upon her was now as gentle and cradling as a grandmother holding a newborn.

A shiver ran over her, followed by another, and another. They were beyond her control, the direct result of delayed fear. She closed her eyes for a long instant.

When she opened them again, Refugio was looking down at her. His eyes were shadowed and his mouth held the suggestion of a smile. "The wrong gallant again," he said.

"I'm not complaining."

"No, you would never be so impolite."

"Or so insulting."

"You can't insult me, my love; it's an impossibility."

"I could thank you," she said.

"Oh, yes, any way you please."

"But you wouldn't care."

"Do you want me to care?" His voice carried soft doubt.

She shifted her shoulders. "As you please."

He bent his head to brush her hair with his lips, and his gaze was pensive. "But that's the question, isn't it? When will I be allowed to please myself?"

She thought she knew what he meant, but could not be sure. It took courage to seek the answer. "Why do you say that?"

"Manifold exasperations and my own too obvious human nature."

"That isn't a reason," she said in acerbic reproof. The exchange, she found, had calmed her as it redirected her thoughts and emotions. She wondered if he had intended it.

"It is," he said, then added as if it was of only slight interest, "and another might be because I discovered on this momentous morning that Don Esteban is on the trail behind us."

She stiffened against him as dismay flooded through her. "You mean he's following us?"

"As fast as he can ride."

"Why? Why would he do it?"

"To bring us grief, no doubt, and because he has a soul lashed by pride. And possibly because we have something, still, that he wants."

"But—what could that be?"

"What else, my dove," he asked in quiet tones, "except you?"

CHAPTER 18

$\mathcal{D}$on Esteban had left Pilar behind in Spain because he thought her discredited, lost to decency and any society that mattered. The situation had not changed for her that she could see. That being so, why would he pursue her now? No, Refugio was wrong. Or if he was not wrong, he had either been attempting to distract her with his suggestion or was trying to conceal something. She did not like to think it could be the last; she did not want to distrust him. Still, he was a bandit, a man used to living by his wits, taking any advantage offered, avoiding the law and most rules of polite conduct. He had a code of his own, yes, but it seemed more flexible than not. There was no way to decide, then, if it was something Refugio had done that was causing her stepfather to follow them in this way.

Of course, if she was right that Don Esteban had twice tried to have Refugio killed, her stepfather's purpose in coming after them might be to finish the task. Perhaps he had lost faith in whoever he had entrusted with the job, or again, might only have lost contact. Regardless, would he really sacrifice his comfort and endanger his own life for the satisfaction of defeating an enemy? Was the hate that drove him that virulent?

The fact that he was back there behind them somewhere cast a dark dreariness over Pilar's spirits. She had begun to hope, and his presence was proof that it had been a useless exercise. It had seemed to her that the vast distances in leagues and time that separated them from Spain, when added to the scant numbers of people in this unending wilderness, must give the band and herself some kind of protection. It seemed possible that the Tejas country could become a sanctuary where they might all start anew. As the long days had fallen away behind her, she had put aside thoughts of riches and revenge and occupied her mind with dreams. They had not been grandiose or even particularly unusual, those dreams, but giving them up was painful.

The question of why Don Esteban was continuing to hound them remained with her, nagging at her mind. There had been little time to discuss it with the others, however, for they had been traveling at speed since the moment Refugio had broken the news to them. It was not just the pursuit by Don Esteban that gave impetus to their progress, but the intelligence that he was not alone. He had joined the Indian traders, those who had been recommended to them in Natchitoches. Since the traders were keeping to the El Camino Real rather than following the more usual northern trade routes, it seemed probable Don Esteban had enlisted these men in his cause. The traders, according to Refugio, numbered a half-dozen men, all well armed. The band would fight this force if it proved necessary, but they preferred to at least choose their own ground.

It was at a rest stop late in the afternoon that Pilar was finally able to ask some of the questions that troubled her. Vicente was wiping down his horse with a handful of dried grass when she came up behind him. She spoke quietly, without the preamble of polite chitchat.

"Tell me the truth, did you really leave the casket of gold behind at Don Esteban's house?"

Refugio's brother straightened from brushing his mount's withers. "I told you so, didn't I? Why would I lie?"

"Gain," she said simply.

"I have no interest in such things."

"Oh, please! Few are immune to the appeal of gold."

"I know that, but still I did not take it."

"Was there anyone else who could have?"

Uneasiness rippled over his features, which had so much the look of Refugio's, though without the chiseled firmness of maturity. "There might have been."

"Enrique? Baltasar? Charro?"

"Any of them, I suppose."

"Did you see anything that would make you think they did?"

He shook his head in slow consideration. "Nothing. But what makes you think it's just the gold the don's after? It might be me."

She did not speak for a moment as she considered whether what she would say might be wounding. "Surely you were only a pawn?"

"Probably. Still, Don Esteban hates being tested at anything, hates it intensely. I wondered many times if he was sane."

"Because of the branding?"

He touched the scar on his cheek as if soothing the memory of long-vanished pain. "Also because of the threats he used to make, to castrate me and send the—the results to Refugio; to sell me into North Africa, where I would be put to use in a harem serving peculiar tastes; to feed me a slow poison for the pleasure of watching my death."

"Dear God," she whispered. Her distress was not just for the nature of the threats, or even Vicente's endurance of the fear that must have accompanied them. It was also for the knowledge that Refugio, during the voyage on board the *Celestina*, must have guessed what Don Esteban was capable of doing, and had been forced to live with his dread until the moment he had found Vicente in New Orleans. It accounted for much.

Finally, she said, "To have injured you would have been to lessen your value as a hostage for Refugio's good behavior."

"Yes, so long as he was capable of thinking that clearly."

"You truly think he's mad, then?"

"I think it's possible that his reasons for following us, for doing anything, may not be rational."

It was an explanation that removed a great many doubts. Pilar did not quite accept it, and yet there was in it a certain undeniable comfort.

The others had accepted the news of Don Esteban's pursuit according to their natures. Baltasar and Enrique swore, one with resignation, the other with disgust. Charro wanted to go back and set up an ambuscade along the trail to get rid of the threat for good, a plan Refugio refused as too risky. Isabel was inclined to cry, while Doña Luisa developed a hunted look and was the first upon her horse when the order was given to mount.

Weathered by sun and wind, callused in places that did not bear examination, they put the leagues behind them. They faced with stolid purpose the knowledge of the long way that still lay ahead. Whether by determination or sheer, dogged persistence, they kept ahead of Don Esteban's party. What that meant was difficult to say; even if they outdistanced him now, they must still confront him when they reached San Antonio de Bexar. At least the likelihood of being surprised somewhere on the spreading plains became more remote.

They were riding single file one morning along a narrow track through a dense, pale green ocean of rough shrubs Charro called mesquite. The Tejas-country native had gone on ahead to scout the way out of the thicket, and to make sure that there were no wandering herds of cattle ahead to dispute their passage along the trail. The drumming sound of hoofbeats, coming fast, was the signal for his return. When he came into view around the bend in the track, they saw that he had lost his hat, his face was red with exertion, and there were red trickles of blood on his hands and on one cheek. As he pulled up before them in a swirl of dust, the others drew up also, bracing themselves for more trouble.

"Don't tell me," Enrique drawled, "that you met another bull, and this one makes the other look like an infant?"

"Not longhorns," Charro gasped, dipping his chin as he tried to catch his breath. "Apache!"

Refugio, who had been bringing up the rear, trotted his horse forward. His voice incisive, he asked, "How many?"

"I'm not sure. All I saw was their sign. No prints of women and children. It's a war party. Twenty braves, maybe more."

"You think they know we're behind them?" Baltasar asked, his large brow furrowed.

"Not behind them, but beside them. They're riding parallel to us. It's their way."

There was silence, until Doña Luisa spoke in shrill disbelief. "You mean they are keeping up with us? Watching us?"

"Exactly." Charro's blue eyes were shadowed and his voice grim.

"We'll all be killed!" the noblewoman cried.

Enrique placed his hand on her arms, which were clasped about his waist, as if to reassure her. Doña Luisa rested her forehead against his back a brief moment before straightening with a furtive look around her to see if anyone had noticed.

Pilar watched Refugio; they all did in one way or another. Don Esteban was behind them and an Apache war party was shadowing them. There were wild cattle to contend with and endless leagues of country where there would be no help forthcoming if anyone should fall ill or be injured. In the midst of these many dangers, someone must decide what they were going to do. That someone, they knew instinctively, was the bandit leader.

Refugio eased his position in his saddle, then squared his shoulders. Turning to Charro, he asked, "When are the Apaches likely to attack?"

"Could be any second. Or at dawn tomorrow. Or midday next week. Or even not at all. It depends on what the war chief decides, and if the warriors with him are inclined to follow his suggestions."

"It's that arbitrary?"

"Leaders among the Apache, including war chiefs, rise to their places because of proven ability and sound judgment. If either of these things seem doubtful, no one follows. They are finished."

The two men stared at each other for long moments. There was between them a subtle undercurrent, a suggestion of significance in the exchange of information that was not apparent on the surface. Charro seemed to have gained stature since entering his home territory, and with it an extra measure of assurance. It seemed that new confidence might incline him to challenge Refugio's leadership, though not, perhaps, at the present moment.

Refugio looked away from the others, his gaze unseeing as he surveyed the finely cut foliage of the mesquite surrounding them. At last he said, "I see no option except to ride on. The Apaches know this terrain better than we do. They outnumber us three to one, or more. If we mount an attack in this kind of country, they would most likely vanish into the scrub at the first sign the fight was going against them, then reappear when we least expect it. If we tarry too long, Don Esteban will be treading on our heels, and while the possibility of leading him into an Apache trap is enticing, I doubt he would take the bait."

"You think he knows we are close ahead of him?" Doña Luisa asked.

Refugio gave her a brief glance. "We have been making little effort to cover our tracks, since there is only one route. It even seems possible the don is aware of the Apaches on our trail, since he is traveling with men familiar with the countryside and the Indians. It could be he's hoping the Apaches will finish us."

Doña Luisa shuddered, falling silent.

"That leaves advancing then," Charro said. "Do we simply wait for the Apaches to attack?"

"Unless you have an idea to suggest that's worth the hazard to eight lives, including three women."

"But Refugio," Isabel said urgently as she nudged her horse forward, "if you are allowing the women to keep you from acting, you know you must not."

He turned his head to look at her, and there was a hint of softness in his gaze. "How can it be prevented?"

Isabel shook her head. "I don't know, unless you stop feeling and only think."

"I'm tired of doing that. It may be I will leave it to Charro." He turned to the other man. "Well?"

Charro hesitated no more than an instant, staring at Refugio with bafflement in his eyes. Then he said, "We ride."

What followed over the next week was a marathon of stamina and wits and ragged, protesting nerves. The band slept little. A double watch was mounted on the horses; it was a favorite tactic of the Indians to leave their prey afoot and therefore easier to overcome. Every inch of their advance was carefully studied, as well as every foot of their back trail.

Perhaps because of their caution, the Apaches seemed aware of their knowledge of their presence. The Indian warriors began to show themselves for brief moments, flitting across the trail, ghosting through the outer darkness beyond the campfire at night, or else allowing themselves to be silhouetted against the skyline after the mesquite thicket was left behind them. The tactic was wearing, for every glimpse could as easily presage an attack as not.

Fear could only last so long, however, before the body rebelled and numbed that response. Exhaustion also did its work, so that after a while they all rode in stoic silence, watchful but once more enduring.

One of the hardest things was losing the illusion of freedom. There had been such pleasure in it, while it lasted, that its lack was painful. Pilar hated the sense of being hemmed in on both sides, of being contained and controlled and observed. Like Refugio, she often wondered in despair if she would ever be able to please herself, ever be able to come and go without trepidation, or build a life solely to suit herself.

They had stopped one evening in a small grove of scrub oaks, the only protection on what had once more become open plains with a hauntingly familiar look of Spain. The shade was welcome, for it had grown hot and dry as spring advanced into early summer. Flies droned around them with a heavy, indolent sound. The leaves overhead whispered in the constant breeze. The grove had long been a favorite stopping place, for the charred remains of old campfires were scattered here and there, and they found a rusted breastplate half buried in the sandy earth.

Pilar and Isabel sat somewhat apart from the others, sharing a seat on a tree trunk felled by some long-past storm while they ate their late meal of beans and bacon. After a time Isabel sent Pilar a glance from under her near colorless lashes.

"Forgive me if I pry into what doesn't concern me," the girl said, her voice soft, "but is there something wrong between you and Refugio?"

"Wrong? What do you mean?" Pilar put a piece of biscuit into her mouth and chewed it slowly.

"You hardly ever speak to each other, almost never touch. You sleep beside him every night and he covers you with his blanket, but if he does more, no one can tell."

Pilar gave the other girl a long look as she swallowed. Her voice cool, she said, "Should anyone be able to tell?"

"You are angry because you think I'm prying. I swear it's only that I'm concerned, as a friend." Isabel tossed what was left of her biscuit away in the direction of a hovering bird before she went on. "I thought you cared for him; it seemed so on the ship."

"A great deal has changed since then."

"Has it? How?" Isabel persisted.

"How can you ask? With the fire, the voyage upriver, Don Esteban, and then the Apaches, there has been neither time nor strength for indulging in . . . lovemaking."

"But would you, if there had not been all these things?"

"What do you care?" Pilar asked in hard tones. "You are only concerned about Refugio. Do you think I should serve him in bed simply because I am with him?"

"It isn't bed I was thinking of," Isabel said in soft reproof. "He needs someone. He needs you."

"I haven't seen he needs anyone, least of all me."

"You are mistaken. You saved his life on the ship. He willed himself to live because of you."

"Don't be ridiculous. All I did was force him to abandon his pose of illness."

"You think so? There was more to it than that, much

more. I don't know what you did, but you changed him. He isn't the same, not at all. I told you once that he is a man more sensitive than most, though he has learned to control it for his own protection. Because of you, he is living much closer to the edge than ever before, and the reason is because he is permitting himself to feel more than since his father and his sister died. You can't desert him now."

"He has you to be his champion. Why would he need anyone else?"

"I . . . don't know the answer to that. I used to think he feared that his love would bring me harm because I might be used as a hostage to entrap him. Or else that he was holding himself aloof because he had nothing to offer except a name that had been dishonored. Sometimes I even told myself that he thought I was not strong enough to bear the great power of the love he had locked inside him. It was all foolishness. The truth, as I have seen since you came, was that he could not feel for me what I felt for him."

There was such pain in the other girl's face that compassion rose inside Pilar. With it was an answering pain. "It may be," she said, "that he feels nothing for me, either. Have you considered that?"

Isabel shook her head. "You have hurt each other, I know. There are things that he has had to do that are hard to understand, much less forgive. He makes a sacrifice of himself so easily that it sometimes seems he doesn't care. That isn't true. You must be careful not to hurt him anymore."

Isabel spoke so logically that it was difficult to remember that she sometimes told artistic lies, that she lived in a world of her own fantasies. Isabel saw things not as they were, but as she wanted them to be. To believe what such a person said would be stupid. Yet for a brief instant Pilar wanted desperately to believe her.

Out of the irritation caused by her own weakness, she said, "What of Baltasar? You are hurting him, too, with this infatuation for Refugio."

"I know, but I can't help it. I didn't ask him to love me. I don't know why he does."

"You could help by not talking about Refugio as if he was your savior."

"But he was!" Isabel cried.

"Was he really, or is that just a story you made up? And even if he did save you in some way, must you talk about it in front of Baltasar? Can't you think of his feelings, even if you can't return them?"

Tears rose, glistening in Isabel's eyes. "I don't hurt him on purpose, it just happens."

"That doesn't make it easier for him to bear."

"I know, I know. But sometimes I have to talk about what Refugio did just to make him notice me for a small moment. Refugio dislikes it as much as Baltasar, I can tell, but I can't help it."

Maybe Isabel couldn't help it, Pilar thought, just as the girl couldn't seem to stop weaving her tales of being swept away from an existence of misery and humiliation by Refugio. People did strange things to soothe the hurting they felt inside, no matter what the cause of it might be.

It was a quiet night. No coyotes howled. The wind whispered in the leaves of the scrub oaks. The piece of a moon sailing overhead was pale and kept its face turned away. Pilar lay wakeful for a long time, though she slept finally with her cheek pillowed on Refugio's arm.

The Apaches attacked at dawn.

They rode down on them over the waving grass of the plains just as the light was turning from dark blue to gray. Charro and Enrique were saddling the horses, which were tied to the trunks of the stunted oaks they had camped underneath. Baltasar was making up the packs for the mules that had been brought in but were still hobbled. The three women were picking up and folding the bedrolls to be placed in the packs, while Vicente scrubbed out the breakfast skillet with sand. Refugio had already mounted and ridden out a short distance. It was he who saw the Indians coming, their bobbing black forms silhouetted against the skyline. Whipping his mount around, he sent it galloping back toward the camp.

They had made their plans, knowing it might be only a matter of time before they must defend themselves. Baltasar, the moment he saw Refugio turn and race toward them and heard the distant, pipping yells, pulled out his musket and shot the nearest mule. Charro dragged the other one into place and killed it. They threw the loaded pack saddles into the space between the dead animals, forming a bulwark. While Baltasar reloaded at speed, Pilar and Vicente yanked the extra powder and musket balls from the packs, then Vicente took up their extra musket. Isabel dug out the two rolls of bandaging they had with them, and she and Pilar laid everything out on a hastily spread cloth. Within seconds they were throwing themselves down behind the makeshift rampart.

Everyone except Doña Luisa. The noblewoman had been instructed in what she should do. It was her job to be sure their water barrel was conveniently to hand and not exposed to fire. Instead, she was standing with her hands clenched and her wide eyes fastened on the swiftly approaching enemy.

"Luisa!" Enrique called. "Get down!"

She turned toward him an instant, but swung back immediately toward the Indians. Her face was pale and her lips writhed in a soundless tirade of impotent rage.

Enrique leaped to his feet and ran to catch the woman's

arm. He dragged her bodily toward the barricade of dead mules, shoving her down beside him. "Get down, I said," he told her in rough tones. "You are to reload. Remember it, and think of nothing else if you value your life."

Doña Luisa gave him an angry stare, but there was also a degree of comprehension in her face that had not been there before. Looking around her, she found the water barrel and rolled it closer behind the nearest pack saddle.

The shrieks and yells of the Apaches had a thin, eerie sound in the cool morning air. It was not a large war party; still, their painted faces, streaked with white and black and ocher, were fearsome in the pale light. Five or six of them cradled muskets across their bodies. One warrior shouldered his and fired at Refugio as he raced ahead of them. The sound of the shot boomed across the rolling ground, though the ball went wide.

Refugio crouched lower over his mount's neck, looking back over his shoulder. The horse was running flat out, his eyes wild. Refugio looked back at the barricade, then swerved hard to his left out of the band's line of fire. A scattering of arrows whistled after him, burying themselves in the ground to one side of him. More arrows followed, whistling in every direction, an arcing fusillade that fell around the barricade in a deadly shower.

At that moment another Apache raised his musket. He held it steady against the motion of his horse, then got off a shot. The blue-gray smoke billowed back over his shoulder. In the same instant Charro gave a shout and the guns of the men of the band roared out in unison. Refugio was struck. The straw hat he wore was whipped from his head. He weaved, trying to stay upright, then fell in boneless grace to land facedown in the grass some thirty yards away.

Beyond Refugio two Apaches threw up their arms and catapulted backward off their horses, and a third reeled back before flinging himself forward to hug his mount's neck. The others came on, whooping and firing and brandishing lances.

Pilar, frantically pushing a patch and ball into Charro's musket, spared the attackers no more than a glance before twisting around to look toward where Refugio lay. He was stirring, lifting his head, trying to drag himself toward the barricade. Pilar rose to her knees only to be pulled down once more by Charro. Beside her Isabel was screaming, the sound grating with grief and fear. As Charro called in impatient haste for his musket, Pilar turned back to thrust it into his hands.

The band fired again at near point-blank range. Two more Apaches were flung backward off their mounts. The rest wheeled in ragged formation, pounding away to their right past the bulwark. They circled in a wide arc, streaming one behind the other in wild and reckless abandon.

"Refugio," Isabel moaned, struggling up from beside Baltasar the instant the way was clear, her eyes blinded by the tears that overflowed down her splotched face. The big man tried to hold her, but she wrenched her arm from his grasp. She put her foot on the top of a pack saddle and jumped over it, running toward where Refugio was hauling himself along. Vicente also threw down his musket and leaped up, sprinting after Isabel. Charro was reloading his own gun, his attention on the Indians galloping in a wide circle just out of range. Pilar rolled away from him and came to her feet. Lifting her skirts, she cleared the barricade to follow Vicente.

Isabel was kneeling over Refugio, sobbing as she dabbed at the blood that gleamed wet and red in his hair. Vicente, as he reached his brother, caught one arm, trying to help him to his feet. Plunging forward the last few steps, Pilar grasped the other to draw Refugio upward with desperate strength.

The Apaches were charging again. The ground vibrated underfoot with the pounding of their horses' hoofs. Their shrill cries pierced the air, making the hair rise on the back of Pilar's neck. They were moving so slowly, she and Vicente and Refugio. They started and stopped and blundered over the ground. Refugio's legs would not quite sustain him, so that he staggered, keeping halfway erect only by fiercely sustained will. Isabel, trying to hold his hand, kept getting in the way.

Abruptly, Isabel released him. "His hat," she cried, and whirled, running back the way they had come.

Pilar swung her head to stare back over her shoulder. The Indians were bearing down on them, screaming and yelling, firing wildly with bow and musket. Their faces were strained copper masks daubed with paint. More naked than not, riding without saddles or bits, they seemed like demonic creatures part man, part horse, and wholly malevolent.

Isabel paid the Apaches no more heed than if they had been a part of the band returning from a morning ride. There was smile on her face as she ran, and joy in her red-rimmed eyes. She reached the hat and bent to pick it up. Turning with it in her hand, she plucked at the hole in its crown where the musket ball had torn it from Refugio's head. The wind flapped her skirts around her legs and sent long tendrils of her hair, teased from the knot on her nape, flying about her face like spiderwebs loosened from their moorings. She started toward them at a slow amble.

Baltasar was shouting Isabel's name, rising to his feet. Charro and Enrique stood up to pull Refugio over the bulwark of the mule carcasses and lower him to the ground. They threw themselves down beside him then, lifting their muskets. Vicente scuttled back to his place. Pilar went down on her belly beside Refugio, trying to look at his wound and keep her head down at the same time.

"Never mind," he said, his voice husky but trenchant. "Where is my musket? Help me into position."

He did not wait for her to comply, but twisted around, looking for a gun. It was then he saw Isabel. "Dear God," he said in soft beseechment. "I ask you, dear God, why?"

Baltasar was still hollering and waving. "Isabel! Look behind you for the love of God!"

The girl heard and started, then turned her head. Her footsteps faltered before she broke into a stumbling run. Baltasar, swearing, leaped over the barricade and started toward her. Abruptly he stopped as a flying arrow came whining down, thudding into him. He bent double as it shafted into his side and through his body so the barb appeared in the back. Slowly, he dropped to his knees.

Isabel screamed. She went on screaming as the Indians thundered down upon her. She was buffeted this way and that, spinning around. The hat was knocked from her hands and trampled, but, miraculously, she did not fall. Dazed, she staggered behind the attackers with her hair sliding from its pins, drifting in her face.

The band opened fire; they had no choice. The powder smoke, blue and acrid, obscured the view for an instant. Then as the wind whipped it away, they saw the Indians swerving away again, while another Apache lay twitching on the ground and a second was being held on his horse by a companion.

The Apaches wheeled, riding at breakneck speed, bending low to snatch up their dead from where they had fallen and haul them across their laps.

Then Isabel's screams trailed to a despairing moan.

There was a warrior riding down on her. He swooped low and caught her hair, twisting it around his hand as he heaved her upward and across his thighs. She dangled with her head down, her arms flopping as the warrior kicked his horse into headlong flight.

Baltasar bellowed out in grief and rage. Charro swore, rising to one knee. Enrique squeezed Doña Luisa's shoulder as she sat white and appalled. Vicente looked sick, but his lips moved in silent prayers.

Refugio reached for the musket that lay, fresh charged, in Vicente's lax grasp. He steadied it on the rump of the dead mule and sighted at the back of the retreating warrior. Carefully, he squeezed the trigger.

The musket boomed. The Indian flinched at the sound, but only bent low over his captive, lying along his horse's neck as he sped away.

Slowly Refugio lowered his head, resting it on the hot musket barrel as he closed his eyes.

CHAPTER 19

They stood listening to the echoes of receding hoofbeats and staring at each other. It did not seem possible that it could be over just like that. It was beyond belief that Isabel could be gone, that the Apaches had taken her with them. Everything had happened so quickly, one terrible thing piling on another, that they could not seem to accept them.

"I should have gone back for her," Vicente murmured almost to himself. "We should have run out to help her. We should have saved her."

"How?" Enrique asked, the word blunt. "Just one second's less attention, less firepower, and the savages might have overrun us. They could be happily mutilating us right now."

"She did it herself, poor thing," Doña Luisa added. "Once she turned back for the hat, there was nothing anyone could have done for her."

"For a hat," Pilar said softly. "She went back for a hat."

Baltasar groaned and bent to the ground with his hands pressed to the side of his belly where blood oozed around the protruding shaft of the arrow. There was horrified anguish in the sound that came from him.

The reminder of his injury jarred them from their dazed introspection into frantic action, as if it would compensate for the helplessness they felt over Isabel. Pilar swung toward the big man, touching his arm to urge him to lie down on his good side. Vicente and Charro came forward to help him stretch out, while Doña Luisa made pads of the bandaging. The two men sliced the barbed head from the arrow and jerked it free. Enrique, standing ready, quickly applied the thick bandage pads to both sides. He held them while Doña Luisa, flinching yet valiant under Enrique's sardonic gaze, wrapped more bandaging tightly around them. The wound was ugly, but Baltasar was tough. Only time would tell whether the arrow had torn anything vital.

Pilar left the others to their task while she turned to Refugio. He had not moved or spoken since he had fired the last shot. He was breathing, however, his chest rising and falling in a steady, if fast, rhythm. With a pot of water in one hand and a cloth and bandage roll in the other, she knelt beside him. Reaching out, she placed her hand on his shoulder.

Refugio raised his head and lifted his lashes to stare at her from heavy bloodshot eyes. He sustained her clear gaze only a moment before he lowered his own. Still, he pushed himself up to lie against a saddle pack, and made no protest as she washed the blood and bits of grass from the furrow in his scalp. The ball had struck at an angle, glancing off the skull. Though the bleeding had been copious at first, it had now nearly stopped. She thought he probably had a headache and would for some time.

There was something odd about the wound, however. She touched it gently with her fingers, drawing back the hair growing on each side to see better, as she tried to decide what it was. Refugio moved restlessly under her ministrations, drawing away from her. Pilar turned to reach for the roll of bandaging. In that moment she knew what was wrong.

She sat back on her heels, her hands clenched tight on

the bandage roll as she watched the slow seep of Refugio's dark red blood from the furrow. It was deepest toward the front, closest to his face. It could not have been made by a shot fired from behind him. Slowly, she swung her head to look at the other men, at Charro and Baltasar and Enrique, and even Vicente. It had to be one of them, for the women had touched the muskets only to load them.

It could not have been an accident; they were all too expert, too drilled in accuracy and the importance of not wasting a shot. Which one was capable of this thing? And why? Before God, why?

Refugio was staring at her, his gaze commanding, insistent. She met his gray eyes, and her own were stark with knowledge, intent with cogent thought. She could see the strain of the past days and of this new injury in the pared-down refinement of his features and the new lines around his eyes. A pervading ache began somewhere deep inside her, rising until she had to grind her teeth against it. How long could he go on? she wondered. How long could she, with this knowledge inside her?

He gave an infinitesimal shake of his head, gesturing with one hand toward the gash. His voice so soft only she could hear, he said, "Cover it. There is cleanliness and decency in that, and none in anything else."

She hesitated a long moment, her lips firm as she resisted the force of his implacable will. It seemed, however, that there was nothing to be done if he would not himself make an accusation. Taking up the bandaging, she made a pad and held it in place while she wound the bandaging slowly around his head. When she was done, he caught her fingers and raised them to his lips. Pilar was moved, though she knew, even as she felt the warm touch, that the gesture was one of gratitude and nothing more.

Charro was also injured, a graze from an arrow in the fleshy part of his calf, though he tended it himself with Vicente's help. Enrique, finished with Baltasar, went to see to their horses. He reported back that they were safe there among the stunted oaks, the only wounds were the scrapes and nicks they had sustained from their own rearing and plunging at the end of their ropes. Leading out his own mare, soothing her nervousness with quiet words and soft caresses, he swung into the saddle and set out to see if he could come up with Refugio's horse, which had bolted.

Doña Luisa called after him. "Don't go far!"

"I won't," he said, waving over his shoulder as if that expression of concern was an everyday occurrence.

He was as good as his word. He returned in less than half an hour, leading Refugio's stallion by its halter. The moment he walked into the camp, it was as if a signal had been given. Baltasar, struggling up to one elbow from where he lay panting against the pain in his side, looked at them all one by one. Finally, he spoke.

"All right," he said. "What are we going to do?"

No one answered. They looked at Refugio, but he was staring out over the plains.

"We have to do something," the big man said, a note of pleading underlying the words. "We can't just let them have Isabel."

Enrique turned to Charro. "What is the war party likely to do now? Do you think they may be back?"

Charro lifted his shoulders. "It's possible. Then again, they may keep riding. There's no way to tell."

"What—what will they do to her?" Doña Luisa frowned to cover her apprehension as she asked the question.

"Maybe nothing except make a slave of her, or a wife

if the warrior who took her grows enamored of her."

Enrique took him up sharply. "But you don't think that will happen."

"They may also stop as soon as they think its safe and . . . take turns."

"And then?"

"And then take her with them back to their camp if she survives, and if she doesn't make too much trouble. Otherwise, they may cut her throat. Or again, they may save her for special torture in retaliation for their defeat here."

Enrique swore. Vicente, sitting with his hands dangling between his bent knees, turned even more pale.

"We're wasting time talking about it," Baltasar growled. "Let's ride after them."

"It would be to risk the lives of all, including the other women." It was Enrique who spoke the warning.

"That doesn't matter," Pilar said quickly.

"But it does," Charro answered, his voice quiet as his gaze rested on her. "It matters to us."

Baltasar spoke again, his voice dogged. "If we can't catch up with them before they reach their main camp or their village, it will be no use. There's no possible way we could sneak in among them, and to attack would be like stirring up an ant hill. We have to go now."

Enrique looked from Charro to Baltasar, then turned his seeking gaze on Refugio. The acrobat gave a backward jerk of his head with a brow raised in query. "Well, my friend? What shall it be?"

Refugio, sitting contemplating his hands, looked up. His voice quietly scathing, he said, "Why is it that I am always presented with the weighing of life and death? Is there no one else who wants to share the failures of good intentions gone awry, or who will bear the guilt of injuries unanticipated, unintended? Someone else take a portion of regret. Someone else decide."

"You are the leader," Enrique answered, as if that was enough.

"I say we go," Baltasar said in tones gruff with concern.

No one else spoke, nor did they meet Refugio's searching glance.

"My gratitude then, Baltasar," their leader said gravely. "It seems we go."

They rode out, following the tracks of the Apaches, less than a quarter hour later. They traveled light, after burying the pack saddles with their supplies among the scrub oaks. If they were successful, they would come back for them. If not, they would have no use for them. In either case, they did not need the extra weight now.

Doña Luisa had her own mount, the one Isabel usually rode. There had been some discussion of leaving her and Pilar behind, but it was deemed too dangerous without a strong guard, and there was not enough of them to take such precautions and still have a chance of rescuing Isabel.

The pace Refugio set was relentless, harder than any they had so far endured. The only reason they were able to keep to it was the certain knowledge that the Apaches were riding just as hard, if not more so. The weeks they had spent in the saddle showed their worth, for none of them were unduly strained, at least in these early hours. How Doña Luisa was standing up under it, Pilar was not sure. For herself, she was determined to bear with anything that the injured men among them were able to tolerate.

They knew that what they were doing was foolhardy to the point of madness; there was no question of that. Regardless, they felt compelled to do something. They had all come so far together, had suffered so much, that it would have been a betrayal to go on without Isabel. No one voiced this truth, but the fact that they felt it was obvious in the lack of real opposition to the quest.

Thinking of what they were actually doing could make the hair rise on Pilar's head. She tried not to think about it. She only set her face forward and concentrated on staying in the saddle, staying abreast of the others. Bodily aches and discomforts were something to be ignored; there were other things more important.

She could not help wondering, however, what Isabel must be feeling, the terror and the pain, the humiliation and despair. Would she expect them to come after her? Would she be watching for them? Isabel knew Refugio was injured, and also Baltasar. She might not think them able to make the attempt. Moreover, she had appeared so confused just before she was taken, and so nearly unconscious afterward, that she might be incapable of realizing anything.

Poor Isabel. There were some people for whom things never went quite right, who never found their way to peace, much less happiness. They always wanted something more, something else, something they could not have. It was a lamentable way to live, but not one that could always be avoided. Pilar was beginning to fear that she herself was becoming like Isabel, always yearning.

They reached the Indian encampment just after dark. It was the smoke, rising from dozens of cook fires, that led them to it. The gray cloud hovered over the shallow valley in which the village lay, with the last rays of the sunset reflecting red on its underbelly.

It was Charro who volunteered to go and investigate. He knew the countryside and the Indian ways; they let him go. He left them on foot, fading into the darkness. The others dismounted in a small draw and collapsed on the ground.

When Charro rejoined with them a short time later, there was an ill and haunted look on his face. They bombarded him with questions, disturbed by the whiteness around his mouth and his silence. When he answered, his voice had the rasp of a file.

"The warriors who attacked us are there all right, along with maybe a dozen others, plus a few older men and twenty or so women. Isabel is with them. It appears she has been given to the women for torture. She—There are burns. And cuts."

Baltasar had been sitting on the ground, holding his side. He struggled to his feet. "What are you saying?"

"You heard me." Charro turned and walked away a short distance, standing with his back to them and his head down.

"Let's go," Refugio said.

They moved as swiftly as they could without raising an alarm. A short distance from the camp they came upon the still body of an Indian sentry Charro had silenced, something he had neglected to mention. A few yards more and they dropped to a crawl, making their way to the crest of a hill overlooking the encampment.

It was not large, just a cluster of huts built of poles and brush set well back from the edge of a tiny stream. There was no order to them, or to the fires which burned like small yellow beacons before them. A herd of horses huddled nearby. There were a few dogs and a number of children scattered here and there. Most of the men were gathered around a single fire in the center. The women were nearer at hand, at the camp's edge.

They were too late. Isabel lay sprawled and unmoving beside a dying fire. Most of her hair had been singed from her head, except for a single strand at the crown of her scalp, and the little clothing she still wore was charred. Great bruises marked her legs, and between them were the red gashes of cuts without number. One leg lay at an odd angle, perhaps an explanation for why she had not been kept alive as a slave.

Refugio lay watching for long moment before he released his breath in a sigh. Turning, he motioned for a retreat.

"Wait! She's moving."

It was Baltasar who spoke in that harsh whisper. His eyes were watering with the intensity of the gaze he kept on Isabel. And he was right. She was twitching, trying to shift her hand. Even as they watched, she made a low, groaning sound. One of the Indian women looked over at her, then reached for a stick which lay close to hand.

Baltasar had his musket in his hand. He lifted it to his shoulder, sighting along the barrel.

"No!" Charro hissed, clamping his hand on Baltasar's shoulder. "You'll bring them all down on us."

"I don't care!"

"I do! It's too late, my friend. Even if we could get down there to her, and then escape with her and our own lives again, she couldn't ride. I doubt she would live more than a few hours."

Baltasar resisted for long seconds, then slowly the tension went out of him and he slumped over the musket. Tears gathered in his eyes, trickling down the sides of his nose. Finally, he straightened once more. "I'm not leaving her like that."

"You have to, there's nothing else. Unless you want to die with her."

"I would, if it would help. But I can at least see she doesn't hurt anymore."

They saw what he meant, saw that there was rightness in it in spite of all the laws against it. No one tried to stop him as he aimed the musket at the woman he loved.

He aimed, but he could not fire. The hands of the big man began to shake. Tremors ran along his arms, invading his shoulders, making his head jar against the stock of his musket. His lips drew back in a grimace as he fought it. Sweat beaded his forehead and ran between his eyes to mingle with the wetness on his cheeks, while his big body shook as if caught in a violent palsy.

He let out his breath in a grunting groan and lowered the barrel of the musket once more. Below them the Indian woman got to her feet and began to walk toward Isabel, swinging her stick. Baltasar shuddered, then slowly he turned his head, searching.

His gaze found Refugio. "El Leon," he said. "You must do it."

The sound of his voice was tormented, pleading. The distant campfires reflected yellow upon his face, shining in the liquid slowly tracking down its broad, weathered expanse.

The spasm that ran over Refugio's face was brief, instantly controlled, impossible to decipher. He closed his eyes, then opened them again.

His voice when he spoke was zephyr quiet, but the edge in it was annihilating. "I will. For you, Baltasar, and no other. But the Apaches will swarm up here when they hear the shot. The rest of you must be ready to ride. Go now. Leave me. I'll catch up with you."

They obeyed. What else was there to do? It was a relief to go, a relief to know they did not have to perform the task that Refugio had accepted. They stumbled often as they hurried back toward the horses, however, for they were waiting for the booming roar of the musket shot.

They had reached the horses when it came. They followed their orders, throwing themselves on their mounts and whipping them into a gallop back the way they had come. They rode as if demons were after them, as if pursued by every childhood horror ever conceived. And when Refugio rejoined them sometime later, riding in from the north after circling wide to elude his pursuers, it seemed they were not sure those fears had not caught up with them. They neither spoke to him nor looked at him, and they increased their pace as they rode on into the night.

They stopped to retrieve their supplies. They did not linger there where the mules lay like discarded mounds of carrion, but continued on. They stopped again for a short while before dawn, to snatch a little rest and cool down the horses before letting them drink. By the time the sun had cleared the horizon, they were moving once more.

It was late afternoon before they ceased looking back over their shoulders. There was small reason to doubt that the Apaches could have found them if they had wanted, or caught up with them if they wished; it appeared that the Indians had abandoned the chase. Whether the reason was the damage the band had inflicted, or something to do with traveling at night, or Isabel's death, they could not tell. They could only be thankful that there was no dust cloud behind them, no one on their back trail.

The trail behind them was clear of Don Esteban as well as the Indians. They could only guess what had happened to him. He could have been attacked by Apaches also, or else had discovered the surveillance of the Indians and turned back out of fear for his own neck. It was also possible that he and the traders had come upon the scene of the battle at the scrub oaks and followed their tracks in the direction of the Indian encampment, then somehow missed their return in the dark. Or, if they had failed to see the signs of battle, since the oaks had been off the trail, they might have ridden past and could now be ahead of them. Another possibility was that the traders, being familiar with the country, could have guessed the band's destination and left the Indian dangers of the Camino Real for some other, perhaps more southerly, route.

The band was thankful for the respite but did not trust it, not entirely. They made no fire when they stopped for the night, and they chose the location for their camp with even more care than usual. Charro, as one of the three able-bodied men, volunteered for the first watch, but in reality they were all on guard. In spite of their exhaustion, they were too strung up to sleep. They shifted this way and that and raked rocks and sticks from under their blankets. They sighed and cleared their throats and flexed sore muscles and counted the stars hanging close overhead. Vicente could be heard muttering prayers under his breath. Nothing seemed to help.

The guard changed, with Enrique taking Charro's place. Finally, somewhere toward midnight, Baltasar began to snore as usual, and Doña Luisa to breathe in a heavy and regular rhythm. Charro turned on his side and gave a long sigh. Vicente was silent while his older brother, as always, lay completely still beside Pilar. Pilar herself, with her eyes tightly closed, began to feel the quiescence that precedes rest.

She was disturbed by a soft rustle. Goose flesh rippled over her. She opened her eyes by slow degrees.

Refugio was getting up. He picked up his blanket and moved soundlessly away, climbing the slope of the small hollow in which they all lay. She heard him speak quietly to Enrique after he was out of sight, a brief exchange. Pilar waited a moment, then she rose also and left the hollow.

Enrique was sitting on a saddle, punching at the dirt with a stick. In a sound just above a whisper, Pilar asked of him, "Refugio?"

The acrobat pointed into the night. She nodded, and moved away in the direction he indicated.

The moon was like a slice of melon with the ends upturned. It floated in benign splendor, not too bright, not too dark, neither retiring nor intruding. In its light she saw Refugio walking ahead of her. Insects, disturbed by his tread, flew out from his feet. Somewhere a night bird called.

At some distance from the camp, near an outcropping of rock, he checked for possible snakes, then spread his blanket. Sitting down, he drew up his legs and leaned his back against the sun-warmed stones.

Pilar stopped a short distance away. She was trying to think of some way to announce her presence when he spoke.

"If you have trailed after me with offerings of pity and reproach, you can save yourself the trouble; I have enough of both of my own."

"I only have my company," she said. When he did not reply, she went on, "If you would rather be alone, I can go back."

"No. Please." The words were stark with appeal. He moved aside on the blanket to give her room.

She took the place he offered, sitting down on the blanket with her back against the rock, and resting her hands on her drawn-up knees. She thought of saying something bland about the night air or the weather, anything to ease the tension, but it did not seem right. Nothing did.

She glanced at him, at the swath of bandaging about his head showing white against his bronze skin in the darkness. She wondered if his head was hurting him, if that was the reason he had got up, but would not ask for fear it would sound like the pity he had refused. Instead, she said, "I'm sorry about Isabel."

His chest rose and fell before he answered. "So am I."

"You cared for her, I think."

"Not as much as I could have. Not as much as she wanted."

"Why was that?"

He turned his head to stare at her in the darkness. "Why do you ask?"

"I don't know. Maybe to make what happened seem real."

He looked forward again. "She was like a bird you find with a broken wing, one that never heals quite as it should. You have to protect such birds, because they can't protect themselves. If you fail, a cat or a hawk comes along, and there is no escape."

"Therefore, her capture was your fault, her death your burden."

"Deny it, if you can."

"What happens to crippled birds who are never rescued?"

"Oh, I'm quite capable of making that rationalization myself, but it doesn't absolve me."

She swung her head to stare at him. "You were faced with an impossible choice, to let Isabel die by cruel degrees or give her the grace of a swift end. There was no release for any of us so long as she lived, and the longer we remained where we were, the more likely it was that we would be discovered and killed. You were elected executioner by default, a position you did not shirk and scorned to try to pass to someone else. If there is guilt, it belongs to the rest of us, because we were so relieved that you agreed and because we left you to do the task alone. And now we are ashamed of our relief and lack of courage."

"I should never have left Spain, never have followed after Don Esteban."

"Now you are encroaching on my regrets."

"Not at all," he said politely. "You are included in them."

"Thank you very much, but I thought we settled this before. I am responsible for what I do."

"I would like to insist, but I'm weary of fighting, Pilar."

"Then stop. This Tejas country is an untamed wilderness so big it stretches to the edge of forever. There must be a place in it where Don Esteban cannot reach and no one cares about El Leon."

"I allowed myself to think so, to even begin to plan, until your stepfather followed after us. But where there are villages, there are authorities, and where there are authorities, there is accountability to the king, and where there is accountability to the king, Don Esteban will have influence and I will always be an outcast, a bandit."

"You don't know that."

"How can it be otherwise? Unless I kill Don Esteban. And I am tired of killing."

"What of your revenge?"

"I have sought it for more years than I can count, and what has it brought me? To live for revenge is a form of death. One by one you lose everyone you love, everything that gives you pride, everything that you are within yourself. All that is left is hate. I am weary of hate and the death it brings. I crave life instead."

"Is this what you have been thinking about today as you rode?"

"You mean, will it pass when I no longer think of Isabel and how she died?" His voice was soft, less stringently monitored than before.

"Yes, I suppose."

"Then the answer is no. No, it won't pass. And no, it isn't what I have been thinking of as I ride."

"What, then?"

He shifted slightly to face her, and his voice was deep and not quite even. "Ah, Pilar, you make it so easy. Is it on purpose?"

"What do you mean?"

He reached to touch her face, drawing his fingertips along the curve of her cheek and down its gentle incline to the turn of her neck before dropping delicately to the round globe of her breast.

"You are life, is what I think, and within you is renewal. I envy you that, for it's a lack in me. Will you let me seek life in you? Will you give me renewal?"

"You mean—you want me?"

"It's what I'm trying to say, in words I can hide behind if you should refuse."

"I'm only a woman."

"I meant that, too, but you are more. You are special to me. I have missed holding you, being held inside you. I need you now, this moment, as I have never needed another human being or ever want to need one again. Love me, or kill me, for without you I am— No. Pay no attention to the babbling of extremity. I refused pity, didn't I? Will you love me for the pleasures of the night if I promise to make them as unending as I am able?"

How could she refuse? Besides, she had no desire to deny him. Why else had she followed him away from the others except for this? He had no use for her compassion or exoneration, but there were ways of offering surcease other than by words.

The ground beneath the blanket was rocky and hard, but they did not feel it. The night air was cool, but they did not know. Nothing mattered, nothing hindered; they were mindful only of each other as they came together under the clear white light of the stars and the melon moon.

With caresses as subtle as their understanding, as exquisite as their concern, they sought the wellsprings of passion and the forgetfulness it can bring. Prodigal of time and selfless in their joint quest, they remembered past lessons and used them well.

Their mouths clung in slow, deep, sweet searching while they undressed each other. They fitted their naked bodies together, the curves and recesses, hardness and softness, with the care of those studying an ancient and exacting craft, and gloried in sensations unforgotten, yet never adequately imagined. The crisp triangle of hair on his chest tickled and was rough to the tongue, while his half-covered paps were flat and satiny until teased to crinkled nubs. The muscles of his back shifting under her hands were like buried silken ropes. The smoothness of her thighs upon his was a thing of revelation, and exultation. His breath made warm, moist tracks on her skin, and raised the goose flesh of anticipation and delight.

Together they moved, reaching for and finding a slow and steady rhythm that stretched time and space and the limits of endurance. He clasped her hands, palm to palm and fingers entwined, and pressed his lips to the throbbing pulse in the tender turn of her neck. He cupped her breasts and spanned her waist with his long hard swordsman's fingers, and reached lower to send spirals of fiery joy to the center of her being. The joining was heated and liquid and fusing; he was a part of her and she of him.

The tumult grew, an invasion of excitement that suffused her body with urgent need. She lifted herself against him, answering his force with her own, striving with him toward the ultimate completion. The shocks of his thrusts shuddered through her. Her breath rasped in her chest. She wanted him deep inside her, immeasurably deep, soundingly deep. She wanted him to reach that part of her that only she knew, the inner sanctuary of her most carefully hoarded self.

He touched it, and the brilliance burst over them. Weightless and beatific, they soared, knowing each other, two parts of a whole, lost in the wonder.

She had given him as near to what he asked as she could find within herself. He had kept his promise.

CHAPTER 20

They came to the Mission San Juan at dusk. The vine-crowned, sun-warmed walls of cream-colored stone that surrounded it enclosed them like an embrace. The sight of the chapel looming in the dimness with the last rays of the sun glazing its belfry, of the padre moving toward them in his dusty black habit while the sound of a choir of rich, beautifully blending Indian voices rose in the evening still-ness, was enough to swell the heart with relief and thankful-ness. Here was safety, for the first time in weeks.

They could have gone to the town of San Antonio de Bexar, or to any one of the other missions strung along the San Antonio River like beads on a necklace. However, their destination was not the town, but the *estancia* of Charro's father. San Juan was not only the favorite mission of Charro's mother, where she had learned her catechism as a child and where her *peninsular* parents, descendants of set-tlers from the Canary Islands, had always gone, but was the last one below the city on this side of the river. The good padre could be depended on to give them a decent meal and a bed for the night, Charro said, and they would be that much closer to home when they rode out in the morning.

The mission was more than just a chapel. It was a complex of buildings built of adobe, including the house of the priest and his assistant friar and the cubicles of the principal Indian workers against the inside walls, plus a granary, stable, blacksmith shop, weaving shed, and a variety of smaller structures such as fowl roosts and outdoor ovens. The church was, however, the central focus of the community, the reason for its being. The padre invited them to enter to give thanks for their deliverance. The entire band complied, partially as a gesture of respect, but also out of very real gratitude. For some it was their first time in a church in years.

The chapel building was not a grand structure nor a large one, but was curiously satisfying with its rough stonework arches, its solid simplicity. The stations of the cross were hand carved, the altar was of native wood barely touched with gilt, the statue of the Virgin was beautifully and brightly painted. There were two oil paintings which had the look of being imported from Spain, but the rest had the vigor and strength that seemed to suggest the new world. It was easy to see why Charro's mother preferred it.

It was strange, seeing the Indians come and go so peacefully about the mission compound. Many were descendants of tribes from farther south, closer to Mexico City, converts who had journeyed to the area as helpers for the first Spanish priests. Others were members of a half-dozen fairly docile tribes of the vicinity, from the Borrado to the Tacame, though a few were Lipan Apaches who had accepted the teachings of the Christ. According to Charro, there were dozens of different tribes of Apache. Not all of them were dedicated to endless war, though most considered it the only route to honor for a warrior.

The band was provided with food, just as Charro had said they would be. He himself ate in state in the priest's quarters, as became the son of an old friend of the church, and Doña Luisa was also included in that invitation. Refugio and Pilar could have participated in the meal also, since the priest was anxious to hear as much as possible about their long overland journey. Refugio had asked to be excused, however, and Pilar had chosen to do the same. Refugio, she thought, felt uncomfortable pretending everything was as it should be with him. All she herself wanted was a chance at the water provided for bathing, without the distracting presence of Doña Luisa in the cubicle she had been assigned to share with the other woman. She had acquired a grudging respect for Doña Luisa in the last days on the trail, but had had enough of her company to last for a long while.

Refugio had not protested the sleeping arrangement. He could not, of course, without branding her as a woman of loose morals; still, she thought he might have deplored it privately if it had mattered to him. She was not sure it did. The nearer they had come to civilization again, the more withdrawn he had become. Since that night after Isabel's death, she had slept in Refugio's arms and he had held her close, but there was seldom anything more between them. She was warmed by his consideration for her, by his refusal to chance exposing their intimate moments to the others sleeping around them. At the same time, his ability to deny himself, and her, was daunting. She was forced to the hurtful conclusion that she was little more to him than another female presence, one comforting at times, but also burdensome now that her value as a hostage for Vicente's safety was past. As a result, there was a small fastness in her heart that she kept inviolate, where she nurtured her doubts and fears and hid her pain.

What was going to become of her here, so far from everything she knew? The question had troubled her on the long journey, but the worry of staying alive had been too pressing for other problems to seem important. Now that they were nearing their destination, a decision would have to be made.

The first consideration would be money, some means of keeping herself. She would have to find work of some kind, and a place to stay. Perhaps the priest at the mission would have some suggestion, or else Charro's parents might be able to advise her. She did not know where else to turn. Of one thing she was certain, she would not depend on Refugio. Pride made that impossible, if nothing else.

Sometimes she despaired of understanding how his mind worked, of knowing what guilts and emotions, faults and obligations moved him to behave as he did. Still, she had to concede that he was not alone in his sense of constraint. She had worried herself that she would be judged harshly here in this harsh land. Somehow, the people of New Orleans, perhaps because they were so French still, had not seemed as likely to be severe over lapses of conduct. The things Charro had to say about his family, and even his own attitudes at times, had made her think those who lived here would be different.

She could not help wondering how Charro's parents would feel about having their son's friends thrust upon them. He said aloud that they would be delighted, quite ready to overlook any little irregularities of past behavior in them all, for the sake of having their son safely home again. Pilar was not sure that was what he really thought.

Such concerns were the cause, she was sure, of her disturbed night. Also, she had grown used to having the open sky above her, and it was difficult to endure the close walls of the cubicle to which she was assigned. She was troubled as well by nightmare images of Isabel as she thought of how the girl had longed to reach safety. Moreover, it was undeniable that lying on a straw mattress next to Doña Luisa was not the same as sleeping beside Refugio. It was a habit, that was all. Habits were strange things.

As she ate the breakfast of fresh-baked bread and hot chocolate served to them, Pilar glanced down the table at the bandit leader. He was talking quietly with Baltasar. The older man seemed to have shrunk in the last days on the trail. His wound had been slow to heal, and he still favored his side. He had spoken little and spent much time riding alone and staring at the horizon.

Refugio appeared rested and fit. He had ceased wearing the bandaging around his head, declaring it was no longer needed. Perhaps if wasn't; the only sign of the injury was the dark path of the scab running through his hair. He rebounded quickly from his wounds, at least those that were physical.

He looked up, catching her eye almost as if he had known she was watching him. He smiled, a faint movement of the lips, before turning back once more to Baltasar. That small instant of recognition gave Pilar an odd feeling. It was almost as if he had looked at her because he could not help himself, but then deliberately relegated her to some portion of his mind where she would not interfere with what he had to do. A shiver moved over her there in the warm summer dawn.

They left shortly afterward, riding out with the blessing of the priest upon them and the farewells of the Indian children ringing in their ears. They crossed the river a short time later and headed toward the southwest.

The dust cloud appeared shortly after midday. It lay ahead of them and was moving at a fast pace in their direction. Their first thought was of Indians; attacks along this road leading to San Antonio were not impossible, or even uncommon. They left the track, except for Charro and Refugio, who circled forward to investigate.

The two men rode back at the head of a cavalcade of horsemen who whooped and hollered and even fired off a few shots in celebration. It was Charro's father and a group of his *charros*. They had ridden out to escort them safely to the hacienda. The priest had sent word the evening before of their arrival, and Señor Huerta had not been able to wait to see his son, nor to bear the thought that some mishap during the last hours of travel might prevent the homecoming. He had set out at dawn to be certain that all was well.

Charro's home, the house where he had been born, was built like a fortress to repel Indian attacks, and had served its purpose well on several occasions over the years. The adobe walls were thick and tall, and everything needed to sustain life over a long period was enclosed within them. The jacales, or huts of the Indian laborers—built with adobe walls and roofs of peeled poles covered with brush plastered with mud—were located outside the walls in random groupings, but there was ample space inside for their protection in time of need. The back wall of the house itself, rising two stories without windows, formed the rear of the stockade, so that the enclosure was like a large courtyard. The stables and other outbuildings were placed around the perimeter, while in the center was a spashing fountain in a basin of limestone.

The main house was of whitewashed adobe and built with a long and narrow balcony along the front of the upper floor, with a loggia of arched openings underneath it. Projecting out from just above the arches was a roof of latticework built of peeled poles. An ancient grapevine grew upon it, its luxurious leaves providing shade, while long runners also grew up to the balcony to make a curtain of greenery around it. On the floor of packed earth under the latticework was set a long, rough-hewn table flanked by benches. Bulbs of garlic and peppers of many kinds hung in strings from the lattice. Enormous clay pots made from cracked ollas, or water jars, were set here and there and filled with the bright red and pink of geraniums. The dwelling was certainly Spanish in design, and yet the roughness of the

materials used, the brilliant whitewash and obvious arrangements for outdoor living, gave it a flavor of its own.

Charro's mother was waiting under the loggia as they
rode through the great double gates into the courtyard. She
came forward as Charro swung from the saddle, a plump,
short woman with a round face creased by a soft maternal
smile. She took her son into her arms, kissing his cheeks
again and again and exclaiming over how he had filled out,
how broad his shoulders were and how rough his hands. She
greeted them all with delighted welcome. Still exclaiming
and thanking God in equal measure, she led them all inside.
Looking around, she beckoned to an Indian maidservant
who hovered nearby, giving rapid instructions for their
comfort.

"Benita!" Charro called out with pleasure, and strode
forward to take the maidservant's hands. Holding her arms
wide, he shook his head. "You've grown up while I was
away, and very nicely, too, I must say. You were always
pretty, but now look at you."

Benita flushed under the cream of her skin, flashing a
glance at Señora Huerta. Then she turned her enormous
dark eyes back to Charro as if she could not help herself.
There was the softness of affection, and perhaps more, in her
square face. Charro grinned down at her in total unaware-
ness of his mother's frowning glance behind him. It seemed
likely that the girl was the Indian maidservant for whose
sake he had been banished to Spain.

"Attend to me, Benita!" Señora Huerta said, her voice
sharp. "There is much to be done if everything is to be ready
for the fiesta."

"Fiesta?" Charro asked, dropping the girl's hands and
turning from her with his face alight. "You mean it?"

"But of course," his father answered as he moved to clap
him on the shoulder. "It isn't every day my son returns,

especially by way of the overland route from Louisiana. We must celebrate such an auspicious event."

"Tonight?"

"Naturally tonight. This is the day of your arrival, is it not? Everyone has asked where you were and what was happening with you so many times since you left that it would be a shame to keep the news from them too long."

The riders with invitations to the fiesta had been sent out at the same time that Señor Huerta had left to meet them. Neighbors and friends began to arrive short hours later. They came, most of them, on horseback, with ladies and children riding pillion or else perched upon gentle donkeys or gaily caparisoned mules. A few came in carts, squeaking along, and there were even one or two in carriages, great cumbersome vehicles built more for durability over bad roads than for comfort. Many of them showed up together. They had traveled in groups for safety, one family merging with another as they joined the passing caravan or overtook each other on the road, so that the final company was some seventy or eighty strong.

They brought guitars and mandolins and concertinas, small drums and castanets and Indian rattles. They brought gifts of ground corn and strings of red peppers, goat's cheese and homemade wine and confections created with milk and chocolate and sugar and nuts. The older women wore black and covered their hair with caps; the younger ones had pinned flowers in their hair and had on dresses with flounces and lace in colors and styles only three or four years behind those of Madrid.

The great wide gates were left standing open until the last stragglers came ambling in. When no one arrived for a half-hour stretch, they were shut tight and the fiesta began.

The food was splendid, on the scale of some medieval banquet. There was beef simmered in a sauce of peppers and honey, flavored with tomato to make it tender, and whole pigs and lambs cooked over an open fire. There were rice dishes and bean dishes and dishes combining something of everything, all of it to be eaten with unleavened cakes of flour and also of cornmeal. The desserts began with the traditional flans and ended with cakes dripping with honey and butter, or else rich with dried fruits and flavorings of rum and vanilla. Everyone ate until they could hold no more, sitting elbow to elbow at tables brought out into the courtyard under the stars and set with flickering pottery oil lamps. Then the music and dancing began.

They played the fandango, the bolero, the Sevillanas, and also the contradanza imported from France by the Bourbons who sat on the throne. When they had need to catch their breaths, they slowed the pace to a gentle minuet. The women in black nodded and tapped their feet and kept careful watch over daughters and granddaughters and nieces while leaning this way and that to hear the latest gossip. The older men stood to one side, smoking foul-smelling *cigarros* and talking of cattle and horses and the latest news to come the long distance from Mexico City. The young women sat beside their mothers or else congregated in giggling, chattering groups. From that safety they sent bright, challenging glances to the young men who leaned against the arches of the loggia and favored them with appreciative appraisals.

Pilar, having been provided with an evening costume for the occasion by Charro's mother, danced with the partners presented to her by the thoughtful lady. Doña Luisa, though given black to wear by Señora Huerta, did the same. Most of the men of the band also performed to the music, as was expected of them as unattached males, and had no lack of partners. The only exception was Baltasar, who retreated to the stables with a plate of food in one hand and a bottle of wine in the other. He was not seen for the rest of the evening.

The night had scarcely begun before the tale of Refugio's championing of Charro during his trials in Spain, of their perilous sea voyage and long overland journey, had circled the courtyard. It added a luster to the band, increasing greatly the appeal they already had by virtue of being strangers in a comparatively narrow society. The gathering was not made privy to the whole story, however. There was no whisper of Refugio's identity as El Leon. This was a part of Charro's past his parents had apparently thought it best to keep hidden.

Señora Huerta, watching the proceedings from a vantage point under the loggia, was seen now and then to rest her gaze upon Refugio with a look of worry in her eyes. It did not affect her manner toward him, however. He was her son's deliverer, and moreover, a man of no small personal attraction. She smiled upon him and introduced him to her neighbors who happened to have daughters. And once, as she and the bandit leader strolled about the courtyard in quiet conversation, she was seen to stop and reach up to make the sign of the cross on his forehead.

Refugio danced with Pilar, a swift bolero that he executed with passion and grace. His dark gray gaze was intent as he watched her, but he smiled seldom and his touch was impersonal. Afterward he permitted Charro to claim her with no more than a mild protest, a token expression of regret.

Pilar and Charro promenaded around the courtyard, speaking at random of his home, the guests of his parents, the pleasures of the fiesta.

"I had not known how much I missed all this," Charro said with a wave toward the musicians and his friends and neighbors. "I wasn't anxious to go when my father suggested it; still, I thought it would be fine to see great buildings, listen to learned men, meet elegant women, do great things. I've seen and done enough. I'll be content to marry and raise little Huertas, and stay here all my days."

"In spite of the Apaches?"

"There are dangers everywhere. If it was not the Apaches, it would be something else, yellow fever, fires—bandits." He gave her a droll smile. "But what of you? What will you do now?"

They were walking near the fountain. She reached to trail her fingers along the deep, damp stone basin surrounding it. "I don't know. Much depends on my stepfather, whether he is coming here and, if he is, what he intends to do. Even if he doesn't try to harm me, what he may say of me could make me unwelcome."

"Impossible," Charro declared.

She gave him a grateful smile. "If all goes well, I thought I might find work, sewing, perhaps."

"Sewing!"

"I was well taught in the convent."

"So were most of the women here; they make their own clothing. But you were not meant for menial tasks."

"I have to do something!"

"What of Refugio?"

"I— Who can say?"

He watched her a long moment. "Yes, I understand. But . . . you know that if it were not for him, and if you were one of the daughters of our neighbors, that walking like this with me would be considered a prelude to betrothal?"

She sent him a swift glance. His gaze upon her was warm. She smiled a little. "I've grown so used to being without a duenna that I hadn't thought how it might look. Shall we rejoin the others to save your reputation?"

"To save me from my mother's wrath, maybe. But you might think about it."

"A duenna?"

"No, Pilar, a betrothal. There will always be a place for you here."

Behind them the music was gay and the shuffling of the dancer's feet light as they moved in time to it. Charro's slender face grew serious as he slowed his pace, moving with a horseman's grace in his close-fitting rider's clothes, which on this occasion were sewn with buttons made of Indian silver.

"That's a . . . very kind gesture."

He grimaced. "It isn't kind at all; I'm thinking of myself. I will say no more because Refugio is my friend. But you will remember, please?"

The declaration, oblique thought it might have been, was warming. She had no idea of taking advantage of it, but she was grateful. She smiled at him in the dimness of the courtyard as they turned and strolled back toward the loggia.

It was when the music was at its loudest, the dancing at its fastest, and the merriment at its highest, that a pounding was heard at the gates.

Charro ran to the wall and swung up onto the guard platform beside the wide entrance to take a look. When he reported back that there was a squadron of soldiers outside, Señor Huerta ordered the gate opened. The soldiers marched inside while Indian servants ran to hold their mounts.

Señor Huerta stepped forward as the military unit dismounted and drew up in formation. "Welcome to my home, gentlemen. You come upon us during a time of rejoicing, as you can see. We celebrate the safe arrival of my son from Spain after a long absence. It would give us great pleasure if you would join us and also accept our hospitality for what remains of the night."

The leader of the squadron, a young captain, bowed. "You do us great honor, señor, and my men and I are most grateful for your kind offer." He stopped to clear his throat. "However, I fear my errand is not a happy one. I am here on an official assignment at the request of his excellency, Governor Ramon Martinez Pacheco."

"How is this?" Señor Huerta's stance had grown stiff.

"You have staying with you, I understand, a man by the name of Refugio de Carranza y Leon, and a woman who is traveling with him, the Señorita Pilar Sandoval y Serna. Is this not so?"

Behind Charro's father the music had come to an end with a flourish. The captain's words rang out loud and clear, so that the dancers turned to stare as avidly as those who had not been dancing. Charro's father answered simply. "It is."

"Then I must ask you to produce them."

"For what purpose, may I ask?"

"The governor orders that they appear before him to answer questions concerning their activities in Spain and Louisiana."

"But they have only just arrived," the older man protested. "How has their presence come to the governor's attention so quickly?"

"Information has been brought concerning them by a traveler, one Don Esteban Iturbide. There are charges, I fear, of grave import. I must ask you again to give up your guests into my custody. If you refuse, I have the authority to take them by force."

It was a formal arrest. The soldiers, armed with swords and muskets, were blocking the way to the gates. To escape, Pilar saw in a swift glance, they would have to fight. It was possible that many of those gathered inside the courtyard would be injured. She saw Enrique exchange a long look with Refugio, then look to where Charro was standing just under the guard platform. He was watching Pilar with his hands balled into fists. Enrique turned back to Refugio, but their leader slowly shook his head.

Moving with a firm tread, Refugio walked forward.

His voice was quiet yet carried as he spoke. "There will be no need for force or violations of hospitality. I am Refugio de Carranza y Leon, and I place myself at your disposal. As for the lady, there is no possible blame that can be attached to her, therefore no need for her presence. You may leave her here."

Pilar moved then, slipping through the crowd to stand at Refugio's side. Her chest was tight with the terrible sense of irony she felt for being caught by Don Esteban at last, here where they had thought they might be safe; still, she did not hesitate. "I do not ask for such consideration," she said. "The governor has demanded my presence also, and it is my stepfather who has attached blame to me by involving me in the charges which require our appearance. I would not disappoint either gentleman."

They were received in the study of the governor's palace. They had set out at dawn, reaching San Antonio during the siesta hours. After a short period to refresh themselves from the ride, they were brought before the official representative of Spain in the province.

The governor's palace was a grandiose name for a low-built, whitewashed building which faced the military plaza of San Antonio de Bexar, with the church of San Fernando nearby. Governor Pacheco's private quarters were in the house, for there were domestic noises coming from beyond the study, perhaps out in the walled patio at the rear, the sound of a woman scolding, the clatter of pots around a cooking fire. The shutters of the floor-to-ceiling windows in the governor's study stood open to catch the evening air. They looked out over the square where the last rays of a red sunset streamed through the trees around the plaza, casting long, vermilion-edged shadows across the dusty quadrangle. People were just beginning to gather there in the first hint of evening cool, young women with their duennas promenading in one direction and the soldiers in faded uniforms walking in the other, so that they met twice each time they made a complete circuit.

Governor Pacheco sat behind a heavy table of dark oak. His chair, cushioned in red velvet and with velvet padded arms, rose up behind him with a back incised with crude carvings of the lions and castles of Spain. Besides him, standing with one hand resting on a corner of the table was Don Esteban. His features were burned by the sun and wind and his clothing lacked his preferred degree of richness. The expression in his small black eyes, however, as he watched Refugio and Pilar take their places in front of the governor with their escort of soldiers around them, was one of malignant satisfaction.

That look turned to wariness as he discovered that they had not come alone. Crowding into the room behind them was Charro, Baltasar, and Enrique, with Señor Huerta and a good dozen of his best horsemen behind him. Though Refugio was unarmed, the others were not, and their stances as they positioned themselves about the room were bellicose.

The governor rose to his feet. "What is the meaning of this intrusion, Señor Huerta?" he asked. "You were not summoned."

"The two who were are friends of my son. But for them, he might now be dead. Therefore, they are friends of mine who deserve whatever I may be able to do to aid them. For the present, I offer only my support."

Don Esteban, his face suffused with dawning rage, brought his fist crashing down on the table. "This is insupportable! I will not have such interference! I demand these people be removed."

The governor turned his head deliberately to give the nobleman a hard stare. In that moment it could be seen that there was some slight friction between the two men. Perhaps Don Esteban had been too demanding since his arrival, or else had tried to overawe the governor with his court connections. Either course must have been unwise. The governor, an austere gentleman with a proud nose, did not look like a man easily impressed by threats.

"I must remind you, sir," the province's highest official said to Don Esteban with icy politeness, "that I am conducting this interview. You will allow me to set the conditions." His lips snapped shut and he turned back to Charro's father. "Since you are an old and respected member of this community, Señor Huerta, I will permit you and your followers to remain."

Charro's father bowed in acknowledgment of the gesture. "I thank you, your excellency, and my son also thanks you."

"Yes," Charro said, bowing in his turn.

The governor dropped back into his chair. "Now that we have that settled, let us proceed."

He shuffled through several sheets of foolscap which lay before him, reading over an item here, an item there. Don Esteban fidgeted at his side, but the governor would not be hurried. Finally, the official placed the sheets aside in a neat pile and folded his hands, resting them in the exact center of a large blotter of Cordoban leather.

"There have been a number of charges made here today. The most serious ones are against you, Refugio de Carranza. Don Esteban Iturbide claims that you are, in fact, the notorious bandit wanted in Spain under the name of El Leon. You are accused of committing a number of crimes against Don Esteban personally. According to him, on a day in December of this past year, you abducted from his keeping his stepdaughter, Señorita Pilar Sandoval y Serna, and made off with her into the mountains, where you kept her against her will."

"That is totally untrue," Pilar interrupted. "I asked Refugio to remove me from my stepfather's household because I was in fear of my life, for I suspected he had murdered my mother. I was forced to stay with Refugio because Don Esteban had my aunt knifed in her bed so I would have no place else to go."

"Preposterous!" Don Esteban exploded before she had finished speaking. "She is deranged from being forced to live with cutthroats and scum such as Carranza and his men. They have totally destroyed her mind as well as her morals."

"Who," Señor Huerta said, taking a step forward, "are you calling cutthroats and scum? I take leave to inform you that my son has been with Carranza, and he is neither!"

"Gentlemen, if you please!" the governor said.

"Señor Huerta is right," Pilar insisted. "I have never seen any of Refugio's followers do a vile or unjust thing, which is more than can be said of my stepfather."

"Thank you, señorita," the governor said in exasperated tones. "May we continue?"

"I assure you it's so!"

"That may or may not be. For the moment, we are enumerating the charges against Refugio de Carranza. Please remain silent."

Pilar swallowed her protests, though anger rose inside her.

"Where was I? Yes. While holding Señorita Sandoval captive, Carranza, it is suggested that you seduced her into immoral and sinful ways. This was done with malice, because of your vendetta against Don Esteban, one of long standing. This gentleman further claims that you followed him to the Louisiana colony, where you consorted openly with his stepdaughter for the purpose of discrediting him in his new position. You then broke into his house with the help of his stepdaughter, whom you have suborned to your will. While there, you searched out the hiding place for the small bag of emeralds that represented the fortune he had amassed over the course of a lifetime, and also tortured him into revealing the hiding place of his ready gold."

"Emeralds?" Pilar said, the word drawn from her by disbelief.

The governor turned his gaze upon her. "A highly portable form of wealth, one to which Don Esteban had reduced a rather large estate."

"And Refugio is supposed to have taken these emeralds?" she said slowly.

"That is the charge." The words were dismissive, as was the way the governor turned away from her. He continued, "Don Esteban also is ready to swear that Refugio de Carranza attempted to murder him in a highly irregular altercation with swords, and when that failed, deliberately set fire to a private chapel for the purpose of making his escape with the stolen goods. This fire subsequently caused the virtual destruction of the town of New Orleans, a result also laid at the door of the accused."

Pilar barely listened to these last charges. She turned her head to look up at Refugio. Was it possible? Was it? Could he have found the emeralds and pocketed them during his search of Don Esteban's house?

But if he had, surely he would have said so. Surely he could not have failed to mention gems of such value when he knew they could only represent what Don Esteban had stolen from her, the reason she had followed after Don Esteban to Louisiana in the first place.

It was impossible to think that Refugio could have had them with him all this time, and yet it made a terrible kind of sense. Why else would Don Esteban have followed them at such risk and effort? Why else, except for that one thing he valued, wealth?

Refugio, as if drawn by her stare, swung his head slowly to look down at her. He met the warm brown of her eyes, and his own were bleak with painful self-derision.

Abruptly, Pilar's doubts left her. Refugio had stolen the emeralds. He had taken them, then had deliberately kept the knowledge from her. He had betrayed her and their joint quest, betrayed every tender moment they had shared for the sake of a handful of gems. He had taken the emeralds, had had them all along. And he had them still.

CHAPTER 21

I am going to put a question to you, Refugio de Carranza," Governor Pacheco said, his voice even, yet with a hard note underneath it. "Are you, or are you not, known in Spain as El Leon?"

Refugio's lips twisted in a smile. "I am no lion, and never was," he answered, "though I may have been, on occasion, a jackal."

"There!" Señor Huerta said. "What you have here is one man's word against that of another. This entire examination has been a disgrace, based on charges brought out of spite, and with the intention to wound."

Don Esteban flung up his head. "Are you accusing me of lying, señor? If so, I tell you the liar is there." He flung out his arm to point at Refugio. "The examination has been too weak, if anything. Carranza should be put to the test."

The governor turned his hard stare from one man to the other. "I see no need for torture to get to the bottom of this affair. It has been conducted with all due regard for both the gravity of the accusations and the welfare of the accused. If, gentlemen, you do not approve of my handling of it, I suggest you take your complaints to Mexico City. Or to Madrid."

Señor Huerta was unabashed. "Carranza is the friend of my son, and a man of great honor and courage. Not one claim made by this nobleman from Spain can be proven against him. Don Esteban Iturbide's actions are nothing more than an attempt to use the official machinery of this province in a private vendetta, one of long standing between his family and that of Carranza. I say it should not be allowed!"

"And who are you to say anything at all?" Don Esteban demanded. "You, señor, can know nothing and less than nothing of this matter, stuck here as you are in this provincial desert. I would advise you to allow Carranza to fight his own battles, or you may find yourself in a war not of your choosing."

Charro's father drew himself up. "Are you threatening me?"

"Take it as you will. As for proof of what I say, there is my stepdaughter at Carranza's side. What more is needed?"

Charro moved forward. "What if Pilar is here with us?" he asked. "A fine care you have for her, when you stand there blackening her name before the world."

Don Esteban sneered. "You ride with Carranza so must be one of his bandits. What possible weight can your opinion hold? Of course you support him, since he may save your skin by saving his."

"A vicious lie!" Señor Huerta cried.

"Come, we are straying from the purpose at hand," the governor said, his expression harassed.

"I must speak," Charro insisted. "Have you never heard, Don Esteban, of the affections of the heart? Your stepdaughter would not be the first women to consort, as you so elegantly put it, with the enemy of her family."

The governor tried ineffectually to call them all to order. Don Esteban ignored the official as he gave a harsh laugh. "Affections? Is that what you call it? You mistake Carranza's sentiments, my friend. He knows nothing except how to hate. He has kept my stepdaughter with him solely to make me look foolish, because her shame is my shame, and it pleases him to have it so."

"No," Refugio said, the single word cutting like a honed sword through the babble of voices as Charro and his father tried to refute Don Esteban's statement and the governor attempted to restore order. "No," he went on in a quieter tone as the voices began to die away. "Pilar Sandoval y Serna has traveled under my protection, it's true, and my behavior toward her has not always been the most honorable, but this much I swear: I never meant to cause her harm. I would like nothing so much as to have her with me, beside me, all my days. It is my most ardent wish to make her my wife."

Silence descended as the men turned toward Pilar. The governor, his tones clipped, spoke first. "Is this true?"

Was it? Pilar didn't know, nor could she bring herself to trust that it might be so. The reason was the emeralds. It was not their value, the wealth they represented, that mattered; quite suddenly that seemed not to count at all. The important thing was that Refugio had not told her about them. He had kept the knowledge from her, allowing her to think she had no way to live, denying her the freedom from want and care that they represented. If he had betrayed her by keeping them to himself, then what else in the long list of charges Don Esteban had made might not also be true?

Had Refugio kept her with him from the beginning merely to bring dishonor on her stepfather? Could he have made love to her, accepted her offer of herself merely for the sake of the added shame to his old enemy? Had he kept her with him, not because he had begun to care, as she had dared hope, but rather because it had suited his schemes of vengeance?

And yet even if it was true, she had only herself to blame. Had she not offered him just such a bargain that night in the patio garden? She had not meant it to go so far. She had thought the embarrassment to Don Esteban would be no more than a few hour's duration, a day at the most, until she could be left with her aunt. Still, the principle was the same. She did not, then, have grounds for complaint.

But she did have reason to put an end to being used. She could do it now, this moment. She clasped her hands together in front of her and drew a deep breath.

"Wait," Refugio said, his voice softly urgent. "There are more reasons than you know, and more pledges."

Charro, standing no more than an arm's length away, turned toward her also. "Let her speak," he said. "She has that right."

Pilar looked from one man to the other. Charro's face was open and calm, with a steady light in his blue eyes. In Refugio's features there was remorse, hope and despair in equal measure, and a hundred other things she did not understand. His thinking was too convoluted, his feelings too complex, for her to meet him easily on common ground. The effort at this moment was too painful. It seemed that the best thing to be done for him—for them all—was to deny that there had ever been anything approaching intimacy between Refugio and herself.

When she spoke, her voice was clear, and edged with the anger that gave her courage. "Refugio Carranza has been of great service to me, and I am grateful. But if he intended more, then he failed to tell me. I am very sorry. I have been previously honored by a request for my hand from Señor Miguel Huerta."

"You mean to marry him?" the governor asked, his voice sharp.

Pilar looked at Charro, gazing into his wide eyes. Still, she was aware of the abortive movement Refugio made as he started to take a step after her, then restrained himself. "Yes," she answered, "I do."

Charro suddenly smiled. He moved to her side, putting his arm about her shoulders, drawing her close against him, away from Refugio. "Ah, *querida*," he whispered, "I will be a good husband."

The governor cleared his throat and straightened the edge of the foolscap near his elbow. "Yes. That seems to dispose of that. May we now continue?"

"Precisely," Don Esteban snapped.

The governor gave the man a glance of annoyance before turning once more toward Refugio. "It appears, Señor Carranza, that you did indeed abduct Señorita Sandoval—whether at her request or for your own purpose is beside the point. The escapade itself seems to indicate that acting outside the law in this manner was not unknown to you."

Refugio was silent as the governor paused. It appeared that his mind was elsewhere, or that if he had any defense to make, he had lost interest in presenting it.

"It is plain then," the governor went on, "that I cannot absolve you of the charges made against you out of hand. It's also true that the fact that you abducted the lady does not prove that you are El Leon. Therefore, I have no cause to hold you."

A ragged cheer went up from the men gathered around, the members of the band and Vicente, and also Señor Huerta's *charros*. Don Esteban cursed and pounded the table, making the governor's papers scatter.

"Quiet," the governor rapped out, straightening his papers once more. "That will be enough. This matter is not settled."

"What do you mean?" Señor Huerta asked.

The governor ignored him, speaking to Refugio. "While I cannot hold you, señor, neither can I, in all conscience, ignore the possibility that there may be some truth in the accusations against you. My only recourse seems to be to send to Spain for a description of this bandit, El Leon."

"This is an outrage," Don Esteban shouted. "I demand that you place this man under arrest."

"Do you, señor?" the governor said, rising to his feet. "And would you also like to remain here in custody in San Antonio until word arrives from Spain on this matter? Just in case Refugio de Carranza would like to bring charges of slander against you if the answer is in his favor?"

"You would not dare!"

"Would I not?" The governor looked down on the don from his superior height. "I would remind you that I am the supreme authority north of the Rio Grande."

"For the interim only. I have friends who can see to it you never receive official appointment!"

"I hope they may, Don Esteban," the governor replied, tight-lipped with rage, "since I want nothing more than to leave here and return to Spain!" The governor swung from the fuming grandee. "You have all heard my decision. I extend my deepest appreciation for your prompt response to my summons, and now I bid you good day."

They were dismissed, and they were not sorry to go. There was much shouting, much riding in circles and general celebration on the way back to the hacienda. The ruling of the governor was felt to be a victory of sorts. The request to Spain for information must go, laboriously, southward across Sonora, and along the twisting trails to Mexico City, then from there to Vera Cruz and across the ocean to Spain. It was always possible that it would be lost somewhere along the way, or else that, on being received in Spain, it would be shuffled onto the desk of some minor official and forgotten. Failing that, it seemed possible that the description of El Leon, even if it finally made its way back to New Spain after a year and a half or even two, might be so vague that it would be difficult to apply it with any certainty.

Of course, it was true that most of the country people between Seville and Cordoba knew, and many town people guessed, that Refugio Carranza was El Leon. However, Spanish officialdom in Madrid might not be aware of it, or else would find it difficult to prove.

Whatever might come of it all, for the moment the threat Don Esteban represented had been reduced to less than nothing. Refugio was free. They were all safe and on their way to good food and a warm bed, and there was going to be a wedding. So they whooped and they laughed and cracked jokes in their joy. The only ones who were silent were Pilar and Refugio, and the prospective groom.

Señora Huerta, once the hacienda was reached, greeted the news of the coming nuptials with something less than delight.

"Is this the truth, my son?" she asked, cradling Charro's face between her two hands.

"Yes, *madre*."

"And you will be happy and remain with us here?"

"Yes, *madre*."

She gazed into his eyes a long moment before she gave a slow nod. "It is well, then. If there is to be a wedding, we must begin to make ready."

"There is no hurry," Pilar protested from where she stood to one side.

The older woman turned on her. "Is there reason to delay?"

"None at all," her son answered for Pilar, "the sooner, the better."

"You agree?" Señora Huerta asked Pilar with lifted brows.

What else was there to say? She summoned a smile, echoing in a whisper, "The sooner, the better."

They began the following morning.

Charro's mother came to Pilar's room with the maid Benita trailing behind her. In the maid's arms was a pile of gowns for evening in pale blue, cream, and yellow, also one of white embroidered with tiny blue flowers. They were the bridal gowns that had been used by members of the señora's family, her own gown and that of her daughter, Charro's sister, who had married the summer before and moved with her new husband to a home below the Rio Grande. There were also one or two other gowns belonging to Charro's sister which she had left behind as too youthful in style for a married woman. Pilar must try them all on. When she had made her choice for a wedding gown, and also for other occasions, Benita would alter them to fit.

As she spoke, the older woman gestured toward the curtained bed, indicating that the maid should lay out the gowns upon it. The señora then walked to the narrow double doors that opened onto the upper balcony. She pulled them shut, closing off the view, then moved away to take a seat beside the large armoire against the wall opposite the foot of the bed. She folded her hands, waiting to see that her wishes were carried out.

It made no great difference to Pilar what she wore; still, she did her best to appear cooperative and to show her appreciation. The gown that had belonged to the señora was far too short for her use. The ones belonging to Charro's sister were too large in the waist, but fitted well elsewhere. After some discussion the white with the blue flowers was pronounced by the señora as suitable for the ceremony. It would be taken up first, with the others to follow.

Pilar stood still with her arms held stiffly out beside her while Benita advanced upon her with needle and thread. Pins were scarce in the Tejas country, it appeared; the maid would use basting stitches to take up the seams that needed alteration.

The girl had nimble fingers. Señora Huerta had time for only one or two questions about Pilar's family and her convent schooling before the girl finished one seam, then moved around to begin on another. She drew the silk and cotton material tight, so that it constricted Pilar's waist, then plunged the needle into it. Pilar felt a sudden excruciating sting in her side. She yelped and jerked away from the girl.

"A thousand pardons, señorita," the Indian girl said, but there was no regret in her dark, red-rimmed eyes.

Pilar, meeting her gaze, recognized jealousy mingled with resentment on Benita's broad face. The girl was in love with Charro; she was forever doing some small something for him, dusting his hat for the sake of holding it, bringing him water or some special tidbit from the kitchen. Pilar was suddenly contrite, for she realized she had not considered what her unexpected announcement might mean to anyone except herself.

Señora Huerta rose to her feet. "Clumsy girl," she said in anger. "You have caused a spot of blood on the gown. Finish what you are doing, quickly now. Then go and soak out the stain."

Pilar did not flinch as the girl approached her once more with the needle. It had been a small act of revenge, that stab, one intended to attract attention. It had succeeded.

The incident was not repeated. As Pilar stood and allowed herself to be sewn into the gown she would wear for her wedding, it seemed that it was her future that was being stitched up, and that she might never be able to breathe freely again.

Pilar was not the only one who noticed Benita's distress over the wedding. Doña Luisa brought up the subject when she joined Pilar later in the morning. "You seemed to have destroyed the little maid's dream world," the widow said to her as she wandered out onto the balcony nibbling a piece of candy. "I just saw her scouring the table in the kitchen and using tears for soap."

Pilar agreed as she stepped out onto the balcony behind her. "I feel terrible about her."

"If I may say so, you don't look much happier than Benita." The other woman's gaze was shrewd in its appraisal.

"I'm trying to catch my breath. Everything is happening so fast."

"Yes, that is it, I'm sure. And you are not at all worried about Refugio."

Pilar moved to the balcony railing. Over her shoulder she said, "Why should I be?"

"He made you a public proposal of marriage and you refused him. Aren't you curious to know how he accepted that affront?"

"He had his purpose for making it; I had mine for refusing. He is very good at deciphering the reasons people do things. I'm sure he understood."

"Understanding and accepting are two different things. But I wonder if you don't misjudge Refugio? He may have a purpose for doing most things, yes, but the fact that his brain functions extremely well doesn't mean that he is incapable of feeling. He is an extraordinary man. I would think carefully before I sent him away."

"Would you?" Pilar said with a great show of indifference.

"I would, though I would probably choose to marry Charro just the same, as you are doing."

"Why would you say that?"

"He has the better prospects at the moment."

"You are forgetting the emeralds, aren't you? I'm sure Enrique told you about them."

Doña Luisa laughed. "So he did, how could I forget? It must be Enrique's good influence."

Pilar turned to face the other woman, with her back against the balcony railing. "You admit it?"

"Oh, yes. Isn't it amusing?"

Pilar frowned. "You aren't just—playing with Enrique, are you?"

"He is not a man for that kind of thing," the other woman said with a wry smile. "Oh, he's droll and funny and tolerant beyond most, but he has high standards and a quick temper. He keeps these standards for himself as well as for me. I find that endearing."

"I see," Pilar said slowly.

Doña Luisa laughed. "I don't suppose you do, but it doesn't matter since I am happy."

"What of your husband's estate? Will you go back to claim it?"

"No!" The widow shuddered, adding, "No, not if the saints are kind. I never want to set foot on a ship or a horse again."

"It's strange that you need never have left New Orleans, that you could have remained without harm from Don Esteban."

"Strange, yes, but some things are meant to be."

Pilar gave the other woman a long look. "But what of the money?"

"Enrique will see to it. He doesn't mind travel, and he will have the right as my husband to handle my affairs."

"Your husband! But what of—" Pilar stopped, unwilling to put something that had only been a nebulous dread in her mind into words.

"Refugio?" The widow gave a comfortable laugh. "He was kind on the ship. He saw how frightened I was of being alone, and how hurt at having been married to a man who only wanted to get an heir on my body while clinging to his mulatto mistress. Later, he ceased to be so kind. He had a reason, of course; he wanted me to turn to Enrique. He is diabolical, but also wise."

Was it possible, Pilar wondered, that Refugio had wanted her to turn to Charro? Did he feel a compulsion to establish all his discarded women with someone else? She did not really think it could be true, but the chance was strong enough that she might be able to use it to help her forget.

"You will remain here, then?"

"Oh, yes, in spite of there being no fabled cities of gold. I suspected that was a trick, you know; I'm not stupid. But I also wanted to see if Refugio was right, if I was stronger inside than I knew. No one was more surprised than I to find it's so. The Apaches terrify me still, but I will be all right with Enrique beside me. When my husband's estate is settled, he and I will find a place where we can grow cattle and babies. I will become fat, and Enrique will not care."

"And you will be content? You will never miss the court at Madrid?"

"Of course I shall miss it! And sometimes I will stamp my feet and cry for my old friends and the parties and fine clothes, and wonder why I ever buried myself in this wilderness. But I will always know that Enrique must live far away from Spain and the past. He will understand, and make me laugh, and it will pass."

"You expect much of him."

"Yes, and he will give me more. That's the way of it."

"Charro will also be a good husband," Pilar said, lifting her chin.

"Yes, probably. But will you make a good wife for him?"

That was, of course, the question. Pilar considered it with care after the other woman had gone. She would try, but would it be enough?

It was late evening when Pilar heard the first strains of the guitar. She wanted to shut out the sound but she could not. The melody was the old Andalusian love song Refugio had played that night in Seville, and again on the ship. The sound went on and on, bringing images of fountains and lemon trees shining in the moonlight, and of other things she would as soon forget. And when she thought she could stand it no longer, he began to sing, the words and the tones soft and rich and incredibly poignant.

She moved from her bedchamber through the narrow doors and out onto the balcony. She could not see him among the scattered shadows of the courtyard below. Still, his voice rose in endless refrain.

There was no one else about for the moment. Charro had ridden out with his father to inspect a herd of cattle the Indian *charros* were gathering, and the two had not yet returned. Vicente, Enrique, and Baltasar had gone to witness a cockfight to be held at the nearest group of Indian jacales. The señora was overseeing the preparations for the evening meal, harrying the servants in the lower regions of a connecting side building. Doña Luisa was completing her toilette for the evening.

Pilar moved farther out onto the balcony, the better to see. She trailed her fingers along the railing as she walked along beside it to change her vantage point. The glow of light from candles left burning in generous display in Doña Luisa's room slid over her as she passed the widow's door, gleaming in the dark honey-gold of her hair, shimmering along the slender turns of her arms and throat, exposed by her evening dress. The night breeze, delicately scented with sage, rustled the grape leaves that fringed the balcony overhead. From some distance away came the lowing of cattle and the cries of the Indian children at their jacales beyond the courtyard. And through it all, like some haunting memory, ran the music Refugio made.

Pilar reached the end of the balcony where the grapevine grew, and turned in the other direction, aimlessly strolling. She had given up on discovering Refugio's location below, since it seemed he did not want to be found. She wished Charro and the others would return, bringing their laughter and teasing to brighten the night. She wished the dinner bell would ring, though she knew well it would not for at least an hour. She wished that Doña Luisa would finish dressing and come and talk to her. She wished that Señora Huerta would find some task that needed her help. She longed for something to happen, anything to stop the music and the singing.

She reached her bedchamber again and stepped inside. Deliberately, she closed the narrow doors behind her. The music faded, dying away. She could no longer hear it.

Or had it really stopped? She stood listening for long moments, but could not quite tell. The walls of the house were thick and the balcony doors so solid.

She drew a deep breath, then closed her eyes and let it out slowly. Lifting a hand to rub the back of her neck, she moved farther into the room.

She busied herself, straightening away her few belongings. However, she was soon uncomfortable. The closed doors shut out the cooling breeze of the night, and there was still heat trapped in the room from the long hot day. It was silly of her to endure it merely because of a piece of music and her own irritated sensibilities.

Turning in a swirl of skirts, she moved back to the doors. She grasped the handles and pulled the solid panels open, letting the night air sweep inside.

With the wind came Refugio. He glided soundlessly around the doorframe and halted with his back to the open door panel that lay against the wall.

"Accommodating and endlessly hospitable," he said, his voice resonant with warmth. "Will you also be loving?"

CHAPTER 22

Pilar backed away from Refugio. Almost afraid of the answer, she said, "What do you mean?"

"I am asking, in my own way of course, if I am welcome?"

"How can you think so, when I am to be married to Charro?"

"As a ploy to persuade Governor Pacheco to feel compassion for me, spurning my suit could hardly have been bettered. I would have foregone the aid, however, if it had allowed me to avoid the rack of it."

"You hid your torment well."

"Practice gives that facility."

"Nevertheless, the decision was made, and I am to be married."

"Then you intend to pledge fidelity?" he said in sardonic tones.

"Of course!"

"I did wonder."

She lifted her chin as she caught his meaning. "You feel that I should have been faithful to you?"

"I had somehow expected it." He shrugged. "I can't think why."

"Nor can I, when you trusted me in nothing else."

"You mean the emeralds," he said in stark acceptance of the change of subject.

She turned away from him, pacing a few steps before swinging back again. "What else should I mean? You kept them from me, knowing full well what they meant to me. You hoarded them over all those long, weary miles, and never said a word. How could you?"

"And what they meant to me, what of that?" His gaze was intent upon her flushed face.

"What do they mean, indeed? The Carranza estates in Spain are gone forever. There might be a hacienda here in the Tejas country, cattle and horses and *charros* to follow your orders. But what do such things matter against the way you betrayed me?"

"Nothing and less than nothing," he answered impatiently. "For me to have given you the emeralds would have put you in danger from Don Esteban the instant he discovered you had them. More than that, they were a way of keeping you with me."

Her eyes narrowed. "If you intended to use them to bribe me into staying, then you have a strange idea of my character."

"Not at all. As long as I had them, your legacy from your mother was safe from Don Esteban. But as long as you did not know it, you would not have the means to leave me."

His features were defenseless as he waited for her answer. He stood perfectly still, leaning on his hands, which were pressed flat against the door behind him as if he would permit himself no gesture of appeal.

Pilar, watching him, felt his meaning penetrate to the center of her being. He had not wanted her to leave him. He had risked everything against the chance of keeping her.

Finally, she said, "You thought, when you came across the emeralds in New Orleans, that if you shared them with me, I would immediately abandon all of you and return to Spain?"

353

"Share?" he said, the word tentative.

"Naturally, I would not have taken them all. You had lost as much as I."

His face tightened over the bones. "So generous. But still, you would have had what you came after. There would have been no way to hold you."

"Must a woman be held by force or money, and never of her own desires? Can't she decide of her own will whether she will go or stay?"

"The temptation to use the means at hand is strong when the alternative is unbearable."

It was, perhaps, an attempt at an explanation, or even justification; certainly it was not an apology. It came to her, fleetingly, that it might also be a declaration, though of what kind it was difficult to say. She had always known that he wanted her, though she had never felt before that, for him, the obstruction of his desire was something he would be unable to bear.

She lowered her lashes as she considered it. "That night after Isabel died," she said, "when you spoke of staying here in New Spain—it was not just idle talk, was it? You knew then that you had the money to do that, if you wished."

He was extremely quick. "I could not have used it without making you wonder where it came from. I would have told you when the time came."

"You would have told me something; I don't doubt that." A hint of irony touched her lips and was gone.

He pushed away from the door, taking a step toward her. "What can I say to make you believe me, to make you understand?"

His words were nearly lost in the clatter of horses' hoofs. It was Charro and the others returning, sweeping into the courtyard through the gates that some servant on watch must have thrown open. Their voices rang against the walls of the house as they exchanged laughing insults and called out in exuberance for drink to clear the dust of their ride from their throats.

"You had better go," Pilar said, meeting Refugio's gaze with steady brown eyes. "Charro will not like finding you here."

"He has become a possessive bridegroom?"

A troubled look crossed her face. "He doesn't say much, but I see him watching us."

"No doubt I would do the same in his place." Refugio's voice indicated acceptance, but he made no move to leave.

"Please," she said, "you really must go."

"Must I? I could also stay. And you could tell Charro that you made a mistake, that you have changed your mind."

"I made a promise." The words were firmer than she felt.

"Promises can be broken, and often are."

"Not without good reason."

"What reason would serve, I wonder?" There was a hard light in his eyes.

"Not the emeralds," she said quickly, afraid that he might offer them.

"Ah, Pilar, you misjudge me. I have better sense than that, and also plans for their use. Señor Huerta tells me there is an *estancia* that joins this one to the south that may be bought for a fair price. The owner grows old and tired of fighting Apaches, and wants to die in Spain. In any case, I have more . . . sentiment within me." The astringency that crept into his voice was a reminder that the last phrase had been used at the meeting in the governor's study. Who had said it? Was it Don Esteban?

Her husband-to-be had entered the house; she could hear his voice below, calling her name as he searched for her.

The sound was followed by the quick tattoo of his footsteps on the stairs. Panic beat up inside her as she thought of the two men coming face to face with each other in her bedchamber. There was something in Refugio's stance, some incipient recklessness in his manner, that fueled it.

On a quick, indrawn breath, she said, "Refugio, please don't do this."

He tilted his head, his eyes steel-gray with the darkness behind them. "Have you no interest in my sentiments?"

"Not at this moment," she said, clasping her hands into fists at her sides. "Not here."

He watched her for long seconds as Charro's tread came nearer, thudding on the floor of the sitting room that connected to her bedchamber. Abruptly he said, "Then I am left to requiems and revenge and my unrequited love. It could be that it's fitting."

There came a thumping on the bedchamber door. "Pilar?" Charro called.

She glanced in that direction but did not answer. Turning back toward Refugio as if drawn by a magnet, she said, "Love?"

There was no answer. He was gone.

It was a moment before she could bring her taut muscles to move, could force herself to reach to open the door for Charro. He stood there looking down at her, studying her pale face, before he searched the room beyond her with a glance that lingered on the balcony door. Finally, he stepped inside.

"What is it?" he asked. "Don't you feel well?"

She summoned a smile. "Yes, fine. I was just . . . resting."

He closed the door behind him with slow care. When he looked at her again, there was the shadow of trouble in his eyes. "He was here, wasn't he? Refugio?"

"Yes," she answered. It would be wrong to persist in her lie.

"Begging you to reconsider? Making love to you?"

"Explaining," she said, "or trying to."

"And that's all?"

She inclined her head. There was no need to tell him that there might have been more if he had not returned.

He moved closer to her and reached to take her hands in his. He caressed the smooth backs of her fingers with his thumbs, his gaze upon that small movement. His voice deep, he said, "Refugio is my friend. More than that, he has been as a brother to me. He took the scared boy that I was when I came to him, and turned him into a man. He gave me back my pride and my sense of who and what I was inside; there is no one I respect more. But, *querida*, I cannot permit him to visit you like this. If I do, it will destroy us."

"I know," she said, her voice coming low and uneven from her constricted throat. "And I would do nothing to—to hurt you. I tried to tell him—"

"I'm sure you did, but Refugio listens to no one when it comes to you. You are his weakness. We always thought he had none, those of us in the band, but that was before you came. He will have to go. He will have to leave the hacienda. We can't stay here together, the three of us."

"Yes," she whispered. "But what if he won't leave?"

"Then he must learn, somehow, to let you go. If he cannot, if he will not, then we will eventually have to fight. And either I will kill him or he will kill me."

"Oh, Charro, no!" she cried, her eyes huge as she searched his face.

He bent his head, lifting her hands to press her fingers to his lips. His voice was hoarse, his warm breath moist against her hands as he said, "There is no other way."

"There must be," she protested.

He made no answer as he caught her in his arms and pressed his mouth to hers. His lips were sweet and gentle, and he held her with care. But Pilar, shivering in the strong circle of his arms, felt only fear.

Pilar did not sleep well when bedtime finally came. The things that Refugio and Charro had said repeated endlessly in her mind. She knew Refugio was right, that she was marrying Charro out of pique. Did that make it wrong when Charro wanted her, and when she had no one else, no other place to go?

She realized also that, in spite of what Refugio had said, he had not offered her a portion of the emeralds. She didn't want them, not really, but it was a damning omission. Or was it? Might he not be protecting her from Don Esteban still?

He had spoken of love, though in his own oblique fashion. Had he meant what she thought, or was there some other significance in it that she could not see? What was it he had said before about his speech? That he used it to hide behind? What was he hiding from now?

The long sleeves and thick linen of the nightgown Señora Huerta had loaned Pilar was too heavy for the warmth of the night. She thought of taking it off, but decided against it. The night breeze coming through the open doors onto the balcony was slowly growing cooler. She jerked the thick folds from under her, straightening the long length that had twisted about her as she turned in restlessness. Closing her eyes tightly, she willed sleep to come.

It seemed endless hours later that she was startled into awareness. There had been a noise somewhere nearby, like the faint scrape of a footstep. She thought it had come from outside on the balcony, or possibly from just inside her bedchamber.

Slow anger seeped over her. That Refugio could think that he might come and go in her bedchamber as he pleased, even in the middle of the night, was past bearing. She would tell him so in words that could leave no possible doubt.

She opened her eyes to slits. The balcony doorway made a gray rectangle in the darkness. There was no sign of movement there, no shape of a man's form. The room around her was dense with blackness, but she could sense no movement in it. Where had he gone? Or had he been there at all? Perhaps she had only imagined that footfall, or else dreamed it.

There came a quiet rustle from just above her head. Before she could turn, before she could move, a thick, smothering blanket descended. It covered her head and shoulders, and hard, rough hands pressed it down over her face. She struck out, and her arms were entangled in the folds. What felt like a knee was thrown across her legs, pinning her to the mattress. She drew in her breath to scream.

The sound was trapped in her throat as a hand came down hard across her face. She felt her upper lip bruise against her teeth. Then the darkness exploded with points of light as a blow smashed into her jaw. The light points faded, and there was nothing.

Pilar roused once. She was lying facedown across the saddle of a horse that was just jolting to a halt. She was wrapped in the close folds of a blanket smelling faintly of sheep's wool and wood smoke. Her feet were bound together at the ankles, and her hands were fastened at the wrists. Her head pounded with a ferocious, pulsing pain. She heard the creak of leather as someone dismounted. Then she was dragged backward, across the saddle. Her midsection cramped and the pounding in her head increased. The double pain took her backward once more into darkness.

Voices drew her toward consciousness the next time. They made a deep rumbling that seemed to have no words. She turned her head slightly, catching her breath as pain throbbed in her temple. It was a moment before she realized that the voices had ceased.

She opened her eyes. She was lying on a floor of packed earth. An Indian trade blanket was wrapped around her, though it had been pulled away from her face. Above her was an unsealed roof of crossed poles. For an instant she thought she was in the courtyard at the hacienda, then she saw that the roof had a hole in one corner through which could be seen the star-filled night sky, and the crumbling adobe walls about her were smoked black from countless fires. There were no furnishings, no bedrolls, no pots around the center fire hole. She was in an abandoned hut, perhaps an Indian jacal.

The light for her inspection was provided by a single lantern of pierced tin. It sat on the floor well away from the sagging entrance door. Two men stood beside it, looking in her direction. For a moment their features were blurred, then she began slowly to make them out.

"So you are awake, my dear Pilar," Don Esteban said. "We were beginning to be worried about you. My large friend, here, feared he had struck you too hard."

She saw the other man standing there, heard what Don Esteban said of him; still her mind refused to accept it. She blinked, trying to clear the odd denseness from her mind. She moistened dry lips to speak, though the word she said was only a whisper.

"Baltasar?" she said.

"Are you really surprised?" Don Esteban said. "I would not have thought he had that much ability to play a part.

It's interesting what people are able to do when they have good reason."

Pilar could find no answer. Her hands were now unbound, she discovered, though there seemed to be a braided leather thong still about her ankles. She closed her eyes, lifting a hand to her head.

"I didn't mean to hurt you," Baltasar said in a bass rumble. "But I had to do something to get you away without any noise."

She lifted her lashes to stare at him. The lantern light below him shone on the white of his shirtfront and made a soft glow under his chin, glinting on his beard stubble. "Why?" she asked.

"My orders," her stepfather answered for Baltasar. "I had to have you, because you are the only one who can bring Carranza—and the emeralds."

"What—" she began, then stopped. Appalled comprehension rose in her eyes.

"You see it, don't you? Just as he went after his little friend Isabel who was taken by the Apaches, he will come after you. He can do no less, because he is El Leon."

She shook her head, a grave mistake. Swallowing upon the sickness the movement brought, she said, "How will he know where to come? He's more acute than most, but not a mind reader."

Baltasar answered her. "I left a note on your pillow giving the place. And I told him to come alone. It may be a long time before the paper is found and taken to him, but he will come."

"On your pillow," Don Esteban said in cold amusement. "That should worry him, don't you think?"

Pilar ignored him, her gaze on Baltasar. "I don't see how you did it, how you got me out of the hacienda, I mean. What of the guard? How did you get past him?"

"It was easy," the large man said with a sardonic look that sat strangely on his broad face. "You are light and the grapevine at your balcony is strong. As for the guard, there was no problem. I was the guard."

"But if you could take me from the hacienda, why could you not just steal the emeralds, if that was what my stepfather wanted?"

Don Esteban laughed, a harsh sound. "Taking the emeralds would have been much more difficult since Carranza keeps them near him at all times. Difficult or not, it would not have been enough. You of all people should know that I don't want just the emeralds."

"It's insane to take this so far," she said, her voice querulous with distress. "You have risked so much, and for what? Hate and a few jewels that came from something you stole in the first place? Why couldn't you have just let us go when we left New Orleans?"

"Because I did not choose to," the portly and graying little man said with a hard glitter in his eyes.

She stared at him for long moments. "Then whatever happens when Refugio comes, that too will be of your choosing."

Don Esteban turned from her, motioning to Baltasar with a negligent gesture, as if her words had no power to disturb him. The two of them moved away, conferring in whispers. Pilar, feeling too helpless lying flat on the floor, pushed herself up by degrees to sit with her back against the wall. After a moment her head stopped pounding and settled to a dull ache. It became easier to think.

Would Refugio really come? The answer to that was simple; of course he would. He would come because he was the leader, and therefore responsible for her plight. He would come, possibly, for the sake of a night spent on a ship at sea, and another beside a rock on the dark plains. He would come because she would not be where she was if it were not for Don Esteban's vendetta against him. Oh, yes, he would come.

Would he come alone?

He well might. It was just the kind of sacrifice that he could consider it his duty to make.

How long would it be before he arrived? It must be close to dawn by now. If no one had seen Baltasar take her away, if no one had discovered her absence during the night, then she would not be missed before breakfast. She had no idea how far this jacal was from the hacienda, but assumed that it was within two or three hours; surely she could not have been brought farther than that. Any closer, however, would have been too dangerous.

The middle of the morning, then, or perhaps midday, was the soonest that Refugio could be expected. Surely there was something she could do to release herself, or change matters in some way, between now and then?

Under the trading blanket Pilar flexed the muscles of her calves slowly, putting pressure on the thong of braided leather knotted about her ankles. It bit into her skin, but she ignored the sting. She thought there might be a little give in the leather. Baltasar may have left it loose because he had not wanted to cut off the blood circulation to her feet. Or he may have only considered the possibility of any attempt at escape as unlikely. What she would do if she managed to free her feet, she did not know, but at least it would help her feelings to do something.

Don Esteban swung his head to look at her, demanding, "What are you doing?"

Pilar gave him her most limpid look. "Nothing."

"Don't think you can fool me. Under the blanket. What are you doing?"

"The toes of my left foot are numb," she complained.

"Too bad. Keep still, or I will see to it you are numb all over. Forever."

Pilar obeyed, at least until he turned his back again. Then she began very carefully to stretch the thong once more.

Refugio came without warning. There was no sound of hoofbeats, no footsteps, no change in the night stillness. The ramshackle door of the hut simply creaked open on its leather hinges and he stepped inside.

Baltasar swung around, instincts honed by years with the band causing him to draw his sword in the same powerful movement. Don Esteban turned with a curse on his lips. Refugio faced them at his ease. With his cloak fastened at the neck and flung back behind his shoulders, it was easy to see that he was unarmed.

"I bid you good evening, gentlemen," he said, "or is it morning?"

"How did you get here so quickly?" Don Esteban snapped.

"I rode, of course. Weren't you expecting me?"

Refugio moved a few steps farther into the hut. His gaze flicked to where Pilar sat. It rested on her for only a moment, but she felt there was no detail of her appearance that he missed; not her hair straggling on her shoulders with strands caught, glinting, on her linen gown; not the shadows under her eyes and the bruise shading her chin, nor the dingy trader's blanket that was bunched around her. She could only stare at him while her heart sank like a weight of stone inside her.

Baltasar, frowning, echoed Don Esteban's question. "How could you have found this place so fast, unless—"

"Unless I followed you? Did it never once occur to you, my former friend, that your midnight abduction was too easy?"

"What are you saying?" Baltasar growled.

"You thought you were baiting a trap, but you were only taking the bait left for you. Didn't you wonder why you were left as the only guard? I trusted you that much once, *compadre*, but that was long ago."

"You wanted me to take Pilar? I don't believe it."

Refugio's smile was placid. "You will think differently, I expect, when you discover that you are surrounded."

Don Esteban exclaimed, his gaze going instantly to the night beyond the open door. He recovered at once. "It's a fabrication, it must be. But even if it were not," he pointed out, "you are unarmed."

Refugio glanced down at himself as if in surprise. "So I am. Will you take that as license to carve my hide into thin slices? Do that, and I can promise you the same fate before you can wipe your sword."

"Empty threats," Don Esteban sneered.

"Possibly. Shall we see?"

Baltasar gave a dogged shake of his head. "You would never let Pilar run the danger of being caught between us and anybody you might have brought."

"You mean because of a few nights of sharing a berth or a blanket? She made a lovely companion for the journey, but all journeys end."

Baltasar glanced at Pilar, then back to Refugio. "I don't think so, not for you when it comes to this woman. I heard you ask her to marry you just this morning; we all did."

Refugio gave a quiet laugh. "It was well done, wasn't it? I'm delighted you appreciated the ruse, since it was for your benefit. Yours, and Don Esteban's, of course. I needed some way to force you, Baltasar, to expose yourself as the member of my band who had turned traitor. At the same time, I needed to persuade Don Esteban to tear himself away from the protection of the governor and official authority.

I rather thought an abduction would appeal to my old enemy, that he would enjoy serving me the same trick I had served him in Spain. I needed to convince the two of you, then, that Pilar would be a worthy hostage. What better way than a proposal of marriage to indicate her value to me? What better way than a proposal to suggest that she was worth the taking?"

CHAPTER 23

Refugio had used her. The knowledge burned in Pilar's mind, along with all the things implied by it. He had risked her life for his revenge; it meant no more to him than that. In that case, he could not possibly love her, and all his half-formed vows meant nothing. They were false coins dredged up to try to persuade her to surrender to him once more. Doubtless his pride had been hurt by her public refusal to be his wife, or else, seeing her on the point of slipping away from him, her value had suddenly increased in his eyes. His desire for her had been rekindled then, and he had sought her out to satisfy it.

None of it seemed like the Refugio she thought she knew, yet he had condemned himself by his own words. The conclusions she had reached had followed inescapably from that fact.

Baltasar was less easy to convince. He asked skeptically, "You will not mind if Don Esteban kills her?"

"What does killing prove, except that the killer has strength and a weapon?"

"Nothing," the big man agreed, "but it would hurt you, as you hurt me. I should have taken Pilar back there on the trail, should have given her to the Indians and made you kill her, too."

Refugio shook his head, his gaze steady on Baltasar. "I didn't kill Isabel at your command."

"No? I remember it different."

"That may be," Refugio said, his voice soft. "For myself, I consider that I was forced to kill her because you failed her."

Pilar, watching them, felt her own confused heartache recede as she witnessed the depths of the pain that lay between the two men. But she saw something more. She saw Don Esteban watching them, saw him smiling to himself.

She spoke quickly, before she could lose the conviction rising inside her. "I don't think either of you caused the death of Isabel. I think the man who is responsible is standing there beside you."

Baltasar turned ponderously to face her. "What are you saying?"

"If it had not been for Don Esteban, none of us would have left Spain. It was he who started the long string of events that brought us here. His interference can be traced back to the death of Refugio's father, and beyond. It includes my mother, but the most important thing is this: if he had not kidnapped Vicente and taken him with him to Louisiana, none of us would have left Spain, and Isabel would still be alive."

"If Carranza had not taken the emeralds—". Don Esteban began.

"An error, it has to be admitted," Refugio said, "one more among many. And yet, Don Esteban, I think that Isabel's death can be brought even closer home to you."

"How's that?" Baltasar's voice was wary, yet rough with suspicion.

"It's a trick," Don Esteban said quickly. "Don't let him confuse you by twisting things to suit his own ends."

"Twisting them how?" The big man's voice was dogged.

"There's no mystery," Refugio said, "only an exercise of logic. Don Esteban was traveling with Indian traders, Frenchmen who were familiar with the various tribes, who spoke their language and had steel hatchets, knives, and muskets to exchange for whatever the Indians might have of value. The Apache war party trailed us first, you remember, tracking us as if theirs was a mission of vengeance—or as if they needed to be certain who we were."

"You are saying they were paid to make the attack?" Baltasar's face was creased with thought.

"In muskets, with more to be provided, I expect, when they produced our scalps."

Baltasar turned on Don Esteban. "You sent those murdering devils after the band? You sent them, knowing that I was with them, and Isabel?"

"Certainly not!" the older man said, drawing himself up as if he would overawe the other man. "You were attacked because you were traveling across Indian country. I had nothing to do with it."

"But you and your party were not attacked," Refugio pointed out quietly.

"A fact that proves nothing at all!"

"Refugio doesn't say things without a reason," Baltasar said, his voice dogged.

"Yes, and his reason is to put us at each other's throats," the don declared.

"Could be that's where we should be," Baltasar said.

"But what of him?" Don Esteban asked, his voice rising. "I thought you said he was the one who decided on the overland trail."

Baltasar made no reply for a moment. In the silence, Pilar met Refugio's gaze. She knew then that what Don Esteban said was true: Refugio wanted the other two men at odds for some reason of his own. Did that mean there was no one else in the darkness beyond the jacal? She did not dare think it could be so, for it would also mean he was unarmed against two men who wanted him dead. And it would mean that everything he had said about setting a trap with her as bait was a lie.

But if it was true, then he might need her help in what he was doing.

Deliberately, she said, "If you are looking for someone to blame, Baltasar, what of yourself? If you had not shot Refugio during the attack, Isabel would not have left the barricade, and the Apaches could not have taken her. But you did, just as you hired someone to shoot him during the attack of the corsairs on the ship, and just as you replaced the mock sword in the duel in Havana with a sharp one. Why did you do it? What in the name of heaven made you join with my stepfather against the band?"

The big man gave a hollow laugh. "Refugio took my Isabel's love and treated it as if it were nothing. He took everything she had, but he would not let her go."

"I tried," Refugio said, his tone reflective.

"Oh, yes, you tried. You brought a lady to the cabin in the mountains to shame her. You brought Pilar to show Isabel how far she was beneath you."

"To show her the kind of woman I needed, to convince Isabel that I meant it when I said that I could not love her. I thought she would turn to you."

"She did, but for comfort, not love. I gave her all the love inside me, and all she had for me in return was pity."

"That isn't true," Pilar said to the big man. "She loved you."

"She loved me as she might a pet dog."

Pilar shook her head. "You think she loved Refugio? It seems to me she worshiped him because he had saved her, because he was the first man to make her feel safe. That isn't love."

"Maybe. But that was what I wanted from her, that worship, and I knew that as long as the great El Leon was alive, she would never be able to give it. She as good as told me so the night you came, when Refugio forced her to accept you by giving you his bed."

"So you offered your help to his enemy."

"That was done weeks before you came, after Refugio let me have Isabel, after I saw how it would be."

"You—it was you who killed my aunt, that night when I came to the hut in the mountains, when you were gone so long?"

"No, how could that be? The don sent others for that. Until that night, I only let him know, now and then, what little I could discover about the movements of the band; it wasn't much since only Refugio knew where we would go, what we would do. Then I saw how Refugio had hurt Isabel by bringing you. I saw she would never love me as long as he was alive, and I wanted him to die. I thought that if I arranged it, Don Esteban would reward me."

"You tried to kill him, after all he had done."

Baltasar looked away from Pilar. "I wanted the money for Isabel. For afterward."

"Now there will be no afterward, for Isabel is dead; Don Esteban has seen to that."

"How affecting," Don Esteban said with a curl of his lips, half hidden by his perfumed beard. "But there will be no afterward for you, either, my dear stepdaughter. Or for Carranza."

Baltasar stiffened, the frown deepening between his eyes. "You promised to let Señorita Pilar go if Refugio came."

"Of course I did, because you would not have brought her otherwise," the don said impatiently. "But it can't be. She would go straight to the governor with the story."

"If Refugio is killed trying to keep you from taking

her from him, that's one thing, since she's your stepdaughter and you can claim to be protecting her honor by saving her from him. But what excuse can you give the governor for killing her? You had better think again."

Don Esteban's face tightened. "She's done nothing except make trouble since she left the convent, and I've been put to enough inconvenience because of her. It can be an accident. Possibly Carranza will attempt to use her as a shield from my wrath, or maybe Carranza himself will kill her in a jealous rage. No matter the story told, I want her dead."

Refugio, his gaze steadfast on the face of the man who was once his friend, said, "You gave me your word in your note that Pilar would go free."

"The note was written by Don Esteban."

"But it was you who left it for me, you who gave me the terms of surrender. I hold you to them."

"Pay no attention," Don Esteban said in strident tones. "Think how glorious a revenge it will be, if he knows she will die with him, because of him."

Baltasar studied Refugio, then turned back to Don Esteban. "It's not right," he said doggedly. "I did give Refugio my word. He would not have come if he had not believed what I said."

"What difference does that make?" the older man demanded, smashing his fist into his hand, his face growing purple. "This is no time for sudden scruples!"

"By all means let us dispense with scruples," Refugio said. "If I can't have an honorable friend, let me at least have a suitably dishonorable enemy."

Baltasar's brows knotted in a frown. "I wanted Refugio dead, but not Señorita Pilar. I don't hold with killing women."

"It would make your revenge perfect, much more than

just killing him," Don Esteban said in virulent persuasion. "If she is first, he will suffer for a few seconds as you suffered when your Isabel died."

Pilar, watching the big man's face, saw the reluctance reflected there. She spoke in abrupt comprehension. "What is it, Baltasar? Do you find it hard to kill a friend when he's facing you? Especially when the friend is El Leon? The honorable thing to do would be to give him a sword and match yourself against him. You never wanted that, did you? You tried three times to kill him, and three times you failed. Are you sure you want to kill him at all?"

"Shut up!" Don Esteban said, the words vicious.

Refugio said nothing, only watching her and the other two men with taut attention.

Pilar went on, her concentration on the big man and the struggle inside him, which twisted his face and made him clench his great hands into vein-corded fists. "It was Don Esteban who caused Isabel's death, just as he killed my mother and my aunt and now wants me dead. He finds it easy to attack women. They don't matter to him; their deaths trouble him no more than if they were animals."

Don Esteban drew the sword that hung at his side. "Yours," he said, "will trouble me even less."

Pilar barely glanced at the naked blade pointed at her, though she spoke more quickly. "Will you let him get away with what he has done, Baltasar? Will you let him use you to get what he wants, even though he would have let you be killed by the Apaches with the rest of us? The solution is easy. Give Refugio your sword. Give it to him and let the two men who have injured you try to kill each other."

"An excellent idea," Refugio said, his voice soft, as if he feared anything louder would sway Baltasar in the wrong direction.

At the same instant, Don Esteban took a step toward Pilar, shouting, "I told you to shut up!"

Baltasar moved quickly to match Don Esteban's stride, and Refugio kept pace at his side. The lantern light ran in a silver-blue gleam down the length of the sword Pilar's stepfather held.

She pushed herself up with her back pressed to the wall behind her. Using its support, she rose unsteadily to her bound feet. She jerked at her right ankle with desperate strength, trying to loosen the thong. She felt the wetness of warm blood creeping down her instep, dampening the leather binding. She increased the pressure, oblivious to the pain. Abruptly, the thong slipped. Her right foot was free, though it was so numb she was not sure it would hold her.

Don Esteban advanced another step as he saw she had loosened her bonds, though at the same time he glanced back over his shoulder at the door. It seemed he was not quite certain whether the jacal was surrounded, not certain he was free to act. He cursed Baltasar, saying in tones of contempt, "You came in with me on this plan. Now stop playing the fool and help me carry it out!"

Pilar said quickly to the big man, "It isn't foolish to admit you made a mistake. You owe Don Esteban nothing—unless it's payment in kind for what he did to Isabel. You could give him that."

"Listen to her, Baltasar," Refugio said in soft entreaty, "listen, and either take your moment of vengeance as Pilar said—or else give it to me."

"Stupid fools, all of you," Don Esteban said, his lips curling in a grimace. He tightened his grip on his sword, moving with it pointed at Pilar's heart. She gathered her trembling muscles, knowing any evasion she might make would be no more than a delay.

Baltasar moistened his lips as he listened to Refugio. "You will kill me for this, later," he said.

"No," his leader said hurriedly. "Escape is through the door."

"Don't be an imbecile!" Don Esteban cried with a sudden note of fear in his voice. "There's no need for this."

The big man shook his head, obviously wavering. "The band will shoot me the minute they see me."

"They may try, so you'll have to be quick. But I pledge you a recompense for Isabel's pain and her blood." Refugio's voice was steady. "And Pilar's life."

"Not if I take it first!" Don Esteban drew back his sword for the thrust.

Baltasar made a strangled sound, muttering, "Pray God the band shoots straight."

He dragged his sword, screeching, from his scabbard, and slapped the hilt into Refugio's hand. In the same instant he whirled around and dived for the door.

Refugio spared him not a glance, but lunged full length with the sword in his grasp, catching the driving blow Don Esteban had begun, wrenching the other man's blade upward in a rasping scrape that showered the dirt floor with orange sparks. The glittering point struck the wall above Pilar's head even as the guards of the two weapons locked together with a vicious clang. Refugio grabbed the older man's shoulder and shoved. The don plunged off balance, coming up against the adobe wall in a scattering of loose dirt, twisting around to face his opponent.

Refugio stepped back. Catching the hem of his cloak, he swirled it around his left arm, out of the way, then stood balanced and ready.

Pilar, her breathing fast and uneven, slid along the wall away from the men. She bent to snatch the blanket up from the floor under Refugio's feet, where it might be an impediment. He glanced at her, a swift and comprehensive appraisal, then he settled into his position, intent only on the man before him.

Don Esteban attacked in fury, trying to take advantage of the small confines of the jacal, to force Refugio back into Pilar or else trap him in a corner. Pilar retreated in limping haste to the doorway, ready to step through. She could not bring herself to move farther, however, but stood watching with her fingers digging into the blanket. From the night beyond came the dull noise of hoofbeats fading away as Baltasar fled. There had been no shots, no shouts.

Refugio had been bluffing. He had come alone.

Don Esteban fought like an enraged animal caught in a trap, using every desperate ruse at his command, every trick learned from the New Orleans encounter between them. Refugio was fighting for two; his defeat would mean death for Pilar. His countermoves were smoothly efficient, but cautious.

The lantern cast their shadows, dancing in triplicate on the wall. It made shifting pools of layered darkness in the corners that were more treacherous than pure blackness would have been. The ceiling was low, and uneven with its sagging poles; both men had to watch above them as well as in front and to the sides, or they were likely to bring crumbling thatch, scorpions, and spiders cascading down the backs of their necks.

Refugio made not a sound. Don Esteban breathed like a faulty bellows, gasping in the warm air. Perspiration appeared on the older man's face, beading on his cheeks and forehead, running down his nose. It made a wet patch between his shoulders on the back of his jacket. Refugio's hairline grew damp and curling, and there was a satin sheen of moisture at the open neck of his shirt.

Their feet shuffled back and forth on the earthen floor,

stirring up dust that glinted in soft gold eddies in the flickering light. Don Esteban grew more aggressive, his footfalls heavier, as if he wanted to slash Refugio to quivering ribbons and grind him into the dirt. Refugio evaded him, giving ground, expending a minimum of effort.

Backing swiftly, the younger man unfurled his cloak from his arm and dipped his left hand into the garment's pocket. He drew it out with his fingers clenched around a small leather bag. His gaze narrowed on the point of his opponent's sword, he put the bag to his mouth and used his teeth to loosen the string that held it closed. With the bag's neck open, he abruptly turned it bottom side up.

Gems poured from it in a stream as green and shining as the new leaves of summer. They hit the floor, bouncing and skittering under the feet of the two men, burying themselves in the dusty surface where they winked like cat's eyes in the dim light.

"You wanted the emeralds in exchange for Pilar," Refugio said. "There you have them. Some may be a trifle marred before we're done, but I do keep my bargains."

Don Esteban cursed in savage fury. He minced back and forth on tiptoe, darting quick, agonized glances at the floor with his teeth set together as if in anticipation of pain.

He trod upon a green stone and it made an ominous crunching noise in the gritty dirt. The don flailed in a sudden desperate feint, circling Refugio's blade, his own adhering, locking with it once more to the hilt. He shoved at Refugio as he leaped back, disengaging.

"Stand clear," he ground out, his chest heaving with effort. "I must pick up my property."

Refugio inclined his head in polite acquiescence. "By all means."

Don Esteban squatted down, reaching out to pick up the sparkling emeralds from the dirt one by one, collecting them up in his left hand. His hasty gathering was clumsy, for he picked up quantities of dry earth with them. As he worked, he snatched quick upward glances at Refugio, as if he suspected him of some ruse or was planning one himself.

Disquiet rose in Pilar's mind. Before she could stop herself, a warning rose to her lips. "Take care—"

There was no need to finish it. Refugio was watching, waiting in long-held knowledge of the sly cunning that underlay Don Esteban's actions.

The don sprang upright, flinging the handful of jewels and dirt into Refugio's face. He followed them with a hard, straight thrust of his sword with all his strength behind it. Refugio bent swiftly under the hail of green stones in their cloud of dust, meeting his opponent's sword with a parry that jarred them both to the elbow, then leading into an Italian master's feint that slipped past Don Esteban's guard like an eel sliding into water.

Don Esteban cried out. The two men held their places while the dust the don had thrown settled, lazily billowing, to the floor. It appeared for a moment that the two were embracing, with Refugio supporting the older man. Then Refugio retracted his sword. Don Esteban staggered back, sprawling to lie in the dirt with a crimson stain spreading over his jacket front.

Pilar let out her pent breath and closed her eyes. Tears threatened to overwhelm her, and she swallowed them down. She felt sick and spent and empty. She had witnessed an execution. She had known how it would be, must be, as surely as Baltasar had known when he gave Refugio his sword and departed. Refugio could have drawn out the agony, could have tormented his old enemy as the wild cat for which he was named might play with a mouse. He had not. He had permitted the don a last chance at escape, a chance to call it even and withdraw from the contest, and even take his stolen property. Don Esteban had not been able to resist a last foul ruse, a last attempt to catch his sworn foe unaware. And so he had died.

He had died, and it was over.

Pilar opened her eyes. Refugio was on one knee in the dust, sifting through it for the emeralds. His movements were deliberate, precise. He cupped the shining stones in his hand, touching them with his long, callused fingers, meticulously counting. A bleak pain settled in Pilar's chest; still, she moved slowly to join him. She sank to her knees, reaching to locate a half-dozen green jewels.

"That's all of them." Refugio's face was still, his eyes shadowed in the dimness.

Pilar held the emeralds to the light, then bent her head to carefully blow away the dust adhering to them. With them lying on the blue-veined white surface of her palm, she held them out to Refugio.

He reached for her hand, taking it in his. With his closed fingers around the emeralds he held, he put his fist over her palm then released his grasp, adding them to those she had recovered. Removing his hand, he curled his fingers around hers so she possessed the whole shimmering green hoard; then he held them there.

"What are you doing?" she said. "I don't want these."

"You did once."

"Not anymore. You're the one who risked your life for them, the one who lost the most; you should have them."

She tried to push them toward him, but he would not let her. His clasp tightened until she could feel the polished edges of the stones biting into her skin. Abruptly, he released her and rose to his feet with decision. He stepped back.

"I don't want to see them again," he said. "They are a

reminder of things best forgotten. I make you a present of them, a dowry. Now, shall we go?"

"But what of you?" she asked.

He was already turning toward the door. He looked back with one hand braced on the frame. His gray eyes were clouded and his face lined with weariness as he answered. "What of me? Dowries are convenient things, I have no doubt, but I . . . have no use for one."

CHAPTER 24

The funeral for Don Esteban was held the following day. They buried him in the piece of hallowed ground beyond the walls of the hacienda where the *charros* and their families were laid to rest, and also Charro's grandfather, who had been given the land. The old man had wanted to watch over his *mercedes*, though later Huerta family members were buried in the cemetery near the Mission San Juan.

It was Señor Huerta who had pointed out that Pilar was now, most probably, Don Esteban's heir. His son was dead and there were no other living relatives of close degree, so her claim should be strong. There was a certain bitter humor in that knowledge. It mattered little to Pilar, however, beyond the fact that there would likely be no one to dispute her possession of the emeralds.

Governor Pacheco had been present at the service. Vicente had been sent to inform him of the death and await his orders as to what he wished in the way of investigation into the affair. It had been a great concession for the governor to come personally to the hacienda, one due to the status of Señor Huerta in the community, Pilar thought. After the ceremony, while the grave was being filled, the governor had convened a hearing. Pilar had not attended for the simple reason that neither she nor any of the other women of the house had been informed of it. It had been of no great duration. The governor, Charro said, had decided after hearing the evidence, that Don Esteban had been killed in an honorable meeting with swords, and that no blame could be attached to Refugio for the tragic outcome. Governor Pacheco had taken a virulent dislike to the don, and was not inclined to waste many minutes of his time in worry over the man's demise. The wonder was not, according to the official, that someone had killed him, but that no one had done it sooner. There had been some suggestion that the death be blamed on the Apaches, with only the arrival of Carranza preventing the usual mutilation of the body. Refugio would not agree. The responsibility was his, and he would not deny it. He had seemed inclined to object to calling it a meeting of honor, but had been prevailed upon to agree to it as the wisest course.

Vicente had been troubled by the findings of the inquiry, though he was glad that his brother was freed from the threat of punishment in the matter. He had felt it necessary to speak to a priest about it. That was not difficult, for the good padre from Mission San Juan had come to the hacienda for the funeral rites and had stayed overnight afterward. The two had sat up until nearly dawn discussing this and a multitude of other theological questions as propounded in Seville, and also the problems of mission life, from persuading the Indians to accept the glories of Christianity to keeping the system of canals that watered the fields open and running. When morning came, Vicente had ridden with the padre back to the mission, as part of his escort. Vicente had not returned. Instead, there had been a message saying that he would return with the priest in two day's time, when he came to celebrate the wedding mass, but then would make the mission his home. There was need for his help there, and it was possible he would become an assistant friar in training to the priest.

The message was a reminder of how close the wedding was upon Pilar. All that was left was this night and one more, then she would be wed to Charro. Pilar wanted to be happy, to feel some anticipation, but she could not. She was fond of Charro. More than that, she respected him and knew he would be a good husband to her. Still, the thought of the wedding, and the night afterward, filled her with dread.

A dozen times she had started out to find him, to beg off from it. A dozen times she had stopped. She was reluctant to hurt and embarrass him by her refusal to go through with the ceremony after she herself had dragged him into it. She hated to admit that she did not know her own mind, that she had accepted his very tentative offer out of pique and desperation. Moreover, she could not think what else she would do, where she would go and how she would get there over the dangerous roads to San Antonio. If she could not leave, could not command an escort, it would be most uncomfortable staying here to face Señor and Señora Huerta, as well as Charro.

She thought Charro suspected how she felt, for she had caught him watching her with concern in his eyes. He was moody and withdrawn, though he kept close beside her when Refugio was near.

When Charro was not with her, he spent much time with Enrique. The two of them, she thought, missed Baltasar. It was not surprising; they had been together for a long time.

The big man had not reappeared, nor had any sign of him been found around the hacienda by the Indian *charros*. No one could say where he was staying, what he was doing, how he was living. He could be anywhere. He was used to living off the land. It was possible, too, that he had gone to San Antonio, or that he had ridden away either south toward the Rio Grande or back east toward Louisiana.

Pilar had thought of him often since the night at the jacal. He had done much that was vile, yet he had saved her life by his refusal to kill her. She would never forget the look in his eyes as he left, or his whispered prayer of hope that the band was waiting outside, waiting to kill him.

Baltasar had wanted to die. It was not just Isabel's death and his part in causing it, she thought, but also his betrayal of the man who had been his friend and his leader. So long as he could hold Isabel up as his reason, he could live with it. When she was gone, he could not. She wondered what would become of him, though it seemed likely she would never know.

She could not sleep. It seemed endless ages since she had really slept. She had been so restless this evening that she had not even donned her nightgown when she retired for the night, but still wore the day gown of gray stripes with a black stomacher that she had put on that morning. She had tried to work on a piece of sewing Charro's mother had given her, a petticoat for her trousseau, but soon tossed it aside. Leaving the candles burning on the table beside the bed, she had pulled her chair out onto the balcony. Somehow, it seemed more restful there in the corner where the grapevines grew in a thick, rustling curtain.

The night was calm, the air fresh and dry yet soft. The stars appeared close. The moon hardly moved in its arcing track across the heavens. There was a guard on the platform near the gate, but she thought he was asleep; there had been no flicker of movement from there in some time. Now and then a moth, drawn by the light, fluttered past and into the bedchamber. She could hear the insects flying against the candle's glass shade, bumping into it with a faint musical chiming.

The first notes of the guitar were so soft she was not

quite sure she was not hearing the moths against the glass. They grew louder by degrees, but still seemed to be coming from far away, perhaps from a room under the far end of the loggia, perhaps even from outside the courtyard wall.

Then, as she recognized the melody, Pilar felt something hot and tight close around her heart, slowly squeezing.

Why? Why did he have to do it? Did he know what pain that sound brought her, what memories it stirred so that they danced, hauntingly, in her head? That night on the ship, the instant the planes of his face softened before he reached to take her in his arms. The way he knelt to comfort the little boy who had been bitten by the parrot. The feel of his arms around her as he lay with her in the bed at Doña Luisa's house in New Orleans. The look in his eyes as New Orleans burned. The infinite grace of his fall from his horse as he was shot during the Apache attack. The stark timbre of his voice as he bargained for the comfort of her body with promises of pleasure. The careless cascade of green gems, shining in the lantern light.

The quiet strumming came nearer, as if the player was walking at a slow, even pace. It almost seemed that Pilar could feel the chords vibrating deep inside her, drawing out the same sweet resonance as before. At the same time, she knew a burgeoning panic. What if Refugio should come to her? What would she say? What would she do? Would she be able to deny him, to send him away? What would happen if Charro should find him there?

How could Charro not know he was there, when El Leon was announcing his presence, if not his intentions, so clearly with his music?

It might not be Refugio. It could be any man with a guitar who had heard the song he had played and remembered it, or been reminded that he knew it.

No, she knew it was Refugio. No one else played with

that combination of precision and hidden fire. No one else could draw out the joy and pathos within the song and make them ring in the air. No one else knew so well how to breach her defenses and, musician and master swordsman that he was, pierce her heart with a single singing note.

She closed her eyes, listening in tight concentration, as if she would memorize every phrase and cadence, every delicate intimation of close-held emotion. She listened, scarcely breathing. She listened and felt, somewhere inside her, the hot gathering of tears.

She could not do it.

She could not marry Charro when every particle of her being could be awakened to hopeless longing by the sound of a guitar. To stand with him before a priest and exchange vows of fidelity and love would be to betray everything she was, everything she felt for Refugio. Where could it lead, except to disaster? For if Refugio came for her, she must go with him. There was nothing that could prevent it except death itself.

Was he coming? Was the music louder, nearer? She got to her feet, drawing farther back among the vines. She could see nothing in the courtyard below except long rectangles of blackness and the faint shimmer of the moon's light among the spattering droplets falling from the fountain. There was no quiet tread, no stealthy movement.

Or was there? Had that been the graceful slide of a shadow along the high wall? She strained her eyes but could not be sure.

If he did come for her, what then? What would become of them? Where would they go? Governor Pacheco might have looked the other way over the death of Don Esteban, but that did not mean he would forget to send to Spain to learn about El Leon. They might have a year, possibly two, and then Refugio would be a wanted man again. They could run away, head farther south in the direction of Vera Cruz or Mexico City, but someday, somewhere, the long reach of the king would touch them and that would be the end.

But they would have the time until then. They would have the glory. A year could be a long time. In a year, there could be a child. In two, there could be another. She would have something left of Refugio to cling to, some living chalice to hold the essence of their love.

If he was coming.

The song was ending. There were only a few notes more. She drew a deep breath, preparing to move forward from her concealment into the moonlight, to beckon to him.

And then the music ceased.

It stopped with a discord, a twanging violation of the strings that rasped Pilar's nerves to rawness and sent a shudder along her spine. She did not move. Disquiet echoed through her. She opened her eyes so wide they ached as she searched the dim corners of the courtyard.

What was happening? Who was out there? The urge to call out rose in her throat, but she held it back. She thought of going inside, of making her way downstairs and out into the courtyard. She hesitated, uncertain it was wise, almost sure her present vantage point was better.

Then there came the rustle of grapevine leaves from the far end of the balcony. They shook again, a movement that set the vines farther along near Pilar to quivering.

The agitation was too violent to be a lizard darting along the vines, or even the kitchen cat ascending them as it stalked some night creature. There was a man climbing up from the loggia below.

He was moving swiftly, without pausing to search overlong for handholds, as if he had done this before. He was hoisting himself up with the athletic ease of hard muscles and well-honed reflexes. It would take him only a moment to reach the balcony railing. Pilar took a step forward.

His head appeared among the vine leaves, a bobbing shadow. He drew himself upward, his broad shoulder muscles bunching with the effort. Reaching for the railing, he grasped it for support as he levered himself close enough to put a foot on the edge of the floorboards underneath.

Pilar moved with a quick tread, stepping into the shafting light of the moon. Her voice suddenly breathless, she called out in soft, tentative welcome.

"I'm here, Refugio."

Below in the courtyard a man ran from the shadows. His head was bare, his features contorted with rage and fear, and he carried a musket in his hands.

"Get back, Pilar!" Charro shouted. "Stay out of the way!"

The man at the end of the balcony was moving now with urgent speed, disentangling himself from the concealing vines, lifting a long leg to put it over the railing even as he braced his hands behind him. In a moment he would vault the top rail and land on his feet on the balcony. Down below, Charro brought his musket up to his shoulder. He sighted down the barrel, ready to fire.

Pilar saw what was happening and could not believe it. A scream rushed into her throat, swelling it to bursting. It tore from her in shrill despair. "No!"

The musket shot cracked out, becoming a booming roar. Orange fire blossomed around the barrel, then was smothered by a cloud of dark smoke. Another musket boomed from a different quarter, and yet another. The vivid, blinding explosions shook the night and drowned every other sound in their thunder.

The musket balls whined, thudding into the man on the shadowed balcony. He grunted as he was flung backward with black splotches spreading on the white of his shirt. He caught himself with his hands on the railing, weaving. Then he released his hold and fell, heavy and lax, into the courtyard below.

Pilar heard the crash as he broke through the lattice over the patio area, then a solid impact as he struck the ground. She swayed, trying to catch her breath in her raw throat, trying to make her mind and her body obey her frantic will while red mist swam before her eyes and she could feel her heart draining.

"No," she whispered, with a violent shake of her head. "No!"

Then as if released, she whirled and flung herself through the door of her bedchamber and across the room. She snatched open the inner door and ran with flying skirts to the salon where the stairs descended. She flew downward and out onto the loggia.

There, she slowed to a jerky walk, moving as in a daze toward where a man lay stretched on the ground with Charro and Enrique bending over him. Behind her the house was blooming with light as voices called out in distress and fear. Through a haze of tears she saw the maid Benita come running from a lower room, saw Señor Huerta walking from a dark corner of the courtyard with a smoking musket in his hand.

Charro turned his head as he heard Pilar approach. His face was gray and his mouth set in a straight line of pain. He straightened, stepping in front of the body. Putting out his hands, he tried to catch her arms, to stop her. "Don't," he said, his voice thick. "Don't look. There's nothing you can do."

She evaded him, refusing to meet his eyes, jerking the

arm he caught from his grasp. She went to one knee beside the man on the ground in a billow of skirts. Her gaze, quick and desperate, ran over the spreading red wetness that colored the whole front of his shirt. A tremor ran over her, quivering in her hand as she reached and turned his face to light.

A small cry was forced from her, and after it a long, tremulous sigh. Tears spilled over her lashes, running in warm wet tracks down her face. She placed her hand on his forehead and brought it down slowly, gently, to close the staring, glazing eyes.

The men above her shifted. There was a soft tread behind her, then a figure knelt in swooping grace at her side. "I pray you are near, *cara* ," Refugio said, "to be the last thing on this earth I see, and to shut out the night for me."

He put his arm around her shoulders, holding her tight against him for a long moment before he drew her to her feet. He was warm and whole and alive, though his face was drawn and there was darkness behind his eyes.

Charro took a step forward. "We had to shoot. Baltasar was going for Pilar again. God knows why—revenge, for the emeralds—but we couldn't take a chance."

It was not only Charro, but also his father and Enrique who had fired. They carried their muskets or else had lain them down near the body. Refugio, Pilar saw, had no firearm. He had only the sword at his side. The leather strap that crossed his chest held a guitar slung behind his back.

"Shall I thank you for exacting my revenge for me?" Refugio said.

Charro blinked as a tide of angry color rose in his face. "It seemed necessary. You would not."

"Maybe for a reason?"

"Yes, because you overflow with misplaced compassion. Baltasar tried three different times to kill you, and might have again the next time self-pity muddled his brain. He manhandled Pilar once, putting her life in danger, and was about to try more of the same. There had to be an end to it."

"I don't think he meant to hurt me," Pilar broke in, her voice husky. "He kept me from harm before, when my stepfather wanted me killed. No, I think he knew all of you were out here watching, waiting. I think Baltasar wanted—"

Refugio's arm clamped down on her shoulders, a warning pressure instantly released. His smooth voice intervened as she faltered. "Baltasar wanted a few of the emeralds, doubtless, to make his path smoother wherever he decided to go. It's the obvious answer."

It might be obvious, but it wasn't correct. Baltasar, she was almost sure, had wanted to die, and had appointed the band his executioners. Refugio knew it as well as she; he had been there to hear the big man's whispered prayer that night at the jacal. To tell the band the truth, she saw belatedly, would not be a kindness. They had enough guilt and pain to handle without adding more.

Charro was shaking his head. "He might have hurt Pilar to get them."

"He might," Refugio agreed, his voice flat with care and weariness.

Baltasar, Pilar thought, had also known that Refugio was not on guard, for he had heard him playing his serenade. He had given his leader, then, this one small mercy, perhaps in return for the manner of Isabel's dying—that Refugio need not share in the death. This also Refugio must know, and bear.

Pilar had thought once that she disliked the complicated mental processes of the man at her side. She was wrong. She loved the complexity that was so much a part of him, for within it were degrees of tolerance and understanding unknown to most. She had benefited from it as much as any, and would, pray God, again.

"It's over now," Enrique said, the brusque words hiding

whatever he might feel. "We should cover him, bury him, and make an end of it."

"Yes," Señor Huerta said with a glance toward where his wife and Doña Luisa hovered, with Benita beside them and the other servants nearby. He beckoned toward one of the Indian men, and also toward the guard squatting on his platform, watching the proceedings. They ran to do his bidding.

"This way," his wife, the señora, said, indicating that the body should be carried into a small room used for guests on the lower floor.

Charro moved toward Pilar. His face was stiff as his gaze rested on Refugio's arm still about her, but he held out his hand. "Come, Pilar. This has been distressing for you. I will see you back to your room and your bed, and maybe find a glass of wine to calm you."

"No."

It was Refugio who spoke, the word simple, final. He did not release his hold, but kept Pilar at his side.

Charro searched his face. "You have no right to interfere. She is my betrothed."

"Not any longer. I have a prior right, and I'm taking her with me."

"Prior right? If you mean because you made her your mistress, I refuse to recognize it!"

"No, my friend. Because of promises and pledges made in two hemispheres, unblessed but no less binding. Because of nights shared and dangers met and two minds that leap as one to a single conclusion. Because she is beauty and strength and truth, and I have need of them. Because she holds my soul in the hollow of her hand and keeps it secure when there is no other who will, or can. Because I must. Because she requires it."

Charro stood tall with the moonlight striking the

prominent bones of his face and leaving his eyes in shadow. "I won't let you take her."

"Stop me," Refugio said quietly, and brought his sword sighing from its scabbard.

Benita screamed. Señora Huerta moaned while her husband swore under his breath. The men removing Baltasar's body put it down and stood watching, alert for orders.

Charro did not move a muscle though his chest rose and fell with his rapid breathing. His voice was strained as he made his answer. "I can command a dozen men with a single word. The gates are locked. There is no way you can win free."

"Fighting is not a favorite pastime, but I can do it," Refugio answered, his sword point steady and only inches from Charro's heart. "There are horses waiting beyond the wall, and Enrique will open the gate."

The acrobat, as Charro turned to look at him, gave a shrug and a nod.

"I forbid it," the son of the Huerta *estancia* said, "and my word is law here."

"Not to me," Enrique said in sorrowful, but measured contradiction. "Refugio is still, and will ever be, my leader. He is still El Leon."

Charro's face tightened. He swung sharply toward Pilar and his eyes narrowed as he tilted his head, studying her pale face. "This was planned, then," he said in grating tones. "I might have known. Did you?"

Pilar began to shake her head, but Refugio spoke first.

"The betrayal is mine alone. An abduction was planned for tonight, but the rest—was happenstance."

"Conspicuously gallant, as usual, but yours is not the answer I seek. You don't protest, Pilar, nor do you beg to stay. If I misunderstood you when you said in front of the governor that you meant to marry me, you might have told me so."

"You didn't misunderstand. It's just—I'm sorry, Charro. I thought it would be best for everybody. I was wrong."

"Then you're going with Refugio?"

She made a small gesture of distress. "Please don't try to stop him. I couldn't bear that there should be any more killing."

"But if you are unwilling—" he began urgently.

"No, not unwilling. Never—quite—unwilling."

Refugio signaled with his sword to Enrique. The acrobat leaped to raise the bar of the gate. Step by slow step, Refugio drew Pilar back with him toward the wide opening. Charro moved after them with his hands clamped into fists and his jaws so tight the muscles stood out in relief. There was indecision in his eyes, however.

"Let them go, my son," came the quiet counsel of Señora Huerta. "You have interfered enough."

"Yes," Benita said in tones laced with anger and gladness as she moved to Charro's side. "Let them go."

Refugio did not wait for more. He swung with Pilar, sweeping her out of the courtyard toward where a pair of horses were tied to a hitching post. He threw her up into the saddle, tossed up her reins, then swung to his own horse. In an instant they had gathered their mounts and sent them pounding away down the long and dusty road that led to San Antonio.

They rode swift and hard. Pilar did not ask where they were going, she did not want to know. It was enough that she was beside Refugio, and the road ahead, silver in the light of the moon, was open before them. The moment was hers, as was the great, swelling exhilaration of love she felt inside her. Nothing could take it away, nothing change it. She would keep the memory always.

They had gone perhaps five miles when she looked back. The road behind was clear, and yet there was a haze rising above it, a roiling cloud that caught the moonglow with a pale glinting. It seemed to be moving fast, caused by a group of horsemen of no small number.

Her eyes were shadowed as she looked toward Refugio. "We're being followed," she called.

"I know." The acknowledgment was grim.

"Apaches, do you think?"

He shook his head. "Charro."

They increased their speed, galloping through the night. The wind was cool in their faces, the air tinged with a sweet, sharp scent of sage. Rabbits sprang from their path and sprinted away. Birds with long legs and longer necks raced beside them for short stretches before veering into the grass. The moon leaned toward setting, then finally, as if letting go, dropped below the horizon. Still, they rode on.

The horsemen behind them kept pace. They did not close the gap between them, but neither did they fall back. On and on they went as dawn spread slowly into the sky, lining it with pink and rose silk and veils of blue gauze. The sun came up, sending its searching, life-giving rays to slant into their eyes. And then, when the world was brightest, they heard floating toward them on the morning breeze the sound of church bells.

Vicente was waiting for them in front of the mission chapel. The two brothers clasped each other's shoulders, both grinning. Vicente, when Refugio released him, stepped forward to salute Pilar on the cheek.

"Enough of that," Refugio said in mock disapproval. "We have need to hurry."

"There's a problem?" Vicente inquired, his humor disappearing.

"You might say so. Charro is coming."

"Then come this way. The padre is waiting."

As Vicente stepped inside the church, Refugio turned to Pilar. There was sudden gravity in his eyes as he offered his hand, and with it an open, unshielded look that she had never seen before. He drew a deep breath, squaring his shoulders. "I didn't mean it to be this way," he said. "I meant to take long hours convincing you that all the things I said to Don Esteban and Baltasar that night were lies meant to preserve your life and my sanity. I meant to woo you with soft words to make up for all those unspoken these long months when I had no right to declare myself, to court you with caresses and promises of eternal devotion. Only if those failed did I intend to steal you away."

"Only then," she said, staring past his shoulder, "because you thought I might require it?"

"Quick, so quick," he mourned. "I knew better than to say that aloud. But can you deny it? Could you have brought yourself to wound Charro's tender pride with a blunt refusal when the wedding was so near? Could you have overcome the outcry of your conscience in order to tell him? I meant to do it for you."

"To save me from making a mistake?"

"I am not so noble. To save you for me."

"I heard the reasons you gave to convince Charro," she said in soft distress as she met the penetrating gray of his eyes, "but are you sure this is what you want?"

"It's what I need, what I must have, or become a raving maniac trying to hold the world at sword's length while I keep you."

"You could travel faster alone." The words were stark with self-denial.

"I'm going nowhere."

"You must, eventually. What of when Governor Pacheco receives word from Spain?"

"He has decided against sending a dispatch; he told me

so at the funeral. The Tejas country needs settlers, and it's not as if there has never been a bandit in the province. According to him, half the officials in the colonial system qualify."

"He knows then, about you?"

"Rather, he refuses to know. So long as there is doubt, he is content. He didn't care for your stepfather. Not only did Don Esteban infuriate him, but he had heard of him, not to his credit, in Madrid. And it seems that he once knew my father."

"Then that means," she said in slow, mounting gladness, "that you're safe."

"We're safe. For the moment. There's still the matter of a jilted bridegroom, and time is slipping away. Shall I be a dead abductor or a dead husband, my sweet Pilar? What will it take to have the answer I seek?"

"Only ask," she answered, her eyes richly brown, perfectly clear as she sustained the intensity of his searching gaze.

He smiled in slow, rich amusement. "I prefer my way," he said, and bent to place his hand under her knees, lifting her high in the strength of his arms. He stepped with her inside the church doors.

There, he halted. His voice deep, he asked, "Will you marry me?"

"Immediately," she answered, for she could hear the drumming of horses' hoofs, a muffled roar above the quick beating of her heart.

"Yes," he said softly, "immediately."

The priest was in his vestments and the candles had been lighted. The kneeling bench was placed before the altar. The smell of incense, dry wood, and sanctity hung in the air. The mission Indians, their faces expectant, filled the hand-hewn pews. The bells had stopped ringing. All was ready.

It took no more than a few scant moments for the names to be repeated for the priest. Their vows were made while candlelight shone on their faces, reflecting serene and golden in their eyes. The priest made the sign of the cross in blessing over them, intoning his command to be fruitful. They were wed. The priest, his voice gentle but hurried, faintly harried, began to intone the final prayer.

The church doors opened. The tread of booted feet could be heard, echoing on the wooden floor. Then came silence.

The priest's voice faltered, but he continued courageously to the end. With a final benediction, he raised his head.

Pilar, with Refugio's arm around her, got slowly to her feet, then turned to face the church aisle.

Charro stood there, with Enrique at one side and his father on the other. Behind them were the *charros*, some twenty strong. There was dust on their shoulders and in the lines of their faces, and they all held their hats in their hands.

"We could not let you ride all this way unescorted, even if we were somewhat tardy," Charro said, his face creasing in a wry smile. "It seemed that it would be a shame if the Apaches were allowed to stop the wedding. It's one we have—all of us—thought should have been celebrated long since."

His father clapped him on the back. "Well said, my son. And we will celebrate it as only we can celebrate weddings here in the Tejas country. My wife and Benita are preparing a feast, and riders have been sent to bring the guests. By the time we return, they will have prepared the nuptial chamber, where the two of you will stay as long as you wish, or as long as you are able! Come now, and let the joy begin!"

It was unending, that joy. The music and the food, the wine and the laughter continued for two days and nights. Enrique and Doña Luisa, watching it, stated their unalterable purpose of taking up residence in San Antonio before they were wed. They were not certain they could survive another *estancia* fiesta.

Charro's gaiety was forced at first, then as the daughters from neighboring *estancias* strolled past him, looking at him from the corners of their dark, liquid eyes, he became more resigned. And he was often seen in dark corners with Benita. Consoling him in myriad ways, with soft words and inviting glances and access to her downstairs chamber, had become the maidservant's most pressing duty.

Benita came to Pilar during the first night. Leaning over the chair where Pilar sat under the loggia, the maidservant whispered, "Tomorrow you must grind corn."

"What?" Pilar turned to look at the girl.

"Among my mother's people, who came with the priests from far south in Mexico, a young man often steals a bride. If she doesn't run away, if she begins to grind the corn, it's all right."

"I'll remember that," Pilar said, smiling.

"Oh, yes, it's funny, but also wise. Shall I bring you a grinding bowl and some grain?"

"Please," Pilar said, thinking of what Refugio would say when he saw it.

"I will," the girl said, and went away to see who Charro was dancing with now.

What would become of Benita? Pilar wished she knew. It seemed unlikely that Charro's parents would countenance a marriage between them. And yet, they had nearly lost

Charro once because they tried to separate them. Perhaps something could be worked out; she would have to think about it.

In the meantime it was growing late, and Refugio, standing with Enrique and Señor Huerta, was ignoring the conversation of the other two men while he watched her with a look that brought heated blood to her face. She made her excuses and good-nights to her hostess and moved with unhurried steps toward the stairs.

Refugio joined her within the quarter hour. She was waiting, lying naked in the curtained bed with her hair brushed and spilling around her on her pillow in the light of a single candle, and the sheet pulled up and tucked over her breasts. He paused in the doorway, the light in his gray eyes becoming steely with intentness. Closing the door behind him, he stepped into the bedchamber.

It was then that he saw the small bag of emeralds that lay in the center of the second pillow of the bed.

"What is this?" he asked quietly as he began to strip off his shirt.

"My dowry," she answered.

"To offend you is my last wish at this moment, but I have to tell you I don't feel like sharing my pillow with them."

"We must decide how they are to be used."

"Must we? Now?"

She ignored the seductive depth of his words. "There is the matter of the *estancia* that joins this one, with an owner who may sell."

"You would like an *estancia*?"

"I thought you might, since you mentioned it before."

"The emeralds are yours. Do what you want." He tossed his shirt aside and began to lever off his boots.

She gave him an irritated look. "How can I buy land

unless you agree? I'm not the one who will have to tend it or fight the Indians!"

"You require that I decide?"

"I don't require anything!" she said, raising herself to sweep the bag of gems from the pillow and fling them at him. "Do what you will with them!"

He left off unbuttoning his breeches to catch the bag in a deft grasp. His gaze went to the expanse of softly curving, pearl-tinted flesh exposed as the sheet over Pilar was dislodged. His voice quietly questioning, he said, "Anything?"

"Yes, I don't care. I never did care, except that—"

"I know, *cara*, I always knew. There's no need for you to tell me." He skimmed from his breeches, then, splendidly naked, sat down on the bed beside her.

She glanced at him, then away again. "Then let the emeralds be ours. Let's decide together what's to be done."

"Eventually," he murmured, taking the sheet she held and tugging it from her grasp before stripping it to the end of the bed. "I've thought of something else to do with them just now."

He leaned over her, supporting himself on one elbow. Pressing her backward so she lay flat on the mattress, he opened the top of the bag he held, then upended it.

She jumped a little as the cool stones touched her skin, rolling into the valley between her breasts, bouncing in a trickle over her abdomen to the flat expanse of her belly, with the last bright stone coming to rest near the the apex of her thighs. And yet, guessing his purpose, she knew the slow surge of excitement in her veins. She watched in bemusement as Refugio bent over her and took between his lips a gem that rested on the side of the mound of her breast, before tasting the skin underneath.

With slow reluctance he lifted his head, then turned and spat the emerald into his hand.

"Gritty," he said, "but unaccountably delicious."

"Unaccountably?" she queried, her voice low.

He smiled with a slow curving of his firm lips. "It's possible I might account for it if pressed."

"I love you," she said, reaching to touch his face, trailing her fingers through the crisp waves of his hair, feeling the rising swell of joy and passion and hope that came from deep inside.

"I know," he answered, his gaze darkening as he watched her face, "but I thought you would never say it. If you tell me a thousand times, it will never be enough."

"Shall we see?"

"Not . . . right this minute."

"Ah. You prefer this other thing you thought of?"

"Possibly." He leaned to take up another stone, but spat it out more quickly than the last. "Very gritty. This idea may have been a mistake."

Pilar lifted a brow, the look in her dark eyes sultry. She picked up the three or four sandiest emeralds in her fingers and rubbed them on the sheet to clean them. Returning them to their former places with care, she reached for the candlestick from the table beside the bed, bringing it to her lips to blow out the flame.

She settled back on her pillow in the darkness. "Oh," she said softly, "I don't think so."

Author's Note

I've never been to Havana; let me confess that at once. I'd have gone willingly, if I could—there are few places I wouldn't go at the drop of anybody's hat—but political realities being what they are, it didn't seem too smart to carry research that far. I did visit Spain and San Antonio, and New Orleans, of course, prior to sitting down to write *Spanish Serenade*. The truth is, the story grew out of a fascination with things Spanish that began on a trip to Spain in 1985. It would never have come into being without the time spent prowling around the patios and cathedrals and country inns of Spain, or the missions, museums, and Tex-Mex restaurants of San Antonio. I hereby express my public gratitude to my close friend Sue Anderson for luring me away from my past preoccupation with French history and culture and encouraging me, and joining me, in my sampling of the flavors and glories that are derived from Old Spain.

There never was, to my knowledge, a noble outlaw known in Spain as the Lion of the Andalusian hills, nor was there a woman called the Venus de la Torre. All other characters in the story are fictional also, with the exception of King Carlos III of Spain, Governor Miro and Treasurer Nuñez of New Orleans, and Governor Pacheco of San Antonio.

The Great Fire of 1788 that nearly destroyed New Orleans occurred much as described. It began when lace curtains near the altar in the private chapel of the house of Treasurer Nuñez caught fire, and was spread by a fierce wind from the south and the explosion of caches of gunpowder. Damage was much greater than it need have been, due to the failure to sound the church bells in alarm because of the religious holiday of Good Friday. All other events in the story are imaginary.

A number of sources were consulted for background in each of the story locales. *Spain, the Root and the Flower* by John A. Crow was particularly valuable for its colorful and concise historical overview, as well as its insights into Spanish character, both regional and national. More character types, plus wonderful samples of atmosphere, were gleaned from the old *Tales of the Alhambra* by Washington Irving. The section on Havana sent me to the Britannica and an atlas and old travel books. Then this summer, in one of those coincidences that happen so often to writers they almost take them for granted, *National Geographic* did a special article on Old Havana, complete with pictures of ancient buildings and a map of the old city. This new information confirmed images I had conjured up from dry, printed descriptions.

So many of my stories are set in New Orleans that I sometimes feel as if I spend half my days perched on top of a ladder in front of the Louisiana section in my own library/study. I pull books out and put them back, read a little here, a little there—some of it actually having a bearing on the work in progress—but it's all so haphazard that I can never recall all of the books consulted for any particular story. Still, two of the most helpful for this book were the wonderfully detailed *Louisiana, a Narrative History* by Edwin Adams Davis, and Leonard Huber's *New Orleans, a Pictorial History*.

The list of books gathered together for the San Antonio section include *New Spain's Far Northern Frontier, Essays on Spain in the American West, 1540–1821* by David J. Weber; *Mercedes Reales, Hispanic Land Grants of the Upper Rio Grande Region* by Victor Westphall; *Cycles of Conquest* by Edward H. Spicer; *Lone Star, a History of Texas and the*

Texan by T. R. Fehrenbach; *A Place in Time, A Pictorial View of San Antonio's Past* by David McLemore; *The San Antonio River* by Mary Ann Noonan Guerra; and *The Indian Wars* by Robert M. Utley and Wilcomb E. Washburn. I am also grateful to Houston-based researcher Linda Hardcastle for her efforts in tracing down the name and circumstances of the governor of New Spain in the summer of 1788, as well as one or two other questions.

Finally, a special thanks to Lynne Murphy of Edmond, Oklahoma, better known as western romance writer Georgina Gentry, for supplying me with the Spanish name of the wildflower known today as Texas Bluebonnet, for an informative and hilarious telephone conversation concerning Plains Indian habits, but most of all for being there in the best tradition of writers' camaraderie.

Jennifer Blake
Sweet Brier
Quitman, Louisiana
August 1989

About the Author

Jennifer Blake was born near Goldonna, Louisiana, in her grandparents' 120-year-old hand-built cottage. It was her grandmother, a local midwife, who delivered her. She grew up on an eighty-acre farm in the rolling hills of north Louisiana and got married at the age of fifteen. Five years and three children later, she had become a voracious reader, consuming seven or eight books a week. Disillusioned with the books she was reading, she set out to write one of her own. It was a Gothic—*Secret of Mirror House*—and Fawcett was the publisher. Since that time she has written thirty-four books, with more than twelve million copies in print worldwide, and has become one of the bestselling romance authors of our time. Her recent Fawcett books are *Surrender in Moonlight*, *Midnight Waltz*, *Fierce Eden*, *Royal Passion*, *Prisoner of Desire*, *Southern Rapture*, *Louisiana Dawn*, *Perfume of Paradise* and *Love and Smoke*. Jennifer and her husband live in their house near Quitman, Louisiana, styled after old Southern Planters' cottages.